WHISPER OF DESIRE

Grant slept silently on the long side of the sofa.

"Grant," she said in a small, hoarse voice barely audible. He didn't stir. Robyn savored the unguarded moment. She enjoyed watching him sleep. She stared at him, remembering their honeymoon and the nights he'd wake her when he came home. A dreamy smile curved her lips. She had missed him.

He shifted again in his sleep, and his hand moved to her arm. His eyes opened but didn't focus. "Robyn, I love you."

Robyn knew he was dreaming, that if he were awake, he would only think of her as Brooke Johnson, but when he pulled her into his arms, she didn't resist. His sleepy mouth found hers in a soft brushing motion. One hand found its way into her hair, combing through it with long, sensitive strokes. Warm waves, like the gentle lapping of a calm sea, washed over her body.

Then, with sudden swiftness, passion flared, and Grant's tongue pushed past her teeth to taste the wet nectar inside. Robyn felt herself dissolving into him as her body was screaming for her husband to make love to her, to give her the fulfillment she'd waited five years to experience again.

ROMANCES ABOUT AFRICAN-AMERICANS!
YOU'LL FALL IN LOVE
WITH ARABESQUE BOOKS FROM PINNACLE

SERENADE   (0024, $4.99)
by Sandra Kitt

Alexandra Morrow was too young and naive when she first
fell in love with musician, Parker Harrison—and vowed
never to be so vulnerable again. Now Parker is back and
although she tries to resist him, he strolls back into her life
as smoothly as the jazz rhapsodies for which he is known.
Though not the dreamy innocent she was before, Alexandra finds her defenses quickly crumbling and her mind,
body and soul slowly opening up to her one and only love,
who shows her that dreams do come true.

FOREVER YOURS   (0025, $4.99)
by Francis Ray

Victoria Chandler must find a husband quickly or her
grandparents will call in the loans that support her chain
of lingerie boutiques. She arranges a mock marriage to
tall, dark and handsome ranch owner Kane Taggart. The
marriage will only last one year, and her business will be
secure, and Kane will be able to walk away with no strings
attached. The only problem is that Kane has other plans
for Victoria. He'll cast a spell that will make her his forever
after.

A SWEET REFRAIN   (0041, $4.99)
by Margie Walker

Fifteen years before, jazz musician Nathaniel Padell walked
out on Jenine to seek fame and fortune in New York City.
But now the handsome widower is back with a baby girl in
tow. Jenine is still irresistibly attracted to Nat and enchanted
by his daughter. Yet even as love is rekindled, an unexpected
danger threatens Nat's child. Now, Jenine must fight for Nat
before someone stops the music forever!

*Available wherever paperbacks are sold, or order direct from the
Publisher. Send cover price plus 50¢ per copy for mailing and
handling to Penguin USA, P.O. Box 999, c/o Dept. 17109,
Bergenfield, NJ 07621. Residents of New York and Tennessee
must include sales tax. DO NOT SEND CASH.*

Whispers of Love

SHIRLEY HAILSTOCK

PINNACLE BOOKS
WINDSOR PUBLISHING CORP.

To Marilyn McGrillies and Patricia Hahn, who believed in Robyn and Grant from the beginning and who helped in ways even a wordsmith cannot express.

PINNACLE BOOKS are published by

Windsor Publishing Corp.
850 Third Avenue
New York, NY 10022

The P logo Reg U.S. Pat. & TM off. Pinnacle is a trademark of Pinnacle Publishing Corp.

First Pinnacle Printing: September, 1994

Printed in the United States of America

Prologue

Most people came to Las Vegas for the gambling, but Robyn lazed outside the casinos in the arid heat of the desert. The pool had emptied since she'd done her fifty laps. Susan was inside at her rehearsal, and Robyn had been given free rein to use the hotel facilities for any of her needs while she was in Las Vegas. She stretched out on one of the blue-and-white lounge chairs that framed the pool of the Mountain View Resort. Huge sunglasses protected her eyes from the glare bouncing off the still water. Her one-piece bathing suit gave her a modicum of decency. In the quiet, her mind went back to Washington and her job. She pushed the thought aside. She wouldn't think about the Major Crimes Bureau now.

Closing her eyes, she rested a moment. Then, instinct told her she was no longer alone. She could feel someone looking at her, staring at her. Without removing the lenses, she searched the rows of chairs. She saw him at the end of the pool: a man in a blue uniform, his arms casually folded over the back of a lounge chair, and his eyes staring directly at her. Robyn stared back. She felt compelled to. She was used to seeing uniforms, due to her work at the FBI, but this was not a military man. His uniform was that of an airline. She couldn't make out which one.

He pulled his gaze away and let it be caught by the beauty of the distant hills. He was so still, like a bronze statue. Suddenly, Robyn wished for her camera to capture his solitary profile. Few people, who came to this gambling mecca, took the time to notice the awesome beauty of the landscape. She followed his gaze, entranced by the burnish gold and red colors that painted the rugged horizon.

He must be a different kind of man, she thought as she gazed at him openly through her concealing glasses. He was lean and tall, over six feet. His shoulders were straight and broad, giving him an athletic look. His hair was cut short and capped by a captain's hat.

"There you are, Robyn." She jumped, not expecting to hear her name. "You've been out here entirely too long." Susan plopped down on the chair beside her, still in her leotard and footless stockings. Her body completely blocked Robyn's view of the man who'd stared so openly at her.

Robyn checked her watch. "It's only been an hour."

"An hour here is vastly different from an hour in Ocean City, Maryland."

"Just a few more minutes and I'll be in," she sat up, shifting to see if the man was still there. He was gone. Robyn checked the area, but she didn't see him. He must have left as quietly as he'd arrived.

"There isn't time," Susan was saying. "We have a lot of work to do."

"Work? I didn't come here to work." Her mind was

still on the uniformed officer. Where had he gone? She wondered if she'd see him again.

"I've got you a job in the chorus line," Susan announced.

Robyn stared at her for a moment then burst into laughter. Susan's face was sober and after a moment Robyn's sobered, too.

"You *are* kidding," she stated positively.

Susan shook her head slowly.

"Susan, I can't dance."

"Yes, you can," she contradicted. "We were in the same dance class for five years, and I know you still go twice a week."

"I don't mean I can't dance. I mean, I can't dance in a show."

"Why not?"

"I'm on vacation."

"That's not a reason."

"I don't want to dance."

"Of course, you do." Susan rejected her reason.

"No, I don't," she protested.

"Well, you have to. I've just spent half an hour convincing Bob Parker you're the best person for the job, and you can't let me down."

"Susan Collins," Robyn shouted, coming to a sitting position. "We are no longer in school. You can't keep getting me mixed up in sophomoric pranks."

"This is not a prank, sophomoric or otherwise. One of the dancers came down with something."

Robyn thought she was being intentionally vague.

"She'll be out a day or so. We only need you for one night, maybe two."

Robyn knew what that meant. Susan had been her roommate through four years of college. They had shared the same apartment until Susan left to get married almost eighteen months ago. When her marriage broke up after a year, she gave up her teaching position and came to Las Vegas. She got a job as a dancer and had been here for the last eight months.

"Why can't you go on without her?" Logic rallied to Robyn's aid.

"This routine requires that we pair off."

"Then, why doesn't one of the girls sit that dance out? Like you. If you could get the night off, we'd have time to talk before your date." Robyn pulled her glasses off, excited at her counterplan, but Susan was already shaking her head.

"A missing pair would create a hole. It would be obvious something was wrong. We'll have all day tomorrow to talk. I don't have a rehearsal until five o'clock." Susan's large brown eyes pleaded with her.

Robyn knew before she said it that she was going to agree. If she didn't, she knew Susan would argue until she got her way. "I'll do it, Susan." Robyn stopped her friend's happiness with a restraining hand. "But I promise you, if I make a fool of myself, I'm holding you responsible."

The darkness of the lobby was a stark contrast to the brightness of the sun. Grant stood a moment to let his eyes adjust. He turned back to check the two women by the pool. They had the same color hair, although copper highlights bounced off of the hair belonging to the one in the bathing suit. Soft, natural curls flowed over her shoulders to the middle of her back, moving like synchronized swimmers as she bobbed her head up and down. She was sitting up now without the glasses that had covered her face like a mask. He stopped in his motion of turning around. She was beautiful. He'd seen her body while she slept, and her face was just as ravishing. Yellow roses came to his mind. Yellow roses that have been tanned a golden brown, exactly as he liked it. A discovery he'd made this very day.

She sat straight, and her legs were long and shapely. Suddenly, she smiled, and Grant was swept away by the intensity he felt. The two women got up and walked toward another entrance. He watched them with a smile—one in a striped dance costume and the other in a bathing suit of bright red. Her legs seemed to go on forever. The angular jut of the building blocked his view as they rounded a corner and disappeared.

"There must be a woman out there," David greeted him with a slap on the back.

Grant moved around to face his friend who leaned toward the door. He knew David wouldn't see anyone. The woman he'd been watching was well out of sight.

Grant didn't tell him about her. For the moment, he wanted to keep her a secret. He didn't know why. He and David had been friends since the air force, and there was little they didn't know about each other. But when he'd seen the woman from his balcony methodically swimming lap after lap, he'd been fascinated by the beauty of her brown body slicing through the water.

Without changing his uniform, he'd gone to the pool. And there he'd found his nymph lying on a lounger in the afternoon sun. Why he hesitated in approaching her he didn't know. He had no problem with women. They seemed to flock to him. But this one looked so serene, as if life hadn't wiped the idealism from her features yet. For the time being, he only wanted to look at her.

"I got the tickets," David said.

For a moment, Grant didn't know David had been speaking to him. "What tickets?" he asked.

"For the show tonight." Four red tickets extended from David's hand like flat fingers. "It's the best show in Vegas. Lots of girls and singing and girls and dancing and girls and girls and girls," he repeated the litany.

Grant laughed as they headed for their room to get out of their uniforms. The show was hours away. They had time to shower and get in some gambling before David saw *his* girls. And Grant knew he had a date with one of the stewardesses but now couldn't remember her name. He also knew David had set him up with someone and would feign surprise when she suddenly showed up. He didn't care, he told himself, but when they reached the elevator he looked back toward the pool and thought of dark brown hair with copper highlights.

This was certainly a better place to work than the Assassination Bureau. Robyn Warren stood backstage, a three-pound headdress of pink fur balanced on her head. In moments, she'd be on stage for the second time in her twenty-five years. The first time had been two hours ago. She rubbed sweaty hands down her hips and waited. The curtain went up, and the lights rose, bathing sixteen scantly clad women in a blinding white light.

With a smile plastered to her face, Robyn listened to the music and counted the beats, as she performed the memorized steps. A single sound of tapping feet worked in unison to the music of *42nd Street*. It was exhilarating. Blood pumped through her system, mixing with adrenaline, restoring the energy her afternoon of rehearsal had depleted.

She felt the nervousness leave her. She could tell by the twinkle in the eyes of the other dancers when they passed each other forming a set of four circles that blended into one larger circle and finally opening into a straight line that she was a part of the group. The audience applauded in the middle of the routine. The sound was deafening to her ears. For the first time she looked beyond the footlights, wondering if the man from the pool was somewhere out there. It was hard to see anyone with the lights in her eyes. Besides she didn't know anyone here, except Susan, who was dancing on her left. She'd only been in Las Vegas two days. The man by the pool had been a stranger. They hadn't even said hello.

The dance ended much too soon, and she followed the line of bobbing fur backstage to change for the next number. There wasn't much time for musings; for as soon as they had switched from pink to white lace, she heard the call of five minutes. It meant they were to line up backstage, according to a preset system. She stood between Vera and Susan, the three of them were the same height.

The second outing on the stage seemed shorter than her first visit. She was breathless from the exhilaration and excitement. Susan had been right, she loved being out there. Almost before she knew it, she was back in the dressing room. The noise level was high as everyone tried to get dressed for their dates. Robyn moved aside. Susan had quickly dressed and was the first to leave the room, smiling at her and telling her she'd see her back at the apartment. She disappeared through the door, her dress changed and her face remade without the heavy greasepaint that they wore against the harsh lights of the stage.

By the time Robyn was dressed, the room was clear. She flipped the switch, throwing the room into darkness and leaving behind the smell of sweat, perfume, and makeup. From the top of the stairs, she saw him— the man from the pool. While there were people moving around him, carrying scenery and lights, he stood still. His black suit, distinctive against the surroundings, made his presence commanding. His white shirt made his skin darker by contrast. Robyn smiled when he looked up at her.

"You must be lost," she said, as she came down the steps.

"I don't think so." His voice was deep and dark like a warm night.

"If you're waiting for one of the dancers, I'm afraid you've been stood up." She could not imagine anyone forgetting about a guy whose brown eyes were so warm they could melt ice. They followed her all the way to the bottom step.

"I'm waiting for you," he said quietly.

"Me!" She didn't know this man, although she wouldn't mind getting to know him. From the distance she had to look up, she confirmed his height to be just over six feet. His hair had been picked until it circled his head like a small halo.

"I saw you by the pool . . . and on the stage, both times."

She smiled, pleased that someone had come to see her one and only performance. "We were staring at each other," she said directly.

"My name is Grant Richards." He stood up slightly straighter, as if he were coming to attention.

"I'm—"

"Robyn Warren," he finished for her. "I asked one of the other dancers," he explained to her questioning look.

"We don't know each other."

"A situation I'd like to remedy." His smile exuded charm.

He took her arm and locked it through his elbow. Several minutes later, Robyn found herself sitting in the casino's restaurant and having a late dinner with one of the most gorgeous men she'd ever met. He told her he'd been a copilot for Trans-Global for nearly four years. By the time dessert and coffee were served, she'd learned he'd grown up in a series of foster homes, before going to stay with an aunt. He and his friend, David, were here for a few days before they had another flight. She told him she worked for the government.

"I didn't know the government had a need for long-legged girls in bejeweled pink tights."

Robyn laughed. "They weren't bejeweled. They were sequined." She told him how Susan had convinced her to replace a sick dancer in tonight's show.

"Well, since you don't dance for a living, what do you do for the government?"

Robyn dropped her head. "I'm nobody important. I'm an analyst in a small Washington department." She was deliberately vague. She'd been taught to reveal as little as possible about her true purpose at the Federal Bureau of Investigation.

"Washington, D.C.!" Grant seized the word. A large smile displayed his even teeth.

"Yes," she nodded, lifting her coffee cup. The liquid was lukewarm.

"I live in D.C., too."

The thrill that shimmied up Robyn's spine couldn't be stopped. She'd only met Grant a few hours ago, yet she was sure she could fall in love with him.

"So where's Susan, now?" he asked.

"She had a date." Robyn came back from her musings. "And where's David now?" she asked, as the waiter served more coffee.

"He had a date. I lost him when I went to the second show."

"Why did you stay?"

He leaned forward, taking her hand in his. "After I saw you, I was devastated. How could I leave?" His eyes twinkled with mischief.

Robyn blushed, knowing he was teasing. "How could you tell us apart. Up there, we all look the same." It was a common complaint of the dancers. With the makeup and costumes, it was difficult to tell one from the other. And with her coloring, she blended in easier than Susan's milk chocolate complexion did.

"I could argue that." This time there was no teasing in his tone. It was deadly serious.

Robyn's throat constricted, and pulling her hand free, she picked up her water glass. The cool water helped only slightly, for Grant's eyes were fixed on her. She felt as if he were setting her on fire. It was all around her, defining her shape, and any effort to break free would cause the flames to incinerate her. But the overwhelming emotion that rocked her more than the thought of burning was that she didn't want to break free. She wanted this new sensation to continue.

"Why don't we go to the lounge and dance?" he suggested.

They had finished eating long ago, but had lingered over the coffee to talk. Now, they rose and went to the small lounge. The soft music played by a combo filled the room, and many couples were on the dance floor.

The hostess led them to a table, and Grant ordered drinks. Without waiting for them to arrive, he pulled her into his arms, and they began circling the floor to the slow beat of the music. Robyn thought she could die now and not be happier. He smelled good, of lemon soap and aftershave. She raised her hand to the back of his head and touched his soft hair. His arm tightened around her waist, pulling her closer to his body.

They moved in perfect rhythm, each matching the steps of the other as if they had always danced together. She didn't think, after the grueling afternoon she'd had learning the steps to the routine, she'd ever want to dance again. Yet, now resting in Grant's arms, her feet barely touched the floor. She was dancing on a cloud.

They spent the evening there. When most of the other couples had opted for the casino and thoughts of striking it rich, she had found her fortune. She swirled in Grant's arms to the sexy sound of a saxophone that played on and on into the small hours of the morning. When he took her back to Susan's apartment on the outskirts of the city, light was just breaking behind the distant hills.

Robyn didn't move when he pulled the rental car in front of Susan's building. It was one of the best days she'd ever had, and she was reluctant to have it end.

"It'll be daylight soon," she said, prolonging his departure.

Grant looked at the pink color spreading in the sky. It reminded him of the early morning horizon when he was flying.

"It's going to be a beautiful day." He knew that, even without the clear sky. Robyn had entered his life, and for some unexplained reason, he knew all his days would be beautiful.

Robyn turned to him and smiled. His arms snaked around her and pulled her unresisting body closer to his. He kissed her slowly, something he'd wanted to do since seeing her asleep in the sun. She moaned slightly in his embrace as she circled his neck with her arms. She played with his hair, her soft fingers combing through to his scalp. Sensation rocked him. He'd never known anyone to make him feel the way she did. He'd loved having her in his arms when they had danced, and now, his body strained for her. When the kiss ended, he kept her close, hugging her tightly to him.

"Do you suppose it's true that you can find anything open in this town at any hour?"

Robyn leaned back to look at him, her eyes dazed. "Is there something you need right now?" Her voice was thick with emotion.

"I know we only met today. All I know about you is that you work for the government, live in Washington, and like to dance. But I was wondering if we could find an open chapel, would you marry me with the sunrise?"

One

Grant was coming!

Robyn squeezed her eyes closed and massaged her temples with the tips of her fingers. Pain throbbed against her hands. Dr. Elliott thought he was delivering good news when he'd told her the blood was on its way and the donor with it. She never dreamed he'd come. Never thought when she'd given information about Grant to the doctors that he'd do anything except go to the nearest hospital and have the blood drawn. But now he was on his way.

Robyn pulled the hair lying on her back into a ponytail, then stretching, she let it go. Marianne came back at that moment with two cups of coffee in her hands.

"I saw Doctor Elliott in the hall." There was a large smile on her face. "He told me they found a donor who's not too far away." She put the two cups on the table and came to face Robyn. "Why don't you try to get some sleep, Brooke. When Kari wakes up, she'll want to see you. And you don't want to have those dark circles under your eyes."

"I'm all right, Marianne." She patted her friend's hand and wandered back to the window. All she could think of was that Grant was coming. He was coming to save his daughter's life. What if he came to see her, too? What if he didn't? She didn't know what to think. It had been five years. Five long, solitary years of thinking and dreaming about him. And now he was going to be in the same building with her.

She longed to see him. See what he looked like now. How he'd changed. Did he weigh more? Was his hair gray? And his smile, was it as she remembered? But she knew she couldn't see him. She knew she couldn't stand being near him the way she felt now—tired and afraid.

"Brooke, are you listening to me?" Marianne asked.

Robyn turned around, at this moment unused to her new name. She hadn't heard anything. Her mind was reeling from the news of Grant's impending arrival.

"I'm sorry, Marianne. I'm afraid I'm not good company. Why don't you go home? You must have a thousand things to do."

"I'm not going anywhere. Now, why don't you lie down here? I'll get a blanket from the nurse." Marianne motioned toward the sofa. "A few minutes' sleep won't hurt you."

Robyn knew she wouldn't sleep, but to please Marianne, she lay down on the sofa.

"I'll be right back," Robyn heard Marianne say and saw a nurse meet her at the waiting room door just before she closed her eyes.

She didn't sleep. She remembered. Remembered her wedding in the Las Vegas chapel, the house in

D.C., and the photos she used to develop. So many pictures of Grant. He was her favorite subject. They'd get up early in the morning and go to Rock Creek Park while the mist was low to the ground. She had to leave them all behind. She wondered what Grant had done with them. Was he still living in their house? Had he remarried? Her mind bubbled over with questions but the one that plagued her the most she had no answer for—would he know her? Under whatever cover the Witness Protection Program had draped her, would his heart still recognize her as the woman who'd loved him with all her heart?

Jacob Winston eased his suit jacket off as he entered the red-brick house with white shutters that he alone occupied on Tamarach Street in Washington's Rock Creek Park. He found it convenient to his office downtown and to the park's quiet solitude that he often needed. The central air conditioning had kicked on at three o'clock, making the dwelling blessedly cool after the sweltering heat of July in the nation's capital.

He headed for the den to check his messages. It was a normal routine whenever he entered his house. The den was set up as an office. While the rest of the house was clean enough to satisfy any mother-in-law's prying eye, his office was cluttered with books stacked haphazardly on the built-in shelves and piles of old newspapers separated into the three languages he read fluently—English, Spanish, and German. Flipping on the switch of his computer, he headed for the kitchen and a cold beer. The refrigerator looked like his office—cluttered with plastic containers of leftovers, Chinese food boxes, and several bottles of imported beer. He'd acquired a taste for German beer when bumming around Europe the year after he'd graduated from Stanford.

Using the bottle opener he'd mounted on the wall between the kitchen and the utility room, he caught the metal cap and tossed it with an exaggerated jump shot into the trash can nearly six feet away. Then, taking a long swig of the dark liquid, he headed back to the den.

Jacob had left his office before noon, spending the rest of the day in meetings. It was unusual for him to come home without checking in with his secretary or calling his electronic mail to any network computer within the FBI confines. But it was well past nine when he'd left, and tonight he'd wanted to get home. He had the urge to go out into his garden, darkness be damned, and spend the rest of the night in the pool.

Sitting down, he rested the bottle on the coaster he'd assigned permanent duty next to his color monitor. Choosing a menu item, the machine automatically dialed him into the FBI network. Typing through three levels of security and waiting while the remote messages traveled to the central processor and back, he finally saw the *access granted* message blinking on the screen.

Quickly, he accessed electronic mail, knowing his efficient secretary had entered his messages on-line. He took another swig of his beer and then stopped with the bottle midway between his mouth and the coaster. The name on the screen paralyzed him. Robyn had called him three times today, using the name Brooke Johnson. *Urgent* flashed like a danger sign next to her name. Robyn had never, in the years since he'd left her at the FBI headquarters in Atlanta right after Kari was born, ever called him. And to add to his paralysis were four messages to call Marianne Reynolds, each with the same urgent light flashing next to her name.

"Damn," he swore, his blood pounding in his ears. Something had to be wrong for both of them to call. Jacob snatched up the phone, punching the clear button for the unused line. He beat out the digits next to Marianne's name. It wasn't her home number. He knew that by heart.

"Buffalo General Hospital, ICU," a soft female voice greeted.

Jacob was jolted. He could hardly speak to answer the greeting. "I'm trying to reach Marianne Reynolds. She left this number." He didn't identify himself. Years of training had made subterfuge an unconscious act.

"One moment, please," the voice went on calmly and efficiently while his blood had begun to boil. In seconds, Marianne came on the line.

"What's wrong, Marianne?" he asked, wasting no time with a greeting or identification.

"You're too late," she whispered. Her voice sounded resigned and tired.

"Too late for what?" His temper was rising along with his voice level. Fear crowded in, making his heart tight.

"I think she's called him." Marianne's voice was stronger. Jacob could tell by the static that she was speaking into a cordless unit. She must have found a secure place to talk.

"Called who?" he asked unnecessarily. He knew she meant Robyn had made contact with her ex-husband. At least that meant *she* was all right.

"Tell me what happened?" He leaned forward, resting his head against the heel of his hand and closing his eyes.

"There was an accident. Kari is in critical condition. We've been here for two days." Marianne kept her words to a minimum. Jacob knew she realized this was an open line.

"What kind of accident?" Robyn had breached security with her phone call. He needed to know how deep the breach went. Marianne had been trained, but she was obviously attached to Kari, and Jacob knew she loved Robyn like a sister.

"An automobile accident, a stupid, purposeless accident." Her words told him there was no reason to suspect foul play. "Broken glass cut through an artery in Kari's arm. She lost a lot of blood."

"What about Brooke?" Jacob tensed, his mind forming pictures of red-stained bandages and broken bones.

"She escaped with minor cuts and bruises. She's been released, but we needed blood. None was available."

"What?" Jacob stood up, remembering a long ago argument he had with the then Robyn Richards over Kari's possible rare blood type.

"The supply is outdated, and no donors could be located."

Breath left Jacob's body in one long exhale. "Why didn't you call the center in Atlanta," he snapped.

The center was the Center for Disease Control. "I did that, Jacob." There was censure in her voice. "Their records showed that the supply is outdated. The closest supply we could find is in Los Alamos, New Mexico. It won't arrive before morning. She'll die by then."

Jacob heard the sob in Marianne's voice. A lump rose in his throat as he thought of the black-haired child. Although he hadn't seen her since she was born in a maximum security center four years ago, he had a fondness for her unlike any other he could define. He supposed it was due to his being Robyn's Lamaze coach for her delivery. After that experience how could anyone not love a child?

"How long has she got?" He spoke slowly, dragging his mind back to the present problem.

"I don't know, but minutes count at this stage."

"I'll take care of it from here. Keep me informed," he said resolutely. "In the meantime, stay with her."

Marianne handed the phone back, giving a weak smile to the nurse who replaced the receiver. "Thank you," she said absently as the perpetually smiling nurse handed her a blanket. She hoped Robyn was asleep. She'd known Jacob would help.

"Jacob would do anything for her," she muttered to herself as she walked toward the somber colored waiting room. Marianne had learned that the first weekend she'd reported to him. She'd been assigned to protect the newly created Brooke Johnson and her infant child. She quickly learned to address her only as Brooke and Robyn never knew she was her guardian angel. It was an easy assignment and Robyn and Marianne got along well together.

But Jacob was in love with Robyn. Marianne wasn't even sure he knew that. But she could tell by the way he gave in to Robyn whenever he disagreed with whatever she proposed. Usually, the outcome was that she got her way.

But in this case Jacob was too late. Robyn had given her ex-husband's name to the doctor, and he'd already been called. There was nothing else she could have done, and Marianne knew, in her heart, if Robyn hadn't done it she would have called herself.

When she entered the room, Robyn wasn't asleep, but had taken up her position in front of the dark window. She was staring out, looking at nothing, seeing nothing. Marianne knew she didn't even hear her come back.

"Brooke," she called softly. There was no reaction. She went to her friend and stood next to her. Robyn continued to stare through the glass.

"Brooke," she said again, her voice slightly louder. Robyn was still lost. Taking her arm, Marianne shook her lightly. The dazed eyes cleared to a somber brown. "I took a call for you," she said, letting her think Jacob had called her. Robyn didn't know that she was Marianne's assignment. Jacob insisted Marianne not tell her.

"Who was it?" Robyn turned, her face blank, her eyes wide.

"His name was Jacob. I told him what happened. He said he could get the blood."

"It's too late." Tears rolled down her face again. Marianne grabbed a tissue from the box on a nearby table and pushed it into Robyn's hand.

"Don't cry, Brooke. It'll get here in time," she told her, being more positive than she truly was. "Kari will be fine."

Robyn nodded. "Yes, Kari will be fine," she repeated, as a fresh batch of tears shook her body.

Marianne couldn't do anything. She guided Robyn to a chair and sat across from her, allowing her friend to sob tears as large as her swollen eyes.

"You should be at the restaurant," Robyn said.

"I'm not leaving until I know you and Kari are all right. The restaurant can survive without us for one night."

Marianne knew it was true. She'd called Yesterdays, the turn-of-the-century eatery they owned together, and found out things were running smoothly.

"Why don't you try to get some sleep? Just lie down here." She tried to get Robyn back to the sofa.

But Robyn was shaking her head. "I couldn't sleep. I keep thinking about when Kari was a baby." A smile flitted across her face, and Robyn began telling her anecdotes about Kari when she first learned to crawl. Marianne let her continue although she had either heard the story before or been there when the incident happened.

Finally, Robyn's eyes were so heavy that she was falling asleep while she talked. Marianne helped her to the sofa and pushed her down.

"The blood is here." Dr. Elliott came in, and Robyn was up immediately.

"Wonderful," Marianne said. "How's Kari?"

"It'll be hours before we know anything," he said. "But I expect God has given us the time we need."

He left them then, and Marianne immediately hugged her friend. "She's going to be fine, Brooke. I'm sure of it."

"I'm sure of it, too," Robyn said, her voice strained. "Now I think you should go."

"Brooke, don't be silly," Marianne protested.

"I'm not being silly. I'm scared and relieved at the same time. But most of all, I think I'd like to be alone for a while."

It wasn't the truth. What Robyn needed was assurance that Grant had come and gone. She didn't expect to see him. He didn't know Brooke Johnson. Then why was she so nervous that she needed Marianne to leave?

"I don't think being alone will do you any good."

"Please, Marianne." Robyn rolled her eyes to the ceiling. "I'm much too tired to argue the point. Go home and get some rest. In the morning, go to the restaurant. I promise if I need anything, you'll be the first person I call."

Marianne gave her a sober look and nodded. "Use the blanket," she said, reluctant to leave her alone. "Things will be better in the morning."

Robyn smiled as best she could. After Marianne left, she sank into the nearest chair and folded her arms across herself in a protective gesture. She waited.

Dr. Elliott would come back when Grant had gone. Tears rolled from her eyes. Five-year-old tears spilled onto her cheeks, reminding her of a time when she'd left everything she loved behind—including her husband. The only thing she'd taken was Kari, and now she might even lose her.

Two

"You've saved her life," Dr. Elliott said, as he entered the emergency room's curtained cubicle. "The sample matches so perfectly you could be of the same bloodline." A nurse carrying the life-giving liquid passed him, carefully holding the sterile plastic bag that contained the Richardses' ancestry.

Grant smiled at the white-coated doctor. He donated blood often but this was the first time the recipient of his rare type was waiting for the extraction as it left his body. "What's her name?" he asked. All he'd been told was that it was for a child.

"Kari Johnson, a beautiful, black-eyed four-year-old with long dark braids and a smile to twist a man's heart."

"Sounds like she's got yours, Doc." Grant laughed a clear, hearty sound.

"Oh, she has. Her mother is in the ICU waiting room, fourth floor. I'm sure she'd like to see you again."

"Again?" Grant slipped off the examination table, rolling his sleeve down and rebuttoning his cuff.

"She gave us your name and told us where to find you. I naturally assumed you knew each other."

"Mrs. Johnson?" Grant slipped his arms in the blue uniform jacket the doctor held out to him. His brows knitted in confusion. Johnson was a common name, but it brought no images to mind.

"Mrs. Brooke Johnson," Dr. Elliott prodded.

The name meant nothing to him. "I'm not sure I remember a Brooke Johnson. Maybe it's her husband I know."

"She's a widow. Her husband died as a result of some military accident before they moved here. I never met him."

"It doesn't matter. I'll say hello before I leave." Grant smiled. Generally, he was good at remembering names and faces. And if he did know Brooke Johnson, it would be rude to leave without seeing her.

"Good-bye, Mr. Richards and thank you for coming."

Grant shook hands with the thin, long-legged doctor whose height matched his own six-foot, two-inch frame. Frank Elliott would have had all the earmarks of a country doctor if it hadn't been for the rush of brown curls that fell over the collar of his long white coat and the diamond stud that pierced his left earlobe. Dr. Elliott thanked him again, as the doors of the elevator slid open. Grant clasped his hand and with a smile, stepped inside.

The hall was clear when the doors opened onto the fourth floor. Grant whistled softly into the quiet as he walked toward the waiting room adjacent to the doors leading to the intensive care unit. Pushing the door open, Grant's heart suddenly stopped, then hammered so hard against his ribs that he thought the woman facing the windows would certainly hear it. He gripped the glass-paneled door. Robyn was dead. His mind told him that, but everything about this woman screamed her name. The way she stood with her arms wrapped across her body as if she were warding off something. The bow of her head and the soft curve of her hips and legs could be duplicates of the woman he'd loved with all his being. The hair falling down her back was the same color as Robyn's had been. The darkness of the outside prevented any highlights from showing, but instinctively he knew they'd be golden, like the copper pennies he collected in the glass bowl on the desk in his den. His heartbeat shot to his throat and lodged there. Beads of sweat popped out on his forehead despite the comfortable temperature of the room. He didn't know how long he stood there, rooted in position. It was like seeing Robyn again, being in the same room with her.

Then she turned. When she did, his heart stopped again. This time in relief. Color drained from his face, and he dropped his head for a second to gain control of his rioting emotions.

When he looked up, sad swollen eyes looked into his as though they could see into his mind. But not even the shape of her face had any resemblance to his dead wife's. In the five years since Robyn died, he hadn't reacted to a woman as violently as he did to the one standing ten feet away. When she spoke, her voice was throaty and choked. Robyn's had done that when her emotions were close to the surface. He braked his thoughts, telling himself he was reading more into this than was really there. Hundreds of women have that hair color. Don't make more of this than is necessary.

Robyn had her back to the door, but she felt the soft rush of air as it opened and closed silently. The goose bumps rising on her arms and legs and the cold fear running the column from her neck down her spine told her that Grant had entered. Even though she knew he was coming, she was not prepared to see him again.

"Mrs. Johnson, I'm Grant Richards." The deep voice that had whispered words of love in her ear had not changed. She didn't move. Her body seemed frozen except for the hot blood that sang in her ears. Five years ago, this man had been her husband. His vital good looks were as she remembered them before his plane had been hijacked to Beirut, and he'd been held prisoner.

His tall, athletically toned body looked more like he spent his days on some California beach than cutting through the air thirty-thousand feet up. His black hair was slightly longer than airline regulations allowed, but his eyes were still sepia brown with dark flecks of gold. The cleft in his strong chin added sex appeal to a winning smile.

There wasn't much different about his appearance. His eyes looked tired, but that could have been due to having extended his day by immediately boarding a flight to Buffalo after his plane had landed at Washington's National Airport. Dr. Elliott had given her this information when he'd located Grant. Several strands of gray had sneaked into his hair near his temples, and a small vertical scar bisected his right eyebrow. The scar added a slightly sinister look to his face. It hadn't been there when she'd last seen him. It had to be a reminder of the time he spent as a Lebanese captive, she thought. Some sixth sense made her ball her hand into a fist behind her to keep from smoothing the separated brows.

"You didn't have to come. They could have flown the blood up. I didn't expect its owner to come with it," Robyn continued. She looked directly at him but made no attempt to move.

Eyes without a glimmer of recognition appraised her from her high cheekbones and shoulder length, dark brown hair to the generous curve of her hips, down her dancer's legs to end at her sandaled feet. She hadn't left the hospital since they brought Kari in. Now, she was aware of the rumpled shorts and blood-stained T-shirt that she still wore from their trip to the beach.

"Doctor Elliott was insistent on the urgency. There was a plane standing by—and here I am. Your daughter should be receiving the blood right now."

Relief pierced through her like physical pain.

Grant saw her step back and brace herself against the window frame. She turned away from him as she began to tremble. Her body shook violently, and no amount of self-determination could stop it from completing the course it had begun.

He watched her fight the fear that the accident must have caused in her. And now that Kari would be all right, delayed reaction to the pent-up stress was setting in. He had seen it before, in Beirut, when they were finally released. Men, who had been paragons of strength for many months, even years, had collapsed in tears when they reached safety.

Grant touched her lightly on the shoulder, then turned her toward him. She went easily into his arms, and he closed them around her as if they had a right to be there. He lowered her to one of the sofas.

"It's all right, she'll be fine now," he said, comforting her, unable to keep himself from stroking her hair.

"Thank you," Robyn said moments later as she pushed herself up. Grant took her hands and held them. The gesture, she was sure, was to comfort her, but what she felt was a magnetism which wanted to push her farther into his arms. "Mr. Richards . . ." she began.

"Grant," he corrected. "Everyone calls me Grant, and we are practically related," he added, a smile crinkling his eyes. "We have a child between us."

Grant had intended the comment to make her laugh. But when the color drained from her already pale face and fear replaced the sadness in her eyes, he was sorry for the joke. His hands squeezed the suddenly cold ones in his grasp. "I'm sorry. It was a poor joke."

Robyn tried to smile, but his words had caught her completely by surprise. "I understand," she managed. "I was . . . I just wanted to say that I appreciate what you've done for Kari. It must have been an inconvenience for you . . . and your family to come all this way." She stood up and walked aimlessly about with no particular destination in mind. The brief moment in his arms was too close to heaven for her to withstand his nearness.

"I don't have a family. I had a wife." He hesitated for the space of a moment. Robyn noticed it. "She died five years ago."

No she didn't, Robyn wanted to scream. "I'm very sorry." Robyn was relieved but somehow sad, too. If he had remarried his leaving wouldn't have been any easier to take than knowing he was still single. It might even be harder knowing there was another woman who had taken her place.

He stood up and came to stand behind her. "How long have you been here?" he asked, moving the subject away from the past. Robyn didn't know why she'd brought up the subject of his family. She knew he thought she was dead. It was how Jacob Winston and his force had manipulated the situation.

"The ambulance brought us in yesterday. No-no, it was the day before."

Robyn had done that, that little quick repeat of the word no, Grant noted with shock. "And I'll bet you haven't had anything to eat except these cups of coffee."

For the first time, Robyn noticed that the table was littered with partially emptied cups of vending machine coffee. Eight tan-and-white striped cups were scattered about the low table, several more looked at her from the wastebasket.

"I'm hungry. Let me buy you a good dinner," he offered.

"No, I need to stay here. Kari . . ."

"Is in good hands." Dr. Elliott spoke from the door. "You need to get out of here and get some sleep." He came toward them. "Kari is sleeping comfortably. She won't wake up before morning."

How could she explain? She couldn't have dinner with Grant. She didn't want to feel the way he made her feel. Spending time in his company wasn't part of the bargain she'd made with Jacob. In fact, it was in direct violation of the Witness Protection Program of which she and Kari were participants.

Dr. Elliott bent to pick up her sweater from the chair while Grant took her elbow and nudged her toward the waiting room door. She was too tired to struggle, allowing herself to be jockeyed by the two men. One part of her wanted to give in, but somewhere inside a part of her shouted to stop before things got out of hand.

"Could I see Kari before I go?" She turned back to the pediatrician.

"Of course, but only for a moment." Dr. Elliott took her hand and spoke seriously. "Kari is taking the blood now. We won't know much until tomorrow. Get some sleep. If there is any change, I'll have the hospital call you."

Robyn nodded, her eyes flooding with tears that she blinked away. The three of them walked down the hall to the room that housed her small daughter and several shelves of monitoring equipment. Grant followed Robyn as she entered the room and stood at the restraining rail. Kari slept quietly. The precious liquid dripped slowly through its plastic tube, linking Kari's fragile existence to the preserver hanging above her.

Tears sprang to Robyn's eyes as guilt filled her heart. Grant, misunderstanding her action, turned her into his arms and rested her head on his shoulder. She savored the moment. He was so warm and solid she wanted to hang onto him. His child lay so close, and her mouth was bound against telling him of her existence.

Grant didn't know what was happening to him. He had her in his arms now for the second time in the half hour since they'd met. She was so soft. Her hair smelled like sunshine and fresh air. He wanted to crush her to himself, let her know her child would be all right. Brooke Johnson was making him feel things he hadn't felt in years, but he couldn't tell her. Her mind was totally on the child in the bed behind them. She was only clinging to him because she was tired and scared.

Robyn gently pushed herself away from him and moved back to the bed. She smoothed back Kari's dark hair. Her bangs had lost all their curl, and her barrettes looked unnatural against the pillows. She was pale. Her skin, usually a golden brown, was a pale gray. Her arms were bandaged, and there was a bright red gash on her cheek. Lowering the railing between them, she leaned over and kissed her daughter. Carefully, she examined the arm where the exploding glass had severed her artery. When she straightened and repositioned the barrier, she stared at Kari until Grant put his hand on her shoulder and slowly turned her toward the door.

"Are there any good restaurants close by?" he asked at the High Street entrance as they waited for a taxi.

"Of course," she said, thinking of Yesterdays for the first time in nearly two days. Although Marianne had been at the hospital, Robyn had not thought of the restaurant. "I'm not very hungry. I don't really want anything to eat."

"Then, I'll see you home."

Robyn nodded. Her head lolled on her neck. Grant put his hand on the small of her back, guiding her down the steps. The taxi arrived, and he helped her into the backseat.

Robyn leaned against the upholstery, her eyes closed. Grant hated to disturb her. "We need your address, Brooke," he whispered.

She was instantly alert. As much as she wanted to fold herself against him, she sat erect.

"This is lovely," Grant said twenty minutes later as they entered the house she and Kari had occupied since coming to Buffalo. A large L-shaped sofa in a soft dusty rose faced the fireplace in her oversized living room. In front of it was a square mahogany cocktail table holding an arrangement of gray and mauve silk flowers. Two wing chairs completed the grouping. At the opposite end of the room was a baby grand piano.

"Thank you," she smiled, somehow glad he liked it. "We find it comfortable."

"It looks more than comfortable." He went to the mantel and lifted a gold-framed photo of a smiling child. Dr. Elliott had been right. He could see how she could twist a man's heart. Except for her eye color, Kari looked nothing like her mother, he thought. Grant looked at the wedding photo on the opposite side of the mantel. He didn't see much resemblance there either.

"My husband," she explained. "He died before Kari was born."

"I'm sorry," Grant said, feeling at a loss of what to say.

Her hands squeezed into fists behind her as Grant compared the doctored wedding photo of her and a man she'd never met to the one of Kari he held in his hand.

"She's got your eyes," he said.

Robyn nodded. And everything else she got from you, she silently amended.

He turned back to Brooke. Grant liked the decor. The room told a lot about its owner. It was cool and serene with a quiet charm. Although the furnishings were modern, the accents revealed a definite traditional flavor. As he looked around further, he saw everything was neatly stored in its proper place, yet there was an air about it which said *you can live here.* He could imagine toys scattered about the carpeted floor or see colored packages radiating from a tall Christmas tree.

It's home. The thought knocked him off guard. He hadn't thought about a home since Robyn died. He'd sold their old house. He couldn't live there without her. Her mother's piano was the only thing he hadn't put in storage, and he couldn't bring himself to sell it. Robyn had loved it too much.

And here was another woman whose placement of inanimate objects had caused him to remember what it was like to live in a home. After the many foster homes he'd lived in before he was twelve, he couldn't remember anything as being permanent, rooted. He was as sure as he could be that this was his idea of what home should look like. He replaced the photo and turned back to Brooke. For a second their eyes locked in a momentary stare. Heat sprang up in the lower regions of his body, a heat he couldn't control. He felt like he was back in high school, but he had turned thirty-seven on his last birthday. Yet, his body was acting as if it had only today learned about puberty. There was no doubt he wanted Brooke. But the signals he got from her were mixed. He felt there was a guard in front of her, someone who edited everything she thought before allowing the words to come from her mouth. He could almost see another presence behind her sad eyes. He wanted to pass through that invisible being and touch the woman behind it.

"Do you play?" He indicated the piano to cover his discomfort. Taking a seat at the keyboard, he ran his fingers lightly across the keys.

"Only enough for my own satisfaction," she lied.

Robyn, sitting at the piano, suddenly intruded. She had played well. Often, her private concerts led to them making love.

Color rose in Robyn's face. She, too, thought of where her piano playing had led. Suddenly, the danger of his presence hit her. It had become natural for her to play the role designed for her, but with the way her emotions danced out of step each time he looked at her, she had to get him out of her life. And before Jacob Winston learned what she'd done.

"I'm not very hungry, Grant," she began in her it's-time-for-you-to-go-tone.

"I understand." He stood, preparing to leave. "Will you be all right?" His voice was quiet, laced with concern.

"I'm fine—really," she reassured him.

After a slight hesitation, he started for the door. Invisible hands squeezed her heart until she thought she'd scream. Robyn clutched her chest, trying to calm it. She reached into herself, searching for some of the courage and reserve that Jacob had promised would be there when she needed it. And she needed it now.

She watched him walking toward the door. The room suddenly seemed bigger, longer. He moved in slow motion, getting smaller as he got closer to the far side of her life. Just a few seconds, she thought. Just a few more seconds and he'd be gone, out of her life. She'd be safe.

"Gr . . . Grant . . ." she stopped him with a stutter. "Don't go."

Three

Jacob hung up the phone and slumped back in his chair. He grabbed his beer and drained the glass bottle. Usually, he enjoyed his beer, but Marianne's call had his stomach churning. Something didn't sit right.

Suddenly, he sat up in his chair as if propelled. His fingers flew over the computer keyboard, racing against an unseen force. Seconds later, he'd passed security and was in the computer of the Center for Disease Control. The records on the screen confirmed what Marianne had told him.

Why didn't he believe it? It was just too coincidental that all the hospitals in the area were out of stock. Jacob didn't like coincidences. He pulled the phone toward him, setting it on his thigh. He dialed the number he knew by heart but hadn't called in years.

"This better be good," a voice gravelly with sleep barked into his ear. Jacob would have smiled if he hadn't been concentrating so hard.

"Carl, this is Jacob," he said.

"I won't ask if you know what time it is."

Jacob could almost see him turning the clock toward himself to check the digital dial.

"It's important, Carl. I need a favor."

"All right what is it?" he asked, seriousness entering his voice.

Carl Logan and Jacob Winston had been partners on the police force. They'd worked homicide in Chicago for six years, until Carl's wife, Amy, was kidnapped and killed by a serial killer who took their investigation personally. Carl had become a computer jockey. Jacob had gone to the FBI, a different kind of law enforcement. The Cynthia Affair had been his reason for needing a change of location.

"I need you to go and check the blood supply at the center."

"What?" Jacob knew Carl was climbing out of bed. He was the closest thing to a best friend Jacob had. Over the years, the two of them had used their respective skills to help each other whenever they could, and Jacob knew Carl wouldn't let him down. "Why don't I just dial in and check the stock? On second thought, why don't you?"

"I've already done that. It says the supply of AB negative is exhausted."

"And you have reason to believe something different?"

"It's just a hunch." Jacob had no concrete evidence that anything was wrong, just a gnawing feeling in his gut.

"Jacob, we keep extremely accurate—"

"Carl," Jacob stopped him before he began a lecture on the methods of making sure the physical stock matched the records. "This is very important."

"All right, Jacob. I'll go over right now and check it out myself. What are you looking for?"

"AB negative. How much have you got?"

"I'll call you back when I get there. Where are you?"

"Home."

Jacob hung up and waited. Suddenly, everything was quiet. He could hear the crickets outside and the quiet hum of the refrigerator in the kitchen. The clock in the hall, that had been his mother's, chimed out the hour. But the phone did not ring. He stood up and went for another beer, dropping the empty bottle in the recycling container.

There were three bottles in the yellow container before the phone rang. Jacob lunged for it, snatching it off the wall before it finished the first ring.

"Yeah," he said.

"This is really weird, Jacob," Carl said.

"How much have you got?" he asked, trying to control his anxiousness.

"Enough to supply a small war if every casualty was AB negative. None of it's outdated. I'm standing in the refrigerator, and the supply is here. Yet, the machines say we're out. I don't understand."

"Try finding out what happened, and let me know." Jacob knew he didn't have to ask the favor. Carl would search without direction. He couldn't leave a puzzle until all the pieces were in place. "Thanks for your help," Jacob continued. "I owe you one."

"Anytime, partner."

Jacob replaced the receiver and leaned his head against the arm that he had propped on the doorjamb. He'd been tracking anything that might jeopardize Robyn and Kari for five years, but something had

started with Robyn's accident. He could feel it. Tomorrow, he'd verify the blood at the other hospitals.
But he already knew, before he'd placed one call, that
the Crime Network was back in action.

Robyn stood frozen. Grant's hand was on the doorknob when she'd stopped him. She hadn't realized the
strangled cry had come from her until Grant turned.
For a heartbeat, there was a sign of recognition, then
it was gone.

"There isn't much food here," she said. "But the
least I can do is make you an omelette and some coffee."

"It sounds wonderful, I'll help," Grant said. A smile
lit his face as he came back into the room. Robyn
thought she saw relief in his eyes. Maybe she just
wanted to see it, she told herself.

"That won't be necessary." She needed time to com-
pose herself and understand why she'd stopped him.
She knew it was safer to let him go through the door,
yet she'd called him back. It didn't matter that it wasn't
a deliberate act. She'd asked him to stay.

"Don't worry," he smiled. "I'm very good in the
kitchen."

"I'm sure you are." She knew how much help he
could be. Many nights they'd spent, side by side, preparing dinner or loading the dishwasher.

"I am, I promise." He raised his right hand in the
Boy Scout salute, then took off his jacket and folded
it over the back of the sofa before following Robyn
to the kitchen. He stopped short at the door. It was a

huge airy room, brightly lit and outfitted for a gourmet cook.

"Maybe I should take that back," he groaned.

Robyn laughed for the first time. Both of them noticed it but neither commented. Filling the coffeepot with water, she poured it into the well of the automatic machine. Her kitchen was a cook's dream. Copper pots gleamed from a rack above the butcher-block counter, two sinks strategically placed for functionality, and a side-by-side refrigerator and freezer still allowed room for free movement.

"I'm sure you'll be able to find the eggs," she said.

This was where her business had begun. She had a degree in history and had thought she'd follow her father into government work, but Jacob steadfastly asserted she could never use it.

"Absolutely everything about Robyn Richards has to be forgotten. She won't exist. Brooke Johnson does not have a degree in history." She could still hear the adamant tone in his voice.

Robyn chose cooking as a career. She loved making art out of food. Since it was a relatively unassuming profession, and Robyn wasn't one to sit around doing nothing, Jacob had few objections.

At first, she and Marianne catered parties and weddings, fashioning elaborate designs with sweetbreads. Fruits and vegetables were transformed into statues. But her trademark was the spectacular one-of-a-kind wedding cake scenes. She met people who recommended her to their friends. Her reputation and fortune grew until she had saved enough money to buy a run-down Victorian mansion that she'd renovated and turned into a restaurant.

Grant found the eggs, and Robyn handed him a bowl and a silver whisk. He began breaking them as she found cheese, onions, peppers, celery, and ham and started dicing them into small pieces. She worked quickly and efficiently.

He watched in amazement at the lightning manner in which she used a knife. "You *will* tell me if you ever decide to use that on me?" he asked lightly. "Should I ask how you learned to use a knife with the skill of a Japanese master chef?"

"There's nothing mysterious about it. I practiced a lot." She smiled at the fun she had playing with him. "I used to own a catering business, now I have a restaurant in town. For a while my partner and I were the only cooks. And practice does . . ." She left the cliché hanging, allowing her proficiency to finish the sentence.

Robyn took the eggs Grant had whisked into a yellow fluff, added the diced vegetables, and then poured them in the omelette pan. Minutes later, they were seated at the breakfast nook where she and Kari usually began their day.

Grant ate hungrily, obviously enjoying his food. Robyn, too, finished a meal she hadn't thought she was hungry enough to eat. They talked quietly about life in Buffalo, the theater, the latest world events. Robyn knew it wasn't important conversation. She also knew he was trying to help her take her mind off Kari. For the most part, it worked until finally all that was left were dirty dishes and memories. She wanted to cry.

"I should call the hospital," she said tears apparent in her voice.

"She'll be fine." Grant put a restraining hand on her wrist. A regiment of electric shocks galloped from where his hand lay on her wrist up to her shoulder. Her eyes found Grant's and held. She pulled her arm away, rubbing it gently to restore normal feeling.

"I'm sorry. I didn't mean to hurt you."

"I'm not hurt," she said a bit too quickly, then tried to hide it by taking a drink from her coffee cup.

"I'm sure Kari's fine. Doctor Elliott promised to call if there was any change in her condition."

"I know. It's just that I feel so helpless." She stood up and began moving the dishes from the table and stacking them in the sink. "If only I'd listened to Kari. She wanted to stay at the beach longer. If only . . ."

Grant came to stand behind her. "Don't do this to yourself." He turned her to face him, dropping his hands quickly. "It was an accident. You can't blame yourself for circumstances."

"I know, but I keep feeling, if only I'd seen the other car . . ."

"It wasn't your fault," he said more forcefully. "There was nothing you could have done to prevent it." She looked at him, her eyes wide and tired. She wanted to step into his arms and let him hold her but she couldn't. "You know, you should get some sleep. You'll feel much better tomorrow." His voice was quiet as if he could no longer argue with her.

"I don't think I could." With Kari in the hospital

and Grant within holding distance, she was sure sleep for the night was not an option.

"Why don't you try a hot bath? It will relax you."

"Tonight, I don't think it would work."

He nodded, understanding. "All right, talk to me. Tell me where we know each other from."

Grant's instincts were excellent, yet he didn't need them to tell him Brooke Johnson was familiar. He recognized the tenseness in the way she held her shoulders, the nervous way she wrung her hands, and the way her eyes widened. She dropped her head for a moment. The smell of her shampoo wafted through the air. He knew it, had smelled it before, but where? A millisecond of memory flashed through his mind, but flitted before he could capture or record it.

There was no single thing about her that leaped forward to force his memory, but the collection of small things, like the way she moved, tipped her head to the side, or held her fork when she ate. He wondered where they had met and if she remembered.

"We haven't met before," Robyn told him.

"Doctor Elliott said you gave him my name; told him where to find me."

"Oh," she laughed, turning back to the sink and busying herself restacking dishes that were already stacked. "It's your blood type. I memorized the names and addresses of everyone with Kari's blood type within a four-hundred-mile radius. When Doctor Elliott explained all the local supplies were exhausted or outdated I gave him your name."

Lie number one, Robyn thought. Thank goodness she'd devised a reason for knowing who he was without telling the truth. If he'd asked her to name another donor she'd be hard pressed to think of one. If she'd done something practical like finding the names of possible donors and committing them to memory, Grant would still be in Washington, and she would be inside the protective world Jacob had set up for her. She'd used Kari's blood type as a reason to settle so close to her former husband, but she'd hadn't considered the real need to contact him. When Jacob told her there would be a blood supply if needed, she believed him. It unnerved her that his promise proved untrue.

Robyn turned on the water and opened the dishwasher. Methodically, she began rinsing and placing the soiled dishes in the dishwasher. Her thoughts went back five years to the days after the trial. She'd been blackmailed into this elite prison. She was angry, and Jacob took the brunt of her bereft feelings.

She and Jacob argued over everything: where she would live, what she would look like, even the color of her hair. The two of them were a battle looking for a war. It erupted the night she told him she was pregnant.

The last saucer had been placed in the rack, yet the water ran unheeded over her hands. Jacob had been angry. He'd told her it was against the law to break up families. Robyn hadn't known she was going to have a baby when she chose to go in without Grant. His life had been uprooted too many times, and he'd have to give up flying, a sacrifice she wouldn't want him to make. Yet, it might not have had an impact if it weren't for Project Eagle. After she found the camouflaged microchip, Grant had been forced to tell her about it.

Robyn had regrets, but she knew she'd done the

right thing. Without Clarence Christopher's fatherlike influence, she'd have chosen to help her husband and the nine other men being held prisoner in Beirut.

"Brooke, where are you?" Grant reached around her and stopped the flow of water. She snapped back to the present. It had been a long time since thoughts of how she got into the program intruded on her life.

"I'm sorry. I'm tired." She grabbed a paper towel and dried her hands. "Since the accident, I've been at the hospital." She fumbled for something to say. It seemed the past and present were colliding, and she had lost control over what would happen. Why hadn't he just given the blood and let it be flown up? Why did he have to come himself?

"Why don't you get some sleep?"

"Maybe you're right. I think I will take a shower and try to sleep."

"Good idea. Go on. I'll clean these dishes and see myself out."

Robyn hesitated a moment.

"It's all right." He knew she was thinking they had only met. He was a stranger, and how could she leave a strange man in her kitchen and go to bed. "I promise to lock the door behind me."

Robyn was struck by how much she still loved him. She walked to the door, then turned for one last look. "Thank you, Grant. I'll never forget what you've done for Kari. Good-bye."

Robyn stepped into her shower minutes later, hoping the water cascading over her tired body would be enough to wash away the aching need she had for the man downstairs. She hadn't thought her feelings would be this intense. It had been five years, and she had been out with several men since Grant. One of them she'd actually considered marrying. She had thought there would be a dullness to her feelings if she ever saw Grant again, but she was wrong. Her feelings had not changed. Her love was as bright and new as it had been when she saw him standing at the bottom of the stairs in Las Vegas. Her heart beat just as fast now. Her throat was dry and her hands were as cold as when he'd asked her to marry him.

She thought of him washing dishes as the two of them had done countless times. She smiled remembering his playful nature as he'd teased her that they'd still be washing dishes together when they reached sixty and their children were grown and gone. A lump rose in Robyn's throat at the bittersweet irony of the situation. Grant was in her kitchen, five years after she'd walked out of his life.

Tears mingled with the running water. This was her fault. It wasn't that Grant was downstairs because of the accident. It had begun years ago, when she had almost begged to get the part-time job at the FBI while she was in college. A fresh batch of tears racked her body. It was impossible to know at the time, but her happiness that day had paved the road to the misery that she felt pouring from her body like the water spurting from the showerhead.

After graduation, she was offered a permanent position as an analyst in the Major Crimes Bureau. She worked hard and had a good memory. It was because of her memory she realized she had seen a dead man, a man presumed dead. Several witnesses, who claimed they had seen the body of this international assassin, had reported him dead. Word had it that he was killed when trying to execute a contract against a drug lord. But she had seen him—alive—at a Washington restaurant. She had instantly recognized him when he bumped into her as she made her way to the ladies' room.

Four years later, she sat across the courtroom and identified him as Alex Jordan, code name: the Devil. She'd known his life as well as she knew her own, including the assassinations credited to him, like the baffling case in Sicily where six American men had died inside a room that had been locked from the inside.

Alex Jordan had only been the beginning. Everything about him made her suspicious, and every piece of information she uncovered drew her closer and closer to her own agency. It was a Pandora's box and she had sprung the lock.

The shower had gone from hot to tepid when Robyn's memory returned her to the present. Reaching for the crystal dials, she switched them off. The plush white towel that soaked the water from her body was thick and soft. It was not at all like the scratchy one she'd used in the dingy motel room only weeks after Alex Jordan was killed, and McKenzie Cranford was exposed as a mole in the department.

Grant watched Brooke go up the stairs. She had a strange mixture of hurt and trust in her eyes. Trust had won, and somehow that made him feel good. Naturally, she assumed he'd fly back to Washington. What else could he do? He didn't know her, yet he felt a strange pull toward her. His body wanted hers. He resisted the tightening of his stomach muscles that the thought produced. But more than that he also wanted to get to know her. He wanted to know what made her eyes so sad. And why did they give off such ambivalent messages? But the feeling that had passed between them when he touched her was shocking. He knew it shot from his fingers into her arm with the same erratic force that scampered up his own arm. Even if she hadn't rubbed it away, he'd have known she felt it.

When he finished the few dishes she hadn't rinsed, he went back to the living room. It was still in the same neat order he'd left it, but he felt he knew it better on second sight. This time he lifted a picture of Brooke, who smiled from a frame which matched the one of Kari. He noticed her eyes. They held the same sadness he'd noticed when he'd first seen her standing in the backlight of the hospital window. She reminded him of someone else, but he couldn't quite focus on who. But of one thing he was certain, Brooke Johnson *would* see him again.

He liked the feelings she evoked in him. He hadn't felt them in a long time. Not since that day he was finally home, back on U.S. soil and moments away from seeing his wife. His best friend had pulled him away from the throngs of reporters, who were shouting question after question about his release, to tell him there had been an accident. His beloved Robyn, on her way to the airfield to greet him, was in a car that had collided with an oil tanker. In his mind, images of billowing black smoke spiraling above the city and the ensuing fire that had burned her body beyond recognition crystallized as vividly as they had done on that clear day in April five years ago.

He replaced the gold-framed photograph and hooked his jacket over his shoulder, preparing to leave. He listened to the silence and assumed Brooke had fallen asleep. His hand was on the doorknob, before it occurred to him to look in on her and make sure she was all right.

He found her asleep in a room at the top of the stairs with muted yellow walls and beneath a blue-and-white bedspread. She looked like a little girl. Feelings he thought were long buried surfaced, making his body warm. Suddenly, he was a knight in shining armor, standing ready to protect her against whoever had taken the light from her eyes and replaced it with an ever-present sadness. Carefully, he replaced the coverlet over shoulders that he had to resist caressing. She stirred slightly but didn't wake.

Closing the door quietly, he stepped into Kari's adjacent room. Switching on the light, he found the room to be a bright, happy one with pink curtains and stuffed toys filling every available corner. One grouping had six baby bears sitting around a toy table. Miniature cups and saucers sat in front of each bear, indicating an end of a good meal. Grant thought of the impromptu meal he'd just had. It was simple but satisfying.

A hutch with children's books graced one corner.

He picked up *Cat in the Hat,* remembering he'd had this book before his parents were killed, and he was left alone. He put it back. The top shelf had more stuffed bears on it. There was a model of an old train. Inside were two bears dressed as nurses. They had their backs to each other as if they were walking in different directions. Another arrangement had seven bears dressed as knights. They were lined up on a replica of the Brooklyn Bridge.

Above his head was a shelf which circled the room. Books and toys stood behind a small, pink newel post fence. Grant smiled as he picked up a small brown teddy bear and placed it on the shelf overhead with others of its size and color. As he turned, he noticed the photo albums. Pulling one from its place, he flipped through it, finding the pages filled with pictures of the child he had seen but once.

Robyn, too, had loved taking pictures. He remembered building her a darkroom in their basement. She'd spend hours there, developing the film she'd taken of everything from flowers to portraits. He hadn't seen it in years, but the person who took these pictures had the same style as Robyn. He noticed how well each one had been framed before the shutter opened to freeze the moment. Anyone of them could have *made the wall,* Robyn's phrase for the best pictures. "This one," she'd say. "This one makes the wall."

Grant wanted to look closer at them. He took several of the albums downstairs so the light wouldn't filter under Brooke's door and disturb her.

* * *

When Robyn woke, sunlight streamed through her windows. She looked at the clock next to her bed. Kari would be in anytime now, bouncing on the bed saying, "I'm hungry." Robyn rolled over smiling, then memory flooded her consciousness. Kari was in the hospital. Rapidly, she jerked herself upright and dialed the direct number to Dr. Elliott's office. The nurse assured her Kari was all right. She had slept comfortably through the night, awakened briefly at six AM, but immediately had fallen asleep again.

Robyn felt a new optimism as she pulled on the matching robe to her full-length gown and pushed her feet into her slippers before heading downstairs to start the coffee maker. Afterward, she would dress and go to the hospital. She wanted to be there the next time Kari woke. Mentally, she made a note to call Marianne and Will, her closest neighbor and Kari's surrogate grandfather. They had taken turns staying with her. She would check in with Marianne at the restaurant. But first the coffee.

Halfway down the stairs, her heart leapt into her mouth. Grant was still here. He slept silently on the long side of the sofa. The coffee table was scattered with volumes of Kari's baby pictures. For a long moment, she stared dumbfounded. Her hands with a strength unknown to her gripped the wooden banister.

She didn't know how long she stood there nailed to the step or what ghosts carried her across the room, but she found herself wedged between the coffee table and the sofa. Slowly, she dropped to her knees. Grant didn't move, but Robyn's world tilted. Suddenly, she was Robyn Richards, and this was her husband.

"Grant," she said in a small, hoarse voice barely audible. She swallowed the painful knot in her throat and tried his name again. He didn't stir. Robyn savored the unguarded moment. She enjoyed watching him sleep. For the first time in five years, she could gaze upon a real person, not the elusive image she was forced to create during the long nights she endured alone. But why was he here? What made him stay? For a moment, fear that he knew who she was crept into her brain. She rejected the notion immediately. After the elaborate plastic surgery and implants nothing about her face physically was the same. Jacob wouldn't allow it.

Grant shifted. His arm fell off the sofa and into her lap. Robyn caught her breath sure her presence would wake him. After a moment, she relaxed, sitting back on her legs. She stared at him, remembering their honeymoon and the nights he'd wake her when he came in from a late flight. A dreamy smile curved her lips. When his hands moved to her arm, she froze. His eyes opened but didn't focus. "Robyn, I love you." She knew he was dreaming, but when he pulled her into his arms, her body had already decided to go. His mouth found hers in a soft brushing motion. Tentatively, it probed, tasted, cajoled. Whatever metaphysical forces kept time and space continuing in a forward motion seemed to have stopped as he continued his slow exploration. One hand found its way into her hair, combing through it with long sensitive strokes that ended in gentle caresses against her shoulders. Warm waves, like the gentle lapping of a calm sea, washed over her melting body.

Then, with sudden swiftness, passion flared, and his tongue pushed past her teeth to taste the wet nectar inside. Her body arched, straining closer to him. Arms she'd forgotten were hers wrapped around his frame. Excitement flowed through her fingers as she felt the play of sinew, bone, and muscle that rippled in response to her searching hands. His chest crushed her full breasts in a wonderfully erotic pain as he shifted position and slid to the floor. Fervently, he ravished her mouth, her neck, and her shoulders. Dark brown erect nipples pushed back against him with unbridled restraint. Her head fell back, allowing him access to the full column of her neck. Torrents of heat invaded her body. She felt herself dissolving into him. She wouldn't be able to stand this assault on her emotions much longer without screaming for him to make love to her. Already her body was hot and longed for him to push her back into the soft carpeting and give her the fulfillment she'd waited five years to experience again.

Four

"Oh, my God!" Grant said forcing his mouth from hers. He slumped against her as he buried his face in her hair. "I'm sorry, Brooke. I had no intention of doing that."

Robyn's breath came in ragged gulps. She was conscious of everything about her body, even feeling the blood rush through her veins. She tried to speak, but opening her mouth only provided an additional vessel for the air she craved. Grant rolled away from her, but the confined space kept them touching from chest to toe. Finally, control returned to her muscles. Robyn pushed herself up.

"You mentioned your wife last night." Her voice was breathless, and she rested her head on the sofa. "It's only natural you would dream of her." Forcing herself to look at him, she continued, "When I woke you, you thought I was her." She was amazed how calm her voice sounded, almost clinical.

"You must be the most amazing woman in the world."

"Why?"

"Anyone else would have slapped my face for calling her by someone else's name and kissing her the way I kissed you."

Color crept up Robyn's face to her ears. She hadn't completely recovered from being lost in his arms, and his comment brought back graphic images of them from moments before. "I thought you were asleep when you did that."

"I was, but you weren't."

"I didn't . . . I mean . . ." She dropped her eyes, at a loss as to what to say.

"Why did you let me go on?" The softness in his voice made her want to tell him the truth.

Robyn looked him in the eye for a silent second, then dropped her gaze to her hands. She couldn't tell him she was his wife and wanted nothing more than to be held in his arms and smothered with his kisses.

"It's all right," he paused, lifting her chin with one finger. "You don't have to answer. But I do apologize for calling you Robyn."

"Apology accepted." She managed a smile. "Now, how about some breakfast?"

"Sounds good to me." He helped her up, and they entered the kitchen together. "Have you called the hospital?"

"Yes, Kari is doing well." Robyn busied herself preparing the food. She usually sat with Kari, laughing during their breakfast ritual and listening to her excited conversation about the day before. Since beginning life as Brooke Johnson, widow with child, she'd changed significantly.

"Ah, maybe I'll get to see the real girl before I go

back. I guess by the look of the living room, you noticed I glanced through a few albums."

"I must admit I did notice one or two." She laughed, realizing it seemed like years since she'd last laughed.

"I planned just to look in on you and leave, but then I saw the photo albums. My wife was an amateur photographer. The pictures reminded me of . . ." He stopped as if the memory was too painful. "Anyway I must have fallen asleep."

"It's all right. I don't mind you talking about her. Robyn, right?"

"Yes, she liked photography. Did you take the pictures in the albums?"

"It's a hobby of mine. Unfortunately, I don't have much time to really get into it."

Grant was quiet a moment. Robyn was sure he was thinking of the Robyn he lost. A pang of guilt hit her. "Tell me about her?" Robyn asked, putting a cup of coffee in front of him, but keeping out of his line of vision as she continued frying bacon and eggs. "How long were you married."

He lifted the morning potion to his lips and tentatively tested the hot liquid. "Two years. We were technically still honeymooners. We had a house in Washington. She'd done all the decorating herself."

Robyn remembered that house. She could still see the beige curtains that hung from the windows of their bedroom. On breezy days, the wind played hide-and-seek with them. Grant had found the house before they were married, just off Connecticut Avenue. She smiled, remembering the two of them walking to the Washington Hilton for Sunday brunch, then her face clouded when she thought how short their marriage had been.

"Do you still live there?" Robyn dragged her thoughts back to the present. Her eyes were smarting, but she kept them averted from his by giving her full attention to the work she was performing. Jacob hadn't given her any information on Grant. He said a clean break was best for all concerned.

"Not anymore. I tried it for a while, but there were too many memories. I kept expecting her to walk into the bedroom or find her in the kitchen at dinnertime. Finally, I sold the house and moved into a condo."

Robyn's heart sank. She had imagined him living in their house. But now she was glad he had moved. He was only thirty-seven, a virile man. She'd hate to think of him and another woman in the house where they had shared so much love.

Giving him a plate and taking the opposite chair, she said, "You must have loved her a great deal."

"I did. I admit it. What we had in the two short years is more than other couples get in decades of marriage."

Something caught in Robyn's throat. For a moment she couldn't speak.

"How did she die?"

It was a question Robyn had asked Jacob, but his answer had been she didn't *need to know*. She could still hear his cocky reply. "The details of Mrs. Grant Richards's demise are on a need-to-know basis, and you do not need to know." End of discussion, file closed. No manner of coercion could get him to release any details that he had not been specifically ordered to divulge.

"She died in an automobile accident. A plane I was flying was hijacked to Beirut. We were held prisoner for five months." He touched the scar above his eye. Robyn noticed the gesture. "On the day I returned to Washington, the car Robyn was riding in hit an oil tanker."

Robyn flinched. All the air threatened to leave her body, but she forced herself under control. For months, she had taken classes, brainwashing lessons, that taught her how to act and react under unexpected situations. So that was how they'd done it. The story they told him must have included her body being burned beyond recognition. Oh, Jacob, she thought wryly, you are thorough.

"Excuse me," Grant interrupted her thoughts. "I didn't mean to surprise you."

"That's not it. I'm so sorry for you. It must have been terrible, being a prisoner. Then, just when you were free, to have your wife die when trying to reach you." She reached across the table and took his hand. The static electricity which began snapping along her arm wasn't at all unpleasant. His hand tightened.

"You're a very perceptive lady. I like you. And there's more meaning in that phrase than the words convey."

Robyn took her hand away, raising her coffee to her mouth. It was cold. She took both cups and moved to refill them. "Do I remind you of her?" she asked when she sat down again. She wasn't afraid of the answer. The changes made to her included everything—even her voice. The implants in her face elevated her voice while eliminating the almost husky quality she'd had when she and Grant first met. However, of all the alterations forced on her, she did like her new voice. Now, when she sang each night in the lounge she owned, she discovered her range had been increased by several high notes.

"Not much." Grant was saying. "Seeing you yesterday, I was taken by your hair color, but today I don't think it looks like Robyn's at all.

"But I can see a warm, sensitive, and sad person." He went on with her character analysis.

"I'd better get dressed now." She could feel the attraction he had for her. She knew it couldn't go on, wouldn't be allowed to grow and blossom into the love she'd locked safely away never to be taken out and held again. "If you'd like to clean up, there's a bathroom Kari's grandfather uses when he stays the night. I believe he keeps a razor there." Robyn remembered she still needed to call Will.

Grant's hand scratched across the stubble on his chin. "I could use a shave."

She showed him to the room that Will sometimes used when he spent the night with Kari, then went to her own room to dress.

Just as she was putting the finishing touches on her makeup, she heard the doorbell.

Robyn slipped the remaining earring through her ear and pushed her feet into the blue pumps which matched her navy suit. She was halfway down the stairs when she saw Will and Grant locked in a bear hug.

They separated but grasped hands and shook them like two ex-soldiers at a reunion. "I haven't seen you in ages. What the hell are you doing here?" Will asked. Robyn noticed that the corners of Will's eyes were moist.

Grant explained Kari's need for blood. "And how do you happen to be here?"

"Been retired now seven years next May. I got tired of wandering about the world and settled here," Will explained.

"Hello, Will," Robyn interrupted, as she reached the bottom step.

"It's a small world, Brooke." The smile on Grant's face showed obvious happiness at finding a lost friend. "This man is a near father to me."

William McAdams was a six foot, silver-haired retired colonel from the U.S. Army. He was Robyn's closest neighbor and had proved to be an anchor after he moved in next door last year. Will was there to fix any inconvenience that needed attention. He'd taken care of Kari when Robyn spent late nights at Yesterdays. Kari thought of him as her grandfather, and Will encouraged it by allowing her to call him "Graffie." Robyn remembered the long conversation her three-year-old had had with Will before they settled on "Graffie" as a name.

Kari was very proud of her Graffie and introduced him to all of her friends at nursery school on Grandparents' Day. Will, too, reveled in delight at having a small child around. He had three married children who did not visit often, and none of them had children or seemed to be interested in making him a grandfather.

Robyn was grateful for his help and attention when she needed a friend. She also thought of Will as the father she had lost.

"I called the hospital, Brooke." Will addressed her. "They told me Kari's much better this morning. I came by to give you a lift."

In minutes, they were seated in Will's LeSabre. Robyn took the backseat to allow the men to talk without having to crane their heads over the front seat. She sat quietly, listening to them. Something about this meeting seemed out of place. Why had Grant never mentioned Will when they were married? Even though their courtship was whirlwind, they were married for two years. In all that time, he'd told her only about his Aunt Priscilla, with whom he finally went to live, and about a special friend he called Ace, but not that there was a man close enough to him to be his father.

Stop it, Robyn. She braked her thoughts. This is some of Jacob's brainwashing filtering into your mind. There is probably a simple, logical explanation for Grant's silence. And she'd be interested in finding out what it was.

When they reached the hospital, Robyn went directly to ICU. Kari opened her eyes as she came through the door. "Mommy," she called, opening her small arms and reaching for her mother. Robyn fought tears. She'd thought she'd never hear that word again.

"Good morning, darling. How do you feel?" She reached over the restraining rail and took her hands.

"My head hurts."

"Well, it won't hurt for long. Doctor Elliott is here,

and I'm sure he'll want to know everything that bothers you."

Kari smiled. Robyn knew she liked the pediatrician. Kari was very pale and weak. Robyn smoothed the wisp of hair that sleep had loosened from her braids.

"Can I have something to drink?" Kari whispered.

Robyn looked around at the nurse. Almost imperceptibly, she shook her head. "Doctor Elliott will be right in," the white-clad woman whispered.

As if on cue the tall brown-haired man entered. His right hand held onto the stethoscope hanging from his neck. "And how is my favorite patient this morning?"

Robyn couldn't help smiling at the exchange. To think, Kari was almost dead yesterday, and this morning she was alive and active as if the accident had never happened.

Dr. Elliott examined her silently, before asking questions that Kari answered in her clear soprano voice. When he finished, he smiled and told her she could have some juice and a light breakfast of Jell-O.

"That's great, Doc," Kari agreed but appeared sleepy. "I like Jell-O."

"I'm going to tell the nurse to give you something for your headache. It will make you sleepy, but sleep is good for you right now."

Kari frowned. "Can I eat the Jell-O first." A pout that would melt any heart crept across Kari's face.

"Yes, darling. You can eat the Jell-O, first." Dr. Elliott ruffled her hair and winked at her.

When he left, Robyn told Kari about Grant bringing the blood she needed and how he wanted to meet her.

For a moment, she stepped out to allow him to visit Kari briefly.

He came back smiling. "We're blood relatives now." Two pairs of eyes looked at him. "I had to show her my bandage. She's a wonderful kid."

"I know. No granddaughter of mine would be anything else," Will said, he passed a stunned-faced Grant and went into the intensive care unit.

"Will is not your father." Grant made a statement, turning his attention to Robyn.

"Will is a very close neighbor and the best friend I've got. He's like a father to me and a grandfather to Kari. But, in actuality, we are not related."

"He does have that kind of effect on people."

In the life she'd been given, Will had no part to play. "Kari and I met him on his moving-in day. That's what Kari called it," she explained. "I liked him on sight." He was the first real person to come into her life since Grant's buddy, David, and her friend, Susan, had dealt her the heart-crushing blow that Grant was being held in a Beirut prison. She supposed she grabbed hold of Will as an anchor. They had been family ever since. "He's been a constant help whenever I've needed him." She finished. "How do you two happen to know each other?"

"I grew up with his family. We all lived in the same neighborhood. Will was a father to all of us, especially the ones prone to trouble."

"You were prone to trouble?"

"Oh, yes. My parents were killed when I was seven. For five years, I went from one foster home to another."

Robyn knew this. Grant had told her about his Aunt
Priscilla. She loved the old woman and remembered
how they relied on each other for strength during the
five long months of Grant's captivity. "Finally I went
to live with my mother's aunt, a woman I'd never met,"
he continued. "She was too old to handle an active
teen-ager. So, like most boys raised by a single parent,
I had more freedom than kids with both parents. Will
would pull rank whenever he thought I was getting
out of hand. Now, I thank him for keeping me on
track. I think it made me a better man."

"How come you lost touch?"

"I was flying by then. Will's children married and
left. His wife died. He was reassigned to the Philip-
pines. I was flying the New York to London route.
Our lives got busy. We just forgot to write. We lost
touch." He hunched his shoulders and spread his
hands in a gesture of unexplained reasoning. "I did
hear a few years ago that his son from his first marriage had died. I never did get the details."

Will joined them after Grant's comment, preventing
Robyn from saying she hadn't known about a son.
"Kari's asleep," he said, taking a seat next to Robyn.
"I'm sure she'll be out of danger soon."

"I can't wait for her to be well and back at home,
playing with her stuffed animals and pestering me to
take her to the park."

"I'm sure it won't be long before that happens,"
Grant assured her. "Unfortunately, I'm afraid I have
to leave now. I have to be back in Washington this
afternoon."

Robyn's eyes met his directly. She steeled her reflexes so as not to give away the turmoil erupting inside her. This was the last time she'd get to see him. And it was a stolen moment. She'd seized the prolonged interlude that she knew had to end sooner or later.

"Will, could you give me a ride to the airport?" he asked.

"Of course. I'll get the car and meet you at the main entrance." Then, directing his glance to Robyn, Will told her he'd be back to pick her up.

Grant stood, nodding at Will as he left them.

Robyn left her seat to walk to the window she'd stood before nearly twenty-four hours earlier. The pale blue walls were designed to be soothing. For her, they were anything but, although outwardly her appearance could have rivaled that of the best secret agent.

"Grant," she began hesitantly. "I . . . Kari wouldn't be alive without you." She heard the unintentional double meaning in her words. "We'll never forget you."

He came up behind her, taking her shoulders and turning her around to face him. "I want to see you again."

"No, Grant, it isn't a good idea."

"Why not? Is there someone else?"

"Someone else? No, there's no one else." No one except Jacob Winston and any number of hit men, courtesy of Alex Jordan.

"Then why?"

"I can't explain it. Let's just say I'm busy. I have a restaurant to run and a daughter to care for. There's no place in my life right now for a man."

"That's not what your kiss said this morning."

Color began to steal under Robyn's skin tone. With incredible control, she forced it to stop before it broke through the neckline of the white tube top she wore beneath her suit jacket.

"You weren't kissing me. It was Robyn you held in your arms. Maybe the man I held wasn't you."

Grant was stunned. "You just said there wasn't anyone else."

"Even though there isn't, I have reasons."

"What reasons?"

"I can't explain them."

"You're a real puzzle, Brooke Johnson. I'll admit you're doing things to me I'd forgotten existed between a man and a woman. I can't walk away with no hope of seeing you again without knowing why."

"Please, Grant. You've only known me one day. We shared a kiss—a kiss that I enjoyed fully and without reservation. But it was only a kiss. It's not like we're in love."

Robyn didn't recognize her own voice. Was that controlled speech coming from her? Was she telling this man, whom she loved with her very breath, that she didn't want to see him again and not falling to pieces?

His shoulders dropped. The hands gripping her arms fell to his sides. "Good-bye, Brooke Johnson." He turned to leave.

"Fair winds, Grant Richards," she said.

"Fair winds, Mrs. Rich—" he answered automatically.

Abruptly, he stopped. Both of them stared at each

other. Grant's eyes widened in surprise. Robyn steeled her expression. She knew it had been a mistake, but the words were out before she could stop them. It was an expression they had used to say good-bye whenever he had had a flight.

"Why did you say that?" he asked, coming to stand in front of her.

She made herself giggle. "You'll laugh if I tell you."

His features relaxed. "I promise I won't."

Robyn hesitated just long enough to make it seem as if she was embarrassed. "I heard it in a movie. It was about a ship captain and a Russian princess. Whenever he left her to go to sea, she'd wish him 'fair winds.' " She paused a moment. "You remind me of the captain."

Robyn gave him a tentative smile. Her acting was better than she thought. She hoped that it would work and that he would buy her story.

Suddenly, he smiled. He and Robyn had seen that movie. And they'd picked up the phrase as their personal message. He was sure it was because she reminded him of Robyn that made her comment suspect.

"Well, fair winds," he said.

"Fair winds," she repeated softly.

Grant turned abruptly, leaving her alone in the room. The same quiet rush of air that foretold his arrival accompanied his departure. Robyn sank onto one of the sofas. Her legs had grown weak with the effort of keeping her body erect and now refused to support her frame any longer. The tight rein she held over her emotions fractured, then crumpled. She buried her head on her knees and softly cried.

* * *

"Tell me about her, Will?" Grant asked, as Will drove expertly through the light traffic on the expressway.

"I met the two of them a little over a year ago when I moved into the house next to them. What in particular do you want to know about her?"

"Everything."

"Ah, ha, she's got ya, huh?" Will teased.

"Never could hide anything from you." Grant smiled. "You've still got a mind like an active volcano." Grant knew Will was remembering a conversation they'd had years ago when he was a young boy in which he vowed never again to let a girl get under his skin. This was after Mary Beth Armstrong dumped him for the captain of the football team.

"I'm afraid there isn't a lot I can tell you. She doesn't talk much about herself."

"I gathered that. This morning I told her all about Robyn and Beirut, but I don't know anything about her except that she has a daughter with a rare blood type and that she owns a restaurant."

"Robyn? Beirut?"

Grant relayed his story. Years had separated them, but he still felt close to Will.

"My God! I didn't even know that you had married. When I retired, I took a long cruise, went to the Caribbean. It was almost a year before I returned. I didn't read any newspapers or watch television while I was there. I knew about the hostages. The papers were full of them for years, but I never heard about your capture or release."

"It's ancient history now." Grant shrugged off memories of his captivity. He didn't want to go into the hardship it had imposed on his life. He knew Will understood that a man could not go through the experience without it having an impact on his life. "And in the last five years, I've learned to live with Robyn's death."

"And now, Brooke." Will was entering Williamsville. Grant noticed the small black-and-white sign that strained against the wind created by the constant flow of cars moving at the fifty-five mile an hour legal speed limit.

"I asked to see her again. She said there was no one else, but refused me."

"Did she say why?" Will glanced sideways at him.

Grant noticed a change in Will. He was leaning closer to Grant as though probing for specific information. "She said she didn't have room in her life for a man."

"Is that all?"

"No, she said there were other reasons, but she wouldn't explain what they were."

"In the years I've known her, all I can tell you is she had a husband, Ensign Cameron Johnson, U.S. Navy. He died of an embolism on his way to the naval base at San Diego. He had the same rare blood as Kari."

"Kari almost died under the same circumstances. No wonder she keeps a list." Grant whispered the last. He saw Will's frown. "Brooke has memorized a list of people with Kari's blood type. It's essentially how I came to be here." There was that subtle interest coming from Will again. "Will, is there something you're not telling me?"

"What do you mean?"

"Twice, now, when I've repeated something, you've reacted as if it were a surprise."

Will was quiet for a moment. Grant knew he was making up his mind whether he should tell him something. "I just wonder why, if Brooke knew the names of several people with the same type, she waited so long to tell Doctor Elliott." He related the search for Kari's blood type.

"There's something else." Will frowned. "I was in military intelligence a long time, and I can see things the average person would miss."

"You think she's hiding something?" Grant shifted to look at his friend.

"I'm not sure. I can't quite focus on anything specific. It's the way she talks about her past. As if she had learned it, not lived it."

"What are you saying? You're losing me."

"I don't know what I'm saying, and believe me I'm lost, too. But it's like Cameron Johnson is made of cardboard. If I hadn't actually checked him out, I'd say the man never existed or at the very least Brooke never knew him."

"But why would she make up something like that?"

"I haven't a clue. I don't know that she did make it up, but I can tell you that Brooke is a smart cookie. I've dealt with some pretty ingenious characters in my career, and I'd match Brooke against any of them. She thinks well on her feet. When I talk to her, I feel like she analyzes every word she plans to say before she allows it to escape her mouth. She's always on guard—against what or whom I can't tell you."

It was strange that Will's assessment was the same as his own. He, too, felt that Brooke planned her words before saying them. "Where did she live before coming here?"

"Atlanta, Georgia."

"Was Cameron with her there?"

"No, he died five years ago, just before Kari was born."

"Kari was born in Atlanta?"

"Yes."

"What about before Atlanta?"

"Texas. It's all there in its proper place. There is nothing that can't be traced. Her entire life is available through public information sources. Like I said, it's nothing that you can pick out. Just in talking to her you get facts, no stories from childhood, no anecdotes on life in general."

"Will, you worked in intelligence. Are you sure you're not making more out of this than there is?"

"Maybe, maybe not. She's a mystery. I guess it's the training in me, seeing spies where none exist."

"Come on, Will. Spies?" Grant grunted a laugh.

"I won't be that melodramatic. I don't think she's a spy."

"Good. But why would someone leave the warmth of Atlanta to move to snow country?"

"I asked her that. Her answer was that she likes snow." He paused. "It's true. I've seen her walking after a heavy snowfall. Once she even fell down like a child and created angels in a fresh drift."

Grant smiled at the image of Brooke's dark hair and her hourglass figure, which her suit fit like a custom-made glove, contrasted against the whiteness of newly fallen snow. He must drag his thoughts away from her body. It made him harden just thinking of her.

No matter what she said, he had to see her again. She'd awakened something in him, and even though it was Robyn he'd begun kissing, he was fully aware of the woman in his arms long before he broke off the hold she had on him. And she, too, had been affected by the kiss. She had lain against him for several exquisite minutes, her breath ragged, her body out of control.

"Grant, I love Brooke and Kari as if they were part of my own family." Will's voice pulled his attention back to the present. "I'd never do anything to hurt them. Brooke has already suffered through a deep hurt."

"I know, I can see it in her eyes." Grant remembered the photograph he'd held. The saddest eyes he'd ever seen had stared back from a face smiling at an unseen camera. "Did she ever say who caused it?"

"No, and I never asked. She's a fiercely independent woman."

Grant agreed. "I could tell that by the way we had to practically carry her out of the hospital to get her to rest."

Will paused a moment. "Don't get me wrong, Grant. I don't mean to sound as if Brooke is hiding anything more than any other person. It's just that she has boundaries she's erected. I'm careful to stay on my side."

"What do you think I should do about them?" They had reached the airport entrance. Will stopped the car at the light. When it switched from red to green, he guided the powerful vehicle into the airport complex, following the directed paths to the terminal entrance. Parking in front of the automatic glass doors, he faced Grant.

"I can't answer that one, Grant. What do you feel?"

What did he feel? Grant turned the question over in his mind. He wasn't sure how he felt. He only knew that she'd awakened something in him and that he liked it. She was the first woman in five years whom he wanted to see again. And she made him hotter than hell. He didn't know where a relationship with Brooke Johnson would lead, but he was certainly going to find out.

Five

Jacob stared at the Capitol through the windows of his office in the J. Edgar Hoover Building on Pennsylvania Avenue. His desk was cluttered with reports that he needed to go over. Yet, he wasn't in the mood for them. Usually, he had no problem with his work. He even liked it. Marianne had left but a week ago. In the last year, her departures had left him feeling lazy, and he had difficulty concentrating. He attributed it to his having worked almost nonstop for the entire weekend, but the truth was the pint-size redhead got under his skin. He'd been uneasy since Sunday—since Marianne had flown back to Buffalo. She'd been reporting regularly for four years, yet something about this time was different. He couldn't put his finger on the cause, but the small redhead had held something back.

It was her eyes. Jacob was accustomed to reading what people meant by the way they moved their hands or shifted in their chairs. But the most expressive feature in all human nature was the eyes. Marianne's were large and brown. They twinkled when she smiled and filled with tears when she was sad. Jacob had seen many moods cross her face over the years, but this weekend's had no predecessor.

Jacob stood up, pushing the curtains aside and pulling the miniblinds to the top of the window. Absently, he toyed with the cord. Traffic below hummed its afternoon song as taxis and cars vied for strategic positions along the wide thoroughfare. Then, her call last night had unnerved him. It was possible that all the blood supplies in the area were exhausted, but he didn't buy that. Not after talking to Carl.

He looked at the white cord still in his hand as if it could answer his questions. Reports on his desk confirmed there was AB negative blood on the shelves of several hospitals in Buffalo, yet all their computers reported it as exhausted or outdated. Someone was manipulating the situation. Jacob had to find out who and how.

Maybe he should call Marianne. He checked his watch. She'd be at the restaurant by now. It was just past noon. She'd be too busy to talk, and Jacob didn't know what he wanted to ask.

Maybe tonight, he thought, maybe he could ask her what she hadn't told him before he dropped her at the airport. By tonight he'd have had more time to analyze the reports on the network. Maybe he would have something for her to watch out for. But more important, maybe he could find out what it was she wasn't telling him.

Dropping the cord, Jacob sat down and pulled the Jordan file in front of him. "Eyes Only" was stenciled across the manila folder. He opened it, reading the top page. A description of the hit man along with a 5" x

7″ color photo. He was holding the photo when his office door was pushed inward.

"Jacob." Clarence Christopher strolled unannounced into his office. The director of the FBI was a man in his fifties with sparkling blue eyes and silver hair. He looked more like an aging screen star than the keeper of the national security of the United States. And he was Jacob's friend. "Are you free for lunch?"

"Of course," Jacob said, eying the director. Jacob often ate at his desk while he read the hundreds of pieces of paper that crossed it daily. "Is there something on your mind?" Jacob was straightforward.

"Yes, I thought I'd get your ideas over a meal."

Jacob quickly closed the files and locked them in his office safe, wondering what would bring his old friend to his office. Clarence Christopher and Jacob Winston went back to Jacob's days on the Chicago Police Force. It had been Clarence who brought him into the FBI after Cynthia was killed, but it was rare for him to show up without announcement.

Twenty minutes later, a taxi had whisked them through the cobblestone streets of Georgetown to O'Donnell's Restaurant on Wisconsin Avenue. Throughout the delicious meal of scallops in cream sauce and a tossed salad with a spicy mustard dressing, Clarence spoke of his family, the humid Washington weather, and the National Gallery's acquisition of a Rodin sculpture.

Jacob knew it wasn't his practice to discuss FBI business openly in restaurants. "Everywhere there are ears" had been a constant caution when he went through the training fifteen years ago. He also knew whatever the reason for the impromptu meal it had to be of national importance.

Jacob sat still but he was getting anxious. He wasn't used to holding back, and this small talk had gone on long enough. He wanted to know what Clarence wanted to tell him.

But he was kept waiting until the check was paid and they left the famous sea food house. Instead of calling or hailing a passing taxi, Clarence turned left and began walking.

"Do you remember the Alex Jordan case from five years ago?" Clarence asked when they reached the corner.

Jacob visibly tensed. "Yes," he nodded.

"There was a woman who uncovered the Crime Network."

"Robyn Richards," Jacob supplied.

"She testified at the trial. In fact, she was the prime witness against Jordan and his assassination network."

Jacob nodded again, not knowing where this was going.

"As I remember it, she went into the program."

"Correct," Jacob said, uncomfortable at Clarence's probing. "Is there a problem with Mrs. Richards?" Jacob had had many problems with Robyn over the years, but none of them had ever made their way to the director of the FBI.

"I'm not sure." Clarence stepped off the curb at the end of the street. "This morning I got a report that someone had been in the files."

"What files?" He hadn't had any such report.

"The Jordan case files."

Jacob knew he meant the deeply hidden, sealed files.

"I got no word of this. Do you think it was a hacker, who found his way in?"

"I don't think we can take that chance."

Jacob knew he wouldn't even if Clarence offered that option. He'd protected Robyn Richards for five years, and he wasn't about to stop until he was sure every member of the crime syndicate had been caught and put behind bars.

"Who do you think it was?"

"I read the Jordan files this morning. Apparently, Mrs. Richards went into the program, because there was a missing link to the network. I think the link has surfaced, but he's a shrewd operator. He was in and out of the files before we could catch him. He even managed to erase the phone number and overlay it with a number for the Washington Weather Bureau so we couldn't locate him."

"What do you want me to do?"

Clarence stopped, then quickly resumed walking. Jacob could tell he was concerned, so concerned he'd nearly forgotten protocol.

"I think you should discreetly find out if anything out of the ordinary has happened to Mrs. Richards in the past few months. We don't want to alarm her, but if someone is out there, she'll be the target."

Jacob forcibly controlled his breathing. His heart pounded in his chest. For five years, he'd known some-one was going to find out that Brooke Johnson and Robyn Richards were the same woman. Yet, time after time, he allowed her to beat his arguments into the ground. And now that there was almost assurance, he knew he couldn't tell her he was actively investigating the Crime Network she'd uncovered. A network that had sent many of the FBI's most trusted agents to jail cells and had cost their leader his life.

And there was her daughter. Kari. If anyone wanted to force Robyn Richards, they could do it through the child.

"I'm just alerting you, Jacob," the director broke into his thoughts. "I'm putting a man on this. I don't want another fiasco like the one Mrs. Richards uncovered."

Jacob knew Robyn's wide-eyed idealism had caused her to stumble onto the plan. It had ballooned into an ugly scandal.

"The president raked me over the coals," Clarence continued, as he walked briskly in the humid air. "I'd never felt so naked as when I walked into the Oval Office that day. I don't intend to ever be in that position again." Jacob could hear the determination in his voice.

The credibility of the FBI had been shaken by Robyn's discovery. And five years later, it was still trying to live down the stigma of an international assassination bureau, with fingers stretching worldwide.

"Clarence, I know this is outside my department, but I'd like this one."

With the sun glinting off Clarence's uncovered head and his blue eyes squinting against the sun, he stopped in midstride and turned to Jacob. "I was hoping you'd want it, Jacob. This one is a can of worms if I ever saw one, and I need someone I can trust."

Jacob sighed. He'd never held anything back from Clarence. "There's been a new development," he told him. At Clarence's questioning look, Jacob related the details of Kari's accident and the dilemma of the blood supply.

"What's being done?"

"Marianne is keeping me informed. Blood arrived in time, and the little girl is expected to recover. And I'm planning to go and personally check out the situation."

Jacob purposely held back the information that Kari's own father was the person who donated the blood that saved her life.

The envelope slipped from Robyn's suddenly numb fingers. Her hand clutched her neck and its rapidly beating pulse. On the floor, partially hidden by the manila envelope, lay a black-and-white photo of Robyn Richards. It had been the sole content of the oversized envelope. Who sent this, Robyn wondered. She stepped onto the porch, looking up and down the quiet street. No one was about, only the soft morning breeze rustling the leaves on the trees.

Robyn stepped back, closing the door and snatching the paper off the floor. Was it Grant? Had he somehow recognized her? Her hand went to her mouth where he'd kissed her. Did he know instinctively that she was his wife? Did her reaction or her lack of reaction clue him into her real identity?

Questions flowed through her mind as she stared at the damning photo, especially the one question she feared most—had they found her? She didn't even know who *they* were. The reason she'd been inducted into protective custody was because a missing link existed in the Crime Network. An unknown threat still existed. Did they know who she was? Had Grant's visit been a signal that Robyn Richards was alive and hiding out as Brooke Johnson?

Robyn paced the room. Someone was suspicious, but did they know for sure. Was this a test? Something to rattle her into making a mistake. She had to do something, but what? She looked at the postmark. The envelope had been mailed from Washington, D.C. Should she call Jacob?

"Hello, Brooke."

Although her senses heightened, not even the flicker of an eyelash revealed surprise at Jacob's sudden intrusion. It had been two days since Grant flew back to Washington. She knew one of Jacob's men was bound to show up. She just didn't think it would be Jacob himself. "I thought you weren't coming back," she said dryly.

His blue eyes flashed. Robyn watched the imperceptible straightening of his shoulders; an indication that he was angry. Jacob stood six feet tall, but he appeared to be taller. His frame looked underfed, but she'd seen him training once and knew his strength and agility were concealed by his wiry appearance.

"Let's go for a walk," he told her, as if he were commanding troops.

Time hadn't changed Jacob. He was still looking over his shoulder expecting the bad guys to come bursting through the door. How he came to be in her dressing room at the back of Yesterdays she'd never know. As much as her logical mind told her he had to have come through the door, his usual method of appearing and disappearing could very well include materializing from thin air.

He took her arm and led her down the back stairs of the restaurant. The July night was warm when she stepped outside. Silently, they crossed the lawn, skipping the circular patio stones like kids playing hopscotch and passing the white gazebo crowded with flowers from today's wedding party. Moonlight shimmered on her sequined gown that clung suggestively to every curve of her lithe body. Earrings, dangling to the soft blush of her bare shoulders, sparkled like fireworks with each toss of her head.

Robyn looked at the staid countenance of the G-man as his height made it necessary for him to duck under the rose-draped lattice portico. The grounds opened onto a small stream that wound its way through the property, creating pockets of picturesque settings.

Jacob swept the area with his eyes as if he had some kind of internal radar detector. He must have decided it was free of any bugs, microphones, plastic explosives, or other incendiary devices, for he turned to face her.

"Is it safe to talk now?" she teased, taking several steps toward the water.

"What are you up to?"

"Me?" She gave him a surprised look.

Jacob rounded on her. "Don't be flippant with me. You know damn well what I'm talking about."

"I'm not up to anything," she said calmly.

"What was he doing here?"

"Don't ask stupid questions." She spoke with anger. "If you know he was here, you know damn well why—my daughter was dying. She needed blood. If you remember, it's a rare type."

"And was that what made him spend the night at your house?"

Robyn's mouth fell open, then shut abruptly. "Is that what brought you out of retirement?" Her voice was savage but barely audible. "You think I slept with him."

"If you did or didn't is not the point."

"You're right, and it's also none of your business." She watched Jacob turn away and push his hands deeply into his pockets as he took several deep breaths in an attempt to regain some of the control that Robyn seemed to have taken away from him. When his shoulders settled back in the position of *G-man-ready-to-deal-with-difficult-female,* she told him the truth.

"Jacob, my thoughts were almost solely on Kari and her chances of survival. I won't lie and tell you I had no feelings for Grant, but I did *not* sleep with him." She thought she saw him relax a bit, as much as he ever relaxed in her presence. "My major concern was getting Kari the blood she needed."

"There were other sources," he said angrily.

"They were dry." Robyn stopped, sucking her breath in an angry hiss. "And why was that, Jacob? You promised me there would always be AB negative blood on hand for emergencies."

"I'm sorry. There was a mix-up."

"Mix-up? Kari could have died over a mix-up?"

"She wouldn't have died. Word got to us in time. We had a plane ready to fly out when news came you had called Grant Richards."

"Just for the record I didn't call Grant. I was surprised to find he was on his way to deliver the blood in person. And just how did you come by that tidbit of information?" Her voice dripped with sarcasm.

"You don't need to know, Robyn." He lapsed back to her given name. A clear signal he felt the area was clean.

"I'm so tired of that phrase. This is my life at stake here, as you've so often told me. Just who decides what I have a need to know?"

"I can't tell you that."

"Oh, Jacob, lighten up. Isn't there any human being inside that spy getup you wear?" She was sorry the moment she said it. "I didn't mean that, Jacob. It's just that you make me so . . ."

"Angry." He finished for her. "I know. You make me angry, too."

"Why are you here? It's been four years. You told me after the operation, we'd never have to see each other again. By now, I expected you to be bureau chief or something."

"That's not far from the truth. But I'm here to extract a promise from you."

"All right, Jacob, I'm ready. Hit me with it." She straightened her shoulders as if he were about to throw her a hard ball. She had to be ready to catch it no matter which side it curved toward.

The tall government agent walked to within a foot of her. "I want your promise, a reconfirmed promise, you'll play by the rules. You won't see him again."

"There was no blood available for Kari and he was my last hope. I only expected the doctors to fly the blood up. I promise you I didn't think there was the slightest possibility he'd come, too." She turned away. "You can't imagine what it did to me to have him so close and not to be able to tell him who I was and worse that the person whose life he saved was his own daughter."

"I do understand. I'm not completely inhuman, Robyn." Jacob's voice was softer than she thought it could be. And it was very close to her ear.

She turned back to him. "I said I was sorry, Jacob. I know you're a man with a job to do. And I know I'm not the most cooperative person you've ever had to deal with."

"Do I have your promise?"

She sighed. "You have my promise."

"Good, now you'd better get back in there. It's almost time for your song."

"How will you get back?"

"You don't . . ."

"Need to know." Robyn knew the answer. This time

she smiled. "Jacob, will you do me a favor before you leave?"

"Of course."

"Smile for me."

"What?"

"All the time you spent with me, teaching me, arguing with me, and shaping me into Brooke Johnson, I've never seen you smile."

"I'll smile if you'll do me a favor, too."

"When have I ever refused you a favor?" Her smile was impish. As close as he'd ever come to a smile changed his features at her obvious comment. Then, he stepped back as if compliance needed room. Slowly, the skin of his lips curved back and upward, revealing clean, even teeth. "You ought to do it more often," Robyn said. "It changes your face completely." Quickly, the mask was refitted and back in place was the G-Man. "Now what's your favor?"

Without a word, Jacob began closing the distance that separated them. Robyn didn't know what to expect. When his arms encircled her waist, she was too surprised to react. His mouth took hers in a slow leisurely kiss. Behind it was no trace of the G-man character, no hard-line military attaché, not even a clumsy adolescent. The man kissing her was experienced and thorough. He held her lightly but securely as if he were afraid his strength could easily break her small rib cage. Hands roaming over the sequined gown brailled her body from her shoulder blades to her rounded bottom that he pulled quickly and surely against the length of himself. The protrusion pressing against her lower body left her in no doubt of why

Jacob had come to find her. Reluctantly, he raised his head but didn't move his hands or step back to remove the imprint of his body on hers.

"If all goes well, Robyn, this is our last time together. But if you ever need me, I'll know and I'll be there." He released her, turned and walked away, his head high, and body at attention, advancing forward, with not even a backward glance.

Stunned, her eyes followed him as he crossed the creek and was swallowed up by the enveloping darkness of the night and the trees. Long after he was gone, she stood there. She found herself wondering if Jacob Winston was married. Did he have a family? Were there two, three children walking around with his face stamped on them? Inside her head, a metamorphosis was taking place. The cardboard spy was dissolving, an outercase eliminated, revealing a real person, with feelings, emotions, and hope. She felt sorry for him. That kiss told her he'd secretly been waiting for her. Hoping that with time and circumstances she'd fall out of love with Grant. But all the time he knew his job would never permit him to have any kind of relationship with her. She was a member of the elite society of protected witnesses. Involvement with her would be tantamount to a full-page ad in the *New York Times*.

As she retraced her footsteps over the moon-washed path, cut out like giant silver dollars against a background of dark grass, she remembered the photograph. She had planned to tell him about it, but his surprising kiss made her forget. She couldn't call him back. He'd said if she needed him he'd know and he'd be there.

Inside, the band played "A House Is Not a Home," reducing the noise of tonight's crowd to a whirling hum. It reminded her of the sound of blank space over an open telephone line. The lights were bright and happy. Robyn needed gaiety. She was caught in a no-win situation. Grant could never be part of her life. And she could never be part of Jacob's, no matter how much he wished it.

For the first time since she'd met him, she identified with him. He was no longer her enemy. She wished she could tell him.

"Where have you been?" Marianne greeted her as she walked into the dressing room. "Do you know you're on in five minutes."

Robyn had forgotten. "Thanks, Marianne. I'll be ready, but would you tell Mike I've changed my mind. I'm going to sing 'Secret Love' tonight."

Marianne's look of surprise wasn't lost on her. Robyn was a very decisive person. She had rehearsed tonight's show for three hours this afternoon. To change it without explanation was out of character, and Marianne recognized it.

"Why the sudden change?"

"No particular reason, just a mood change."

"Mood change? My mood would change, too, if that handsome man I saw at the hospital looked my way."

"Hurry and tell Mike," she said. It was rare for Marianne to pry into her life. Robyn was sure it was what had kept them friends for five years.

Robyn repaired her hair and reapplied the lipstick that Jacob had so expertly wiped off her mouth. With only seconds to spare, she took her place under the artificial setting of a moonlit garden, much like the one she'd vacated only minutes ago. As the orchestra began to play the introduction, she raised her head and remembered the smile Jacob had given her. Then, taking a deep breath, she began to sing.

Tonight, her voice was closer to her old voice. The tone was deeper. The words were rich and round as they floated on the small wisps of controlled air before spreading about the lounge. She kept the image of Jacob in her mind as she repeated the refrain.

Only Jacob couldn't tell anyone. She didn't know why he'd chosen to let her know. It didn't change anything—couldn't.

She ended the song slowly, thinking of the tall, khaki-coated man giving away his secret to the only person who had to keep it.

"Listen to that applause." Marianne's voice was choked as Robyn met her backstage after her third curtain call. "I've never heard you sing like that before."

"Marianne, you hear me every night."

"But tonight was—different." She hesitated as if the word didn't hold as much meaning as she meant to impart.

"Different good or different bad?" Robyn teased, deliberately misunderstanding Marianne's meaning.

"Good, of course."

"Thank you." Robyn smiled at the short redhead who reminded her of Little Orphan Annie with her mop of unruly curls and sprinkle of freckles.

Marianne followed as she moved toward the stairs.

"I'm not being kind. There wasn't a person here tonight who wasn't moved by you—and that includes the staff."

Robyn entered the small dressing room. The lighted mirror was almost obscured by a huge vase of red roses.

"Who are you, Brooke?"

Thoughts of the flowers left her as she swung around to confront the restaurant manager. "What?"

"Brooke, I'm your friend, your partner. Yet, the woman who walked out on stage tonight bares little resemblance to the one I thought I knew."

"Nobody ever knows anyone completely—not even husband and wife."

"Is it him?"

Robyn didn't have to ask who she meant. Marianne had run into Will just before Grant came out. She'd burst into the waiting room, bubbling over with questions, one following rapidly on the heels of another.

"I told you he came because of Kari's blood type. I don't expect to ever see him again." The words fell like slow rain, washing away a chalk drawing on the sidewalk.

"Why not? He's male, attractive, and unmarried."

"We live in different worlds." It might as well be different planets, she added silently.

"How do you know that? You've been alone since your husband died. Don't you think five years is enough time to grieve?"

"I'm not grieving," she denied, pulling a red-and-black bustled gown with a slight train from the closet.

"What do you call it? You haven't been out with more than six men in the past two years."

"I'm very discriminating." Robyn threw flippantly over her shoulder.

"Discriminating, hell! You're turning yourself into a corpse."

Robyn swung around to face her friend. Every feature of her perfectly made-up face was in place.

"I'm sorry, Brooke, but you are burying yourself. First, in Kari, then in this restaurant. You won't leave any room for a man."

"I don't need one. Kari and I like our lives the way they are."

"Is that really true?" Marianne frowned. "You mean to tell me that Greek god physique with a smile brighter than sunshine, has no effect on your hormones? Honey, you are a corpse."

"Unzip me." Robyn turned her back. Grant had a definite impact on her. He was the reason she was held prisoner in this shell of an existence. She'd exchanged her grasp at happiness for a defense system and the lives of ten men, among them her husband. With her eyes wide open she'd followed the one-way signs and passed uninhibited through the portal to this life. Eventually, it had been sealed. Behind her was a door with no handle and no key. She was trapped, irretrievably imprisoned in a new world. A world where she had to tell a practiced set of lies until they became truth and truth became a lie.

"If he does come back, Brooke, would you go out with him?" Marianne pulled the zipper down from the top of the gown. Robyn stepped out of it and hung it on a hanger.

Marianne went back to the bouquet of roses. She bowed her head to take in their fragrance. "What's his name anyway? It's probably not a good idea for me to address him as Mr. Tall, Dark, and Handsome."

"Grant Richards. He's an airline pilot."

Robyn waited for a response. When she got none, she continued. "Anyway, I won't be seeing Grant again. His routes don't come this way."

"Maybe."

Robyn snapped her belt closed. Marianne stood in front of the flower arrangement. A small white envelope extended from her hand like a bridge to the past.

Robyn's fingers closing over it completed the link between the past and the present. Pulling the card from its casing, she read it silently.

> Seeing you, again—
> is a very good idea.
>   Grant

She wanted to smile, but she knew Marianne was expecting a reaction, and she'd been taught too well to allow any of her personal feelings to sneak out through the cracks in the armor that she had carefully placed on her new life.

Six

As the week went by, Robyn's optimism waned until depression gripped her. Seeing Grant for a short while, then not being able to see him again, had cast her back into the role of grieving widow. The only bright spot in her day was Kari. She'd recovered quickly after the blood transfusion, but the doctors kept her in the hospital for a week while her other injuries healed.

"Mommy!" Kari wailed, running across the room and into Robyn's arms.

"Hello, darling." Robyn dropped to the floor, arms open to receive the ball of energy flying toward her. She planted a swift kiss on her cheek, noting the bandage on her arm, residual evidence of the accident. "I'm so glad to see you." She hugged the soft child, pushing her hair into place. "Here, look what I brought you."

Kari exuberantly ripped the white wrapping paper, decorated with teddy bears, away from the box. Inside, she found a white stuffed Care Bear. "Oh," she smiled. "Two more teddy bears."

"Two?" Robyn looked at her daughter, then around the room. She spotted the pink furry creature sitting on the guest chair. "Is that from Doctor Elliott?" she asked.

"Oh, no. That's from Uncle Grant." Kari left Robyn, still sitting on the floor, to go place the white bear next to the pink one. "He said I could call him that if it was all right with you."

"He was here." Robyn issued the inaudible statement to herself. Her heart began to pound.

"He went to get us something to drink. Is it all right, Mommy?" Kari asked.

"What, dear?" Robyn's disoriented attention focused.

"If I call him Uncle Grant?"

Robyn looked at Kari as if she hadn't heard the question. Her mind kept hearing *he went to get us something to drink.* "Kari, was Grant here—in the hospital?"

"Hi." Robyn's eyes followed her daughter's stare. Grant's unmistakable vitality blocked the door, a cup in each hand.

Don't react, don't let surprise register in your eyes, don't move your eyebrows. Breathe normally, make sure that when you speak your voice is normal. Jacob's voice seemed to whisper the repetitive instructions in her ear as he'd so often done.

"Here, Kari." He walked around Robyn and handed one of the cups to the little girl, then set the other one on the table. "Let me help you up."

Robyn had forgotten to move. He was having the same effect on her that he'd had when she found him asleep on her sofa. "I didn't expect to see you again."

"Well, I couldn't fly away on the day my newest

friend goes home." He cast a friendly smile at Kari who returned it before continuing to play with her bears.

"I didn't know you two had become friends."

"Oh, yes, Mommy. Uncle Grant came to see me three times." She held up three fingers. "He's got the same kind of blood as me."

Robyn's eyes came back to Grant. "I must admit I did come to see Kari, but I hoped we'd run into each other again."

"Grant, I thought I made my feelings clear."

"Mommy, Uncle Grant's going to take us to Crystal Beach." Kari's excitement communicated itself to her. The child was oblivious to the tension mounting within her. Grant appeared amused at her discomfort.

"Not so fast, sweetie, Mommy has to agree first." He smiled at the child.

Robyn threw Grant a look that said they'd discuss this later.

"Can we go, Mommy?" Kari's small voice tugged at her heart.

"Kari, Doctor Elliott isn't going to let us go to the beach for a while," she said coming down to the child's level. "You're leaving the hospital, but you still have to get well."

"What about after I get well?" she persisted.

"How about we talk about it then?" Robyn smiled, opening her arms, knowing her daughter would immediately agree with her and run into them.

The nurse came in with the wheelchair then. "I get to sit in this," Kari said, leaving Robyn and running to the chair. She sat down and looked up at Grant.

"Uncle Grant is going to push me," she announced. "He said he would go with us, Mommy."

Robyn's gaze joined her daughter's. Grant stared at her with a helpless expression on his face. She clenched her teeth and helplessly followed the small group as they left the hospital room.

Kari chatted between them as Robyn drove silently through the light traffic. Robyn admitted she was glad to see Grant. Seeing him standing in the doorway made her want to react. She wanted to jump into his arms, cover his face with kisses, and tell him she loved him. If she hadn't been conscious of Jacob's words guiding her, she was sure she'd have followed her impulses. And, now, she had to go through another good-bye scene.

"Mommy, are we going by the restaurant?" Kari had turned her attention to Robyn.

"No, darling, we're going home. Why, are you hungry?"

"Only a little."

"Good, Graffie is at home and he's making your favorite."

"Spaghetti, ooh, goodie." Kari's two favorite words bubbled from the small body sitting between her mother and father. Robyn could suddenly and clearly see her former image and Grant's clear good looks like a time exposure reflected on the miniature face smiling at her.

"Hey, watch out." Grant's husky voice, intoned with panic, broke her concentration.

Robyn's foot jammed the brake to the floor as she stopped the car just short of a busy intersection. "I'm sorry. Are you all right?" Grant nodded, but Robyn noticed Kari's hand grasp her arm in a harsh grip. Her eyes were wide and filled with fear. She remembered the accident that had placed her in the hospital. Robyn cautioned herself to pay attention and drive carefully. "It's all right, darling. Mommy will drive slower." Kari returned the smile Robyn gave her and relaxed her fingers.

"Here, Kari, you can hold onto me while Mommy drives." Grant took hold of the child's hand. A pang of jealousy sliced through Robyn at the ease with which her daughter released her arm and curled up in Grant's. Robyn berated herself. She'd never had to share her daughter before, and Kari and Grant seemed to get along so well. She had to allow them this time together. When he left tonight, they could never see each other again.

She turned her attention back to the road. The remainder of the journey was accomplished without incident.

"Graffie," Kari screamed as she came through the door.

Will opened his arms, and Kari ran into his arms as she had into her mother's. "I missed you, my little munchkin." He lifted her into the air and swung her around. Kari's tinkling voice drifted about the room.

"I missed you, too, Graffie. Mommy says we're having spaghetti."

"That's right. And it's all ready." He kissed the dark head moving toward the kitchen.

Robyn noticed the table was set for four. Will must have known Grant would be here. They all sat down to a delicious dinner after which Will excused himself, saying something about a TV mystery he wanted to see.

Robyn spent the next several hours with Kari and Grant. She read the child's favorite books and played a few cartoon tapes. Kari said she got to see a lot of new tapes while she was in the hospital. Grant joined right in as if he was part of the family. Finally, Robyn could see Kari was tiring.

"It's time to go to bed, Kari."

"How about some hot chocolate?" The child didn't argue that it was still daylight.

"Okay. You go get ready, and I'll make the chocolate."

"Will you come with me?" She invited Grant to her room. For the second time that day, jealousy tugged at Robyn's heart. Her daughter was usually reserved in her acceptance of strangers. Grant, in her eyes, must be different.

Robyn could hear the rhythmic beeps of a computer game while she made hot drinks in the kitchen. She smiled at Kari's animated laughter. To think that only two weeks ago she'd almost died. She pushed the thought away like removing a dark cloud as she poured hot chocolate for Kari and Grant, but made hot apple spiced tea for herself.

"Mommy, I beat him, I beat him," she shouted excitedly when Robyn entered the room carrying a tray.

Robyn looked sympathetically at Grant. "Don't worry she beats me, too."

"I can't believe a four-year-old has beat me at a computer game."

"Just how often do you and the Super Mario Brothers get together?" Robyn's eyebrows went up along with the curve of her lips.

"At least once a lifetime." He smiled, accepting the cup she offered.

Kari continued to jab the joystick back and forth, destroying the electronic space monsters that blocked her path. In less than a minute, she had topped her previous score.

"Okay, Kari, it's time to drink your chocolate and get into bed." The pink clad child frowned but accepted the cup.

"He's not bad, Mommy, but Graffie is better." Kari had a chocolate mustache that she licked in her childish way and completely circled her mouth with the brown liquid.

"Everybody's a critic." Grant set down his cup and tickled the Care Bears on her pajamas. Gales of high-pitched laughter flowed from the child.

"Come on, champ. Let's go to bed." Robyn turned the spread down on the bed and pulled back the sheet. Kari stepped out of Grant's grasp and went into the bathroom to brush her teeth.

"Goodnight, darling." Robyn whispered after she kissed the clean pink cheeks and settled her in the bed.

"Goodnight, Kari," Grant echoed.

Robyn felt good as she walked down the steps. She was glad Kari had gotten along so well with her father. But she knew in the next few minutes she was going to have to tell him she could never see him again.

"You look much more relaxed," Grant told her when

she'd deposited the tray in the kitchen and returned to the living room.

"I am. I was extremely worried about Kari, but she's going to be fine."

"How about you?" Concern was evident in the softly spoken question.

"I'm fine, too." Grant had given her a perfect lead-in. Robyn sat down in one of the wing chairs. "Grant, why are you here?"

"I came to see you."

"I thought I told you it wasn't a good idea."

"But you didn't tell me why."

"You don't need to know." She didn't believe she'd said that.

"You're wrong, Brooke. I do need to know." Grant moved. He came closer, sitting on the coffee table facing her. "I need to know everything about you."

Robyn refused to drop her eyes. She looked directly into his dark black orbs. "There isn't a lot to tell. I'm plain, ordinary. I have a child, and I work. We live a perfectly ordinary life in this house."

"What about me? How do you feel about me?"

"I don't feel anything for you." She was amazed at how well she could lie and keep her face straight.

"Who taught you to do that?" he asked.

"Do what?" Maybe she wasn't as good as she thought. He'd thrown her a fastball. She didn't expect it.

"Tell such complete lies without blinking one beautiful eyelash." He outlined her eyes with his thumbs forcing her to close them.

"I'm not lying." She struggled to keep the shudder that passed through her from bubbling out.

"No?"

Robyn stood up, moving away from him. She waited until she got behind the sofa before speaking. "Grant, I'm very grateful for what you did for Kari, but I'm not going to have an affair with you."

Grant didn't answer her. He stood, too, and followed her around. Robyn backed away. She didn't know what he was going to do. Slowly, he stalked her until she backed herself up against the wall. He stopped. Barely three feet separated them. Grant looked deeply into her eyes. She could see the desire in his. In her own, she refused to let it show. Fire began a slow burn in the pit of her stomach and quickly spread throughout her being. Immeasurable seconds passed. Electricity snapped around the room. Her body ached for him. She knew she couldn't hold out much longer, when suddenly something propelled her from behind. Her arms were around his neck, pulling his mouth to meet hers in a ragged, life-threatening kiss. Grant took charge, burying his hands in her hair, trading one passionately wet kiss for another. Neither of them appeared to be in control. Need to touch, taste, possess each other led them on. Robyn was exhausted and tears filled her eyes when she finally pulled her mouth away and collapsed in his arms. She felt like crying, something she hadn't done in years. She wanted him, but he had to go. She'd promised Jacob she wouldn't see him again. She'd resolved her life without him, and now, here she was wrapped in his warm arms, loving him, loving the sight and feel of him holding her.

"You taste like—apple spiced tea."

This wasn't Robyn he was holding in his arms. This was Brooke. Grant knew it. It had been two weeks since she had sent him away. During that time, he'd tried to forget her. He'd only known her for a weekend, but for some unexplainable reason her image kept creeping into his thoughts. He admitted he liked having her in his arms, but he'd had many women in his arms, and only Robyn had left an impression until now. Three times he'd flown in to see Kari, hoping he'd run into Brooke. It wasn't until Kari told him she was leaving the hospital that he came back knowing if he stayed he had to see Brooke again.

And this time he'd hit the jackpot. She had made a move toward him, but even in doing so she had pushed him away. He liked the feel of her, the way her slight little body seemed to fit perfectly with his frame. Even though he held her, he knew she was pushing him away. Her mouth said "go away," but her body screamed for him to stay.

And he could go on holding her. She reminded him a little of Robyn. A twig of conscience pulled at him for the comparison. It had been years since he compared anyone to his wife. It was unfair to Brooke. It had to be the tea. Robyn liked herb teas. Most of the women he'd known since hadn't drunk tea at all. Brooke was refreshingly different.

Why she wanted to push him away he didn't know. He also knew he couldn't ask yet. She wasn't ready to answer that question. Why? Was her husband the man who had spoiled her for him? Had she had a bad marriage? Did he beat her? All he had were questions, and he couldn't ask any of them. Not yet, not to this beautiful woman. But in time. He'd come back often. No matter how much she objected. She stirred him, made him feel alive, and he suddenly, like a desperate man, wanted to be alive again. He wanted to feel, even hurt if he had to, but he'd conquer Brooke Johnson.

"I have to leave now. But I will be back." He still held her.

She tried to push herself away but he tightened his grip, holding her more securely against him.

"Please, don't come," she pleaded. "Just go and leave us alone."

"What is it, Brooke? Can't you tell me what's wrong?"

"No, I can't. Just go and not come back. There is so much you don't know, and I'll never be able to tell you. It's best if we just drop this association right now."

"After the way you kissed me. There's got to be more here than you're telling me."

"Grant, please. Don't ask me any questions." She couldn't keep the pleading quality out of her voice.

"I'm flying to Europe. I'll be back in a week, and I'll be here to take you to dinner at eight o'clock." He ignored her request. Releasing her slightly, he looked down into her face. It was glowing with the remembrance of recent kisses. For an uncontrollable moment, her mouth reminded him of Robyn's, swollen with spent passion. Rapidly, he pushed the thought from his mind. "Don't be late. I hate to be kept waiting."

With that, he smiled and dropped a swift kiss on her upturned mouth before pulling the door open and disappearing through it.

Robyn slid down the wall. Tears flowed from her eyes slowly. In a little less than ten days, she'd promised Jacob she wouldn't see Grant again, and already she'd broken her promise. She didn't know what to do. She wanted him desperately. Part of her rejoiced in knowing she would see him again, while the other part of her cried at the injustice of the system that had put her in this position.

"Mommy, are you all right?"

Robyn instinctively moved toward the small voice. Her hands wiped at the tears in her eyes. "Of course, darling. Mommy is fine. Are you all right?" Kari was standing halfway up the stairs. The bear Grant had given her hung from one hand as she wiped her eyes with the other.

"I woke up." Robyn smiled at the three-word explanation.

"Did you have a bad dream?" She sat down and pulled her daughter into her arms.

"No. Is Uncle Grant gone?" She asked, snuggling closer to Robyn.

"He had to go back to his airplane."

"Will he be back in time to go to the beach?"

She frowned. How was she going to explain to a four-year-old that they could never see him again? "Kari, he's a very busy man. He has to fly his plane a long way."

"But he promised. If it was all right with you. You like the beach don't you, Mommy?" Kari pumped her

head up and down, giving the answer to the question
she had asked.

"Of course, but we have to wait until you feel better
and Doctor Elliott says it's okay."

Kari smiled the smile that would break men's hearts
in future years. "Doctor Elliott likes the beach. He
told me." Her head continued to bob up and down.
"He'll say I can go."

"Well, we'll just have to wait and ask him. Now,
back to bed young lady."

Robyn wished her problem could be solved as easily
as a trip to the beach. That she could get her doctor's
permission and everything would be fine. But her doctor had an office in Washington, D.C., and he only
made house calls under extreme circumstances.

Seven

Grant rarely got the chance to play in the air. But, today, the horizon had called to him as clearly as if it had a voice. He pulled back on the stick in his hand. The motion was light-years different than the computer controlled jets he usually piloted. His air service was a business, and for years, he'd put in twenty-four hour days to make it a success. But it had paid off. Today, he appreciated his work as he soared over the airfield in the World War I fighter plane he'd bought at a recent auction. The wind whirled through his hair as he executed a three-hundred-sixty-degree loop and hung upside down for a moment.

He grinned, slapping his thigh and letting out a whoop of laughter. This was flying. He felt like the Red Baron. Next time, he'd get a scarf to wear like the legendary German flier. There was just him and the wind. He controlled it with the stick in his hand. He pulled it back, and the rotating blades that controlled the single engine had the small double-wing plane climbing toward the heavens.

It was like the first time he'd flown—when he'd found the freedom of the sky. Everything he wanted, all of his love and feelings were there in the limitless horizon. After not belonging anywhere, not being wanted by the foster families he stayed with, the sky was his love. The families were kind, but he knew he was an outsider. At twelve, he went to stay with Aunt Priscilla. At first, their relationship was uneasy, but eventually, they began to tolerate each other. Now, he loved the old woman, and she loved him. But it wasn't until he met Will and took his first flight that he'd learned where he belonged. He hated to imagine what would have happened to him if he'd never learned to fly.

"Richards's Air calling 1701–Nancy."

Grant heard Adam Carpenter's voice crackle over the radio that his mechanic had insisted on adding when they restored the plane. Grant wanted to leave it out and be as authentic as possible, but Adam was a product of his time, the age of high definition television, air phones, and computers. He wasn't about to let Grant get out of communication distance with the ground.

Lifting the old-style handset, he depressed the speaker button and answered, "Go on, Adam. I'm here." Grant wasn't on a scheduled flight. He was playing and didn't answer in the customary fashion.

"I have a call for you."

"If it's not an emergency, take a message." Grant didn't want to be disturbed. Flying was his life, and today, he didn't want anything to interfere with the way he felt toward the sky and the plane.

"I think you'll want to speak to this little lady." There was a smile in Adam's voice. Grant immediately thought of Brooke. His grip on the stick tightened.

"Put her on," he said.

"Hi, Uncle Grant." Kari's high-pitched voice crackled over the radio phone.

Grant laughed at where his thoughts had been. "How's my favorite blood relative?" he asked.

"I'm fine. Graffie said I could call you."

"I'm so glad you did. What are you doing? Beating Graffie at Space Invaders or Super Mario?" These two games made up Grant's entire repertoire.

"No, Graffie's on his computer in the basement. I'm in the kitchen having a sandwich." Her small voice sounded as if she'd accomplished something big. Grant could imagine peanut butter and jelly smeared around her beautiful mouth.

"Will you make me a sandwich, too?"

"Of course, when are you coming to see me again?"

"I'll be there tomorrow," he said, feeling the anticipation of seeing Brooke again warm his loins.

"I'll make you lunch," Kari volunteered. "We can have oysters on the half shell as an appetizer." She faltered on the last word, but continued in her childlike voice, "followed by Crab Imperial and Mommy's special iced tea."

Grant laughed. The child was precious and definitely the daughter of a restaurant owner. Brooke had taught her a proper menu for lunch.

"Kari, I'm afraid I won't be able to make it for lunch, but I'd like a rain check." He couldn't keep the laughter out of his voice.

"All right, we'll have lunch another day."

"I promise, sweetheart."

"Good-bye, Uncle Grant."

"Good-bye, Kari."

Grant released the speaker button and replaced the handset. He was smiling at Kari's confidence. To think she could have died. He'd never even have met her if they didn't have the same blood type.

And he'd have never met her mother, Brooke. The smile left his face, and his brows knitted together. Brooke was an enigma. He was sure she wasn't a spy as Will had suggested, but she *was* hiding something. He didn't know what, but each time he'd been with her, he could feel there was something behind everything she said and did. And her constant refusal to see him wasn't hurting his ego, he joked to himself. It was as if she were afraid to continue seeing him. But why? Before that night in the hospital, they had never met.

He remembered that night. He'd thought she was Robyn. It was more than a thought, he knew she was Robyn. But how? Robyn was dead. And when she'd turned, his knees would have buckled if she hadn't been white as a sheet and looking nothing like his wife.

And, then, he'd taken her home. What happened on the sofa the next morning had started as a dream but hadn't ended that way. Yet, there were so many similarities between Brooke and Robyn: the way she moved, how she phrased her words, and even the lyrical way her hands stirred the air as if they were playing the piano.

Grant pulled hard on the stick in his hand. The plane climbed straight up until it looped over in a complete

circle. It was how he felt. Brooke was driving him
crazy, and his life was running from one circle to another, never finding a solution, just continuing along
the same path.

Well, he'd change that tomorrow. He'd find out what
it was she was hiding.

"I've decided not to see him again," Robyn
pounded the dough for Yesterdays's famous dinner
rolls. It was the third decision she'd made in as many
days.

Marianne stood at the counter across from her.
"You think you can hold to that?" she asked, throwing
her a disdainful look while she dabbed white stars on
a bunny cake.

"Of course," Robyn said, punching at the mass of
dough in her bowl. In truth, Robyn wasn't sure of
anything anymore. In just one day, Grant had upset
the normal operation of her orderly life. She remembered how he'd upset her life that one day in Las Vegas
when she'd met and married him within hours. She
regretted her decision not to take him into the program
with her, especially after she discovered her pregnancy.

Grant had been bounced from one foster home to
another. He never developed a sense of belonging,
never allowed himself to love anyone for fear they
would leave him. Even Aunt Priscilla had told her he'd
never opened up after he came to live with her. Flying
was his freedom. Up there among the clouds and the
wind was as close as he could get to the people who

really loved him, and he'd never give up flying. He'd
die if he couldn't fly.

Robyn knew firsthand what it was to give up something you loved. If it hadn't been for the microchip
her decision might have been different. And it was
only by chance she found it. Grant's uniform had
needed pressing. The iron passed over a lump in the
lining. She could find no rip and thought the uniform
was flawed. Gently opening the fabric, she found the
microchip. It was concealed inside a fake diamond.
Anyone else would have thought it was an unset gem.
Robyn noticed the flaw wasn't natural, but man-made.

Grant had told her the project was called Eagle, and
it had national security implications. She immediately
thought he was spying. He explained he wasn't but
couldn't tell her anything more. When she found out
her testimony would put her in the Witness Protection
Program, she started digging for information on Project Eagle. Director Christopher found her one night
and invited her to his office. He explained the position
Grant held. He had been friends with one of the men
who'd stolen a vital component of a defense system.
Grant had been trying to get enough information to
ensure the government would find the device. His position was unique, easy access in and out of the country, no association with any government agency, and
a prior affiliation with the prime suspect.

Robyn had been stunned. What were the odds that
her Grant could be working undercover for the government? The director could give her no definite time
that he might complete this project, but that it was
vitally important. When he was released from the

Lebanese jail, they'd wanted him to continue his assignment. Afterwards, he could join her in the program, but there was no telling if that would be one month or one year.

Robyn had left his office with the weight of the free world on her shoulders. It was history now, Robyn shrugged. There was nothing she could do about it. She mentally shook her shoulders. Jacob *was* right. She couldn't be protected if she ignored the rules.

"When do you plan to let him know?" Marianne broke into her thoughts.

Robyn was jarred. Let who know? Then, she remembered her decision not to see Grant again.

"I thought I'd call his air service and leave a message." She expected to hear Marianne call her a coward, but the redhead remained silent, concentrating on dabbing the inner ear of the rabbit with dark pink icing.

"Marianne, you're awfully quiet. Why aren't you trying to talk me out of this?"

"It's your decision."

"What happened to all those speeches you gave me about dating? Not leaving any room in my life for a man?"

"Do you *want* me to talk you out of it?"

Robyn was silent for a long time. "I guess it's best if I stick by the decision I've made."

"Which one? Today's, yesterday's, or the one you might make tomorrow?" Marianne sounded unusually cynical.

"I thought you liked Grant, Marianne?"

"I like him as well as the next guy."

Robyn's head came up to look at her partner. "As well as the next guy," she repeated. "This, from the woman who referred to him as the man with the Greek god physique."

"You don't need me to talk you out of this. You're doing it yourself."

She *was* talking herself out of her decision. Robyn sat down. Her arms and face were coated with flour. Usually a neat cook, today she'd made a mess of the floor and herself.

"What would you do in my place?"

"I'm not in your place. And you haven't explained why you think going out with him will ruin your life."

Oh, Marianne, if only I could, Robyn wanted to say. So many times since she and Marianne had become partners, she had wanted to confide in her friend, but she'd remember one of Jacob's lectures and work out the problems for herself.

"Well, since you won't tell me, maybe you should stop killing that bread and go expend some of that energy through your feet." Marianne had finished the cake. She cleaned her hands and took the bowl of dough.

"You're right. If I practice, maybe it'll take my mind off Grant." She tried to smile as she cleaned the flour from her face and arms. Robyn paused next to the pink and white rabbit cake. "Who's this for?" she asked, licking some of the excess icing.

"Carrie Snodgrass. She feels about rabbits the way Kari does about bears."

Robyn smiled. "Will has just added to her collection."

"What did he make this time?"

"A trolley car full of bears. Kari loves it." Robyn smiled, and left Marianne in the aftermath of her mess.

In the lounge, the chorus line was busy working on a new routine. Sue-Ellen, the newest recruit, was having a hard time. Robyn slipped out of her warmup suit and joined the line. She wore a navy blue leotard with white footless stockings and beige pumps.

The music began, and she felt like Sue-Ellen. She kept missing the steps. Several times, the line stopped because of her mistakes. Then, she put her mind to it and finally found her footing. Every measure of energy she had, she channeled into the dance steps, giving no conscious part of her mind over to Grant.

"Take a break, everyone." Pete, the music director and choreographer, called.

Robyn grabbed a towel and patted her face. She hung it around her neck and left the stage. At the bar, she poured herself a glass of water and drank deeply.

"Brooke, do you want to dance the solo?" Pete asked, taking the seat next to her.

"No." Her brows went up as she faced him.

"I've seen more energy in your steps today than anytime in the recent past. What's going on?"

"I'm sorry. Am I causing a problem?"

"Of course, not."

"I think you should let Sue-Ellen dance the solo."

"Sue-Ellen," he laughed. "She's falling all over her feet."

"She's just nervous. She needs a little confidence. And giving her the solo will do it."

"There you go being kind hearted again. But you

know I love it. After all, where would I be if you hadn't been kind to me." Pete leaned forward and squeezed her hand. "Now, how about going through your song?"

Robyn smiled. She felt a lot better. "Fine," she nodded.

"Set up for the 'Time' number." Pete hollered to the stage crew. "I think we should try the dancing water with this."

"What do the sets look like?"

"There will be a huge moon, and the water will be backlit. On the stage will be you and the piano."

Robyn watched the movement on the stage. The grand piano was rolled into place, and the lights dimmed until the back wall was the only source of illumination. She went to her mark in the arm of the piano. Pete followed her to his seat at the keyboard. He raised his arm like a baton. Violins began the first notes of "One Moment in Time," and a spotlight highlighted her.

Robyn listened to the introduction, then took a breath and came in clear on the first note. Behind her, the water danced to the rise and fall of the piano and her voice. The words took on a secondary meaning as she went into the chorus. She knew where she stood at that moment in time, and it was up to her to decide where the rest of her life was going.

When the music ended and the house lights began to brighten the room, Robyn froze as the familiar form of Grant Richards stepped away from the bar and came toward the stage. He stopped near the four steps to the elevated platform. She was glad the piano was behind her. It provided support since her knees were suddenly weak.

"You're early," she said, coming to the end of the stage. Pete called the chorus back, and activity started behind her. "You're not due back for days. Why didn't you call?"

"If I'd called, you'd tell me not to come, right?"

Robyn leveled her gaze. "Yes," she said.

Grant spread his hands in answer and smiled.

Robyn didn't return it. "We have to talk." She walked to the barstool, retrieving her clothing, and then led Grant toward her dressing room. Before she reached the stairs, his hand took her arm and propelled her past the stairs and through the kitchen.

"Marianne, Brooke is leaving. She won't be back tonight."

"Yes, I will," she contradicted, as he hurried her about the counters laden with food for tonight's menu and through the door.

"Decision number four?" The redhead pushed her hands through her hair as she sat down on the chair behind her.

Washington National Airport was alive with activity. It was Friday. The sun hung low in the afternoon sky, and weekend travelers scurried to escape the city. Jacob leaned against the wall of windows in the waiting area of US Air. The tarmac was hot, and he could see the waves of heat rising off the black surface. A steady stream of planes entered and left the retractable jetways. Marianne was due in for her once a month report. Usually, she made her own way to the Watergate Hotel, and a car would pick her up on Saturday morning. For the rest of the weekend, they'd work in his office.

Today, he wanted to talk to her as soon as she arrived. He stood up straight moments later when he saw her short bob of curly red hair appear. He took a step forward then stopped when he noticed she wasn't alone. The man with her was tall and muscular, with straight black hair cut neatly above his shirt collar. He was dressed in a business suit instead of the jeans and T-shirts that were the uniforms of American travelers. Something around Jacob's heart tightened. He refused to acknowledge it as anything except disappointment at not being able to execute his plan.

The couple walked briskly toward the indoor runway that led to the baggage claim area, ticket counters, and taxis waiting outside. Jacob followed at a discreet distance. They both went to baggage claim. Jacob lifted a courtesy phone and had Marianne paged, leaving a message that a car was waiting for her. He watched as she found her bag, shook hands with the man, and made her way through the maze of people waiting at the carousel and its endless circle of luggage. He went outside and was there when the automatic doors opened and she came through them alone.

"Jacob," she greeted. "I didn't expect a car." Her smile was radiant.

"Let me have that." He took her suitcase and garment bag and led her to the government cars parked next to the entrance of the north terminal. "I wanted to talk to you," he said after he'd helped her inside, stored her luggage in the backseat, and slid into the driver's seat.

He started the car and reversed out of the space. He didn't go far before turning onto Boundary Drive and heading for Lady Bird Johnson Park. Puzzled, Marianne looked at him when he bypassed the entrance to the George Washington Parkway that would have been the route to the Watergate Hotel.

"Let's walk," Jacob said when he'd parked in the empty lot.

Marianne followed him down a path that led to a railing along the Potomac River. They were in the direct flight path of outgoing planes, and overhead, a huge jumbo jet thundered on its route toward an unknown destination.

Jacob rested his arms on the rail. He looked out over the water for so long, Marianne thought he had forgotten she was there. Jacob was different. What had made him come to the airport? He had never done that before. Not even the first time she came to report to him. The last time she'd been here she thought he acted slightly out of step, but this time he was totally out of character. Marianne wondered what had happened to change Jacob? She stepped closer to him, but he made no move to acknowledge her presence.

"Jacob," she called quietly. "Is something wrong?"

He didn't turn immediately but kept staring across the water. Then, he shifted and looked at her. Marianne had the feeling that he'd never seen her before and that he found it strange that she was standing before him. She reached for him, touching his sleeve.

"Are you all right?" she asked again.

He nodded covering her hand, then resumed his position at the rail.

Marianne let her hand stay where it was. She would have liked to explore the emotions rioting through her system, but she had an important report to give. With her free hand, she opened the large purse on her shoulder and pulled out a folded piece of paper.

"Have you ever seen this?" She handed it to Jacob.

He took it, letting go of her hand to open the fold. "Where did you get this?" He glanced at the photocopy of the picture of Robyn Richards.

"I found it in the safe at the restaurant, hidden behind some papers we keep there."

"Did Brooke say anything about this?"

"No," Marianne shook her head. "If she hadn't folded the envelope it was in, I'd never have noticed it." Marianne pointed to the bottom part of the photocopy where she'd copied the envelope and an enlargement of the postmark.

Jacob squinted in the bright sunlight. "This arrived before my visit. Why didn't she tell me about it?"

"I don't know. Since Kari's accident and Grant's arrival, she hasn't known which way to turn."

"But she must know someone has discovered who she is." He looked at the grainy photo. "That her life is in danger."

"Her life has been in danger for five years," Marianne hesitated. Jacob looked at her, waiting for her to continue. "She could think Grant sent it."

"Do you think she told him?"

"No," Marianne said without hesitation. "If she'd told him, she wouldn't be flip-flopping on whether to see him when he comes."

"She's still seeing him then?"

Marianne knew about Robyn's promise to Jacob. "Brooke doesn't invite him. He just shows up, and how can she refuse to go out with him? He's handsome, sure of himself, and he makes her feel like she's the only woman in the world." Marianne realized she was talking about herself as well as Robyn. "Beyond that, she's in love with him."

" 'Wars have been lost and won over love,' " Jacob quoted some unknown poet. Marianne had no idea who. She knew how Robyn felt, wanting something she couldn't have.

"I'm going to have to act on this," Jacob said, his gaze moving from Marianne to the paper and back.

Marianne nodded. She knew he'd have to do something.

"Come on, I'll get you to your hotel."

He took her arm and led her back to the car. The drive to Watergate was made in silence. Traffic over the Fourteenth Street Bridge had more than the usual amount of snarl for a Friday. Jacob cursed under his breath as they inched along at five miles an hour. When they hit Constitution Avenue Marianne could see the flashing lights of police cars ahead. Jacob banked left and took the streets through downtown until they reached P Street. Since Rock Creek Park at this hour flowed West it was apparent they were taking a route through Georgetown.

Marianne turned her attention to the cobblestone streets. The silence bothered her. She wondered what Jacob was thinking, what he would do with the information she'd given him and how Robyn would react when she found out he knew. Over the years Robyn had not known anything about her reports to Jacob. Until Kari's accident there hadn't been much to say. Now she felt like a traitor.

"Jacob—," she began intent on asking him the question uppermost in her mind. She stopped suddenly, whipping her head around to stare at the back of a man walking up Wisconsin Avenue. His back was to her and crowds of tourist thronging the narrow pavement swallowed him up. She was sure—.

"What is it?" Jacob glanced over his shoulder quickly, then at her before giving his attention to negotiating the trolley tracks lining the broad avenue.

It couldn't be, Marianne thought. She thought she'd seen Will McAdams.

"Nothing," she finally said. Turning back she resettled her seat belt and stared at the shops and street vendors interspersed with a moving sea of people. Shaking her head she resolved the image as someone who looked like Will. After all, she'd only had a glimpse of him and she couldn't see much because of the people in her way. Will was probably fixing spaghetti for Kari. It was the child's favorite food and Marianne knew he watched her while Robyn ran the restaurant.

At the hotel she filled in the records card and smiled at the familiar clerk as she accepted her computer-coded key. Thoughts of Will had evaporated by

the time the doors to the mirrored elevator opened.
Jacob followed her, carrying her garment bag and
suitcase. He'd just dropped them on the king-size bed
and turned to leave when the first bomb exploded.

Eight

Grant had finished checking in, and the green-and-white clad agent smiled and handed him the keys to his rental car. Heading for the automatic doors, he saw her. Marianne looked strained and pale as she awkwardly pulled her suitcase from the circling carousel with her left hand. She dropped it next to her feet as if the action hurt. He made his way toward her. She looked surprised and frightened when she saw him.

"Marianne, what happened to you?" he asked. When he picked up her suitcase and garment bag, Grant noticed the bandage on her arms. Her face looked as if she'd been in a tanning machine where the lights worked only on one side. And part of her lower jaw was covered by a gauze patch.

"I'm fine," she said by way of explanation. She offered a smile but it didn't seem to work. Her eyes misted, but she blinked the tears away.

"You don't look so good. I have a car. Let me give you a ride home." Grant didn't want to mention how badly she looked. He guided her to the area where the agent had told him he'd find the car and stored her suitcase and bag in the trunk. She dropped her head and looked close to tears.

"Can I help?" Grant offered.

"No," she answered with a long sigh and lay her head against the upholstery. It had been a long time since someone had tried to kill her. The first and only other time it had happened, she'd threatened to leave the service. She didn't want to be an undercover agent. It was then that she had been transferred to the program and had taken the assignment of protecting Robyn and Kari. The assignment had been easy up to yesterday. If Jacob hadn't come to pick her up, she would have gone back to that room and been killed. She shuddered.

"Are you cold," Grant asked. He reached for the air conditioning setting and raised the temperature of the digital display. Grant had reached Route 33 and was heading toward the restaurant.

"You'll have to pass the turnoff for Yesterdays and take the Parkside Avenue-Zoo exit," she directed.

Marianne sat quietly afterward. The car took ten minutes to reach the location, and at that point, she sat up and directed him past the park and onto the quiet tree-lined street where she lived. Her house was unlike Robyn's in that it was a tall but narrow Victorian. The paint, a soft blue trimmed in salmon pink, set it apart. It sat nestled among other Victorians of bright and muted colors.

Grant pulled into her driveway and got out. He went around and helped her out. She was wobbly at first, and for a moment, Grant was about to lift her and carry her up the five steps that led to the small front porch. She regained her balance and walked across the grass to grasp the handrail. Getting her suitcase, he followed her.

Inside, the rooms were dark since the windows were hung with heavy drapery. The furniture was sparse, giving the rooms an airiness when she threw every drape open.

"I'll be fine now," she told him.

Grant wasn't so sure. "What happened, Marianne?" he asked for the second time since leaving the airport. "You've obviously been in some sort of accident. I can keep a secret, if that's a concern, but you look like you need someone to talk to."

She hesitated, her chin shaking, as if she wanted to say something but was forcing herself to remain quiet. Her action reminded him of Brooke and her determined effort to control her words. "Would you like me to call Brooke?"

"No!" she shouted too loud and too quickly. "Don't call Brooke. She's much too busy right now." Her voice was lower.

"How about some tea?" he suggested. It was a trick Robyn used to use on him to make him tell her things he didn't want her to know. "A cup of tea will make you feel better."

In the kitchen, Grant filled the kettle sitting on the stove with water and searched the tea canister. It was filled with individual bags, but in the cabinet next to the sugar he found a box of loose apple spiced tea. Searching further, he found a tea ball in the drawer and used Robyn's recipe to make hot apple spiced tea. The aroma filled his senses and momentarily brought Robyn back to life. Then, he remembered the sad

woman in the other room. He placed several spoons
of sugar in the hot mixture and took two cups back
to the living room.

Marianne was curled up on the window seat. Her
arms were wrapped around her body tightly as if her
life force would escape if she didn't hold it in. She
stared vacant-eyed through the glass at the gray day.
Grant could tell that her mind was miles away. Maybe
she was back in her weekend. Something had happened there that had frightened her. He called her
name. She didn't respond.

He set the two cups on the window ledge and took
the seat next to her. "I'm not leaving until you tell
me what happened."

She came back then. His voice drew her from the
sound of the shattering glass and from Jacob holding
onto her to prevent any harm from happening to her.
Without his quick thinking, she shuddered to imagine
where she would be now, dead or in the burn unit of
George Washington Hospital Center.

"There was a fire," she told a half-truth. A bomb
exploding in her hotel room had set it to burning. "My
hotel room caught on fire. I barely escaped."

"Are you all right?" Grant's eyes went to the bandages.

"I wasn't burned badly." Her voice was monotone.
"I was just scared, and my arms have a few blisters.
The doctor said they won't scar." She swallowed a sob
and lifted her chin.

"What started the fire?" he asked in a whispered
tone.

"Electrical wiring," she lied. "It was a faulty switch

in the room. Everyone escaped unharmed." Marianne sipped her tea. Life seemed to be returning. She felt better now that she was back on familiar ground. But if someone knew her exact hotel room in Washington, they also knew where she lived. Jacob had her house checked out. He'd been on the phone, barking orders since they'd left the hospital, and he'd taken her to his house in Rock Creek Park.

It was Jacob who had sent a message to Robyn telling her Marianne would be staying an extra day. He didn't explain anything, and Marianne knew Robyn wouldn't pry. The two of them had come to an unspoken understanding years ago, and neither of them interfered in the other's life. At least not until Grant had come to donate blood for Kari. Then, Robyn appeared to open up a little, giving Marianne glimpses of her feelings, but Marianne had been forced to keep her own feelings to herself.

Grant watched her. She was nervous and needed someone to help her. She drank the tea methodically. It must have been a trauma to find yourself in a burning room. Grant hadn't known any burn victims, but he'd seen films of plane crashes and had been required to take classes to handle emergency landings. The greatest hazard in force landing a plane was the likelihood of fire. Case studies of survivors had told him the trauma lasted long after the victims were safe. And Marianne had all the symptoms of delayed shock.

She finished her tea, and Grant coaxed her into going to bed. When she climbed the stairs, he used the phone to call Brooke. She was there in minutes.

"How is she?" Robyn asked the moment she came through the door.

"I'm not sure. She's has bandages but doesn't appear to be in any physical pain. She looks like she needs someone."

"I'll go up."

Grant kissed her lightly on the mouth. "I'm going to the hotel. I'll call later."

Robyn nodded and headed up the heavily carpeted stairs. Marianne was lying on the bed fully dressed. She took one look at Robyn and burst into tears. Robyn ran to her, cradling her head in her arms and letting her cry. Her body shook in spasms. Robyn knew she had to let fear run its course. She spoke in a whispered voice, telling Marianne it was over. The fire was out, and there was nothing to hurt her now. After a long while, she stopped crying. Exhaustion made her sleep. Robyn covered her with a light blanket and went to the kitchen.

The tea Grant had made was sitting on the warming plate. Robyn poured herself a cup. She started for the pedestal table when the phone rang. Quickly, she snatched it from the wall, hoping the sound had not jarred Marianne from her much needed sleep.

"Hello," she answered.

At the other end, someone coughed then cleared his throat. "I'm sorry, I must have the wrong number." A muffled voice spoke into her ear. She was about to say something when the line went dead. Robyn looked at the phone before replacing it. There was something familiar about the voice, but it was disguised. Somehow she knew it.

She took her tea to the table and sat down. Her brows knitted together in thought, trying to focus on the sound she'd just heard. There had been something authoritative about it, almost military in nature. The only man she knew with a voice like that didn't know Marianne. That man was Jacob Winston.

She was all right. She was safe. Jacob told himself over and over. Marianne had stayed an extra day, but when he'd driven her to the airport, she was still pale and fearful. He'd had her house checked, and it was clean. But he didn't want her to return. He wanted her to stay with him where he could keep her safe, but she'd told him she couldn't do it. Her obligations were to Robyn and Kari, and there was no way he could do his job if he had to continually check on her.

Jacob knew she was right, but he didn't like the way she looked. Her vibrant personality had been changed by the bomb. The façade of control she tried to show was cracked, and he could see it. And he was sending her back alone. There was no one she could tell what had happened. They had gone over the story she was to tell to explain the bandages. He'd squelched any mention in the news services, and the official version spoke of a faulty electrical switch that had been replaced that afternoon.

The truth was a small bomb had been placed over the door. He hadn't seen it until he'd turned to leave. And there it was, hanging inches from Marianne's head. It was amateurish, but the second blast that had been set off by the first had all the marks of a professional demolitions expert. Jacob had the room combed. His findings proved the professional theory. There wasn't enough left of the bomb to fill a thimble. But he knew it was a calling card. Alex Jordan has risen from the dead, and this time he was after him.

Well, his attention was fully focused. Marianne was an innocent. She had nothing to do with the Crime Network. This was meant to be a warning that they were close. Icy fingers skittered up Jacob's spine. It was personal now.

The private elevator to Clarence Christopher's office reminded Jacob of the Hoover years. Although J. Edgar Hoover died years before the first shovel of dirt to build the block size building bearing his name was ever turned, the elevator would have afforded the notorious director the cover of secrecy to hold his nocturnal meetings. As far as Jacob knew, Clarence had never held a meeting after dark. There were conferences that flowed over into darkness, but the clandestine reports of Hoover's era were not part of the Christopher culture.

Jacob stepped into the room. Clarence looked up from his massive desk.

"How is she?" he asked.

"A little pale, but Marianne's a strong woman. She'll be fine." Jacob remembered Cynthia, another strong woman. He'd never seen fear on her face as he'd seen on Marianne's when she couldn't breathe or felt the surge of protectiveness that came over him at the hospital when she'd put her arms around him.

"Has she returned, yet?"

Jacob took the chair opposite Clarence. "This morning. I put her on the plane myself." She insisted on returning against his wishes. He knew she was scared and returning alone was her way of dealing with it. He had called her this afternoon and Robyn answered. It was lucky he recognized her voice before he spoke. But Robyn was smart. He wasn't sure he'd fooled her.

Clarence picked up the pen in front of him and looked at it for a long time. "What have you found out about the explosion?"

"The bomb hanging over the door was crude and of no consequence. It was placed there as a decoy to prevent anyone from leaving the room. But the one behind the bar was the work of a professional. The plastic explosive was army-issue and experimental. It was designed to both explode and incinerate, leaving no trace of itself behind. It's cropped up in several terrorist attacks in recent years."

"Where do you suppose he got hold of it?"

"We're working on that. So far, the only place we've come up with is an out of the way air base in northern Canada."

"Canada?"

Jacob nodded. "We picked it up during the computer search that cross-referenced the blasting caps and the plastic explosive. Apparently, there's a research unit up there working on thermodynamics." Jacob knew that translated into bomb.

"Have they discovered any of their supply missing?"

"Not according to their records, but I have someone checking the physical inventory."

Clarence nodded his assent, then looked down at the report on his desk. "I've read your reports on activities in the last five years related to the Crime Network. Do you believe they are still in operation?"

"All the evidence points in that direction. Before Jordan was found, the targets were specific and expensive. The unit must have needed money to keep everyone in the elaborate lifestyles they were living. In the past five years, the actions have bordered on revenge. Each of those assassinated, we think, had an association with the other. Several members of the same army unit, three men who were roommates at college, and seven business partners. The list is short but there is a connection. I have the feeling we're looking for a small group of people or even a single man who's doing the hits."

"Any idea who or why?"

Jacob shook his head, frustration evident in the cast of his shoulders.

"What of Mrs. Richards?"

Sitting up straight, he looked directly at the FBI director. "She hasn't mentioned the photo Marianne brought. Someone could have discovered her identity, and then again it could be a false lead."

"You think her husband sent it?" Christopher asked.

"He could have." Jacob shrugged. "We haven't been able to prevent him from continually seeing her. We gave his service a greater work load, but he still manages to sporadically appear. There was a sale of surplus aircraft scheduled for next month. After last night's bombing, I had it moved to this week. He'll be too busy with it to have time to make trips to Buffalo."

Christopher nodded.

"Do you think he might be of use to us?" Clarence asked.

"As an unwilling pawn?" Jacob's brows went up.

"You don't like that idea? It's how we got Mrs. Richards to testify five years ago. And I know you don't approve of those kind of tactics, but sometimes it's the only way to get the job done."

"Maybe," Jacob said. "But if we'd just asked her she might have considered it her civic duty and helped without coercion."

"We didn't have time for that. Jordan was well connected. As it was, we had to protect her during the investigation.

"What about resettlement? We could give her a new identity; have her start over. This time her husband could go, too." Christopher suggested.

"That would be very hard on Kari, her daughter. She's four."

"What's your suggestion? She's either a target for some unknown assailant or uprooted." Christopher spread his hands. "It's your call."

Jacob didn't want to call this one. He remembered the first time he'd seen Robyn. She had looked like a frightened little bird about to be eaten by a giant cat. But she fought valiantly, if in vain. This time, she had to make the choice. It was her life. Too many people were running it without her knowledge.

Marianne was winning. She woke up without the burning pain that had plagued her arms and face. The room was dark, and she knew she'd been asleep a long time. Looking at the small clock with two white cherubs on it that Robyn had given her for Christmas two years ago, she found it was after eight o'clock. The crowd at Yesterdays would be spilling onto the porch. She should be there to help Robyn. A shaft of pain in her head as she tried to move warned her not to consider the possibility.

She raised herself up on her elbows. Pain shot up the back of her skull and threatened to blind her. The pain killers the doctor had given her were sitting on the night table. Suddenly, she remembered Robyn had been there. Robyn had given her the pills, and she'd fallen asleep. She reached for the lamp and turn it on. Her eyes squinted against the brightness that swept over the room.

Swinging around, she placed her feet on the floor. The pain in her head intensified to white hot. A wave of nausea threatened her, and she remained still until it passed. Gingerly, she stood up and went to the bathroom.

Robyn heard the movement from downstairs. She'd just finished making another cup of tea. Marianne would certainly be hungry by now. She poured a second cup and placed both cups on a claw-footed silver tray. She added a plate of the muffins that Grant had dropped by and climbed the stairs to the master bedroom.

Knocking lightly, she opened the door. Marianne was standing in the bathroom doorway, a paper cup in her hand. "Have you been here all day?" she asked, dropping the yellow flowered cup into the wastebasket.

"Most of it," Robyn nodded. "Grant came back to make sure you were all right. He told me what happened. I'm so glad you're going to be all right. But you should have called me. The message Pete took only said you would be a day late in returning. Nothing about an accident."

"I'm sorry," she apologized, knowing Jacob wouldn't volunteer any details that weren't absolutely necessary. "The hospital was busy with all the people coming in with minor burns and injuries."

Actually, she didn't remember much about the hospital. Just Jacob holding her.

"How do you feel now?" Robyn watched Marianne make her way back to the bed and sit down.

"I have an awful headache, but my arms don't hurt anymore." She looked at the bandages that were still on her arms. Underneath, her skin had first- and second-degree burns. Most of the covered area was red, and part of it was blistered. She knew it was time to change the dressing. Jacob had wrapped them for her this morning before he took her to the airport.

"Would you like me to change those?" Robyn appeared to read her mind.

"I brought some gauze back with me. It's in my suitcase."

Grant had left the case in the downstairs hall.

"I'll get it. Have some tea and muffins. You must be hungry, too. Would you like me to order you some food?"

Marianne shook her head. "The muffins look good."

"Grant brought them by before he left," she explained.

"He's gone, already." Usually, he stayed a few days when he came. She yawned. The pills she'd taken were making her drowsy.

"Something came up suddenly, and he had to go buy some planes. He didn't have time to explain it to me."

Robyn left to get Marianne's suitcase. Marianne understood Grant's departure. Jacob was manipulating his presence. The fire bombing had told them that danger was closing in. Grant had to be kept away from Robyn.

"You must have been a nurse in another life," Marianne said minutes later as Robyn cut the surgical tape and secured the last wrapping in place. She slid down in the bed.

"I don't think so, but I've bandaged my share of scraped knees," she smiled, thinking of Kari.

"Where is Kari?"

"She's with Will. The two of them have been inseparable since last weekend."

"What did they do?" she asked. Her question was more than gentle curiosity.

"Saturday, Will took her to the beach. She fell asleep in the sun and came home with a slight sunburn, but she was too tired and too happy to do anything but sleep. On Sunday, they went to a kiddie play at Studio Area. She can't stop talking about it."

Robyn smiled, and Marianne returned it. She remembered the man she'd thought was Will McAdams in Georgetown. Robyn's story had told her where he was. She had to be wrong. A man couldn't be in two places at one time.

"Who's managing the restaurant?" Marianne changed the subject.

"Would you believe Pete?" she laughed. "If we ever sell that place, we'll have to give it to him. He's playing king tonight."

"And who's playing queen?" It was Robyn's role.

"Sue-Ellen." Both women laughed. Marianne's eyes widened then held her stomach.

"Sue-Ellen!" She was the clumsiest dancer Marianne had ever seen. Yet, Robyn liked her. "Do you suppose she'll fall over the dessert cart or snag her dress on one of the tables?"

"She's not that clumsy," Robyn defended her.

"You know she's a runaway." Marianne put her hand over her mouth as she tried to stifle another yawn.

Robyn nodded. "But she's over twenty-one and answerable to no one."

"I can't see why you keep her around."

Robyn stopped a moment, then she said, "She reminds me of myself a few years ago."

"You could never have been that clumsy," Marianne stated.

"It's not that she's clumsy so much as lacking confidence. Given a little time, she'll begin to believe in herself."

Marianne didn't ask, but she thought Robyn was speaking about herself and not about Sue-Ellen. And she hadn't missed the slight hesitation Robyn had made before she had begun speaking. It was the first time Robyn had mentioned a past outside of the prepared one Jacob had ingrained in her when she entered the program.

"Give her a chance, Marianne."

"I promise, I will."

Robyn smiled at her friend who was obviously tired. "You should go back to sleep." She got up. Marianne didn't protest. Robyn found a pink gown in the top drawer and helped her into it. Within minutes, she was asleep.

Ladened with the silver tray, Robyn tiptoed down the stairs and into the kitchen. She thought about Sue-Ellen. And thinking of her brought her own past back, when she was Robyn Warren, dancing briefly in a chorus line, nervous and unsteady until the other dancers let her know she was one of them. Then, her steps became sure and easy.

And it had been like that when she'd been approached to testify in the Alex Jordan trial. She was unsure and nervous. Grant being in Lebanon added to the pressure she was feeling. Then, the government came along and offered to get him out in exchange for her direct testimony. But to do so meant to suddenly and completely disappear from her friends. Even Susan didn't know where she had been sequestered.

When she'd arrived at the court, she was bombarded with flashbulbs popping in her face and an opposing attorney who was known worldwide for winning cases that had been considered open and shut. She, a twenty-five-year-old, was up against that. And she had needed someone to believe in her. That someone had been Jacob Winston.

Then, she didn't know he would also be the man who would coach her in the program and the man who would protect her life and that of her child.

Nine

"Where are you taking me?" Robyn asked, as the sleek car sped through the afternoon traffic. Grant had shown up unexpectedly. His comings and goings were hard to predict, and no matter what Robyn did, she ended up at his side.

"Someplace I can talk to you without continually hearing you say you don't want to see me. When everytime I look at you, all I can see is a bedroom in your eyes."

"That's not true," she lied, looking away from him. She, however, knew whenever she looked at him, all she wanted to do was run into his arms and have him make love to her.

"Liar." His accusation was tempered by the smile on his face.

Robyn was silent. It had been two weeks since she had last seen him. Marianne's burns were almost healed, and she was back at work. Grant had called to say he'd bought some new airplanes and was busy getting them in operating order since his work load had also increased. Robyn didn't know if she was happy or sad. When he wasn't there, she missed him, but his presence meant danger.

They left the city behind and traveled up Route 33 to the airport. Grant guided the car into the airport driveway and proceeded to an area for small planes and helicopters.

Minutes later, they were seated in a helicopter flying over the city.

"When did you learn to fly helicopters?" She spoke into the headset Grant had given her. The noise prevented them from hearing each other without amplification.

"When I bought the air service, it came with helicopters."

"Is it the same as flying a plane?" Grant had taught her to fly a small plane years ago.

"It's quite different. There aren't nearly as many controls, but it is more difficult to fly."

"But you like it." She could see it in his face. It took her back to when they were first married. Flying had been his life, he'd told her. It was the only thing he loved that loved him back before he met her. He'd said he couldn't live without flying.

"I love it almost as much as I like breathing. I feel like I can do anything when I'm up here." He was proud.

"What would you have done if you weren't a pilot?" For some reason she needed to affirm her decision, to make sure her decision had been the only one that could have been made at the time.

"Not fly. I don't know. I was sixteen, still in high school, when I went on my first plane ride. It was then that I decided I had to fly, and since then it's been the only thing in my life." He paused a moment before adding. "I have to admit, if it weren't for flying, I'd probably have lost my mind when Robyn died."

"Look there's the Liberty Bank Building." Robyn, changing the subject, pointed to the twin statues at each end of the famous landmark. Further down Main Street, she could see the War Memorial Auditorium, and then Grant flew directly over Yesterdays.

"Have you ever been in a helicopter before?"

"Never, not even to sit in one."

"How do you like it?"

"It's wonderful." She offered a smile. "I didn't know you could get so close to things. I can actually recognize streets."

"Maybe one day you'd like to learn?" Grant asked.

Robyn sat back in her seat. "No, I don't think so. I do very little traveling, and I have no need for a helicopter."

"How about just for the fun of it? Someday, you could just soar off into the sky and leave everything behind you. Up here, it's just you and the sky."

Robyn had the sense he wasn't speaking to her anymore. He was in his own heaven. The sky was his world. The place where nothing else mattered, where he could go to solve his problems. A place to come to grips with anything the outside world threw at him. Even the death of his wife.

"Grant," she called to him tenderly. "This is not my world. It's your world. And I can't be a part of it."

"Why not? What happened to you that spoiled you for me? Where you beaten as a child? Where you so in love with your late husband, no other man can ever hold a candle to him?"

Robyn averted her glance, once again looking out at the blue of the sky and the clouds that contrived to make it a beautiful scene. She didn't want it to look like this. She'd rather the day be cloudy and wet instead of brilliantly alive. She felt like she was dying again. Everytime Grant flew into and out of her life, he took a little part of her with him. This time would be no different.

"Nothing traumatic happened to me," she lied. Death was always traumatic. "We don't travel the same paths. You're a pilot with government connections." Deep connections, she thought. "I'm just a restaurant owner with people to support. When you set me down again, we're not going to see each other so there's no need to make future plans."

"You're either very good, or you've been trained well," he observed.

"What do you mean?" Robyn asked.

"Your mouth says one thing but your body doesn't speak the same language."

"I mean what I say."

"Liar," he said again. Grant banked right, and Robyn noticed they were no longer over the city. Below them was nothing but green counterpanes of fields ready for harvesting. She'd only seen it once from this angle. Grant was right in his assessment of the flight. In the air, she felt like she was floating. She didn't need the metal casing around her. All she needed was the man sitting next to her, and he could take her to heights greater than any aircraft could.

"Does that stick control everything?" Robyn made another subject change as she pointed at the control Grant held.

"It controls the rotors, the blades on the top." He glanced up as if he could see through the roof. She followed his gaze.

"Are there elevators and ailerons and rudders to control?"

"You know how to fly!" A surprised smile curved his lips.

"No, I just took some ground lessons long ago."

"But you've never had the controls in your hands."

"No," not to a helicopter, she amended silently.

"How long ago did you take the ground course?"

"Before Kari was born."

"Did you want to fly then?"

"Yes."

"What changed your mind?"

"Nothing. I guess I'd still like to fly, but I'm no longer interested in taking lessons or flying planes. I had a fear then. I think I've conquered it."

"What scares you now?"

"Nothing." Robyn stole a glance at Grant. Had she said that too quickly? She was frightened. Afraid of a faceless, nameless person who knew her movements. She'd received the photo several weeks ago and done nothing about it, hiding it as if that would eliminate the problem. Then Marianne's room caught fire. Did that happen because of her friendship? And yesterday the poison . . .

"There is something." Grant broke into her thoughts. "Something that terrifies you. I see it in your eyes. Something scares you so badly you don't want to confront it."

Fear knotted in her stomach. She pushed herself into the upholstered seat, her body tight to keep from trembling. She was losing her edge. Grant read her all too clearly. "Can we drop this? It's none of your business."

Grant set the helicopter down in a field and pulled a picnic basket from behind his seat. He ducked under the rotating blades and came around to open the door for her.

Robyn looked around, pushing all thoughts of yesterday out of her mind. They must be a long way from anywhere. "Is this legal? I mean, can you set a helicopter down anyplace you want?"

"Not in our country. We're in Canada."

"Canada?"

"I checked with the Canadian authorities before we left. That's why we had to answer those questions at the airport."

Robyn remembered the man asking her nationality, and how long they planned to visit. At the time, she was too caught up in her argument with Grant to recognize the questions were the same as those the customs officials asked when she crossed the Peace Bridge.

Grant spread a red blanket on the ground and proceeded to sit on it.

"You may as well enjoy it. You'll notice we're quite a ways from anywhere. You can't run away. I have you at my mercy until I decide to fly you back to civilization."

Robyn wanted to be angry. She also wanted to drop down on the blanket and rummage in the basket with him. It was warmer since they'd landed, and her temperature rose just by being in his presence. She slipped the white jacket that matched her warmup suit off her arms and placed it on the edge of the blanket.

"We have Coke, iced tea, ginger ale." Grant offered her one of the aluminum cans.

"Ginger ale," Robyn took the canned beverage. She hated canned tea, preferring her own home-brewed concoction. She sat down as far away from him as the blanket allowed. "How long do you plan to keep me here?"

He sat up straight. "I didn't mean it to be a prison. If you'd like to leave, we'll go." He placed the can he held in his hand back in the basket, making ready to go.

"Grant," she said hesitantly. "I'd like to stay for a while."

He stopped, shifting his gaze to look directly into her eyes. Smoke clouded them. He didn't know how he was going to keep his hands off her if she looked at him like that. And he knew if he made a move in her direction, she'd freeze.

"Where are we?" she asked.

"Ontario, about thirty miles east of the beach Kari likes."

"Crystal Beach. It's really an amusement park." She took the sandwich he offered.

They ate in silence. He liked looking at her and didn't want to break the silence. She shifted several times, and he knew her back was uncomfortable with nothing to rest it against. Grant lounged against the back of a tree watching her. Then without him knowing it, he reached for her and pulled her against him. She fit into the cradle of his arms and didn't say a word. She turned her eyes to his, and he thought he'd lose himself in them.

"If you keep doing that I'll kiss you."

Robyn dropped her gaze and laid her head on his chest. She could hear his heart beating. It was going faster than normal, and she smiled at the obvious arousal she knew she caused in him. Settling comfortably, she watched the billowy clouds in the distant sky.

"Did you ever draw cloud pictures?" she asked.

"Everybody's done that. I used to paint them with bright colors."

Robyn laughed.

"Don't laugh. I was very good. With my fingertip, I had all the paint I needed, and I'd use vast amounts of red to draw smiles and big baggy pants. Tell me something you used to do?"

"I didn't paint the clouds. I used to let them form their own pictures, and then they'd talk to each other in foreign languages."

"Do you speak a foreign language?"

"No, but when I was ten I was going to learn every one I could—French, Spanish, and German." She shifted against him. He took her hand and brought it to his lips.

"I had a friend who could speak six languages. She'd been a service brat and lived all over the world. I envied her." She remembered Linda Sawyer fondly.

The last she'd heard Linda married a captain in the air force, and they lived in Germany.

"What about you?" she asked Grant.

"Only enough to get me a good dinner and a hotel room with a shower in just about any country." The tinkle of Robyn's laughter had him fitting her closer into the crook of his arm. "When I flew for Trans-Global, I learned the rudimentary phrases."

"Do you miss flying for them?"

"Not anymore. I did at first, but I needed the air service. The time was right." If it hadn't been for Robyn's death, he might have never left. He'd been alone, devastated, and needed something to occupy his time and energy. During the long months in Beirut, when they tortured him and tried to get information he didn't have by inflicting pain on other crew members, thoughts of Robyn had kept him sane. At first, he was sure the hijacking had something to do with Project Eagle, but no one had questioned him about that. Then Robyn was gone—and with her, his will to live. Shortly after Eagle was safely put to bed, the air service deal began falling in place. He gave it everything. Night and day he'd worked until David and Susan thought he was killing himself.

Maybe, he really did want to die then, but it had passed, and now he wanted to go on living. He wanted to live with Brooke Johnson and discover all the mysteries that made her who she was.

"Tell me something else you used to do," Robyn broke into his thoughts.

"Well, when I was eight," he smiled, his eyes bright and dancing. "I had only seen the U.S. as a map. I thought the lines defining the boundaries of states were really there."

Robyn started laughing. He could feel her body shaking against his. She sat up and looked at him. Her laugh continued until she could barely control it. "When did you find out they weren't there?"

"When I met Will and he arranged my first flight." He joined her laughing. "I admit it's silly, but I believed it. Don't tell me you never believed anything silly."

"Me, of course not." She straightened her face. "I was a model child." She snickered. "I never believed anything silly." Her face cracked.

"Come on what was it?" He straightened, too. Sitting with his back fully against the tree.

"Promise you won't laugh."

"No," he said leaning toward her. "Give, what was it?"

"I thought the wind carved out Mount Rushmore."

Grant threw his head back and laughed. Robyn stared at him. Then, she laughed, too.

"And when did it dawn on you that it wasn't a natural occurrence?" He could hardly stop the tears coming down from the corners of his eyes. When he looked at Robyn she had tears in the corners of her eyes, too.

"I was in high school. Must have been a slow learner." She touched her head.

Grant caught her arm then and pulled her back against him. "Didn't you ever wonder why the wind," he stifled another laugh, "picked those particular men to carve into the side of a mountain?"

"Not until I saw an article in the newspaper when I was in high school. Then, it all sounded so silly. How could I ever have thought the wind could do such a thing?"

Grant laughed again. "You're wonderful, wonderful." He hugged her closer.

Grant's laughter died. Robyn looked up into his eyes. The playful whimsy that had been there was replaced by raw desire. She knew her own had to reflect the same burning rapture in their depths. Her skin was warm, but when his hands on her arms urged hers upward, fire burned into her.

"Grant, don't," she whimpered. "I'll be lost."

"I'm already lost." His mouth took hers. His kiss was scorching. Her lips opened to him, like a dry river seeking water. Thoughts of being Brooke Johnson intruded for only a second before she pushed them aside and became Robyn Richards. Her fingers tangled in the soft hair above his shirt collar. She pulled his mouth closer to hers, shifting her position as he pushed her gently back onto the blanket. Grant covered her with his body. She felt his arousal hard against her as his mouth left hers to travel down her neck and pause at the neckline of her leotard.

His hand came up to pull the fabric aside. The cool air pushed against her nipple. The pebble hardness of her breast thrust against the warmth of his palm as it traveled in circles. Robyn gasped at the excitement coursing through her body. Whimpers of delight escaped her mouth.

She smelled good, like flowers. Grant wanted to taste her. His tongue slid over her nipple, and he was rewarded as she arched closer to the pleasure he evoked. Her fingers slipped into his hair, and heat surged through him. He wanted her, wanted her now in this grassy meadow, under the shade of this tree. He wanted to know that she was his, to hear those sounds she made when he touched her in the right spots.

When his mouth found its way back to hers, passion gripped him in her strong clutches, and he ravished her mouth with as much force as she used to violated his. He pushed at her clothes, wanting to tear them from her body. He hadn't wanted to do that to anyone since . . .

Suddenly, Robyn was free. The weight on her had lifted, and cold air touched her where Grant's hands and body had been. She was disoriented and angry. Her breath came in short gasps. She pulled her clothes into place as she fought for control.

"What's wrong?" she finally asked. He stood several feet away staring into the distance, his back to her.

"It's time we left."

"Did I do anything wrong?" She walked behind him.

He turned to look at her. Robyn saw torture in his eyes and wanted to relieve it. "It's not you," he said. "It's me." His hand came up and gently touched her cheek. Robyn didn't move, although she wanted to lean into the gesture. She was sure he would pull away if she made any advancement.

Robyn and Grant were back in the air minutes later. He was a changed man, and she didn't know why. She didn't know if she'd done or said something wrong. One minute, he was crushing her to the ground—she warmed at the thought of his body stretched the length of hers—then, he was as closed and tight as a tin can.

How could he explain? For the second time, he'd had her in his arms and thoughts of his wife had intruded. Grant wasn't used to comparing women to Robyn. After her immediate death, when he tried to be a one-man love army, he compared everyone to Robyn. But he'd long since gotten past that, or so he thought. Then why? Why were thoughts of Robyn continually intruding whenever he saw Brooke or thought of her? Even in the dream, the two women kept merging into one and he couldn't tell them apart. But making love to one woman and imagining her to be someone else was something he would not do.

"Yesterdays, may I help you?" Robyn spoke automatically into the telephone while she watched Sue-Ellen continually miss her cue.

"I certainly hope so." The dark voice glided through her veins, elevating her blood pressure. Robyn's breath caught, and her heart started to pound. She wavered between depression and joy. Joy won. Clasping her palm over the mouthpiece, she allowed the tiny cry to escape as she turned away from the action on the stage to face the mirrored wall behind the bar.

"Are you still there?"

"Yes," she faltered. "I'm here." She hadn't heard from Grant for nearly a week, since that day they'd flown into Canada and had the impromptu picnic. She thought he was out of her life. He was so different after he kissed her. She didn't know what to think, and she refused to ask. Since she couldn't explain her own actions when he probed into her past, she couldn't ask him to explain.

The dull ache in her chest had become a hard pain and now hearing his voice made the ache even harder to contain.

"Where are you?" she asked.

"I'm still in D.C. but—" he paused. "I want to see you."

"Grant," she cut him off. "I've had a lot of time to think this week."

"Brooke, please don't say no so fast. Give it a chance? Give me a chance?"

"I can't, Grant."

"Why not? What's so wrong with me?"

"Grant there's nothing wrong with you." Words came hard. She wanted to asked him to fly in. She wanted to rush to the airport and be there when he came through the cabin door. She wanted nothing more than to fall into line with his plans, but somewhere out there was a loose end. Hiding within the protective walls of this program told her the Network was alive, and she knew someone was lying in wait for her. All she needed to do was to make a mistake. And around Grant, she'd be sure to slip up soon.

"I'll be there at six. We have reservations for eight."

"Grant . . ." The phone clicked in her ear. He wasn't listening to her. She replaced the receiver, looking at the black instrument as if it were the reason for her split decision.

She'd been so happy to hear his voice. Yet, every word drove daggers into her heart. She couldn't allow this relationship to develop. Somehow, she had to get that across.

She kept that thought uppermost in her mind as she slipped into her jogging suit and headed toward the kitchen.

"Marianne, I'm leaving and I might not be back tonight."

"Decision number nine?" Marianne asked. She looked up from the cake she was decorating.

"He called. I'm going to have to see him." Mixed emotions at the prospect vied for dominance, but confusion outweighed them all.

"But you intend to tell him this is the end." Marianne used the pastry bag in her hand to punctuate the point.

"That's my intention." Robyn's voice was decisive.

"Do you think it will work this time?"

"Marianne, before I came here something awful happened to me." Robyn noticed Marianne set down the pastry bag. Her full attention was directed toward Robyn.

"Come in here." Marianne led her into the office off the kitchen where they usually did the monthly accounts. The redhead closed the door and sat down next to Robyn in one of the two chairs stationed in front of the huge desk. "Now what happened?"

"Something I don't like to remember. Grant was indirectly involved. He doesn't know anything about

it. Yet, if I continue seeing him, something may happen
to him, and I can't be responsible for that."

"You love him that much?"

Tears fell from Robyn's eyes. "I love him." She had
said it out loud and to another person. She loved him.
She wanted him safe, away from her. The people looking for her had no statute of limitations on betrayal,
and they could reach her through Grant. Worse, they
could hurt Grant. She had to stop seeing him for his
own safety.

Marianne was still thinking about Robyn and Grant
when she let herself into her house after the restaurant
closed. It was nearly three in the morning, and she
was tired. She began her nightly ritual of showering
and washing her hair before she went to bed. When
she stepped out of the shower, the phone was ringing.
It was unusual for anyone to call at this hour unless
it was an emergency.

Draping the short towel around herself she padded
into the carpeted room and lifted the receiver.

"Hello," she said.

"Hello."

Her knees immediately gave out and she sat down
on the white comforter, ignoring the water dripping
from her legs.

"Jacob!" she said in a surprised whisper. "Is anything wrong?"

"No, everything is all right."

Then why was he calling? He only phoned when

there was something he needed to know, and she'd been feeding him his reports at the appointed times.

"How are your arms?"

"They're nearly healed. The scars are there, but they will fade."

There was silence on the other end of the line. Marianne was beginning to think something *was* wrong.

"Did you find anything more about the fire?"

"I have a report for you to read. It'll be here when you come again."

That would be another week. She was looking forward to seeing him. Their time together had been different since the fire. They spent most of it together, talking about everything. Jacob liked basketball and coached a team of young boys.

"I'll be there on Friday."

"I'll pick you up," he said.

Marianne was glad. He'd been there the last two times she'd arrived.

"And Marianne," he paused. "There's a party this weekend. It's an official function. I have a duty to attend. Would you go with me?"

Marianne was speechless. She forgot she had no clothes on until the towel slipped away and the cold air touched her skin. He wanted to take her to a party. Her heart began to pound, and it was difficult to speak, but she managed to say, "I'd love to."

"I'll see you then. Good-bye." He hung up.

She replaced the receiver, but didn't move. Jacob had asked her for a date.

* * *

Robyn looked around as the cold wind whipped her hair out of place and smacked her in the face with it. Grant was obviously going the wrong way, there was nothing this way but planes and the runway. She turned, taking his arm, intent on leading him back toward the terminal, but instead he swung her around, until she was again walking in the opposite direction. A wry smile split his face reflected in his dark eyes.

"We're going the right way," he shouted above the noise of airplane engines and helicopter blades.

"Where are you taking me?" Robyn stopped, her gown a cloud of white enshrouding them.

"Out to dinner," he smiled.

"Out to dinner, where?"

"You said I could pick the restaurant." He took her arm and pulled her into step with him.

"There's no restaurant this way." Robyn saw the small plane loom in front of her. The roar from the motors made her scream to be heard. The wind plastered her gown to her, pushing the fragile whisps of chiffon through her legs and making walking difficult. She had to take two steps to keep up with Grant's stride.

"We're going to Pier 7."

Robyn stopped, yanking her arm away. Pier 7 was in Washington, D.C. It sat on the Potomac River at the mouth of M Street in the fashionable southwest section of the city. She couldn't go there. She had missed D.C. in the five years since she'd left it. She couldn't go back. There were too many memories there pulling at her past.

"What's the matter?" he asked facing her.

"I can't go."

"Why not? Kari's with Will, Marianne's got things under control at the restaurant, you're free for the evening."

"But why D.C.? There are plenty of places to eat here. Why must we go four hundred miles for dinner?" Robyn pushed her hair back. The long curls, that had looked so perfect in her mirror, were tangled tendrils playing cat-and-mouse with the enhanced wind generated by the thrust of huge engines preparing to leave the airfield. Ceasing movement had given her gown time to release her legs only to veil them both in a billowing fog of white material.

"Come on, we can't talk in this wind." He shouted in her ear before once again taking her arm and leading her back into the terminal. The Cessna-110 sat outside, a looming enemy to Robyn's eyes.

"I thought I'd surprise you. Marianne and Will told me you hadn't been out of Buffalo for as long as they've known you. I thought this would be a nice surprise. I guess I'm a little out of practice when it comes to what women like."

Robyn felt small. She knew he was ignorant to the reasons she couldn't go to the Capital.

"We'll go someplace else. Where would you like to eat?"

It was against everything she knew she should do, but Robyn heard herself saying, "I know a nice restaurant on the Potomac River." She was rewarded with his smile.

"I promise to have you home before morning." He took her arm before she had time to change her mind, but instead of ushering her into the plane, he swung her toward the helicopter sitting several yards away. She felt like she had five years ago when he'd rushed into her life like a hurricane, and before she knew it, she was Mrs. Grant Richards. That couldn't happen this time. This time there was more at stake. There was Kari and the restaurant and the life she'd left behind.

Grant took the controls. Robyn heard the rotor blades begin their high-pitched whine as they started to turn above her head. The helicopter lifted off the ground. He took the stick and glided them through the air traffic until they were over downtown Buffalo. The glass and steel structures looked smaller from this vantage point. Lights flickered on and off in the buildings, and cars traveling along the roads inched by without confusion or congestion.

She pointed out the General Motors Building and Liberty Bank. Robyn smiled, and Grant dipped closer to the two statues holding lighted torches on the top of the hundred-year-old building. Further along, Main Street ended in the Niagara River. Grant abruptly banked right and headed north. Robyn looked at the compass.

"Where are we going?" she asked. "You've turned north."

"I thought of another restaurant. Do you have any objections to Toronto?"

"None," she smiled.

Fifteen minutes later they had covered the eighty miles and were en route to Captain John's Harbor Boat Restaurant. Robyn had never been to Toronto, but she'd heard a lot about it from Will and Marianne. Both had suggested she go there for a weekend and take Kari. Robyn never took the time to go.

Grant wondered what it was about Washington that made her almost frantic. He'd lived in Washington for fifteen years and loved the city. It had a beat unlike any other city he'd visited. Aside from congress and presidential parades, he loved the crowds. Every spring, the tourists came to town, eager to see Lincoln's bed, the Watergate Complex, and the cherry blossoms circling the tidal basin around the Jefferson Memorial.

Unlike most residents, he didn't mind the tourists getting lost in Rock Creek Park or holding up traffic during rush hour when certain streets suddenly reversed direction or became one-way.

Grant wanted to see Brooke there. He could almost picture her eyes wide and amazed at the national treasures bathed in white light. But for some reason going to D.C. terrified her.

"Why did you change your mind?" Robyn asked after Grant had landed the helicopter and rented a car. They were traveling up the Queen's Quay.

"It frightened you," he paused. "Do you want to tell me why?"

"I wasn't exactly frightened." She stole a glance at him.

"Why didn't you want to go?" Grant reached the restaurant and pulled the car into a parking space. "You were nearly frantic." He cut the engine and extinguished the lights. Around her, the car seemed to go dark. Grant made no move to leave the confines, and Robyn kept her place.

She held her breath for a moment, then got out of the car. Grant came around to stand in front of her. "It was a long time ago," she began. "Before Kari was born. Something happened while I was in D.C. It's just bad memories. Nothing important." She lifted her head and flashed him a smile. "And certainly nothing worth spoiling dinner over."

Grant took her arm and led her toward the restaurant. Whatever had happened there was significant. She'd chosen her words well. He could tell. But she wasn't ready to trust him with the information. He was convinced now, that whatever it was, it was the reason for the underlying sadness in her life.

Dinner proved better than he thought it was going to be when he first had seen the dark look in her eyes at the airfield. She'd been standing there waiting for him when he'd landed. The white dress that she wore gleamed against the dark tan of her arms. She looked like a portrait waiting for him. He liked the feeling she evoked.

She had smiled when he kissed her lightly, but there was no fire in her eyes like there had been on the blanket in Canada. She didn't know why he'd pulled back so abruptly. It was the sounds—Robyn's sounds. No matter what he did, he couldn't get Robyn out of his thoughts. Even when he held Brooke in his arms and began to make love to her, somehow his wife intruded.

Why? It hadn't happened in years. Why did she remind him so much of Robyn? Even now, he could tell she had something on her mind. Something she'd wanted to tell him since he saw her. He knew it was another one of her I-don't-want-to-see-you-again speeches. This time he was determined to get to the bottom of it.

"Grant, dance with me." His eyes focused on her. The fire was in them. They left the dining room and went into the bar. Several couples were already on the dance floor. The waiter led them to a table and brought her a drink. Grant had only tonic water with a lemon twist. He was flying, he explained.

They took up position on the wooden floor. She went easily into his arms. Robyn closed her eyes and let the music carry her away. She danced on a cloud high up in the air with Grant. Around them, the music tantalized and spun a fantasy world. She wanted it to go on and on, but she suddenly realized it couldn't. She pushed this thought aside. For the next few hours, she'd pretend she was back to being Robyn, and she'd enjoy the last night with her husband. They danced and danced. She was too wrapped up in being in Grant's arms. She whirled and whirled until finally they were the only people left in the restaurant.

Grant tipped the waiters generously as they left. He took her back to the airport, and they boarded the helicopter. The flight back was a blur. She could only stare at him. She was glad she didn't have to worry about working controls and coordinating the powerful machine through the air. Even though the trip was short, it was more than she was able to contend with tonight.

But when Grant parked the bird next to the hangar,

the fantasy she'd been living vanished. The rotors turned slowly after Grant cut the power, their whine elongating into rhythmic puffs of air. When they finally stopped, the silence was deafening.

"Well, it's time for your speech," Grant gave her the lead-in.

"You know what I'm going to say?"

"Yes."

"Then, do I have to say it?" She looked through the glass windows toward the terminal. Everything was quiet. Lights from inside filtered through the windows in an attempt to brighten the night. She concentrated on the glow.

"You're going to have to tell me. I won't stop coming to see you unless there's a good reason."

"There is a good reason, but I can't tell you what it is."

"Why not?"

"Grant, I can't tell you." Frustrated anger crept into her voice.

"It has something to do with Washington, D.C., doesn't it?" he demanded.

"Please don't ask me any questions. I can't answer them." Anger filtered through her voice.

"Can't or won't?"

"It doesn't matter. The reason has little to do with you, and for all concerned, it would be best if we didn't see each other again."

"That's not good enough. Tell me the truth." It was a command.

"Grant, go home, find another woman, get married, but leave me alone."

"I can't." His voice dropped.

Robyn refused to look at him. "Can't or won't?" she screamed.

"Both," he shouted. "I can't and I won't. I'm in love with you."

Ten

Marianne had a lighter step to her walk when she entered the terminal at Washington National Airport. Jacob would have a car waiting outside the terminal. And they had a date. Even the news of the poisoning incident didn't dampen her happiness. Her bags were the first off the flight, and she hurried to the exit. Quickly, her things were stored in the car, and they were speeding toward the nation's Capital.

"We've had another incident," Marianne began an hour later when they were seated side by side on top of a picnic table in Rock Creek Park. Jacob raised a taco to his mouth, and Marianne munched on a hamburger. "Two days ago, Brooke and I made one of our special chocolate desserts. Just as we finished, Pete's cat came into the kitchen. The cat has as bad a sweet tooth as I do and especially for chocolate. Brooke dished him the last of the icing we'd used. Not more than a teaspoon. In seconds, the cat was dead."

"Poison?" Jacob took a drink of his soda.

"Arsenic," Marianne confirmed.

"Did you call the authorities?"

"No, Brooke and I were the only ones who knew.

I suggested it, but she wouldn't let me. We disposed of the dessert and had the cat autopsied. Brooke tried to cover it up, by claiming she'd picked up the wrong box. But we don't keep arsenic in the restaurant."

"Did you notice anyone strange hanging around."

"No one we don't already know. We have several people with records working at the restaurant, but I'd vouch for them. They're fiercely loyal to Brooke."

Jacob concurred. He'd had them checked out, and they were first time offenders, shoplifters, kids gone the wrong way. Robyn's trust in them was returned unquestioned.

"How's she taking this?"

"It's hard to tell. The shell around her is thick. She hasn't mentioned it since."

"What about the photograph."

"Still in the safe."

"Keep a close eye on her. I have a feeling something is going to happen soon, and I don't want her without help when it happens."

Robyn sat comfortably in the cabin of the Lear Jet. Outside, the plane cut through the air at more than four-hundred miles per hour, yet she felt very little motion. The "fasten your seat belt" sign had just been turned off. She loosened hers but kept the lock fully secured. Grant had explained to her years earlier, when he taught her to fly, the value of using a safety belt.

He had taken to dropping by unexpectedly and taking her flying. She loved it, and occasionally, he'd allow her to take the controls, complimenting her ability. Robyn had tired of trying to send him away when her heart wasn't in the task.

Since the night he'd taken her to dinner, he hadn't mentioned being in love and neither had she. She was too scared. This couldn't happen, she told herself. They had no future together, but she couldn't get him out of her life. She'd tried it once, and it hadn't worked. He was her other half—the part that made her alive, not just existing.

And she was glad he ignored her attempts to get rid of him. She loved his surprise drop-ins. Sometimes, days would pass without a word, then just as she was feeling low, he'd show up and take her on a picnic or out to lunch. She'd seen more movies in the past six weeks than she'd seen in five years. Once, they even went bowling, something she hadn't done since leaving college. But today was the first time he'd called to ask her out.

"Would you like something to drink?" Grant asked, moving from his seat to stand behind the bar facing her. His white shirt was in stark contrast to the black of his dinner jacket.

"Martini and Rossi," she replied, appraising how his tanned skin set her pulses running.

He poured the sparkling wine into two goblets and passed her one before lowering himself into the plush oversized chair at her left which swiveled to bring them face to face. Robyn raised her glass, feeling the tiny bubbles tickle her nose, as she sipped the chilled liquid. "Is this one of your planes?" she asked, the soothing blue-and-white color scheme making her feel comfortable.

"Do you like it?"

She could hear the pride in his voice. "It's beautiful. You must get a lot of requests for this kind of plane." Grant had shown her around before they took off. The plane seated twelve and was equipped with a private bedroom. The passenger seats were fully reclinable, and a low semicircular sofa flanked the sunken bar. Tonight, they were alone except for the pilot and co-pilot locked away behind a door at the front of the aircraft.

"I've been fortunate," he answered. "The District of Columbia has a great need to fly people in and out on short notice. I've flown United Nations dignitaries, government officials, rock stars, and once, Princess Diana was my passenger."

"I'm impressed." Robyn smiled, releasing her seat belt and walking to another seat. She sat down and got up, repeating the procedure until she'd sat in all the seats. "To think," she said, lounging on the sofa, "I've sat in the same chairs as one of the most beautiful women in the world."

Grant laughed, a clear happy sound.

"Where did you take her?" She grinned feeling happier than she had in years.

"New York. She had a schedule to maintain and trouble developed with her own plane."

Grant picked up her wine glass and joined her on the sofa. Robyn accepted it, noticing his arm slide behind her along the back of the sofa. She sipped the liquid that added heat to the temperature rising in her blood. "Well," she began. "Now that we're traveling four-hundred miles per hour, and I'm dressed in my formal gown, as you requested." She smoothed the peach-colored chiffon that highlighted her dark skin. "May I ask where we're going?"

"We're going to a very special party."

"Great, I like parties." Lights registered in her eyes.

"It's an engagement party for an old friend."

As quickly as it had come, the light was dashed. Her body, that had been warming comfortably, was suddenly cold. David's face flashed into her memory. Her senses were alive and alert.

"Washington, D.C." she gasped. "Are we headed for Washington?"

"Yes." He took her hand. It was trembling and clammy with unexpected sweat. "It's only for a few hours, Brooke. I promise to have you safely back in Buffalo before breakfast."

"Why didn't you tell me?" she whispered, attempting to control her wildly beating heart.

"I've told my friends so much about you, they wanted to meet you."

There was nothing she could do about it now. Grant didn't know what he was doing. His subtle little trick could mean someone's life. She only hoped everything would work out, and no one would know she was in town. Somehow, Jacob always knew when she broke the rules. She was surprised he hadn't shown up again. Robyn had promised not to see Grant, yet in the past month, he'd been in and out of her life constantly.

"I'm sorry, Robyn. If it means that much to you, I'll have the plane turned around."

"What's your friend's name?" she asked cautiously.

"David Reid." Grant confirmed her silent fear.

Things would work out, she told herself. She was sure everything would be all right. It was just a few hours. She'd enjoy them. She was going to see David again.

"We used to fly together before I started my air service."

"Does he still fly?"

"He'll help me out in a pinch. But his flying is mostly for pleasure these days. He and Susan . . ."

"Susan?" Robyn interrupted at the mention of her old friend's name.

"Susan used to be my next door neighbor. She was my wife's best friend. She and David are engaged. Three years ago, David and Susan began a small business that has exploded." Grant spread his hands to demonstrate.

"What did they do?"

"They started a jewelry store."

"That's wonderful!" Robyn's exuberance was evident in her voice. She'd known Susan made her own jewelry. She'd done it since college. Many times, Robyn had encouraged her to sell it. She was pleased to hear Susan and David were to be married and that her friend had finally taken her advice and was making a living, selling the jewelry she designed.

Meeting them again was another story. If she'd known they were going to D.C., she'd never have boarded the plane. But she had to admit the idea excited her. For so long, she'd wanted to return to the Capital, but she knew better than to try. She told herself it was better to create new memories than to try and return to old haunts. She knew if she'd returned she'd end up in her old neighborhood, trying to get a glimpse of Susan or find out if Grant was still in their old house. The problem with her was she knew she couldn't stop herself if she started down that road. It was like being on a roller coaster and wanting to get off just before the momentum plunged the cars on the downward incline. So she avoided the temptation by not visiting D.C. Now, she was going to see them.

She was confident they wouldn't recognize her. If Grant didn't, surely David and Susan wouldn't know her. But they weren't the people she was concerned about. Jacob Winston was somewhere in D.C. Even if he wasn't, he always knew what was going on in her life. Up to now, she hadn't minded or even thought about it, but now she didn't want him knowing about this trip. She hoped luck was on her side, and by some miracle, Jacob's sources of information were investigating some other witness. She thrust thoughts of Jacob out of her mind. Tonight, she wanted to enjoy herself.

"You're doing it again." Grant's voice captured her attention.

"Doing what?" Her eyes opened in wide surprise.

"Going off on trips without benefit of transport."

"I'm sorry. It has nothing to do with the company." She smiled, hoping it would disarm him and lead him away from questioning her thoughts. "I was thinking of all the lovely pieces of jewelry I've stared at in store windows. One day maybe I'll get to visit one of Susan and David's stores." She tried to pronounce their names as if they were strange to her tongue. "What's the name of the store?"

"Trifles." Robyn knew the answer before he spoke. She and Susan came up with it one rainy Sunday when Grant was flying to England. After Vegas, Robyn tried to convince Susan she could make a living selling her own jewelry instead of continuing her boring job working in the commercial art department of the city's newspaper.

Robyn could picture the store. Even though Susan had shrugged her suggestion off, Robyn had insisted she sketch out a drawing of the store.

"Have they decided on a wedding date, yet?" She dragged her thoughts back to the present. She didn't want to be caught daydreaming again.

"Late August."

Robyn pictured herself dressed in a white gown, floating down the aisle as she took Grant's arm. It was the wedding every bride wanted, but for her, it never happened. She wasn't sad about missing the orange blossoms and a warm Saturday in June routine. She'd been completely happy with the justice of the peace in the Moonlight Wedding Chapel in Las Vegas.

"I've told them you'd come with me." Again, the deep voice snapped her dreams.

Grant caught her off guard. She couldn't go. She knew she couldn't. She was making this trip unannounced. There was no way she could have known he was taking her to D.C. when she boarded the plane.

And in a few hours, she'd be safely back in Buffalo. But to make plans to return to the city where she had enemies sworn to kill her was dangerous. Yet, she was excited by the idea of spending time with Grant, and seeing Susan and David again.

"Grant, I can't. You know I have to take care of things at the restaurant."

"Marianne can handle the restaurant, and she told me you need a change."

Robyn rolled her eyes to the ceiling. Marianne was playing cupid. "I don't even know the bride and groom. I'm sure they won't miss me." Lie number three, she thought. "And that's Marianne's weekend away."

For as long as Robyn and Marianne had been friends, she went away on the third weekend of every month. Robyn never asked where she went. When her own life was such a mystery, how could she ask questions of another person. And Marianne never volunteered anything about her time away. The only indication was that on the Monday after she returned her moods were more somber, as if she'd had a fight and was trying to get over it, without involving anyone at the restaurant.

"It's not them I'm thinking of." Robyn returned her attention to Grant in time to see the wry smile play at the corners of his mouth. Heat, like the airplane, defied gravity, and spilled up her raw shoulders and neck to deepened her face.

"Honestly, Grant. The restaurant is very busy on Saturday nights. It's too much work for one person."

"What about tonight?" he asked, finishing the last of his wine.

"I'm not blind to Marianne's motives, Grant. Tonight, she's playing cupid. It's been a long time since I went out with anyone. She thinks that if I continue to see you, something will develop."

"Will it?" Fear made him ask, and he was holding his breath, waiting for her to answer. He looked directly at her. She returned his gaze, not wavering. Nothing in her eyes showed any emotion. Yet, he knew how he affected her. Since that first morning he'd kissed her, he longed to do it again. Yet, there was something about this woman. Some mystery he couldn't unravel, and she had yet to confide in him. He wanted her, but he wanted more than she was ready to give. He wanted her to trust him enough to tell him what it was that kept her pushing him away.

"It's impossible, Grant." He knew she would say it. She'd told him that before when she sent him away. But he hadn't been able to stay away. He was totally consumed by his love for her. She haunted him, and she didn't know it. He'd done nothing but think about her since he left. David and Susan's engagement party gave him another excuse to see her.

"Okay, it's impossible."

Robyn was nonplussed. She'd expected to argue with him, and he'd calmly accepted her decision. It didn't make her feel good. In fact, she hated how she felt. She wanted to run into his arms and tell him their relationship could go on eternally, but she was prevented. The wall around her was carefully in place, and nothing could pierce it. She sat quietly, sipping the last drops of wine from the heavy crystal goblet.

The house at 2430 Kalarama Road was alive with light, and a festive air penetrated the confines of the limousine that slowly made its way down the narrow street and delivered them to the circular driveway. Robyn gave her hand to the gloved chauffeur who provided support as she exited the car. She had learned as they left the plane and Grant showed her into the limo that he not only owned a charter service but also a fleet of limousines. He explained the need to get people to the airport in order to fly them to their destinations. The plush accommodations were as expensively decorated as the customized plane had been.

Tonight, she was getting the royal treatment. Grant took her arm and led her into the hall. Music greeted them as they stopped briefly to give her wrap to a uniformed maid. Her eyes were hungry for a glimpse of Susan, and she looked around trying to cover her excitement and keep anyone from noticing. Finally, she spotted Susan on the other side of the room. She was thinner. Her hair, that Robyn remembered as being shoulder length, was a short crop of curly ringlets. Her face was radiantly parted in a happy smile. David was by her side. He looked the same. Not even a gray hair had changed his appearance. But he looked more confident than she had remembered. From somewhere, the image of Don Quixote tilting at a windmill came into her consciousness. She could imagine David fighting for the woman by his side. They were talking to a couple whom Robyn didn't know.

In the back of her mind, guilt tugged at her thoughts. She shouldn't be here. She knew she was tempting fate. Tonight, she could make a fatal error. With a slight shrug, she pushed it to the back of her mind. Tonight, she was going to have a good time. Tonight, she wanted to be Robyn. For a few short hours, she wanted to slip back into the comfortable role of Robyn Warren-Richards and tell her husband she loved him. She wanted to rush to her friends and tell them that she'd missed them and spend the evening catching up on the past five years.

But Jacob's face loomed in front of her. The wall was back. Like a living part of her existence it stopped her. She couldn't go back. She had to be more on her guard than ever. These were people who knew her, knew everything about her. They were the ones most dangerous to her. She couldn't afford to let any word, any gesture from her past slip out and condemn her.

Squaring her shoulders, she walked toward them, Grant at her side. Susan looked up, smiled at Grant and came forward. David followed her. Susan hugged Grant, and David shook his hand. "This is Brooke Johnson." He introduced her.

"Hello," Susan smiled widely. "Grant has told us about you."

She gave him a questioning look. "I hope it was all good." She joked covering her embarrassment. "Congratulations, he tells me you're to be married."

Susan turned her gaze to the man she loved. Robyn's heart muscle tightened. She wanted to be able to openly look at the man she loved with the same unmasked emotion.

Robyn knew David had been married before. He told her it only proved he never wanted to be married again. She could see his meeting Susan had changed that. It was wonderful to be able to see them.

She felt like she were on the window side of a one-way mirror. She could look into their lives but they couldn't see hers. She smiled to herself.

"Would you like something to drink?" David asked them.

"Darling, I'd like a glass of wine." Susan responded, and Robyn nodded when Grant asked her. The two women watched as Grant and David headed for the bar.

"Will you be staying for the weekend?" Susan asked conversationally. She moved toward the edge of the room. Robyn walked with her until she stopped near a mahogany table. Above it was a large gold-framed mirror, ornate with cherubs, capturing the activity in the room.

"I'm afraid I have to get back." She watched as her friend's face seem to fall slightly. Robyn knew the expression. There was something on Susan's mind, and she was trying to hide it. For anyone else, it was unnoticeable, but they had known each other since college, and Robyn recognized it immediately. It couldn't be David, not after the way she'd looked at him. It had to be something else. "Is anything wrong?"

Susan smiled. "I'm sorry. Actually, it's none of my business. It's just that Grant has been alone so long, and then, you came into his life. We're . . ."

"I understand." Robyn took over. "You're his friends, and since his wife died, you've been his protectors. Suddenly, I show up, someone you don't know, who doesn't live here and can't be watched to tell if my intentions warrant approval?" She was rewarded by the look of surprise that replaced Susan's smile.

"If I didn't know better . . ." Susan began but appeared to stop speaking when she realized words were actually coming from her mouth.

"Excuse me." Robyn prompted, looking at the room from the mirror above her. Grant and David were talking quietly at the bar on the other side of the room.

"It's nothing, just that no one's read me so clearly since . . . well, in a long time." She corrected herself but Robyn knew she was about to say Robyn. "I'm surprised to find my thoughts so visible."

"I didn't mean to be unfriendly." Robyn wanted Susan to like her. In the back of her mind, she wished to tell her who she really was. Suddenly, the need to confide in someone was so strong she could barely contain the force that wanted to pull Susan into a room and pour her heart out to an understanding ear.

"I think I'm going to like you, Brooke."

Suddenly, her heart was full. Even if she had another face and a voice several notes higher than her former one, that invisible bond that reaches across time and keeps memory alive was shining in Robyn's eyes.

"I know I'm going to like you."

"I'm glad to hear that." Grant stood behind her. He set the glasses that he held on the table and placed his hands on Robyn's bare shoulders. Warmth washed over her, and she had to visibly keep herself from blushing. "Come, dance with me."

Robyn floated away, riding on her own cloud as Grant led her to the dance floor. The small band, hugging one wall of the large room, had just finished playing Billy Joel's "Piano Man." As she and Grant reached the temporary wooden floor, the band reached back in time and launched into Barry Manilow's "I Write the Songs." Her step faulted slightly before Grant turned her into his arms and glided her effortlessly around the floor. Robyn matched his steps, knowing the routine and following the feel of his lead as though their minds had merged and she knew what he would do before he did it.

Grant closed his eyes. She felt like Robyn as he held her in his arms. He lied to himself, saying it was because she was a dancer that she reminded him of Robyn. But he knew it wasn't true. In so many ways, she was like his wife. There was nothing he could see, and nothing she said, but there was something intangible about her that seem to bring Robyn into the picture.

He felt guilty about it sometimes. But there didn't seem to be anything he could do about it. He dreamed of Robyn, and his waking hours were filled with thoughts of how her hair had bounced when she'd moved her head or how her voice had sounded when she'd laughed. He smiled at the images he created. Robyn had been the only other person in his life who could make him block out everything and everyone else. He rationalized that this was the reason he couldn't stop comparing them.

The music stopped, but Robyn was too absorbed in being in Grant's arms to notice. It wasn't until someone bumped into her that she realized couples were leaving the dance floor. She and Grant made their way back to their drinks where she tried to cover her disorientation with the drink she raised to her lips. Susan and David were busy with other guests.

"Tell me what you think?" Grant asked.

"What I think about what?"

"Susan. You and she were having quite a conversation earlier."

"I think she's a wonderful person. I'm glad to see she's so happy." Robyn's eyes found Susan. She was laughing at something someone said to her. "Tell me how they met?" She brought her eyes back to Grant.

"Susan was our next door neighbor. When I was captured and taken to Beirut, David got her to help let Robyn know. They saw each other frequently at our house while Robyn waited for the state department to finish negotiations. After I came back and Robyn died, they started seeing each other."

"What's taken them so long to get married?" It had been five years since that day in her kitchen.

"I guess they were both being cautious. David had a bad marriage and so did Susan. This time, they wanted to be sure everything would work."

Robyn's gaze found Susan and David. They looked at each other as if each person's world centered on the other. "I'm sure it will work."

Dinner was announced then, and she found herself seated next to David. On her right was a thin, red-headed, woman who owned a fashionable dress shop in Georgetown. Robyn had a lovely time talking to her about styles, colors, and using fabric to decorate. She found out that the woman had a hobby of using the excess fabric from making her own designs to make doll clothes. She said she did it for her grand-daughter, but the hobby turned into a business and now she sold the designs in a toy store on M Street.

"I'll have to visit it when I'm in Washington again." Robyn told her.

"And when might that be?" David captured her attention.

"I'm not sure." She turned to him. "I have a business to run in Buffalo."

"Grant tells me you own a restaurant, and you sing and dance there."

"I only sing one song, and I dance to fill in if one of the regulars is out. My role is managing."

"Who's minding the store tonight?" He raised a cup of coffee and drank.

"I have a partner. She's doing everything tonight, and I'm sure she's very busy." Robyn thought of Marianne coping with everything that could possibly go wrong. When they were both there, each had someone to depend on to handle things. Just the thought of not having to take care of everything made the operation run smoother.

"Susan and I are planning our honeymoon in Toronto. Maybe, we can drive down and have dinner one night."

"That would be wonderful." Excitement seemed to ooze from her. She'd love to see them again. And on safe territory. "I'll have the chef make your favorite foods."

David smiled at that. "Now, we'll have to come. And speaking of coming, can we count on seeing you at the wedding?"

Robyn took a deep breath. "I'm not sure. I do need to be at the restaurant."

"Can't you make arrangements? One day can't make that much difference."

"I'll let you know." Robyn knew she couldn't come. She had no right being here tonight.

"I'm sure Grant would want you with him."

"I promise, I'll try." She'd like nothing better than to attend her best friend's wedding. But the situation was impossible. Tonight's visit had been an unexpected one. But to plan to return to the city where men would kill her if they knew her identity . . . And where Jacob was only a few miles away.

David patted her hand and smiled, his arguments curtailed for the moment. Robyn spied Grant at the other end of the table. While she sat at David's right, Grant sat on Susan's right at the opposite end of the table. She wondered if they'd been placed that way for some strategic purpose. Grant was engaged in conversation and not looking at her. Then, the woman next to Robyn captured her attention and monopolized it through the rest of dinner.

After the meal, the dancing resumed and promised to go on late into the night. Robyn found herself at the bar with David by her side.

"Are you having a good time?"

"Yes," she answered truthfully. She was enjoying herself. She'd danced with Grant several times and talked to Susan. She felt like a ghost, able to see into the lives of her friends without them knowing who she really was.

"What's that smile for?" David asked, guiding her away from the bar. They walked into another part of the huge house where small groups of people nodded as they passed. Robyn recognized several of their mutual friends and former neighbors. David led her to the farthest corner of the crowded room. She knew he was about to feel her out.

"You're not going to ask me if my intentions are honorable?" she asked, lightly challenging him as she dropped into one of the maroon velvet chairs that dotted the room.

Throwing his head back and laughing loudly, David captured the attention of the room. For a brief moment, all eyes focused on them. He quieted and normal conversation resumed.

"You've been talking to Susan." It was a statement.

"We've decided to become friends," she smiled.

"I like you, Brooke Johnson. You're direct." Robyn dropped her head a moment before bringing her eyes back to his. "You're like Susan," David continued. "She, too, can't manage to stop saying what's on her mind."

"You love her a lot." Robyn didn't need to say it.

She only had to look at them to see that they each were absorbed in the other.

"Fortunately, what comes out of her mouth is also what's in her heart and I love her—a lot." Robyn knew the small phrase came from his heart. It made her feel warm inside. She had liked David from the first, and Susan was her oldest friend. The two of them married would make her immensely happy.

Robyn raised her glass to him and toasted, "I wish you a lifetime of memories—created today, remembered today, created tomorrow, remembered forever." The look on David's face stopped her heart. How could she be so thoughtless? That was the toast he'd given to Grant and herself at their wedding dinner in Las Vegas. In the last five years, she'd been so cautious, now she was forgetting herself. She had to be careful. She promised herself it wouldn't happen again. In a few hours, she'd be safely back in Buffalo, away from everyone who'd been so important in the life she'd left.

"I gave that toast to Grant and Robyn. He must have told you."

She raised her glass, giving a noncommittal shake of her head and hoping her error would be covered.

He leaned closer to her as if the words he was about to say were for her ears only. "Grant is a changed man since he met you."

"What do you mean, a changed man?"

"More relaxed, smiles a lot." David leaned back in his chair. "The only change has been his frequent trips to see you."

"What was he like before?"

David's brows furrowed, and he sipped at his drink before answering. "I don't mean to sound like he was unhappy. He's told you about Robyn?"

Robyn nodded. "She died five years ago."

"After Robyn died, Grant burned the candle at both ends. He put everything into the air service. Sometimes, we didn't see him for weeks."

Robyn's heart contracted. Guilt over the pain she'd caused him washed over her like scalding water. Forcing herself not to shudder, she continued to listen.

"Finally, when the business began to prosper, we thought Grant would begin to take it easy."

"But he didn't?" Robyn asked.

"Not by a long shot. He wanted to fly every contract himself."

"That's not like Grant . . . I mean he doesn't seem like the type who wouldn't know how dangerous that could be. Couldn't you convince him?"

"We tried. Susan thought . . . well, I agreed . . ."

Robyn watched him fumble. She knew what he wanted to say. But she let him struggle a while before she helped him.

"You thought he needed a diversion, a woman, maybe."

"Exactly," David smiled, probably relieved she understood.

"Did it work?" she asked.

"Too well. He found a replacement for the energy he put into the business. About a year later, it stopped. He seemed like his old self."

"Did anything happen to cause the change?"

"I thought it was a resolution of Robyn's death. You

see he never talked about her. Suddenly, he just began. I thought he exorcised all the demons keeping her alive. But it wasn't until a few weeks ago when he came back from Buffalo that I really think he began to let her go." The last sentence he spoke very slowly. Then, he paused as if he wanted the effect to sink into her.

Robyn's eyes bored into her friend. "Why are you telling me this? I'm a complete stranger."

"Grant's my friend. I want him to heal."

"Five years is a long time. You think that he's still grieving for Robyn?" Robyn asked herself that same question. Hadn't she found fault with every man to come into her life since she went into the program? Hadn't all her energy gone into the restaurant? Both of them were still grieving.

"I wouldn't want to see anything happen to cause him any additional pain."

"You think I would hurt him?" She moved to the edge of her seat.

"Not intentionally." David moved closer, taking her hands in his. "Please don't take this the wrong way," he hesitated. "You remind me of Robyn."

Robyn clinched her hands and immediately regretted it when she realized they were clasped in David's.

"You don't look like her, except for the hair. Your voice is different, but there's something about you that reminds me of her. And if Grant sees that, you could damage his healing process."

"What do you think I should do?" she asked.

"I have no solution, you could be the medicine he needs or . . ." He left the sentence hanging.

"Hey, you two have been hiding a long time." Susan came up behind Robyn. "And holding hands, too. What's going on?"

"I've just been trying to convince Robyn to come to our wedding."

"I'd consider it a personal favor if you'd come," Susan said.

"How can I refuse such an invitation." Robyn couldn't believe she'd let herself be talked into returning to Washington in three weeks. This was the last place on earth she should be.

"I've been looking all over for you." Grant joined the group. "Have they been ganging up on you?" He smiled at Robyn, and she returned it.

"No." Robyn looked at Susan before her gaze rested on David.

"Good, let's dance. Susan left me to Marsha Watson and I need someone to give me a sense of balance."

Grant took Robyn back to the dance floor. "Tell me the truth, were David and Susan giving you the third degree?"

"No, they're just concerned about you. And they wanted to invite me to the wedding."

"What did you say? You will come, won't you?" Grant circled the floor easily, and Robyn found it easy to combine her steps with his. "I know Susan will be the bride, but you'll be the prettiest woman there."

"I told them I'd come."

"Wonderful." Grant took the news by executing a series of turns that had her chiffon gown spinning about her legs.

The rest of the night seemed to pass in a blur. Grant

stayed by her side, introducing her to his friends and keeping her busy on the dance floor. She smiled and laughed constantly and enjoyed being with him. It was like slicing a piece out of time. She was newly married and dancing the night away with the man of her dreams.

"Grant." David tapped Grant on the shoulder. "You might think this was planned, but you have a phone call. You can take it in the library."

Grant gave his friend a sarcastic look and ignored him. Again, he tapped. "I swear." A teasing smile pulled at his mouth. Robyn watched the exchange. Reluctantly, Grant left her, and David took his place.

David was not as tall as Grant, but was a good dancer. He swung her effortlessly about the dance floor, causing the chiffon skirt she wore to create a fabric cloud through which she moved. Memory made her match his steps. She couldn't remember the last time she had so much fun. When the music ended, she was excited and relaxed. Smiling and winded, David led her toward the bar.

"You dance well," David commented, after ordering another wine for them both.

Robyn smiled her thank you. She'd always enjoyed dancing with David. He usually gave her a good work-out, and tonight was no different. His routine, however, was decidedly different. She realized when she went into his arms that she could not dance the way she remembered. And thankfully, she hadn't had to hold back her sure steps or fake the routine.

Grant's face was clouded when he re-entered the room. Robyn excused herself to go to him.

"Is something wrong?" she said, coming face-to-face with him.

"Come outside, I have to talk to you."

He took her hand, and she followed as they weaved through the crowd making their way to the terrace. There were couples meandering about, and Grant continued down to the lawn toward the back fence.

"What is it?" she asked, as a finger of fear slid down her spine.

"The decision will be totally yours. That was the airport calling. Apparently, there's been an emergency, and they need to use the plane."

Robyn let out the breath she was holding. "My God, Grant, you scared me. I expected something awful had happened."

"It'll mean you have to stay the night."

Eleven

Grant's condo was on the top floor of a pre-World War II building on Connecticut Avenue. Robyn stepped from the foyer into the spacious living room. It wasn't the typical male's apartment she'd expected. The room was color-coordinated as she figured was the rest of the apartment, indicating he'd hired a decorator.

Although it looked like something from *House Beautiful,* there was no life to the room. Paintings hung from the walls, detailed huge splashes of flowers that shocked the eye more than coordinated with the light-colored carpeting. The furniture was gray, upholstered with the same flower element, only a smaller version.

On the gleaming chrome and glass coffee table was a large vase with fresh flowers and several magazines. The flowers made her feel comfortable, and she smiled at them.

"My housekeeper, Mrs. Alexander, changes the flowers once a week," he explained, following her eyes.

Robyn nodded, her attention moving to the piano that sat in front of a wall of windows leading to a rooftop patio. She couldn't see the kitchen, but the dining area matched the living room. The tables continued the same glass and chrome scheme.

"It's a beautiful piano," she said, feeling breathless.

"I keep it tuned, but play it very little."

"You play?" The surprise showed in her voice. Grant hadn't played when they met.

"Not really. I hired a teacher once. He taught me only one song," he said.

Robyn returned her attention to him, "Just one."

He nodded.

"It must be something very special. Play it for me."

Grant dropped his keys in the bowl by the door. "I haven't played it in a long time," he said. "You'd laugh at me."

"I promise not to. In fact, if you want, I won't even look."

Grant sighed and went to sit at the keyboard. Robyn walked to the bar and found a bottle of champagne chilling in the small refrigerator. Her head was below bar-level when the first notes of Chopin's Nocturne in E-major filtered into the room. Numbness gripped her. Suddenly, she had no feeling in her fingers, and her knees turned to water. The bottle fell from her hand as she tried not to fall over in the confined space. Grasping the bar, she held on, trying to control her ragged breathing. Her arms had little strength, but she pulled herself up. Grant's back was to her. He sat erect, his fingers moving expertly across the keys. Music filled the room. Coming around, she collapsed on a barstool and listened to the haunting music. The Nocturne in E-major by Chopin was her favorite song.

In high school, she'd listened to a radio station, WNIA. Every night at midnight, they'd play Chopin's Nocturne in E-major. It was sign-off music for the station. Robyn would stay up, listening just to hear this song. Then, she'd fall peacefully to sleep.

She remembered the first time Mrs. Ross let her pick a recital piece. She'd chosen this song and worked hard to perfect it. And Grant had remembered enough to learn to play it. Tears gathered in her eyes.

When the last notes of the refrain died, water streamed over her cheeks like the fingers of time.

"You're crying," Grant came to her, taking her hands and closing her in his arms. "It wasn't that bad, was it?" he tried to joke.

Robyn was too choked up to speak. She tried opening and closing her mouth several times but found her throat closed by a clog of tears. Grant drew her closer. She buried her face in his shoulder and closed her eyes. Years melted away.

Few women were moved to tears by music, Grant thought, as he held the soft body in his arms. She smelled delicious. Right now, he wanted to lift her off her feet and carry her into the bedroom. But he just held her, allowing her to cry softly against him.

"I'm sorry," she finally said. "It's been a long time since I heard that song. And you play it beautifully."

"Why did it make you cry."

"Memories."

"Bad memories?"

Robyn shook her head. "No, they were wonderful memories. Why did you pick that particular song?"

He didn't want to tell her. He didn't want Robyn to intrude on them. But she was always there whenever he held Brooke, like he was doing now. He'd smell her hair and memories would flood through him. He'd kiss her neck, and it would be Robyn's neck. It wasn't fair, but he couldn't stop. When they were separated, she was always on his mind. Yet, when he was near her, he couldn't help the comparison.

Robyn stopped crying and pushed herself back. "Well, aren't you going to answer?"

"It's just something I liked?"

"Now, who's lying. No one hires a teacher for just one song unless it means a lot to them. It was her favorite, wasn't it?"

For someone so mysterious, she was extremely perceptive. He nodded. "Robyn loved it."

Grant stepped away then, going behind the bar and finding the discarded bottle of champagne. He opened it and poured two glasses. Robyn accepted one and sipped the bubbly liquid.

Her tears were dry now.

Robyn moved away from the bar. Carrying her glass, she opened the door to the patio. Night air and noise rushed into the room. Walking to the edge of the rooftop garden, she looked out. The length of Connecticut Avenue stretched before her. Even at this early hour of the morning, traffic brightened the famous thoroughfare.

"It's beautiful," she murmured.

"Yes, it's one of the reasons I bought it."

Robyn missed the city. She had loved living in Washington. The city had a life to it, a beat that seemed to mesh with the rhythm of her heart. She never thought she'd have to leave it. And although Buffalo had lots of snow in the winter and great summer sports, it lacked the opulence of Kalarama Road, the quaintness of Georgetown's cobblestone streets, and the frantic energy of Capital Hill.

She felt Grant behind her. He slipped his arms around her waist, and she stepped back. Her head fell against his shoulder. Grant's body hardened. Fire began a slow burn deep in her belly. Grant's hand came to cup her breasts as his mouth moved wetly across her uncovered shoulders. Where he touched her, small volcanoes erupted. She shuddered at the excitement that ran through her. Unconsciously, she moaned at the effect his touch had on her. She felt washed with a consuming heat, a heat that intensified and burned but didn't scorch.

His fingers flicked easily across the fabric of her gown, bringing her nipples to hard peaks. Robyn felt a scream rising. Her breath came in short gasps. Guttural sounds broke from her throat as Grant's hands burned her body. They left her breasts, that pushed and strained against the soft fabric of her dress, to cross her stomach and rub down her thighs. The heat between her legs doubled its intensity as his fingers beat a primal message to her.

Robyn's body felt light, almost liquid inside Grant's influence. Sounds coming from her grew louder as her need for him gained strength. She knew she couldn't take this pleasure-pain for any length of time.

The wind around them picked up, blowing her hair and lifting her gown in a puff of peach chiffon. But it was no match against the flames Grant ignited in her.

In one swift movement, she turned in his arms, seeking and finding the wetness of his hungry mouth. The passion between them had been held for too long, their need for each other kept at bay too long. Robyn poured everything into her kiss. It told him who she was. How much she loved him, had always loved him. How sorry she was for letting him go. She told him of their child and her years of loneliness. Nothing was left out as Grant's mouth fused with hers.

They were alone on a rooftop, but between them, they were alone in the universe. Grant found the zipper at the back of her dress and eased the metal fastening free. Robyn felt the cool breeze on her bare back for a moment before Grant's hands probed her sensitized skin. He lifted his head a second and looked into her eyes. There was no question there. Only a dark passion neither of them could deny. He stepped back just enough to let the dress separating them fall to their feet. His eyes devoured her breasts, making them thrust forward.

Bending, he lifted her and carried her through the apartment to the bedroom.

Slowly, he allowed her body to slip down his frame. Like two dancers in a private ballet he eased her down the long line of his thigh to the soft carpet. His eyes never left her face. It seemed to glow with a yellow-gold light. Tangling his hands in her hair, the velvet soft strands slipped through his fingers. He held her head and angled her mouth back to his.

Robyn felt his hard body next to her softer one. New levels of excitement rioted through her. She was burning with desire and could barely stand the intense moment of separation. She stood between his legs. His dark body pressed into hers. Her hands found the buttons on his shirt, and quickly, she peeled it away from his strong shoulders. Her fingers were frantic as they undressed him. When he stood before her naked, he took her hands in his and drew her back into his arms. His mouth took hers on a gasp of pleasure.

She didn't remember moving until she felt the bed against the back of her legs. Together they lay on it, Grant pulling her closer. Keeping her from leaving even the smallest space.

She touched him, running her hands against powerful shoulders, down subtle arms, across his muscular stomach and even lower. He felt like raw silk. She loved how he even made her palms sensitive whenever they came into contact with skin that rippled under her tutelage.

Grant's moans mingled with Robyn's until she didn't know from which one of them they came. Grant's mouth slid away from hers. He buried his face between her shoulder and neck for a moment. His body trembled against hers. Then, he rolled away and sat on the edge of the bed. For several moments, he looked at her, as if he were trying to memorize every dimension of her body. Robyn felt no embarrassment at his appraisal.

Grant reached across her to the drawer of the nightstand. Out came a foil covered pouch. "Here let me," she said, taking the silver disk from him. She left the bed and kneeling in front of him, pulled the covering away. The rubbery protector felt cool against her fingers. With her index fingers and a slowness borne of anticipation, she watched its length shorten as she gathered it. Keeping her fingers inside, she slipped it over his erection and rubbed the skin of her fingers against him. She felt the strain in him communicated through the motion of his throbbing maleness. Ever so slowly, she brushed her fingers up and down. Grant's hands grabbed her shoulders and squeezed. She dared to look at him. His eyes were closed, and his teeth were clamped on his lower lip as if he was holding back sound. With eminent slowness, she continued to pull the opaque rubber over his hardness, while her fingers reveled in the heat and throbbing energy of the instrument she covered. In a ritualistic finger dance, she made a ceremony of the protective covering. When she finally reached the fullness of his body, her hands went to his thighs. The thread of control that he held over himself was ready to snap. She felt the muscles of his legs bunch under her palms and heard the small cry of pleasure break from the big man sitting above her. She forced herself to maintain a steady pressure, to control the precision and speed with which she raked her thumbnails down his inner thighs. His hands tightened about her shoulders and found their way into her hair that fell down her back. It was exhilarating. When she reached his knees, she lowered her mouth and brushed her tongue over the surface.

Grant hooked his hands under her arms. He hauled her back onto the bed and rolled on top of her. He sought her mouth in an uncontrolled kiss that plunged his tongue deep into the well of her mouth. His legs tangled with hers, and his hands stroked her body drawing heat as they passed over her tip-hard breasts, stomach, and into the center of her being.

Finally, his knee separated her legs, and he hovered above her for a second. She knew he was forcing himself not to plunge into her. With expert direction, he lowered himself into her, but stopped as the heat of his body made contact with the throbbing need in her. A violent surge pushed through Robyn, and she moved forward, opening her body to swallow Grant inside her. But he kept her at bay. And just as she'd created a ceremony with her fingers, he made her groan as he pushed and retreated at the entrance but refused to take the full measure of her offering.

A scream from deep within her was rapidly working its way to the surface. Robyn didn't know if she could keep it from breaking. Pleasure spasms rioted through her. Grant continued his exercise. She squeezed her eyes shut and drew her hands into tight balls against his back.

"Grant," she called as she raised her knees and met his erection. This time he entered her fully. She felt her body close around his hardness, and then, response was out of control. Grant's easy strokes were quickly replaced by frantic movements. Their tango was a pristine dance, each knowing the other's wants and needs. Each pressing the right buttons, making the other cry out with delight as every pleasure point was erotically discovered and exploited.

Robyn couldn't help calling Grant's name. And hers broke from his lips more than once.

The climax was wild, savage, uncontrollable. Grant collapsed against her. She was unaware of his weight as she took long breaths. She felt good, unable to stifle the smile that lifted the corners of her mouth. Her arms tightened around him, and she pressed her lips against his sweat-soaked shoulder.

Grant reacted with a shudder. He turned on his back, pulling Robyn on top of him. Her hair tumbled in his face, and he brushed it away, hooking it behind her ears and holding her face between his hands.

"Even if your mouth doesn't say it, your body knows."

"Knows what?" She rested her elbows above his shoulders. A playful smile curved her lips. Her fingers stroked the scar above his eye.

"That I love you, and you love me." He cradled her head against him and held it, next to his heart.

They lay like that for a long time. Robyn felt happier than she had in years. Grant shifted, keeping her close to his side and gently running his hand up and down her arm. Robyn closed her eyes and reveled in the cocoon of love he weaved.

"Are you sleepy?" he asked. She felt his jaw move against her head.

"No," she answered.

"Good, tell me something about yourself?"

Robyn steeled herself, but didn't tense. She didn't know how to answer that question, and she had to be cautious about what she said. Lying here while the need to trust mingled with the aroma of passion; she wanted to tell him the truth. But did she dare? She thought she'd try lightness.

"Do you want to know when I had my teeth straightened, or how I went from being the skinniest kid in school to the one with the most zits?"

He chuckled as he drove his fingers into her hair. Then, he turned her face to his. In the semidarkness, it was difficult to see.

"Tell me about him?" Grant asked. The seriousness in his voice was unmistakable. "You don't talk about him much."

"I didn't think you'd want me to spend time talking about another man." Robyn tried to buy herself some time. She moved away, needing room if they were going to talk about Cameron Johnson.

Grant smiled and pulled her back into his embrace. "In most cases, that's true. I'm guess I'm just interested in everything about you and what made you the person you are."

Robyn stilled her reaction. How she'd like to answer all his questions, pour her heart out to him, satisfy the unknown questions she could see in his eyes. Tell him who she was, and plead for him to understand and forgive her for leaving him and taking his daughter with her.

Then, her eyes fell on the photograph of him standing next to *The Salt Box,* the plane he flew his first solo in. It was standing on his crowded desk in the corner of the room illuminated by a shaft of moonlight. No other photographs were present. Grant's happy grin poked into her guilt, and slowly, the air seeped out of it. She had made the correct decision. Even today, she couldn't take his love of flying away. It was the one thing in life he couldn't live without.

Grant touched her cheek, causing Robyn to shift her gaze from the hypnotic effect of his smile to the hypnotic effect of the real man beside her. "Tell me, Brooke Johnson, who is the real Brooke Johnson?" If it hadn't been for the mischievous grin he flashed her, she'd be concerned he knew more than she wanted him to know. Outwardly, her features responded, yet her calculatorlike brain went into action. "You don't talk very much about yourself, do you?" he continued.

"I'm not really that interesting," she hedged.

"I can argue that. You're the most mysterious woman I've ever met."

"Isn't mystery the definition of *woman?*" She attempted to redirect the conversation from herself to women in general.

"Every man likes some mystery about a woman. It keeps him interested. But you," he hesitated, searching for words to explain his meaning. "You make intrigue an art."

"What do you mean by that?" One part of her mind told her to steer clear of this avenue, while the other rushed hurriedly toward it.

"In the past month, I've told you about Lebanon, Robyn, and my charter service, yet, all I know about you is that you have a daughter with a rare blood type, you own a restaurant, and you're a widow."

"And you want me to fill in a few of the details." A ready smile traced her even teeth.

"No."

"No?" Her eyebrows went up.

"No, I want you to fill in *all* the details. I want to know everything about you." The eyes that searched hers were serious.

Robyn climbed out of the bed. She found his shirt and pulled it over her nakedness. "My husband's name was Cameron." She began the familiar tale she'd learned and relearned and relearned. "We met during spring vacation our junior year in college. We were married the day after graduation."

"And you lived happily ever after."

Robyn moved toward the curtained windows. She felt much like an actress playing a part. "Not exactly. We were so naive. We believed because we loved each other every problem could be solved."

"It didn't work out."

"It's not what you're thinking. We were so poor. We had no money at all. Getting jobs with no experience was impossible. Cameron joined the navy and had allotments sent to me. It made it easier for us both. When his ship was going to sail I went to San Diego for a week. We called it our honeymoon." She smiled exactly as she'd been cued to do. "On our last day there, he saw me off at the airport. On the bus back to the base, he died. Apparently, he had an embolism. The doctors said it was a blood clot too large to pass through a vessel in the brain."

"I'm sorry." Grant sat fully up in the bed.

"It's all right," she said turning to him. "I've come to terms with his death." She paused a moment. "Which is more than you've done." His gaze narrowed as he stared at her. "You keep Robyn alive. You and your friends."

Grant left the bed then, pulling his pants on and coming to stand in front of her. Robyn could hardly stand not putting her hands on his muscular chest and outlining the clearly defined sections of his torso.

"When David and I went to get the drinks, you and Susan were deeply engaged in conversation for a long time. And later, you disappeared with David. What did they say?"

"Susan was concerned that I could hurt you. And David told me about your life since you lost your wife."

"I see," he let the words out with a heavy breath of air.

"I apologize for their actions. They—"

"You don't have to apologize for them," she interrupted. "They're loyal, and they love you. They don't know anything about me except suddenly you're showing an interest in another woman, a woman they didn't pick and choose for you. I guess they want to make sure you're protected."

"I don't need their protection."

"Of course, you do. Everyone needs someone's protection. Before David met Susan, didn't you scrutinize every woman he saw?"

"Not exactly."

"Men are no different than women. We all want the one we love to like our friends. And have our friends like them. It's very important."

"I suppose you're right. I just never thought of it that way before."

"What about when you married Robyn. Weren't you pleased David liked her and she liked him?"

"I was more than pleased. David told me she was like the sister he'd never had. When she died, he was almost as broken up as I was. I guess that's why it seems she's still alive. Would you want your friends to forget you if you died?"

"I wouldn't want to be forgotten, but I'd want them to go on with their lives. I'd want them to live in the present, not the past."

"You think I'm living in the past, that I'm refusing to go on with my life because I never really let Robyn die?"

Robyn didn't know what answer she wanted to hear. "Is it true?"

"A month ago I'd have said, no. But since I walked into that waiting room, I'm no longer sure." He stepped around Robyn, giving his full attention to the street below for several long moments. Then he turned away. "You remind me of her."

The statement was short, but it hit her like a nuclear missile exploding in her brain. She could see her years of training and the false sense of security she'd made herself believe evaporate into a mushroom cloud of reality. David had seen the similarities in her, too, and Grant had confirmed his friend's fear that she could hurt him by being a constant reminder of his wife.

"It's not your voice, or the way you look," he continued. "In fact, it's nothing I can actually see. But in some way, when I'm with you . . ." He stopped. "I know that's an insult, and I apologize, but . . . it's true." The last was said quietly.

Robyn wasn't insulted. If she and his Robyn weren't the same woman, she would have been. But more important than being insulted, she knew the danger of her situation. She couldn't pull off this kind of charade. She wasn't a good enough actress. Sooner or later, she'd tell him who she was, or he'd guess.

She knew she had to stop. She'd known it since the beginning. And now that he was starting to recognize things in her that the identity of Brooke Johnson could not hide, she had to break off their relationship.

"Say something. Scream, shout, throw something. But don't subject me to your silence."

Robyn turned around and looked in his eyes. Desperation was reflected there. She didn't want to leave him, but it was inevitable. She would return home, and somehow, she'd make good on her promise to Jacob. She wouldn't see Grant again. But now. Just one more time.

"Take me back to bed," she said.

Twelve

She came easily into his arms. Her hands were like hot wax dripping along his shoulders as she caressed him. She seemed to revel in the feel of his skin, just as he came alive under her tutelage. He could feel his muscles bunch and relax at her touch as if they were under her orchestration. She pressed her mouth to his breast. Fires of emotion rocketed through him like a G-force, pressing his body against a stress factor too strong to ignore. He'd lifted her lithe body and carried her back to the bed. He slid her to the floor, her body tracing his on its journey. She was electrified. He felt jolt after jolt of energy pass through him as his tongue paused and rested in the contours of her sensually sculpted body. Standing her on the floor, he kissed her lightly, rubbing his lips gently, caressingly over hers. Heat emanated from her in vast waves. He knew she wanted him to deepen the kiss. Her hands were frantically working in his hair and across his shoulders. But he held back. He wanted to tease her, tease himself, make her want him so badly she'd be blind with urgency when he finally took her. He could barely stand not to devour her. Then, his hands went to the buttons on the shirt she wore, his shirt. He slowly undid them. Moon-drenched skin was exposed inch by inch.

He put his mouth to the exposure. Small whimpering sounds came from her as her fingernails dug into him. Lower and lower, he slid down her his hands memorizing her body and his tongue tasting her. The sound acted like an aphrodisiac, boiling his blood and driving him toward the edge. When all the buttons were released, he slipped the covering off her shoulders, and silently it fell to the floor. He stood back and looked at her, his eyes as hungry as his loins. She was beautiful. In the filtered-light of morning, she was the most beautiful woman he'd ever seen. She didn't appear aware of her nakedness. He discarded his pants, his erection hard and ready. He took her in his arms and lowered her to the silk sheets, joining her there.

He tangled his hands in her hair gently pulling her to him. He fit into the well of her body as if he had been constructed for no other reason. He took her mouth with a hunger that had worked its way from deep within his belly. Tongues and lips battled each other for dominance. He rolled over on her, extending his length, feeling her softness beneath him. Then, his hands ran over her body. She was warm and pliant, and with each touch of his fingertips, he drove her into a frenzy. Finally, he spread her legs and entered her. He knew it would be wonderful. She fit tightly around him, pulling him in and releasing him only to suck his body back to hers. He tried to be gentle, but she was too hot, too ready, and too out of control, writhing beneath him.

And, then, it happened. The soaring came suddenly and without preparation. She lifted her legs around him, and he scooped her buttocks in his hands, rocking her savagely. Fingernails grazed the sensitive skin of his back. He cried out at the fierce pleasure that tore through his body with widening radiation at the feel of her body taking him into it. He held on for as long as he could. The pleasure funnel spiralled upward with an ever widening vortex. He wanted the pleasure to continue forever, but finally, with one maddening cry, white heat tore through him and the night exploded. For the space of an eternity, she held him in that semiworld where life begins and ends. Then, he collapsed. His breathing was ragged as he took short gulps of air, trying to fill his lungs. His body was bathed in sweat, and his limbs felt as heavy as boulders.

What had she done to him? Never had he lost such complete control. Never had his bones turned to powder or his muscles held less substance than water. With his last ounce, of energy he rolled his weight off Brooke. He cradled her in his arms and together they slept.

Grant's internal clock woke him. The summer sun shone through the curtains and brightened the room. Brooke was still imprisoned in his arms. He held her tenderly as if she were an endangered species. And indeed she was, at least to him.

He'd awakened in this room every morning for four years, but today it felt complete. This morning, Brooke was here, by his side. He smoothed the hair away from her face. She stirred, a dreamy smile lifting the corners of her mouth.

He wanted to kiss that mouth, wake her gently, slowly, ease her into the day, then make violent love to her until his name broke from her lips in shattering finality. He groaned as his body began to harden at the thoughts coursing through his mind. For a moment, he hesitated, then quietly left the bed. He dressed in the guest bathroom and headed up Connecticut Avenue at a leisurely pace. He smiled and whistled for the twenty minutes it took to reach Dupont Circle and the small Italian house of confections. The smell of sugar had his mouth watering the moment he opened the door. There were people ahead of him and suddenly he was impatient. He thought of Brooke waiting for him. It was unreasonable, but suddenly he was sorry he'd left her.

When it was his turn, he bought muffins. They were still warm from the oven and smelled delicious. Brooke would probably be asleep when he got back. He'd make coffee and crawl back in bed with her. They could eat, read the paper, drop crumbs on the sheets, and make love. He didn't care what they did as long as they did it together.

The doorman touched his hat and pulled the hydraulically operated glass door open when Grant returned to his condo. Grant smiled as he passed him. He took the first elevator. At the fifth floor, he got off. Everybody in the building must have decided to go out for pastries this morning, he thought. The small room was full of smiling faces, and every button was lighted. The smell of warm bread wafted through the confined space. He'd walk the last three flights. Holding the box in front of him, Grant took the steps two at a time. Waiting for the elevator to climb one floor at a time was too taxing while the woman he loved still wallowed leisurely beneath the white silk sheets of his bed. He was too excited to stay crowded in the elevator.

"Brooke," he called, pushing the door closed behind him. His smile was wide and welcoming.

Stopping midway through the living room, he turned around. His smile faded and was replaced with a frown. His heartbeat increased. Somehow, the apartment was different. Sterile was the word that came to mind. It had a hollow sound despite the gray carpet muffling his footsteps.

"Brooke?" he called again. No reply bought her voice or her person into view. Grant went into the kitchen, then to each of the bedrooms and the den. She wasn't in any of the rooms.

Dropping onto the piano bench, he tried to determine what had happened to the apartment. He got up and walked through the rooms again. Everything was as he had left it, almost. It was neat and clean—too neat and too clean. Brooke had cleaned the coffeepot and cup he'd left on the counter yesterday. The pot was back in its place on the stove, and the cup was neatly stored in the cabinet.

The bed had been made, and the living room furniture looked polished. He lifted the flower vase on the dining room table. No dust ring was present. Then, he went to the coffee table, repeating the procedure. Again, no dust ring. It was as if the apartment had been sucked clean. Everything was in the exact place that he expected to find it, yet nothing was the same.

And where was Brooke? Somehow he knew she was gone for good. Why hadn't she left a note? Maybe she'd gone to Susan's. She seemed interested in the store when he'd told her about it. Grant reached for the phone and quickly dialed the number.

Susan hadn't seen her.

Where could she have gone? And why? Why did he know she wasn't coming back? The cleanliness of the apartment told him, she wasn't just out, she had wiped herself out of his life.

But how could she? After the night they had spent together, didn't she realize how much he loved her? She'd asked him to take her back to bed. And they had made love. She'd shown him how much of his life was missing. He wanted her more than he'd ever wanted another woman. She couldn't disappear from his life.

Robyn didn't know how she got there, but suddenly, she found herself in front of 1651 Gayle Street. She smiled at the pregnant woman working in the garden. Her old house looked happy. A young couple, probably having their first baby, lived there now. In the front yard, a young woman knelt, pulling weeds. Robyn was glad to see her taking care of the flower bed she had planted before her first anniversary. A moment earlier, a young man had left. He'd kissed his wife and reversed the Honda Civic out of the driveway with a happy smile and a wave to the woman on her knees.

Robyn wondered if they could be moles, planted by the men searching for her? She watched the pleasant looking woman for a while. Her body, in full bloom, had a glow that shown radiantly on her oval face. Robyn decided she was all right and took the chance of crossing the street and calling out to her.

"Hello," Robyn greeted, standing on the outside of the white picket fence that surrounded the carefully manicured lawn.

The woman turned, shielding her face against the morning sun.

"Good morning," she called, brushing the dirt from her knees as she approached Robyn.

"Do you know if Susan Collins will be back soon?"

"Susan Collins?" the woman repeated, her brow furrowing. "I'm afraid I don't know anyone by that name."

"She lives in the house next door." Robyn pointed to the white viny¹ sided ranch-style house with black shutters and window boxes spilling over with yellow and white mums.

"We haven't lived here very long, but Mike and Cara Evans live there."

"Oh," Robyn managed to sound sorry and look sincere. "I've been away a long time. I used to live here and Susan was my next door neighbor. I didn't realize she'd moved."

"You lived here?" The woman seemed surprised. "In our house?"

Robyn nodded. "It was a very long time ago. This is my first trip back."

"My husband's just gone to his office for a few hours. Why don't you come in and have some tea with me?"

"I couldn't."

"Of course, you can. I'm Jenny Bryant, and I love making tea." She pulled her gloves off and offered her hand.

Robyn smiled. "I'm Brooke Johnson." She took the soft hand.

"Brooke, what a wonderful name."

Robyn couldn't believe her luck. When she crossed the street, she had expected to talk briefly and leave. Being invited in was like grabbing the golden ring. Moments later, she found herself sitting in the spacious kitchen where she'd received the news of Grant's hijacking. The walls had been yellow then. Now, they were a Wedgwood-blue. The china cup and saucer holding the steaming cup of dark liquid was blue.

"I'm into names at the moment." Jenny rubbed her bulging stomach. "I like Brooke, but Brooke Bryant is to many B's."

She had to agree with that. "When is the baby due?" Robyn sipped her tea. It was bland to her taste. She always spiked hers with apple spice.

"Three more months. But I feel like a cow."

"You look wonderful. Enjoy the time. It's one of the best there is."

"You have children?"

"Only one. A daughter. Her name is Kari."

"How old is she?"

"Four. Have you decided on a name?" Robyn steered the conversation away from herself.

"Yes, I like Margaret Elizabeth if it's a girl and Warren Michael if it's a boy. My husband, William, likes Joann and William, Jr." Jenny frowned at her husband's choice of names.

Robyn envied them. It was something they could share. She had made the decisions alone. Grant wasn't with her, didn't even realize there was a child to name.

"William is an engineer," Jenny continued. "Unfortunately, he had to work today. I'm sure he would have liked to meet you. He has so many questions about the house."

"Maybe I can help answer some of them."

"Finish your tea, and I'll give you a tour. I'm sure you're dying to see what's happened to it since you left."

"You're right," Robyn confirmed as she obediently drained the cup.

Jenny led her through to the living room. It was nothing like she remembered. The plantation white walls were gone, replaced by a pale yellow that picked up the scheme in the multicolored sofa. On the walls hung several paintings which looked of the variety you find in any department store's glass and mirror section. They did coordinate the room and make it warm and cozy.

One of the walls in the dining room had been pulled out and in its place a glass door led out to the patio with brightly colored chairs surrounding an umbrella table. Robyn liked it. It gave the small room air and a sense of additional space. She had entertained Susan and David there often.

Grant's den which had built-in bookcases and a case for his collection of airplanes, was now filled with engineering books. Now, a drafting table sat in one corner, and the posters of airplanes that he'd hung on the walls had been replaced with photographs of bridges and tunnels.

Robyn's eyes misted over but she blinked them away. Jenny led her up the stairs and into the master bedroom. Here, everything was as she had left it that April morning five years ago. A gentle breeze floated through the windows, blowing the white sheers into the room.

It was then that she saw it. In a flash, she was across the room, lifting up the small carriage clock from the night table.

"Do you recognize it?" Jenny asked. "I found it wedged in a drawer of the desk downstairs. The desk was left with a drawer nearly sealed closed. When I finally got it open, I found the clock."

Robyn couldn't speak. It was the clock Grant had given her on their first anniversary. Tears misted her eyes, and she sat down on the queen-size bed.

"It's obviously yours," Jenny said, her voice quiet as if she knew the reverence Robyn placed on it.

"No-no." Robyn cleared her throat. "I just thought it was like one I used to have." Replacing the small gold-plated timepiece made her sorry she'd come. She had better leave.

After a second necessary to pull herself together, Robyn got up and straightened the coverlet. "It's time

I was going. I have to meet someone, and I'm late now."

"I'm sorry. It was good visiting with you." Jenny walked her back to the front door. "If you're ever in town again, I do hope you'll visit me."

"I'd like that." Robyn smiled.

"Maybe next time, William will be here. He's working on a very important proposal. Something to do with building a dam in South America. Otherwise, he'd have been here today and could have asked about the tiny room in the basement."

"The darkroom. I used to develop a lot of film there."

"Oh, that's what it was. We thought it was an unfinished bathroom."

They reached the front door. "Thank you, Jenny. I enjoyed the tea and the tour. Good luck with the baby."

Robyn waved good-bye as she walked toward the car she'd parked a couple of blocks away. She envied the young couple. They loved her house and for that she was glad. She was also sad that she and Grant never got the chance to finish the things they'd planned when they had moved in.

Inside the car, Robyn inserted the key and turned the ignition. Then, she turned it off and leaned her head against the steering wheel. Suddenly, her hands were cold, but her body was burning. She liked what Jenny had done to the house. She could leave it now. She knew it was in good hands. Grant had left the memories behind, and now, she felt she could, too.

The only thing that haunted her was the clock. She'd

wanted it. It was a piece of Grant, but it was also a part of another life. She didn't live that life any longer.

Robyn began to sit up. Suddenly, the door was yanked open, and something was pushed over her head. She fought whoever was attacking her. But the arms fighting back were stronger. She tried to scream, but an unknown hand came across her mouth, stuffing the fabric covering her head inside her mouth and cutting off her air. She kicked and fought blindly but was dragged from the automobile and pulled along the street. She couldn't tell how far she went, since all the while she tried to scream and hit out at the person forcing her to go someplace she had no intention of going.

The hand holding her mouth didn't move, but a knee kicked her in the back, edging her on until another hand pushed her head down, and she was catapulted into an unseen car. Immediately, the door snapped shut, and the car sped away, slamming her against the upholstery. She fought the confining fabric, which smelled of a strong detergent. At least it was clean she thought, realizing now that no one was trying to stop her from pulling the black bag from her head.

Finally, she was free of it.

"Jacob!" she screamed at the familiar face. She didn't know where the strength came from but she was fighting mad and began pummelling him with her fists. "I might have known you'd be behind a stupid stunt like this." Each word was punctuated by a blow.

Jacob grabbed her wrists and shook her. "Stop it!" he yelled. "What the hell do you think you're doing?"

For an immeasurable moment, they glared at each other. Then, he released her, dropping her wrists as if they had suddenly become hot. He straightened his tie, and the mask of G-Man slipped comfortably back into place.

"What do you want?" Robyn asked.

"I want to know what the hell you were doing in that house?" He didn't even try to hide his anger.

"Don't you know, Jacob?" Robyn straightened her borrowed dress, pulling the fabric that had ridden six inches over her knees back into place. "Aren't you privileged to everything that's happened to me for the past five years? Is there any moment of my life you don't touch?"

"Answer the question. Evasion will do no good."

"Damn it, Jacob, don't treat me like a child."

"Then stop acting like one," he shouted. "You have no right to be here at all. Coming back to this house. Didn't you think it would be watched? Did it occur to you that the residents could be planted there for just this kind of happening?"

"Of course, it occurred to me. But I met Jenny Bryant, and I saw her husband, William. Jacob, they're nice people. Jenny's going to have a baby, and her husband is an engineer."

"I know. He's bidding on an engineering project in Argentina." Veins popped out on Jacob's temples. "You just assured him of getting it."

"What?" Robyn turned to stare straight at him. "How? And if you tell me I don't need to know I swear I'll hit you." Robyn reached for her shoe. She needed something stronger than her hand.

"We keep tabs on this house, too. I believe the couple living there are exactly as they appear." Jacob sat back, straightening his tie. Robyn felt as if he were straightening his identity. "For that reason alone," he continued, "I'll make sure William Bryant gets that job, and in record time they will be relocated to Argentina."

"What about the baby? Will there be sufficient medical facilities for her?"

"She'll be fine." Jacob's voice was low. "You have my word on it."

Robyn looked into his eyes. He smiled at her and diffused her anger. "Do they really have to go before the baby?" She thought of all the doctors and sterile equipment that had been on hand in case of emergency when Kari was born. Would Jenny Bryant's baby have the same chance?

"You should never have come here." Jacob was nodding. "Now, we have to try and rectify any presence that could have an impact on your safety."

Robyn slumped in the corner of the luxurious car and sulked. Why couldn't she act like Jacob wanted her to? Why did she allow Grant to manipulate her life? Suddenly, his smiling face focused in front of her. It was that disarming smile that had her forgetting all of her promises and flying around the world with him, when she knew sooner or later Jacob would find out.

"Would it make any difference if I said I was sorry?" Robyn asked, not turning to look at the figure sitting stiffly beside her.

"Not much, but I would like to hear it."

"All right, Jacob, I'm sorry."

"Why did you lie to me?"

"I didn't lie to you. At least at the time, I wasn't lying. And I did do what you asked. I tried to resist him, Jacob." Robyn turned then and took hold of Jacob's arms. "I'm in love with him. Haven't you ever been in love with someone, Jacob? So in love you'd do anything for her?"

Damn, Robyn! I don't want to remember. Jacob looked at the misty eyes imploring him to forgive her. He knew he couldn't deny her request. Yes, he'd been in love before. Cynthia. He hadn't wanted to think about Cynthia, but Robyn made him remember. When he'd seen Robyn and known she had to be made over, the thought of stamping Cynthia's face on the scared woman was uppermost in his mind. He had resisted, knowing if he had tried, Clarence Darrow Christopher III would have pulled his hand.

Wrenching his thoughts back to the air-conditioned car, he answered softly, "I've been in love," he paused. "Robyn." He called her by her real name.

The tears Robyn had been holding spilled down her face, and she shrank into the corner of the luxury seat.

"Where are we going?" she asked, patting her cheeks and seeing the 14th Street Bridge outside the car window. The limousine was heading for northern Virginia.

"The airport."

Grant was at the airport. When she woke and found herself alone, she knew he'd gone to check on the plane. It was why she left. She wanted a quick tour before he returned. What would he think when he found she'd left without a word? Robyn whirled around just as Jacob pulled the familiar red, white, and blue airline envelope from his pocket.

"Your plane leaves in an hour. Marianne will pick you up when you arrive."

"Is she in on this, too, Jacob?"

"No," he answered directly. Robyn was so used to his evasions that she believed him.

"What about the clothes I left at Grant's apartment?"

"They're waiting at the airport."

"What's happened to his car? And this is Susan's dress." Susan had hastily packed her something to wear before she left last night. Robyn hadn't thought of anything but staying the night with Grant. While Susan had remembered practical things, reminding her how strange she'd look in a formal gown at ten o'clock in the morning.

"I'll see to it," Jacob told her in his usual noncommittal style.

"All the loose ends will be tied?" Robyn leaned forward. Her hair swung over her shoulders, separating her view from Jacob. She shifted in the seat and came back to stare directly at the man next to her. "Jacob, I promise to comply with all your conditions."

"Without exception?" One eyebrow went up, the only indication of his disbelief.

"With one exception."

"Go on."

"Susan and David are getting married the third weekend in August. I want to go to the wedding."

"No!"

"Jacob, she's my best friend. She asked me to her wedding. I want to go. Then, I promise, I'll do whatever you say."

"No, Brooke. You're asking the impossible. You should never have come here in the first place. You should not have made contact with any of them."

"But it's too late, Jacob, I've already passed that point. We've seen each other, talked to each other. They've invited me to the wedding, and I want to come. After that, I'll go back into hiding, and you'll never have cause to argue with me again. If you want me to move, I'll move. If you want Kari and I to change our names and disappear, we'll do it. I'll become the compliant female you always wanted me to be."

Jacob stared at Robyn. He found no comfort in her words. He'd tried to make her do what he wanted, but she never was the typical inductee. She was temperamental, feisty, alive, and wonderful—everything he'd ever wanted in a woman. Now, for a few hours at a friend's wedding, a friend who didn't even recognize her, she was willing to become a docile protectee.

"All right, you can go to the wedding."

"Thank you, Jacob." For the second time that day, she flung herself into his arms.

"Hold it, there are conditions." He pushed her away.

"Anything."

"You arrive shortly before the ceremony. Afterwards, you can spend only enough time at the recep-

tion to be considered socially acceptable. Then, you'll
be flown back. Acceptable."

She heard the take-it-or-leave-it note in his voice.
"Acceptable." She looked at her hands. "Is it all right
if I bring Kari."

His heart went out to the baby he'd once held. Jacob
hated to think of putting her in danger, but the child
could be used as a barrier to keep the plan intact if
anyone tried to change it. By anyone he meant Robyn.
"Yes, bring Kari."

"Then, what, Jacob? Are we going to have to move,
change our names and our faces again?"

Jacob ignored her question. "Why didn't you tell
me about the poison or the photograph?"

Robyn lifted her head and directed her gaze at him.
"How did . . ." She didn't complete the thought,
knowing Jacob wouldn't answer.

"Has there been anything else I should know
about?"

Robyn hesitated, refusing to drop her head. "My
wings," she said quietly. "The day after the poison
was found, a delivery was made to the restaurant. Inside the box were a pair of plastic wings. Grant had
given them to me the night we got married. They were
in my jewelry case when I . . . when we left for the
airport." It was the day Grant came home. The television had been full of the reports about the hostages
being released. Robyn had held the plastic wings in
her hand. Then, she had dropped them in the box and
closed it.

"How do you know they were yours? There must
be thousands of those given out every year."

"The right side of the wing had a chip in it. Grant had offered to get me another one, but I wanted that one. On the back side of it, he had carved my initials and the date I flew solo." Robyn was quiet for a long while. "Jacob, I'm scared. He knows who I am."

"Brooke, we're aware of what's happening. We'll keep you safe. I promise."

Robyn stared at him. His face was open and honest, something he rarely showed to her or the world. What was going to happen to her? "Are we going to have to move, Jacob?" she asked again.

"Your plane is waiting."

The car had stopped, and the driver was holding the door open. Robyn looked out at the familiar terminal entrance to Washington National Airport. She took the driver's extended hand and slid out of the limousine. Jacob followed her. He led her straight through the terminal and to the departure gate, showing an I.D. as they bypassed the security machinery.

"Don't worry about anything, Brooke. We'll handle it." Jacob looked at her without the veil that always clouded his eyes. He was close enough to touch, yet the distance between them could have been miles.

"Grant. He'll be all right?" Tears gathered behind her eyes.

"I said we'd handle it."

"How?"

He took her arm and rushed her down the gangway. "You're holding up the plane."

At the entrance to the steel aircraft, she stopped. "Tell me? How are you going to stop Grant? He'll call or fly in."

"I'm expecting you to discourage that." The phrase was a definite threat, implying if she didn't—he would.

Thirteen

Jacob needed a drink. He hadn't felt this gnawing hunger to drown his feelings in a bottle since *she* had died. Robyn had asked him if he'd ever been in love. Cynthia wasn't his first love, but she was the woman he'd wanted to marry.

It was dark in the nation's Capital. The streets outside his office window were wet from a light rain. Car lights were reflected on the street's damp surface, making a picture postcard of Pennsylvania Avenue.

He looked back at the desk. The computer screen beckoned. With several keystrokes, the monitor flickered, and she was there. It had been over nine years since he'd looked at Cynthia. Yet, there she was, hidden behind three levels of computer coding and several passwords. Tonight, Jacob needed her. He needed to remember. He hadn't been responsible for Cynthia's death. If she'd only done what he told her, she might be alive today. But she was too headstrong for that. She hadn't stayed hidden in the basement of the farmhouse where he left her, and she'd been killed.

Just like Robyn. She, too, wouldn't take direction. She defied him at every turn. Yet, he loved Robyn. But not the way he'd loved Cynthia. The two women were alike in temperament and beauty. Both of them got into his blood, and both refused to live the comfortable lives set up for them.

He had to admit he liked that in them. The majority of people he'd dealt with since becoming part of this program were too complacent, eager to get away and start an easy life at the government's expense. Robyn hadn't been one of them. She'd given up everything and fought valiantly to carve out a life for herself. But she wasn't living. Jacob knew that. She was going through the motions, giving everything she had to enhance someone else's life, but not her own. She'd hired an alcoholic music director, giving him the chance to pull his life together. Some of the waiters had prison records or were former juvenile delinquents.

Jacob had them carefully screened. Currently, nothing about them posed a threat. Most of them were too young to have been involved with Alex Jordan or the Network. Need to intervene in her hiring practices hadn't been necessary, yet. And the latest one, an aspiring actress named Sue-Ellen. What he'd noticed happened with the people she helped was that they developed a fierce loyalty to her. He knew if anything were to jeopardize her, he could press these people into service, and without question, they'd rally to her aid.

Yesterdays had been a red wooden structure with ornate wrought-iron balustrades when Robyn bought it. Vinyl siding in light blue with white accents now supported the exterior frame. A single sign of rich red, deeply etched with gold lettering, denoted the name of the restaurant.

Robyn went up the walkway. She noticed everything tonight. The grass had been cut that morning, and the smell reminded her of fresh watermelon. She watched the wide expanse of it perfectly cutting out a circular driveway as it led to the front door. She rarely used this entrance, but tonight, instead of driving, she'd decided to walk the short distance from her house to Delaware Avenue. Arriving just before sunset, she could see the play of rays on the distant sky. It was red like spilled wine.

A couple, laughing as they passed her on their way to the door, brought her out of the suspended state she was in. Taking the last few steps to the canopied door, she entered. The old walls that had made the foyer narrow and dark had been removed. The area opened up on thick red carpeting that her feet sank into as she smiled at a group sitting on the comfortable chairs to her right. It was the usual meeting place for friends arriving at slightly separate times. From above, a huge chandelier brightly lighted the dark panelling and threw out arrays of prisms from the cut glass.

Upstairs were the small dining rooms and private party rooms. Robyn went toward her dressing room. The show wasn't due to start for an hour, but she liked to be prepared. At a moment's notice, she could be called upon to handle an emergency.

Tonight, she'd chosen a gown of black satin. It had a high neck and long sleeves. The gentle folds of the fabric fell about her legs like silk and ended at the black high heels she wore. From the left shoulder to the hem, glittery beads formed an exotic bird. The dress reminded her of flying. And, tonight, she felt like flying. She'd spent the last week depressed, going over and over in her mind what to do when Grant returned.

But he hadn't returned. He hadn't called. And she had survived seeing him, survived kissing him, even survived him making love to her. Although she had to admit, making love still reduced her to idiocy.

Marianne had been telling her for ages. It *was* time she stopped grieving over the past and went on with the future. Robyn had lectured Grant about keeping his dead wife alive. She was no better. For five years, she'd lived in the shadow of his memory, refusing to look forward. It was time she thought about her own life and what the future could bring. She would go out with other men. Somewhere out there was a man she could spend her life with and love, if not in the same way, enough to forget. She just had to find him.

"I know that look." Marianne stopped her on her way through the kitchen. Robyn looked at the desserts, her favorite.

"What look is that?" she asked, admiring the cake replica of the leaning tower of Pisa. The buttercream icing smelled deliciously of lemon. She remembered when she and Marianne were caterers working out of her kitchen. She had run out of white vanilla when she was making icing. As a substitute, Marianne had suggested they use lemon. The cake had smelled wonderful, and the guests loved it. Every since then, she'd made it a part of her recipe.

"The look that says you've made up your mind. What is it this time? Do we change the drapes . . . remodel the lounge . . . or have you resolved never to see Grant Richards again?"

Marianne was remarkably perceptive. She wondered what other aspects of her life her friend knew about and had not exposed.

"I didn't have to decide anything about him. He's gone." She wanted to leave it at that, but Marianne had other plans.

"With or without a little help from you?"

"I don't know," she answered truthfully. He hadn't called since Jacob had taken control. She didn't know if he'd agreed to her plea not to see him again, if he'd been too angry when she didn't return, or if Jacob had *taken care of all the loose ends.*

"What happened when you went down there for the party? When I picked you up, you looked like someone had died." Uncharacteristically, Marianne pressed on.

"Nothing much happened. I told you an emergency came up, and he had to use the plane. I came back the next day."

"By commercial air." Something significant had happened. Jacob had called to tell her to pick up Robyn. She'd known her friend had left with Grant, but how she had ended up in D.C., Marianne could only speculate.

"He was busy, and I didn't want to leave you here alone."

"You're lying."

Robyn gasped. Marianne had never called her a liar

before. The two women stared at each other over the leaning confection.

"Why did you say that?"

"Something happened. I could see it in the dark circles under your eyes. And I knew you'd been crying before you got off that plane."

"All right, I was crying. And Grant didn't send me home. I came alone, without his knowledge."

"Why?"

"Marianne, why are you asking? You don't even like Grant."

"I don't dislike Grant. I'm concerned about you. We've been friends a long time, and I hate to see you so unhappy."

"I'm not unhappy."

"You were certainly doing a good imitation of it until Kari had that blood transfusion. Then, you went from unhappy to miserable."

"Well Grant and I won't be seeing each other again. You were right the other night when you said it was time to stop grieving. It's time I got on with my life."

"Then why are you putting a barrier in front of Grant. He's the best looking man I've seen in years, and he came back to see you."

"He came to see Kari."

Marianne frowned. "Brooke, grown men don't travel four hundred miles to see a child unless it's his."

Robyn controlled her emotions, containing her re-action. "Marianne, you're confusing me. Are you say-ing you want me to see Grant? I thought your opinion of Grant was that he was just another guy."

"If he's what you want, he's not another guy to you."

"Then why did you say it? I can't keep up with you anymore. You're behind him, then you're against him."

"I'm for you, Brooke."

"It doesn't matter anyway, Marianne. He won't be back."

Robyn gave her a crooked smile and walked away. It was nearly time for her song. Marianne didn't know how to protect her friend. Since she'd been assigned, her job had been relatively easy. There were no complications or threats to Robyn's existence. There was also no life. The two of them ran the business and watched Kari grow.

Her own life was different, but just as unhappy. While Robyn gave everything to the restaurant and her daughter, Marianne had many dates, and there were several men in her life. It wasn't until Grant made an unscheduled appearance that Robyn began to live. It was also then that her life with Jacob had taken on a different flavor.

What were they to do? Robyn, for reasons that concerned her own life, could not go on seeing the man she loved. And her association, she refused to label it love, with Jacob was an added conflict that could jeopardize several lives. She shuddered to think of the hotel room and the explosion that nearly killed the two of them.

She needed to talk to someone about her problems, but there was no one. She couldn't tell Robyn, the person she protected, and, she couldn't tell Jacob, the man who protected them both.

* * *

Three weeks passed, and Robyn's life settled into a routine. She threw herself into Kari and the restaurant. It seemed Marianne was working out her own problem if the number of chocolate desserts could be counted. Each day, the ache in Robyn's heart dulled a little. Grant hadn't called, and she was sure he never would. She didn't know whether or how Jacob had contacted him, but she was sure he had a hand in his silence.

Susan and David's wedding was this weekend. She'd promised to attend but early in the week had decided not to go. How could she explain her actions to Grant? How could she look David and Susan in the eye after promising not to hurt their friend and doing just that? It would be best to avoid further contact with any of them. Yet, as the days passed, she found herself longing for one more glimpse into her past.

Pulling into her driveway for her afternoon with Kari, she found a strange car.

"Name's Hammil, Ma'am. Thomas Hammil." The man getting out of the blue Chevrolet extended his hand by way of introduction. Robyn took it. He gave her a quick, hard shake and dropped it. "I'm from the Bureau."

She knew without him telling her. He was from Jacob's office. She wondered if somewhere in Washington they had a factory where they molded these clones.

"Come inside." The tall blonde followed Robyn with the cadence of military training.

"The wedding's tomorrow, Ma'am. I'm here as your escort." The drawl was definitely Texan, she thought as Thomas came straight to the point.

"Jacob sent me an escort?"

"Yes, Ma'am. He's sorry he can't pull the duty himself."

"You can relax, Thomas, and call me Brooke."

"Thank you, Ma'am." Robyn didn't think he knew how to relax. He looked just as straight as before. "We have plane reservations for fifteen hundred hours, that's three o'clock this afternoon, Ma'am."

She hesitated slightly, turning away from Thomas Hammil. She knew what this was. It was a crossroads. One of those places where one decision changed your life. If she stayed here, she'd never see Grant again. If she went . . . she didn't know what lay ahead.

"Ma'am?" Hammil called.

Robyn turned back. "I'll be ready," she told him. "I just have to go next door and pick up, Kari. Would you like something to drink? Or eat?"

"No, Ma'am," he declined.

"Thomas, if we're going to spend the weekend together, don't you think you're going to have to relax a bit?"

"Sorry, Ma'am."

"I promise not to give Jacob a report on your behavior."

At that, he actually smiled.

"Then, if it's all right, Brooke, I would like a soda, if you have one."

Robyn remembered that people from the District of Columbia call pop, soda. It was one of the colloquiums Jacob insisted she learn, and for which he cautioned her never to mistake.

She handed Thomas Hammil a can of cola and filled a glass with ice. "I'll get Kari," she said, leaving him to walk the short distance to Will's house.

Kari met her exuberantly as she always did. She reminded Will of David and Susan's wedding. "I'll be gone overnight."

"I never heard you mention them before. And you're going to their wedding."

"They're friends of Grant's."

"Yes, I remember now."

"Will, are you all right? You never forget anything." She went to him and placed the back of her hand on his forehead as if he were Kari's age.

"Just getting old I guess." Will laughed, moving his head away from her touch. Robyn smiled but concern creased her brow. She loved the old man. In many ways, he was like her father. She wondered if he just didn't want them to go without him. Since he had moved next door, when Kari was just learning to crawl, they'd been friends.

"Will you need a ride to the airport?"

"I have a ride," she answered not bothering to explain the FBI agent waiting for her in her house. "Come on, Kari. You still have to pack your toys."

Kari was immediately ready. She'd been looking forward to going on the trip since Robyn had mentioned it to her.

"Will Uncle Grant be there?" Kari asked, as they walked across the connecting lawns.

"I think he's going to be in the wedding, darling."

"What's a wedding?"

"It's like a big party. First, a woman with a long white dress and a man in a suit swear to love each other for the rest of their lives, then everyone has a party and gives them gifts to start their life."

"Oh, like the picture on the mantel."

Robyn smiled. She stopped, going down to Kari's level. "Kari, that's me in the picture. I'm wearing the long white dress."

"It doesn't look like you," her childish voice said.

"I was a lot younger then."

"Was I a lot younger, too?"

Robyn hugged her with a laugh. "Yes, darling. You were a lot younger."

"What about my daddy?"

Robyn had answered that question before. Kari had asked about her father many times. She knew the same story Robyn had learned. Why did Robyn find it so difficult to lie to her daughter now?

"Kari, don't you know what happened to your daddy?" Her voice was serious.

Kari's youthful soprano was proud and sad. "He died before I was born."

"Yes, darling, he died."

Robyn stood up then, covering the distance that brought her to the kitchen door. She was about to take her daughter to see her real father, yet she had to tell her the figure of a man she'd never seen was her father.

Cameron Johnson, a man who happened to have the same rare blood type as Kari and who died in the service without parents or other relatives, was given to Robyn as her husband. This cardboard figure was Kari's father, while the flesh and blood man whose body had joined with Robyn's in love to produce a dark-eyed, dark-haired child could never know what he had done.

Inside, Robyn introduced Kari to Thomas Hammil and told her he was going to see they get to the wedding. While Kari went to pack her toys in her backpack, Robyn noticed Thomas had cleaned his glass, dried it, and replaced it in the appropriate cabinet. The can that had held his soda had been rinsed, crushed, and discarded in the appropriate recyclable container. It was as if he was erasing his presence from the house.

The fragrance of roses filled the church at Sixteenth and Gallatin Streets. It was a small intimate cathedral nestled off the busy northwest thoroughfare. The stone building had stood for over a hundred years and was covered in ivy as if an artist had sketched it out for a painting. Robyn sat near the back of the church on the right side. Thomas Hammil sat next to her on one side, while an excited Kari fidgeted on the other. Robyn and Kari had matching dresses of pink silk. Her hat was large and floppy. Thomas must have approved of the outfit for he made no comment.

The organ began, and Grant and David came from the vestibule in the front of the church. Robyn's heart lurched when she saw him. Suddenly, a restraining hand took her arm. Thomas Hammil was stronger than he looked. Robyn settled in her seat, but Kari was more vocal.

"Mommy, there's Uncle Grant." She pointed toward the front.

"Don't point, Kari." Robyn pushed her finger down. "I see him, dear."

"Does he know we're here?" she whispered.

"No, darling. Now, be quiet. The bridesmaids are about to come in."

Tears clouded Robyn's eyes when she saw several of her college friends float through the door. They shimmered down the aisle, a sea of golden yellow reflected through her tears. Baby's breath ringed their heads, and they carried baskets of silk flowers, picking up the yellow color scheme. When the organist played "The Wedding March," the congregation stood. Robyn helped Kari, lifting her onto the seat and holding her in the crook of her arm. While she waited for the bride to come through the door, she glanced at the front of the church. Grant's eyes caught and held hers. Anger shot daggers at her. She couldn't drop her gaze as a tremor ran the course of her body. Thomas Hammil came to her aid. He touched her elbow gently as Susan came through the door.

She was beautiful. Exactly the bride she should be. Her dress was covered in lace and pearls. The bodice fit snugly, dropping past her waist, then fanning out in layers of white lace and crystal pleating.

A fresh set of tears streamed over her cheeks. Susan smiled happily and began her slow procession toward her future husband. When all were settled in front, Thomas handed her his handkerchief. Robyn dried her eyes and hazarded a glance in Grant's direction. He had turned to face the minister.

The ceremony was short, and soon, the brightly clad women on the arms of black-tuxedoed men followed the bride and groom up the aisle. Kari waved at Grant as he passed. He lifted his hand to her but did not include Robyn in his welcome.

When the church was nearly empty, Robyn turned to Thomas. "Should we go to the reception now, or wait until after the bridal party has settled?"

"We can go now."

Robyn was not looking forward to coming face-to-face with Grant. The look he'd given her clearly told her that he was angry over her unorthodox exodus.

People gathered at the reception hall before the bride and groom arrived. Thomas found them a table and went to get Robyn and Kari drinks. He came back with a Coke for Kari, a piña colada for her, and something for himself that looked like a martini. They waited an hour before the bridal party finally arrived. Robyn did not join the well-wishers as the party came through the door, but Kari slipped out of her seat before Robyn could stop her and padded across the dance floor to be lifted into Grant's arms. His smile toward her was warm and genuine. He swung her around several times then kissed her on the cheek. Robyn sat stonelike, watching the gentle exchange.

After several minutes, he set her down, and she returned to the table. "Uncle Grant's coming to see me, Mommy," she announced. Fear ran through Robyn. She'd made a bargain with Jacob, and this time she was going to keep it. Grant hadn't come to see them in the last few weeks. Why would he come now? Maybe Kari meant he was going to come to the table. Wasn't it customary to say hello to old friends, old enemies?

The reception line formed. Robyn rose and joined it, Thomas Hammil at her elbow. The first person in line was Marsha Jennings. They had been at college together. When Robyn and Susan lived next door to each other, they had often met Marsha for lunch. Marsha smiled, taking her hand. She suddenly froze, then fumbled as she looked from Robyn to Kari and back.

"Hello, I'm Brooke Johnson," she introduced herself. "This is my daughter, Kari. And this is Thomas Hammil." She turned slightly to include Thomas. And, hopefully, Marsha would think she was mistaken.

"How do you do?" She smiled down at Kari and shook hands with Thomas, then passed them along. When Robyn got to Susan, she was close to tears. How she would have liked to be a part of the ceremony, but it was enough to be present. She hugged her friend and whispered how lovely she thought the dress was. Then, she hugged David and congratulated him.

She placed her hand in Grant's. "What, no hug for me?" He held onto her hand, pulling on it slightly. Robyn had no choice, if she didn't want to snatch her hand away. She leaned forward, and he hugged her tightly, but briefly. His release didn't come until after he felt the tremor run through her.

Reaching down, he swung Kari into his arms. "Hi,

precious. How's my blood doing? You're keeping it safe just in case I need it?"

"I'm keeping it safe," she chimed.

Robyn reached for her. But Grant dodged her grasp. "She's all right. She can stay." He'd won again. He knew she wouldn't fight over the child. The line behind her was long, and she was holding it up. Thomas edged her along, and she left Kari, returning to the table. She took a seat, her back to the raised dais where Grant and the bridal party would sit. She knew she couldn't take him glaring at her when they took their places. Moments later, the bridal party was led to the dais, and Kari was honored by being able to sit on Grant's lap for a while.

When Grant rose with a champagne glass in his hand, Robyn knew the toast. It was the one David had given them and she'd repeated the night of the engagement party. While the room saluted the bride and groom, Kari left the dais to return to her mother.

"I'm ready," she told the FBI man.

"Wait until after the first dance," a remarkably quiet Thomas whispered.

The wait was long. Robyn ate the meal but couldn't remember tasting anything but Grant's wrath against her back. Finally, the meal ended. David and Susan rose to lead the first dance. Other couples joined them, several stopping with words of congratulations. After the dance, Susan and David were immediately surrounded by people. Robyn waited, aware that Grant still sat on the dais. He talked quietly to the woman on his right. Several times, he smiled at what she said.

Robyn could stand it no more. She took Kari's hand

and made her way to Susan and David. "It was a lovely wedding," she said with tears in her eyes. "I hate to have to leave so early, but Kari and I have an early flight."

"But—" Susan began.

"I do hope I'll get to see you again." Robyn cut her off. She hugged Susan and David in turn and found Thomas waiting for them by the door. The car was waiting. She and Kari were whisked away before anyone had a chance to stop them.

With the efficiency of a military maneuver, Thomas had her back in Buffalo and in her home before dinner had begun at Yesterdays. Kari was tired, and Robyn put her to bed early. Thomas excused himself and disappeared, leaving only the feeling that a ghost had been present.

Robyn was restless. Her thoughts scattered and unfocused. Why had Grant hugged her? What did he think, and why hadn't he called after she left? Even at the restaurant, there were no messages waiting when she called. She moved about the house like an automaton. Finally, she took a shower and dressed for bed. She tried reading a book, but after fifteen minutes she hadn't remembered a single word. Turning the light out, she tossed and turned for hours. At midnight, she got up. Maybe a hot drink would help. She'd make herself a cup of tea. It was soothing, and then, she'd be able to sleep. Leaving her bedroom, she opened Kari's door and checked on her. She was sleeping soundly. Pulling the door closed, Robyn crept down the stairs.

The doorbell rang just as she poured the boiling

water into the tea pot. Robyn went to it. Through the
sheer curtains covering the small panes that flanked
both sides of the door, she saw Grant. She pulled the
door in.

"What are you doing here?" she asked, backing
away from the expression she saw on his face. He still
wore the black tuxedo, but the bow tie was gone, and
his ruffled shirt was open at the neck.

"I want to know why?" He came in the door, slamming it behind him. Robyn stepped backward. His expression was angry.

"What are you talking about?"

He reached for her. She sidestepped him. "I'm
talking about three weeks ago. I'm talking about everything since I've met you. I'm talking about why
you keep asking me to go away, and I'm talking
about what happened when you hugged me this afternoon."

"Nothing happened." She turned away, putting the
distance of the room between them.

"You're an awful liar," he sneered.

"Grant—," she began, but his raised hand stopped
her.

"You don't have to answer everything," he shook
his head as if in resignation. "Just tell me what happened to you? I came back, and you were gone. Everything about you was gone. Even the hairbrush
showed no sign of your hair. If I hadn't been with
you, I'd swear you'd never been there."

The picture of Thomas Hammil cleaning her kitchen
suddenly loomed. "I had to go, Grant. I told you there

was no future for us. I asked you to go away and leave me alone."

"Why? After the night we spent together. I love you, and you love me."

Their entwined bodies on his silk sheets crowded into her memory. "I don't love you," she said over the lump in her throat.

"You do."

"Grant, go away."

"Say you love me." He came toward her. There was no place for her to go.

"No." Robyn took refuge behind a chair.

He stalked her. She backed away, moving around the room. "Say it," he demanded.

"It won't make any difference," she pleaded. "There's no place in my life for you."

"Say it!" he shouted.

"Grant you'll wake Kari."

"Say it!" He reached for her as her back came up against the piano. Strong hands drove into her hair, taking fistfuls and twisting it until she was forced to move into the heated area that surrounded his body.

"I don't love you. I don't love you," she chanted, closing her eyes against stinging tears.

Grant pulled her closer. Her eyes flew open. She could see his mouth descending. She knew he was going to kiss her, and she knew she would tell him anything if he did. But she couldn't stop him. All she could do was wait, while his mouth hovered over hers.

"Darling, can't you find the champagne? I put it in

the . . ." a deep male voice came from the dark stair-well.

Robyn and Grant separated as if they'd been pulled apart by giant magnets. Their two heads swiveled around toward the stairs.

"Jacob!"

Fourteen

Robyn's gasp went unheard by Grant whose eyes were riveted to the partially dressed man at the top of the stairs. Jacob stood there, wearing a black kimono and nothing else. Her eyes were fastened to the man who stood in the light flooding from her bedroom. The front door slammed behind her. Looking around, she found Grant had gone. For a split second, she started after him.

"Brooke!" Jacob's voice halted her attempt.

She turned on him, her face red with anger. "What the hell are you doing here?"

Jacob closed the robe and went back through the door. Robyn raced up the stairs and followed him into her bedroom.

"He was a loose end."

"And you had to tie it? You couldn't trust me to do it?"

"I gave you the chance." Jacob picked up a pair of blue bikini briefs and stepped into them. "I heard what was going on downstairs. You couldn't control the situation."

"Jacob, it was none of your business."

He stopped, grasping her arm. She was sure he'd

leave a bruise. "You are my business. You became my business five years ago when you stepped into a witness box."

He let her go. Robyn took two steps backward as he suddenly released her. Jacob continued to dress, putting on his pants and shirt as if he were alone.

"Don't I get a reprieve, Jacob? Is every facet of my life to be controlled by you or some unseen agent as long as I live? Did I give up the freedom of choice, of independent decision, when you walked into my life?"

"Damn you, woman." He turned, taking her upper arms and shaking her. "You're the worst nightmare I've ever had to contend with."

"Then drop me, Jacob. Leave me out there hanging alone. You've done your job. For five years, you've protected me. I'm the one who's changing the rules now. I'm the one putting myself in danger. Let me choose how I'd like to live the rest of my life. Because this shell of an existence is too much. I've coped with it too long. I've got cracks, Jacob. And each day they get wider. I want to stop. Let me?"

"I can't." This time he turned from her. His hands pushed deep into his pockets. "I can't do that, Brooke." He sighed. "If only I could."

"Why not, Jacob?" She went to him, taking his arm. The muscles tensing under her fingers surprised her. Jacob covered her hand with his own. His eyes were soft in the half-light. "The taxpayers can't be expected to take care of me forever." Her voice softened. She could take him angry, but his tenderness destroyed her.

He was silent, too silent. It was like the times after

she'd testified. Signals would pass between him and someone else just before a bomb would drop. She could feel it. It passed through her. Robyn pushed herself back far enough to see his face.

"It's not over, is it, Jacob?" She was amazed at how calm she could be. Jacob shook his head—no placating comments about her not needing to know. Suddenly, she began to tremble. When she was telling him to leave, she'd be responsible for her own mortality, they'd been false words. The reality hit her. There was someone out there, tracking her, trying to kill her. Still, after all these years, someone wanted her dead.

Jacob grasped her trembling body and lowered her to a seat on the bed. "When the Network was uncovered, we knew at least one man or woman escaped our net. That's why we put you through the program."

"Who?" She looked into his eyes. His arms were still holding her as he knelt on the rug.

"We don't know. But in the past five years, discreet inquiries have been made about you."

"What kind of inquires?" Her heart beat with a fear she hadn't ever known.

"Computer files mostly, cross-referencing your name with people from your past." He couldn't tell her about Kari's accident. He could feel the terror rising in her.

"Grant—" she stopped. "What about Grant?"

"He's not as easy to track. He flies in and out of the country regularly. It's very difficult to protect him."

"But you've been trying." Her eyes were wide and glassy with unshed tears.

Jacob nodded. "We think something is going to happen soon. That's why I did what I did tonight. You've got to be careful. One word in the wrong place could get you all killed."

"Oh, Jacob, I'm so sorry. I tried to send him away."

"I know you did." He could hear the agony in her voice. "I know how much you love him." He ran a finger down her cheek. He understood how it was to love someone and not to be able to tell them, not to be able to make any plans together. He knew the gnawing feeling it left in your stomach when the situation was out of your control and totally manipulated by someone else. "Now get some sleep," he told her.

"I can't go to sleep," she protested.

"Try," Jacob said.

"Jacob, you can't really expect me to sleep now?" She was too agitated, wired. How could he expect her to sleep when her life was in danger?

"I'll get your tea." He was gone before she could accept or refuse. In minutes, he was back with a steaming cup of the apple spiced tea that she had gone to make. It now seemed hours ago.

She accepted the hot liquid and sipped it cautiously.

"Now, get in," he said, when she'd drained the small cup. Robyn got into bed, and Jacob pulled the covers up. He sat facing her. "You look like the scared little girl who was trying to appear brave, the first day I met you." He reached over and turned off the lamp. "Go to sleep. I'll be here for a while." He moved to the head of the bed and leaned her forward, making room for himself to sit down. Pulling her back, his fingers massaged her skin, relieving some of the tension bunching her neck muscles together. She was forced to relax.

"What was her name, Jacob?" The darkness seemed to disembody her voice.

"Whose name?"

"The woman you were in love with? The one you tried to pattern me after."

His fingers stopped momentarily, then continued their confident rhythm. "Cynthia." He sounded far away.

"Where is she now?"

"She died."

Robyn closed her eyes, forcing her breath to remain even. "How?" she asked.

"I was protecting her. She didn't follow orders." His answers were short but not cryptic.

"Why do I remind you of her. Do we look alike? I mean before."

"No, physically you're very different. But you are alike."

"You mean I won't follow orders either?" She dropped her head letting the magic in his fingers take some of the stress from her tired muscles.

"No, I mean you're a very strong woman. You won't let life beat you down. You fight for what you want. I didn't pattern you after her."

"I'm sorry, Jacob," she yawned. "How long ago did she die?"

"Nine years."

"I won't be like her, Jacob," she yawned again and turned in his arms, pillowing her head in his lap. "I'll follow orders." Robyn slept.

Jacob sat holding her in the darkness much longer than he needed to. He continued stroking her hair, loving the feel of the lustrous silk. It was her hair that was like Cynthia's. Although, hers was dark and rich, and Cynthia's had been the color of sunshine. Cynthia's face had a scar angled across her chin. Robyn's face was flawlessly clear. Yet, the two women had one thing in common, a vital spirit, and Jacob loved that in them.

He shifted Robyn to the pillow and moved to the chair across the room. He watched her until the dark of night reached its zenith. Then, taking the black kimono, he left the house as silently and unseen as he had entered it.

It wouldn't be long now. They had the blood bank computers, and soon, they would be able to trace the phone number that had manipulated the records. Hammil was covering the explosive since he was an expert himself. Each day, the circle closed a little tighter.

Thank God, Grant thought, as he shut down the engines of the cargo plane. If it hadn't been for the sudden spurt of government contracts, he didn't know if he could have gotten through the past three weeks.

He'd stormed out of Brooke's house with murder on his mind. When that guy came from her bedroom, wearing next to nothing, something snapped in him. There could be an explanation, but if there was, she would have called. In twenty-one days he'd heard nothing.

He'd also seen the man leaving her house in the early morning hours.

"Damn," he had cursed, remembering the scene as if it were unfolding before him now. He was still angry. If problems hadn't developed with the plane, and he'd been able to sleep, he wouldn't have been up to see the figure quietly steal out of Brooke's kitchen door.

But when he got to the airfield, he found he had a problem with the fuel pump. When that was fixed, something had gone wrong with the hydraulics that support the landing gear. On a ladder, he had gone at the problem. He had dropped the wrench he was using and had to climb down to pick it up.

Going back up the ladder, he had tried again to unhinge one of the joints. It wouldn't bulge. Hours had passed. He felt all his fingers had turned to thumbs, and he was no closer to solving the problem. His mind hadn't been working on the plane, it was dwelling on a six-foot figure with dark hair and a black kimono.

Frustration had egged him on. When the second wrench slipped from his grip, he finally had jumped down from the ladder and kicked the ladder. Pain had torn through his leg, but not enough to deaden his awareness. He then had taken on the metal hull with his bare hands. With clenched fists, he had beaten the ghostly image of the man in the black kimono, pummeling the painted hulk.

Several mechanics had had to wrestle him to the ground to prevent him from damaging the plane or himself. He had fought them, lost, not aware where he was. Finally, one of them calling his name, had gotten through. He had agreed to calm down, and they had released him.

It was then that he had called Will McAdams and had gone there for the night, leaving the repair to the mechanics. Why hadn't he slept in the plane? Why hadn't he gone to a hotel? Anywhere away from *her.* But the taxi had dropped his oil-stained frame only thirty paces from Brooke's door.

Will had looked at his swollen knuckles and, without question, had gone to get the first-aid kit. Grant had been a lot calmer after the fight with the airplane. But his hands had hurt like hell. Dried blood and lacerated skin so swollen that he couldn't close either hand, had been cleaned, medicated, and draped in gauze bandages. He had winced when Will applied the iodine. Nothing, however, had compared to the pain created by the vise grip squeezing his heart.

"Maybe I could get the story straight if you'd sit down and stop trying to wear away the carpet," Will had said, when Grant had finally showered and worn one of his old robes.

Grant had sat down. Then just as quickly had risen. He had taken his highball glass between both hands and had drained it.

"I wish I knew, Will. I came to work things out. But she's so damn mysterious. And then there was a man."

"A man? Who?"

"I don't know. I didn't get a good look at him. He came out of her bedroom, and the light was behind him. All I saw was a black kimono." Damn, Grant had thought, he still wanted to hit something. It had been as if some invisible force was conspiring against him, when all he wanted was to get as far away from Brooke Johnson as he could.

But there he had been, thirty feet from the woman who'd turned him into a raving lunatic. He hadn't made a lot of sense to Will. He hadn't known who the man was.

"She doesn't entertain a lot at home," Will had said. "Occasionally, Marianne comes by or one of Kari's friend's parents, but for the most part it's Brooke and Kari. I wonder who he could have been?"

"I have no idea," Grant had said. "She called him Jacob."

"Jacob." Will had repeated the name.

"Do you know him?" Grant had asked.

"No," he had shook his head. "Friday afternoon, when she left for the wedding, there was a strange car in the driveway. She said she had a ride to the airport. I thought one of the waiters was taking her. The same car returned earlier tonight but left after a short time."

Grant had poured himself another drink and immediately had swallowed it. He had snapped the glass onto the bar with an angry thud. As the night wore on, Will had gone to bed. Grant drank until he passed out. He couldn't remember what he'd said to Will or what Will had said to him when something had woken him. He had been in a chair in Will's den. His mouth had felt like cotton, and his head had been about to explode. A clock had ticked on the wall. It had been four o'clock. He had known sleep would not come again. Even the vast amount of alcohol he'd consumed wouldn't have dulled his senses enough for him to sleep.

He had gone to the kitchen for coffee. That was when he had seen the man leaving Brooke's. He had been tall, at least six feet, with dark hair. His face had been averted, and Grant couldn't have seen it, but he had moved with an assurance that made Grant sneer. Anger had rifled through him, and he had wanted to burst through the door and beat him to a pulp.

But he had remembered, Brooke had never said she loved him. He'd told her he was in love with her, but she'd never returned the sentiment. She was a beautiful woman. Why would he assume she spent her nights alone? There were probably many men in her life. Yet, Will said she rarely entertained at home. It didn't mean she didn't entertain elsewhere. Maybe this man was the exception.

Grant's head had been heavy, and the feeling around his heart had become more familiar each time he thought of Brooke and this man. He had watched him walk down the street. He didn't go to any of the parked cars but had disappeared around the corner. Who was he?

"Jacob! What are you doing here?" Marianne yanked the door open after finding him standing on her porch. His tie was gone, and his jacket was hooked on a finger over his back. "Do you know what time it is?" She finished tying the pink sash that held her robe closed.

The question seemed silly until Jacob glanced at his

watch. His face was pale as if he were fighting off an infection. Marianne knew what the infection was—Robyn. Something must have gone seriously wrong. He'd come to her house before, but this was the first time he'd ever shown up at four o'clock in the morning.

"Come in?" she invited. She stood back, giving him entry. Jacob walked past her. He slung his jacket on the seat of the high-back chair that graced her foyer and went into the living room, a determined pace to his steps. Marianne sighed. He looked like a lost little boy.

Usually, they met in the kitchen, keeping everything businesslike, but tonight was different. Jacob needed someone, a friend or maybe only a compassionate ear to listen. She wondered if he'd approached Robyn; told her how he felt, and she rebuffed him. Marianne knew Robyn would be kind, but Jacob might not see it that way. Grant was definitely a factor with which to contend, even though he may have to be told to keep his distance for the safety of his family.

Jacob paced the narrow room like a big cat. His hands were thrust deep in his pockets. She watched him for several moments. He didn't seem to remember she was there as he fought a private battle.

"Can I get you something to drink?" she asked, quietly. He turned at the sound of her voice. Jacob wasn't much for alcohol. Carrot juice was about as heavy as he got. He was a man who needed to be in control. Alcohol would dull the senses. As far as she could remember, she'd never seen him drink anything more than an occasional glass of wine. But, by the look of him, two fingers of straight bourbon was exactly what he needed.

"No," he said, dropping onto the dark green sofa. Marianne went to the kitchen anyway and popped two cups of milk in the microwave. She made some hot chocolate. It was more for her than him, but it would give him something to hold onto and possibly soothe the feelings that were so visible he seemed to wear them on his sleeve. Hot chocolate was one of her mother's remedies. Whenever she had a problem that made her silent and withdrawn, her mother would make two cups and sit down. Eventually, they'd begin to talk.

"Do you want to tell me about it?" she asked quietly, handing him the warm cup.

He shook his head, accepting it and looking at the marshmallows that garnished the top looking like miniature snowballs.

It was just like him, she thought as anger burned within her, to bury his feelings and never express them.

"What did you do tonight?" She wasn't sure he'd tell her. He paused for a long time, staring into the cup. Then, he took a drink and looked at the floating confection.

"I learned a very valuable lesson."

"What was that?" Marianne took a drink. The chocolate was delicious, but she had no taste for it tonight.

"I've learned in this life, there are only two ways to live, either you're a loner or you're on guard twenty-four hours a day."

"And you've resolved to live like that, never having friends or a family? Never having children of your own?"

Jacob stared at her as if the thought had never occurred to him.

"Don't you want to have children? You always ask about Kari. Do you know your voice changes then. There's a tender note in it that has nothing to do with your duty or her involvement in the program. Your eyes light up, and you smile."

His lips curved. "Kari's easy. I've loved her since the minute she was born. I was there, you know."

He had never told her that. "I didn't."

"I was Brooke's Lamaze coach. I saw Kari before she did." Jacob paused. "After her delivery, the doctor laid her in my arms. She was so pink and so tiny. I remember asking why she wasn't brown." Cradling an invisible baby, Jacob was quiet for a long time. "The nurse told me she'd eventually be the color that ringed her ears." Finally, he picked up the cup and drank some of the hot liquid.

Marianne knew the feeling. She had been a surrogate coach for one of the women at the embassy in Thailand on her first assignment. Her labor was premature, and her pains came too quickly to get her to a hospital. When she held the squirming little life in her arms, her heart was as full as an olympic-size pool.

"Don't you want to know that feeling again, with your own child?" she asked, immediately regretting the question as an image of herself and Jacob, clad in surgical green, holding their own child leaped into her mind.

Jacob did want to know that feeling, but not tonight. Tonight, he couldn't think about anything like that. Tonight, he was miserable.

"Marianne, I feel awful." There was a raw quality to the pain in his voice. "I don't know that I can forgive myself for what I did. Brooke certainly will hate me for the rest of my life."

"What did you do?" She refrained from leaving her seat and going to comfort him.

Quietly and without emotion, as if it had been drained from his body, he related the story of discovering Grant had left Washington and was on his way to see Robyn. He told her what he'd done in coming from her bedroom as if he were her lover. Laughter and horror warred within her—laughter that Jacob, with his stiff-as-a-board personality, would play such a role and horror that her friend had been so humiliated in front of the man she loved.

"I feel like a heel," he finished. "Like some rookie with no idea how to handle the situation. My choices weren't thought out or analyzed. They were—"

"Emotional," she finished for him.

The word was foreign to Jacob. Marianne could tell by the blank expression that took over his dark features. For too many years, he'd suppressed any and all feelings for people, living only for the job. She had been sure she was getting through to him on a different level. But whenever he could, he'd crawl back into his shell, and the world would pass by him like a battalion of retreating soldiers.

"How is she?" Marianne asked.

"I put Valium in her tea. She fell asleep immediately."

"Jacob, are you in love with her?" The question surprised Marianne. She hadn't intended to ask it. But it was out, and she couldn't take it back. She sat straight in her chair, her body poised for his answer, afraid of both yes and no.

Jacob didn't think he'd heard her right. Then, he remembered how well Marianne read him. No matter how often he refused to react to situations, she always could tell what he was thinking and feeling. He sat forward and looked her directly in the eye.

"I suppose that was very apparent."

"Only to me." She shook her head. "I'm sure most people don't know. I'd be surprised if Brooke knew, and she's very perceptive." Marianne had to force herself to breathe normally. The air in her lungs wanted to rush out as if they'd been punctured.

"I knew it was impossible," he told her. "I've always known, but I couldn't stop feeling the way I felt. As director of the program in which she is a participant, I couldn't possibly have any relationship with her."

Marianne stared at him as he studied his hands. It was true. A dagger stabbed into her heart. A white-hot heat tore through her, forcing her to clamp her teeth together to keep from screaming. She hung her head and placed the empty cup on the floor. Her fingers were shaking too much to hold it. Chocolate smears coating the sides looked like dirty snow. Jacob could have no relationship with a witness, just as she could have no relationship with him. Not because of Robyn or her love for him, but because of who he was and who she was. They both worked for the Witness Protection Program and had a certain fiduciary relationship to the participants. Any alliance between them was suspect. There was no written rule to keep them apart, but Clarence Christopher would frown on any attempt to exercise the practice.

Leaving her chair, she went to the sofa. She sat next to Jacob, their knees only inches apart. She took his hands. He looked at her, and she wanted to melt.

"I'm sorry," she whispered as if she was trying to soothe the wounds of a child. "Jacob, I'm your friend. I'll always be that." If she could have nothing else, she'd offer friendship.

"Thanks," he said, a twisted smile curving his lips.

She shivered slightly. He misinterpreted the action and pulled her toward him.

"You're cold," he said.

She wasn't, but to be in his arms was better than telling him the truth. Marianne let her head fall on his shoulder. "How did you come to work for the FBI?" she asked, no longer wanting to talk about Robyn or Jacob's love for her. She wanted to hold onto him just for the night, keep herself wrapped around him until the sun rose. For she knew in the light of the coming day, her life would change irrevocably.

"I was on the police force in Chicago. A case I was working went bad." She felt him stiffen and knew it was a subject he didn't speak of much, like so many of the subjects Jacob had buried. "Clarence asked me to join the government when I came off leave. It gave me a chance to change my life." There was a special relationship between Jacob and the director of the FBI. Marianne had even heard of it from some of the other agents with whom she'd trained. It was no secret. Jacob was envied but respected. He might have known Clarence Christopher, but he was solid in his performance.

Marianne snuggled against him. He slipped his arm around her shoulders. "Are you glad you went there?" She closed her eyes, imagining herself next to him on her bed upstairs.

Jacob hadn't thought of that before. Was he happy he'd gone to Washington after Cynthia died? Where would he be now if he hadn't taken the job? He wasn't used to thinking about what might have been. He only had time for what had happened to bring him to this point. And, usually, his mind was on someone else, never himself.

"I don't know," he finally answered. "I've never given it much thought." He yawned and slid down on the sofa. Marianne was practically lying across him, but she didn't move. She just kept her eyes closed.

"In Chicago," she said. "Before the FBI, there was a woman."

It was a statement. Jacob was used to Marianne knowing him. He even liked it that she did. "Cynthia," he didn't hesitate. He wanted her to know about Cynthia. "She died before I left."

"You were protecting her when she died."

It wasn't a question. Jacob didn't have to answer. He knew an answer was unnecessary. Marianne knew the truth. He slipped his fingers into her hair. His thumbs gently massaged her head. She stirred against him. Her hands passed over his legs and hugged his waist. And there she slept.

Jacob wasn't used to waking up next to anyone. His effort to turn over had brought him up against a soft, warm body. His eyes flew open, and in the draped-darkness of morning, he saw the wispy red curls rioting over her head. He smoothed them back, but they had a mind of their own. Marianne didn't move. He looked at her as she slept soundly.

He liked Marianne. She was an honest woman and a true friend. She'd never tell the things she knew about him, and with her, he could be open and honest. With her, there was no guard, no reason to hold his tongue or be careful of his words. He trusted her with his life.

Fifteen

Friday night, the restaurant was crowded. It had been this way for weeks, and Robyn was thankful for the work. She had been too busy to dwell on the night Jacob had come from her bedroom and Grant had jumped to the conclusion that she was sleeping with him. Of course, that was exactly what Jacob had intended.

She wanted to call, explain, tell him the truth, but each time she picked up the phone, she thought of Kari and of Jacob telling her how both their lives were still in danger. Would this ever end?

Sue-Ellen passed her with a timid smile. She was helping out at one of the receptions. There had been a wedding in the afternoon, and two receptions were presently underway. For the first time in weeks, both Robyn and Marianne were on hand. For several months, either she had been gone, off with Grant, she amended, or Marianne had been away on one of her mysterious weekends. Robyn assumed she was seeing a married man. She never mentioned the trips, and of late, her returns didn't warrant a new chocolate dessert. She was glad Marianne was happy. She even envied her. While Robyn was unable to go from one relationship to another, Marianne appeared to bounce back without the slightest damage to her ego. There must be a new man in her life.

"Now, that's the first genuine smile I've seen on your face in weeks." The subject of her thoughts whispered from a point behind her.

"Well, we certainly cannot say the same of you." Robyn tempered her sarcasm with a broad grin. Marianne blushed. "Tell the cook I need some Alaskan crab legs and a two-pound lobster." Before Marianne had time to question her, she turned her attention to the couple standing near the end of the bar. "Susan, David," Robyn called. She rushed to hug them as if they were long lost friends she hadn't seen in years, instead of the three weeks since their wedding. "I'm so glad you came by. You look wonderful."

"So do you," Susan said. "Has Grant ever seen you in that outfit?"

Robyn's face fell slightly. She wore a black lace dress with a high bustle. "No," she answered quietly. "Why don't we sit over here." Robyn ordered a bottle of champagne, then led them to a table next to one of the windows.

"We didn't know the restaurant had a theme." David covered Susan's comment when they were seated.

"I think people like it," Robyn smiled, swallowing her pride. "They can look at it as a trip back in time or as a Halloween party. But to tell you the truth," she leaned closer, "I just love getting dressed up. In any case it seems to work."

"It's beautiful." Susan looked at the mirrors and photographs of the 1920s flappers above her head.

"I'll give you a tour before you leave," Robyn offered.

"I'd like that," David said.

The waiter arrived with the champagne. He went through the ritual of showing her the label with a flare of ceremony that made Yesterdays stand out from other establishments. Then, he poured the pale sparkling liquid into the three fluted champagne glasses and left the bottle in a stand next to the table. David lifted his glass and toasted the two women.

"You will be staying for dinner?" Robyn asked. Their presence had lifted her sagging spirits. And, if only she'd admit it to herself, she was starved for news of Grant. Spending the evening with them would be like getting a little of her old life back. And this wasn't breaking the rules. She had invited them before she'd promised Jacob anything.

"And the show," David said.

"We're not going back until tomorrow," Susan volunteered.

"You'll be my guests." Robyn lifted her glass and sipped the wine. "Anything special you'd like for dinner? I'll have the chef make it."

Both of them shook their heads. "We plan to order straight from the menu." Susan took David's arm and smiled at him. It was obvious these two were in love. Robyn had never seen her friend look so soft or David look so protective. They were still on their honeymoon. All the signs of being newlyweds were there. Robyn had seen a lot of newly married couples. In her garden, weddings were performed every weekend during the summer.

"How's Kari?" Susan asked. "We only got to see a little of her at the wedding. But she's a sweet little girl."

"She's fine." Robyn beamed. "She's home with her grandfather."

"She's certainly taken with Grant," David said.

"And he with her," Susan added.

Robyn dropped her eyes to her empty glass. She knew how much Kari liked Grant. She'd mentioned him several times in the past three weeks. But Robyn couldn't explain to a four-year-old that some relationships weren't always for the best. She told Kari that Grant was very busy and he couldn't come and see them.

"More champagne," David lifted the bottle and re-filled their glasses.

"It was a lovely wedding," Robyn said moving the subject away from Grant.

"I'm sorry you had to leave before we had a chance to talk," Susan said.

"It was a big weekend here," Robyn provided an excuse. "We have weddings booked, and with the restaurant, both of us really need to be here." Robyn hoped they bought the story. She'd fallen back on the restaurant so often. Either Marianne or Robyn could run it alone if they had to. With the staff they had now, most problems were solved before they became a crisis.

"It is very busy," David looked at the number of people in the bar. It was crowded and the dining room was fully booked for the evening. Robyn was proud of the work she and Marianne had put into the business.

"How is the jewelry business? I'm told your designs are beautiful." She sidestepped mentioning Grant's name.

"Yes, it's how I spend the better part of the day." Susan looked pleased. "David is good with the public, but I like the background work."

"Well, women do like a good looking man telling them they look great in expensive stones." Robyn smiled at the man next to her best friend.

"You two talk about the store. I need to find a phone," David said.

"You can use my office." Robyn stopped one of the waiters and directed him to take David to her office. She looked after the man who slid his hand along his wife's neck before leaving the table. Turning back, she said, "You really look happy, Susan. I'm so glad for you."

"Thank you. I love David more than anyone else in the world."

"So tell me about the store. I want to know everything."

"I don't want to talk about the store. Tell me what happened," Susan began without preamble. "After the engagement party, Grant was frantic when you disappeared. Where did you go?"

"I came home. It was important that I get back."

"I know we haven't known each other long, but we agreed to be friends, I can tell you're not telling the whole truth."

Robyn's head snapped up.

"I promise not to tell David or Grant anything you say," she continued. "Speak freely. Did you two have a fight?"

"No."

"Then what happened? At the party, you two couldn't keep your eyes off each other. Then, suddenly, Grant wouldn't even mention your name. And everytime we mention his, you cringe. Now, he's off flying until he is too exhausted to do anything but sleep."

"Susan, he isn't doing anything dangerous, is he?"

"Grant knows the rules. He won't endanger himself or any passengers."

Robyn released the breath she'd held.

"You *are* in love with him. Don't deny it," Susan said when Robyn opened her mouth to protest.

"Yes, I'm in love with him," she admitted.

"Then what's standing in your way?"

"It's not that easy, Susan. There are things he doesn't know about me. Things I can't explain. Believe me, it's best if Grant and I don't see each other again."

"Brooke, there are few things in this world two people can't settle if they talk about it."

"Not this." Robyn was shaking her head. "It happened a long time ago."

"Nobody expects you to be a saint. Believe me Grant's not a saint either."

"It's not that. I can't go into it. Just leave it."

Susan sipped her champagne. "I don't believe you for a moment. I've never seen Grant so happy as he has been in the past few months. Then suddenly you two won't even say each other's name."

"Susan, drop it!" Susan's head came up abruptly.

"I'm sorry. I didn't mean it, but please let's talk about something else. Tell me about the store?"

"We have two of them . . ." Susan began talking after a long silence, and although Robyn was interested, she couldn't keep her mind on what her friend was saying. Grant couldn't say her name, and she'd tried desperately to forget she'd ever seen him. But it was impossible. He was always in her thoughts.

"Well, it's all arranged," David said, slipping back into his seat.

"What's arranged?" Robyn asked.

"We'll stay at the Sheraton downtown and tomorrow visit Niagara Falls, then fly home tomorrow night."

"You can just flat out cancel the hotel," Robyn ordered. "You'll stay at my house. I have a guest room that's dying for visitors."

"But—"

"No buts," Robyn cut David off. "I won't go to Niagara Falls. It's good for honeymooners, but I'll see you get to the airport tomorrow night."

"That won't be—"

"That's a wonderful idea," Susan cut in.

Robyn lifted her champagne glass and toasted the couple. She sipped the dry wine. Her eyes went down when she lifted the glass to her mouth. Otherwise, she'd have seen the looked that passed between her best friend and her new husband.

The day was unusually warm for the second week in September. Usually, the sky was overcast. The days began to get gray in anticipation of the harsh Buffalo winter. But this Saturday morning had dawned like a beautiful summer day, clear and warm.

Robyn and Kari had a wonderful breakfast of strawberry crepes and sausages with Susan and David. Will surprised them by coming in for coffee. Then, he and Kari joined the newlyweds for their trip to the falls.

Robyn was enjoying a brief rest in the late afternoon sun on her patio. Susan and David were due back by six. Their flight was scheduled to leave at eight, and Robyn wanted to take them to the airport.

That must be them now, she thought, hearing sounds inside the house. "I'm out here," Robyn called. Seconds passed, and Kari didn't come to find her. No one came out. "Kari," she called, standing up.

Suddenly, her hand went to her throat. She recognized the flight jacket and cap immediately. Grant stepped from the darkened kitchen to the sunlight of the patio. Her knees went weak, and her heart beat so loudly it drowned out all other sound. She caught hold of the back of the patio chair to support herself.

"What are you doing here?" she whispered.

He looked her up and down. She was wearing shorts and a T-shirt, but under Grant's gaze she felt naked.

"I went to the Sheraton. There was a message saying David and Susan were at this address, and the phone has been conveniently—busy," he spat the word.

"What?" Robyn hadn't been on the phone since she'd come in from the rehearsal. In fact, the phone hadn't rung either. She found the strength to move. Going into the kitchen, she lifted the receiver of the wall phone. Silence greeted her. The line was dead. The kind of dead you hear when a phone has been off the hook for a long time. It had passed the point where the recorded messages cease, and the high-pitched whine was long gone.

"There's a phone off the hook somewhere," she explained, replacing the receiver. "Excuse me." Going through the living room, she went upstairs. In the guest room, the phone was only slightly ajar as if it had not been properly replaced. She touched it slightly, and it fell into the cradle. A second later, she lifted it and was greeted with a dial tone.

Robyn replaced the receiver. For a moment, she wondered if Susan had done it on purpose, then rejected the idea. Suddenly, she remembered the way her friend had cut off David when he started to say something about going to the airport. He must have called Grant and said they were flying home with him.

She found Grant still in the kitchen when she came down the stairs. "Are you here to fly Susan and David back?"

Grant turned from the patio door to face her. The light silhouetted him. "David called me last night."

"They went to Niagara Falls. I expect them any moment now. David put their luggage by the front door." She sounded extremely polite as if the man standing a few feet away was not the man she'd spent a lifetime loving.

"I'll wait outside," he turned away as if he couldn't bear the sight of her.

"Would you like a drink?"

"I'm flying."

"Iced tea, orange juice, cola."

"Iced tea will be fine," he said and went through the door. Robyn's movements were stilted, and her thoughts were numb. She took down a glass and filled it with ice. Then, she poured tea into it from the pitcher in the refrigerator.

Outside, Grant sat on the edge of a lawn chair. When she handed him the glass, their fingers touched. She felt the electricity and snatched her hand back so fast she nearly dropped the glass. Grant placed it on the small table next to him.

Robyn walked to the other side of the patio. "Would it matter if I said I was sorry."

"No!" The monosyllable exploded in the still air like an electric bulb bursting. He was on his feet, his back to her.

She came up behind him, wanting to reach out and touch him, but was afraid. A wall of granite separated her from him. "I am sorry, Grant."

"Who was he?" He turned on her. His hands grabbed her upper arms like steel shackles. "After the night we spent together and me finding you'd just disappeared. All you have to say is you're sorry?"

"I can't explain, Grant." She swallowed tears, wanting to cry but refusing to give in. He dropped his hands and presented her with his back again.

"I do want you to understand."

"Then, tell me." He swung around glaring at her. Robyn dropped her head like a four-year-old. "Make me understand how you could spend the night in my arms, making me feel like I was the only man in the world and then leave without a word."

"Oh, God, don't, Grant. I had to leave." She looked at him, spreading her hands, pleading for understanding.

"Why? What was so hellfire important here that you couldn't wait for me to bring you home?"

"Grant, please. I had no control of the . . ." she stopped.

"Go on. Who had control? The man at the top of the stairs in the black kimono?"

Robyn winced. "It happened a long time ago."

"What, Brooke. What happened a long time ago."

Robyn turned away. "I can't tell you."

"Can't? Or didn't you think of a good enough excuse yet? You've had weeks to do it."

"Please, Grant." She turned away from his dark anger. "Just trust me."

He took her arms and swung her around to face him. "Trust you, trust *you!*"

"Grant, I love you." Robyn felt the tremor run through his body. Then everything went still. "I love you," she repeated.

Grant's eyes bore into hers. There was fear there. She was afraid he wouldn't believe her. In his eyes was anger warring with some other emotion. His hands had tightened on her arms, and she felt like crying out but couldn't.

Then his mouth was on hers, and he was crushing her to him. "Why did you have to say that?" he asked against her lips. "Why do you have to be so beautiful?" His hands threaded through her hair as his mouth rained kisses over every peak and valley of her face. When his mouth came back to hers, it was druglike in its intensity. He plundered her mouth, his tongue dipping deeply into her vessel and extracting all the passionate emotion she had to give. He held her to himself, controlling the movement of her head, refusing to allow her to break contact even if she wanted to.

Robyn didn't want to stop. She wound her arms inside his jacket and around his waist, pulling his body into closer contact with hers. The shudder that quaked her body was both violent and explosive. At last, they collapsed against each other, each supporting the other. Robyn's legs were so weak she was sure she couldn't remain standing if he moved.

Grant clung to her, holding her tightly against him. Breath came in ragged gasps. Robyn's body was damp, and she could feel the moisture through the material of Grant's shirt.

"Grant," she said after a long while. "You have to go."

He was motionless for a long moment. Then, he pushed her away from him. His eyes were depths of deep hurt. Robyn didn't think she would be able to go on. She moved away from him, giving herself room to speak. She wanted to turn away so as not to have to look into the hurt that she knew her words would produce. But she kept her gaze steady. He must believe her.

"I can't tell you the whole truth. But please trust me when I say, lives are at stake. If you don't leave and never come back, it could be dangerous for me and Kari."

"Damn, Brooke." He took a step toward her and

stopped. "You can't make a statement like that and stop. What the hell is going on here?"

"Grant, I can't tell you." She turned away. "I should never have given Doctor Elliott your name." She turned back. "Please, *please,*" she begged. "Leave us alone.

"How can you ask such a thing? You've just said you love me, and I love you."

"It isn't enough," she cried. "Grant, it happened five years ago. I can't tell you anything more. Just that your continued presence could cause people to find me whom I don't want to know I'm alive."

He came to her, taking her shoulders. Robyn stepped away, swinging around to face him. His touch was like a fire in her blood. It would be her undoing if she let him get close to her. "Are you in some kind of trouble?"

"Yes, the worst kind. And I've said more than I should. I know it's intriguing, and I know you want me to tell you everything, but I can't. It's too dangerous. All I ask is that you not come back."

Robyn heard a car door close. "Will must be back. Promise me you won't come back?"

"No!" His hand came out to grab her arm. Robyn moved away.

"You have to." Her voice was a whisper as if her guests were standing nearby. "Susan and David will be here in a moment. This is no joke, Grant. Don't come back!"

Robyn left him then. She went into the living room and through it to the foyer. When Susan and David came in with Will and Kari, she was composed enough to greet them as if nothing had happened. They talked for a brief while, promising to visit each other again and extracting a promise from Robyn to visit whenever she was in Washington. Grant joined them but remained quiet. Robyn almost fizzed under the stare he gave her. He lifted Kari into his arms and nuzzled her close. She laughed her usual high-pitched sound, and clasped her arms tightly around his neck when he held her.

When he set her on the floor, Grant took one of the suitcases sitting in the foyer and started for the car. David followed him.

Everyone hugged each other good-bye. Robyn had an excuse for the tears that curved down her cheeks. Robyn held Kari's hand as she waved good-bye. Grant reversed out of the driveway without a backward glance.

Will left shortly afterward, and Kari and Robyn went into the house. Kari happily chatted away about her day at Niagara Falls. She told Robyn about playing in the arcade and how she had beaten everybody on the Video Monster machine. After a long tirade, Kari said she was thirsty. Robyn went to the kitchen to get her a drink. On the counter, she noticed the empty glass of tea she'd given Grant. The ice had melted, leaving an amber liquid graduated in intensity at the bottom of the glass. Next to it was a piece of paper.

Robyn went to the counter and lifted it. The paper fell from her fingers as if it were fire. It floated to the floor, crossing the fine line that kept the present and past separated. At her feet was the recipe for apple spiced iced tea:

2 Regular Tea Bags
1 Apple Spiced Tea Bag
Pinch of Baking Soda
Sugar
Pitcher of Cold Water

Drop tea bags in boiling water. Boil for three minutes. Add pinch of baking soda (as much as can be held between two fingers) and remove from heat. Pour hot liquid into pitcher of cold water. Sugar to taste. Serve over ice cubes. Makes 1/2 Gallon.

He knows.

Sixteen

Grant's office was a tiny cubbyhole at the back of a private terminal at National Airport. As the air service had grown, he'd remained walled up in the small room with only a dinky window looking out over the planes. He never seemed to catch up on the paperwork. Adam Carpenter had urged him to hire an office manager. He was right. They needed someone to keep the records in order. Grant had time. For the past ten days, he'd had nothing but time.

He leaned his elbows on the desk and rested his head on the steeple of his hands. Ten days he thought, ten miserable days without Brooke. Since he'd flown away from her, he was still as confused. Was she or wasn't she? But how could she be? Robyn was dead. All he wanted was to be as far away from Brooke Johnson as was humanly possible. Yet, there were so many similarities. Beginning with the hair color and the eyes and the photographs of Kari. It was Robyn's style. She flew his plane with the same sureness he'd taught Robyn. She knew the fair winds signal and the song. His and Robyn's song had brought tears to Brooke's eyes. But the worst had been the times when they'd made love. The sounds were Robyn's sounds.

Then the crowning blow—the tea, apple spiced tea. It wasn't unusual for people to drink it hot, but not iced! It was a recipe only Robyn had been able to duplicate. David and Susan had both tried making it. Even he had tried, but Robyn's tasted best. She had a patent on the formula. Just ten days ago when she'd left him alone on the patio and he'd lifted the innocent glass to his lips, he'd sampled that patent. It was all the damning evidence he needed.

He had been too angry to talk. David and Susan must have thought his rage was directed toward them for tricking him into coming to Brooke's house. As it was, he was too confused to speak. What could he say. *I just drank a glass of iced tea Robyn made.* Surely, they would think he'd lost his mind. And he wasn't sure he didn't agree with them.

They couldn't be the same. Why would Robyn leave him? How could her features be so drastically changed? And why? And, then, there was Kari. She had Brooke's hair color, but her other features were nothing like her mother's. If Brooke was Robyn then Kari was his daughter. She'd be the right age. He compared the happy child's features to Robyn's as if he held two photographs. He couldn't see her in Kari. But that was a minor point. Adults bear only a resemblance to themselves as children. There were too many unknowns, too much circumstance.

Brooke had told him life and death were related to their continued association. What was going on? All he knew was that she was scared. He could see that in her eyes. They had a fear he'd never seen before and one he couldn't erase no matter how much he tried.

Could she be alive? He doubted the truth as he knew it. David had told him the body was too badly burned for viewing. He wanted to spare Grant the ordeal of seeing the charred remains of the woman who had filled his life and whom he had lived for during the long months of his captivity. She'd been identified by dental charts. But he'd never seen her. Could they have made a mistake? His head snapped up as if a puppeteer had pulled his strings. A metal shelf holding books and an odd assortment of fighter plane replicas stood directly in front of him. He didn't see it. His mind was somewhere in the past.

If there had been a mistake, and Robyn was alive, why hadn't she called him? She'd told him his seeing her could put her and Kari in danger. What kind of danger? Who was after her and why?

He had to go back. He had to find out if Brooke Johnson and Robyn Richards were in fact the same woman. He stood quickly, galvanized for action. He came around the desk and pushed his arms into his jacket. Reaching for the door, his hand poised in air. What if she was?

"Who the hell are you?" Grant snarled, upon seeing a strange man step into the cabin of his aircraft. He was a man of action, and he'd made a decision to see Brooke again. The fates and his plane conspired against him. Maintenance was being done to the plane he needed. The others were scheduled, and Adam convinced him not to throw the schedule off unless the reason was paramount to the operation. Logic and Adam's expression penetrated his brain, and Grant agreed to wait for the mechanics to complete their work.

Several hours later, he got the final okay. Grant, who should have been able to calm himself during the wait, was as tightly wound as a spring and in no mood for a stowaway.

The man watching him hadn't answered his question. Reaching into his inside pocket, he took an identification folder out and dropped it on the wood-grain shelf separating two oversized seats. The leather pouch made a dull thud as it flopped onto the shelf. Grant stood in the front of the cabin near the door. He lifted the pouch and read the cards inside. Not tonight, he sighed, pushing his cap further back on his head. After everything else, he didn't need an impromptu inspection from the FBI.

"I already have security clearance for this aircraft and for flying government officials. I don't deal in drugs, contraband or illegal aliens. The FBI knows that, so why are you stowing out, away on my plane, Mr. . . . Winston?" he consulted the I.D.

"Jacob," he said from the bar where he'd begun, without permission, to mix drinks. *Jacob.* Grant froze. It was the last word he'd heard Brooke utter before he'd turned and slammed her door.

"I was there," Jacob confirmed Grant's unspoken suspicion. "My purpose was to get you out of her life." He finished mixing the drinks and offered one to Grant. "Scotch and water," he said. Grant made no

move to accept it. Jacob set the glass down and re-
trieved his I.D.

"I don't want a drink. I'm flying out of here in a
few minutes. What I want to know is why you're here
and how soon you'll be gone?"

Jacob picked up his own drink, a whiskey and soda,
no orange juice tonight. He needed courage for breaking the rules—even if it was Dutch. He took a seat
facing Grant, propped his ankle over his knee and
sipped the icy drink.

"I'm here to talk to you about your wife," he finally
answered.

Tension grabbed hold of Grant at the mention of
his Robyn. Grant took a seat. "What do you need to
know about my wife. She's dead. She died five years
ago in an accident. It's all in my records. And to tell
you the truth, I'm in no mood to talk tonight."

"She told you then?"

"She?" What was he talking about? Told him what?
Grant watched the FBI agent. Unease crept up his
spine. He didn't know why.

Jacob knew what he was doing was against policy.
It was a flagrant disregard for rules, and he lived by
rules. But he'd made this decision. "I'm not very good
at being gentle," he said. "So I guess I'm just going
to have to give it to you straight."

Grant sat forward in the chair—waiting.

"The woman you're flying off to see, Brooke
Johnson . . ." Jacob had a copy of Grant's flight plan.

"What does Brooke have to do with Robyn?" Grant
seized the question before Jacob could continue. His
hands were suddenly cold. He was going to confront

Brooke with the similarities between her and his wife, and now this man had connected them, too.

"Brooke is Robyn."

The statement was spoken quietly, but to Grant's ears, it was like cannon fire. He felt like he'd been punched in the stomach and then had an elephant sit on him. He couldn't catch his breath, and he was paralyzed in his seat.

"Robyn . . . is . . . alive?" His voice croaked as he asked the question.

Jacob took Grant's hand, pressing the cold glass against Grant's palm. "Yes," he paused. "The accident five years ago was staged."

Grant threw the drink down his throat and swallowed it. The cool liquid stung his mouth, then radiated warmth as it coursed through his chest and into his stomach. Its heat relieved some of the pressure. Yet, Grant couldn't concentrate. He put his hand up and stopped Jacob when he tried to speak again. Then, he had to get up. He needed to relieve the pressure that was threatening to suffocate him. Yet, he was unsure of the strength of his legs. It couldn't be true. He clutched his chest, taking long gulps of air as he stumbled to the bar for support. The confined space seemed devoid of air. Going to the door, he sucked the oxygen into his lungs, but it wasn't enough. His hands and feet were suddenly freezing. He knew what it meant to have cold fear. He paced back and forth in an attempt to focus on something that would make sense of what he'd just heard. But nothing came, and he found himself covering the same strip of carpet time and again.

Suddenly, rage consumed him. He'd been right. He wanted to throw something. Anger at the absent Robyn filled him. His body seemed to coil and snap. Finding the glass still in his hand, he threw it at the bulkhead. The exercise acted as a catalyst, and suddenly, he was throwing everything that wasn't bolted down. Glasses, dishes, coffeepots, pillows, blankets, magazines—all went flying at the sturdy walls of the airship. And there was an animalistic sound. The sound of a wounded creature howling. It was almost a death cry.

Exhaustion caused him to collapse onto a seat. Jacob moved to sit next to him. He placed another drink in Grant's hand. He drained it.

"How?" Grant finally asked. His face was a pale ashy color, and Jacob thought he was going to pass out, but after several moments, he began to focus on reality.

"Five years ago she was a material witness in a federal case. When the case was over, she went into the Witness Protection Program."

"Five years ago?" Grant's brain refused to register. He could remember nothing.

"Before you were married, Robyn Warren worked for the FBI. She worked in an area she called the Assassination Bureau."

"She worked there after we were married, too. She said she liked what she did, especially working with the computer." He began to calm, but feeling didn't immediately return. His body was numb.

"In the process, she uncovered a group called the Crime Network. We don't know where they were based. But they only dealt on the highest levels. Robyn identified a mob hitman whose photograph she had seen. All previous reports said he was dead. But she saw him, and through her research she uncovered the plot to kill a man called Anthony Gianelli."

"Gianelli, I remember the name." Grant thought for a moment.

"When you were released from Lebanon, his trial was just ending. He was sentenced on the day you returned to Washington. Media attention for the release of the ten hostages pushed him off the front page."

"What did Robyn have to do with Gianelli?"

"Gianelli sponsored a modern day massacre. The plot was to assassinate massive numbers of racketeers in major cities across the United States at the same time. She uncovered the plot and the Network in time to prevent them from carrying it out. As it happened, her research also led her into the highest levels of government. In capturing Gianelli, records were uncovered which put many of his connections behind bars including some high ranking members of the FBI. Gianelli was tried and convicted, and the organization was uncovered. Their leader was also convicted, and the Network disbanded."

"Then why would her life still be in danger?"

Jacob left his seat. He poured himself another drink. "Did she tell you that?"

"She told me nothing, except not to see her again. And that her life and Kari's life could depend on it."

"We know someone or some group is looking for her."

"But if this guy, Gianelli, was put in jail, and it was

his plot to massacre other families, why would anyone still be after Robyn?"

"It isn't the mob," Jacob said, returning to his seat. "It's the Crime Network."

"Didn't you say you disbanded the group?" Grant moved to the bar and made himself another drink, half of it disappearing in one gulp.

"We did what we could, but we knew her life would always be in danger. The number of departments she reached were many and varied. And there was always the possibility of parole or release. In the past five years, discreet inquiries have been made about Robyn Warren-Richards. Some references to Brooke Johnson have also been intercepted. But so far we haven't been able to find out who's doing it. But whoever he is, he knows the system."

"What does that mean?" He resumed his seat in front of Jacob.

"Everything is computerized these days. But the man accessing information can penetrate deeply into our files and those of some outside data banks. Robyn was one of the people who figured out how hackers were getting in to view sensitive data. Of course, the holes she found have been plugged, but a new one opens for every one we close."

"How are you controlling it?" Grant asked, taking a swallow of his drink.

"Robyn's file does not exist on any of the computers, but she does have a file. It's kept secured, accessible by very few individuals, and they must have top secret security clearance."

Grant was quiet for a long time. This man wasn't

here telling him this for no reason. He wanted something. "What do you want from me?"

"Five years ago, Robyn made the decision to go into the program alone. Now, you have to make a decision. In order for us to continue protecting her, she and Kari must continue living their lives as they have in the past."

"Kari!" Grant stood but supported himself against the seat back in front of him. "She's my daughter?" He asked the question slowly as if each word took all of his breath.

Jacob nodded.

Grant dropped his head onto his arms and took several deep breaths.

"Robyn found out she was pregnant after she went into protective custody," Jacob explained.

"Damn her, *damn* her!" Grant shouted, hitting the cushioned chair. "Why the hell didn't she tell me? How could she take my child away and never let me know she was alive?"

The sound of Jacob's glass crashing into the mirror over the bar snapped up Grant's head. "Damn you!" Jacob took a menacing step toward Grant. "Robyn Richards gave up her existence so nine men could go home to their families. Nine men, whom she didn't know, could resume normal lives. She gave them back to mothers and wives who loved them. They don't even know her name or that she played any part in their release. And she gave you the right to do the one thing you would die without—fly."

"What are you talking about?" Grant interjected when Jacob stopped for breath.

"The government pressured her into testifying by using you as a pawn. You were a prisoner in Lebanon. They knew that, and you know the policy concerning terrorists."

"The United States government does not negotiate with terrorists," Grant quoted the same policy Robyn had quoted years earlier when David had told her about Grant's plane.

"Robyn Richards loves you so much she went through pregnancy alone. Then, the trauma of a new face and new identity. She settled in a town where she had no friends. She had to be careful of her words, look over her shoulder, and watch for double meanings in every stranger's conversation. All of this she did for nine unknown men. And her husband, a man whose past had been so unhappy, except when he was flying, that she couldn't take his love for the sky away from him. And you want to damn her."

Grant stared at the man before him. His eyes widened in understanding. Jacob Winston was in love with his wife.

"Robyn's in love with you," Jacob said.

"Then, why did she go alone? Didn't she know I'd choose her over flying? Didn't she realize she meant more to me than any airplane?"

"She understood. She also knew about Project Eagle."

Grant stared at Jacob not moving. Jacob read his reaction. Grant had shut down his responses as any good agent would do.

"I didn't tell her." Grant was adamant.

Jacob ignored the comment. "She knew when she made the decision."

Grant knew what Robyn would have done given the facts of his part in Project Eagle. He'd flown away that day with the chip concealed in his uniform. He was to meet his contact in France. It was set up, and it was a friendly reunion. When it was over and he found out the full magnitude of the system he'd saved, it was overwhelming. If someone had told Robyn only a fraction of what he was doing, she would have made no other decision.

"She did it out of love," Jacob told him. "The kind you read about, where one person sacrifices everything for the other. Most love is never tested the way yours and Robyn's has been. I admire her greatly for what she did."

"So what happens now?"

"There are two choices open. You can join her in the program. We'd have to give you all new identities, including Kari."

"Kari's only four. She wouldn't understand what would be happening to her."

"I agree," Jacob nodded. "You'd have to move to a new town and begin again."

"Or?" Grant prompted.

"Or we could relocate Brooke and Kari." Jacob held back the fact that they may have to do that anyway. The net closing in on Robyn was getting tighter, and so far, he had few clues as to who was trying to find her.

"What about this person trying to find Robyn . . .

Brooke?" Grant was confused as to which name to use.

"There's always the chance something could alert him when the process takes place. But we'd take extra precautions."

"I see." Grant needed another drink. His capability to fly tonight was gone.

"Five years ago, Robyn had to make this decision alone, Grant. Now, it's your turn to decide whether you can go on living as you have since returning from Lebanon and let Robyn remain in her own life, or join her in the program."

"I either uproot her life or give up my wife and child." Grant dropped into the nearest seat. "It is a hell of a decision."

Jacob walked to the barstool opposite Grant. "It's the same decision she had to make."

"Let me think about this." Grant felt as if the world had fallen on him. He'd been in love twice in his life and with the same woman. Now, she was the last person on earth he had a right to see. For her own safety and that of his only child, he had to decide to live without them or have them make another change. What would this change do to Kari? Brooke had a business, a partner, a life she'd made for herself. He'd worked around the clock to get his service off the ground. She must have done the same. What would she think if he wanted her to give it all up and start over?

Seventeen

Grant woke up, reaching for Brooke. An agonizing groan had him grabbing his pillow and hurtling it across the room when he opened his eyes to find the other side of the bed empty. How was he going to survive this grieving? It was worse than when he thought she was dead. To know she was alive and he was barred from seeing her, holding her, making love to her, was a sadistic decision. He couldn't live like this.

Swinging his feet to the floor, Grant hung his head in his hands. It throbbed with a blinding intensity. The sheets were twisted and tangled as if he'd battled demons in his sleep. The headache had been with him for over a week, since the night Jacob Winston had invaded his airship and opened his eyes to the real danger he could cause his wife. *His wife.* He couldn't really believe Robyn was still alive. For five years, he'd lived without her, finally coming to terms with her death. Finding out she was alive was like opening a wound. And Kari. He had a daughter, a child he wouldn't be able to see grow up. A wife and a child, all he'd ever wanted.

Yet, Jacob had given him no choice. For their safety,

he had to leave them alone. Grant made his decision. He'd made several decisions, and each one was as quickly reversed as the first. Pushing himself up, he went to the bathroom. He swallowed two pain pills before turning on the shower. Cold water hit him, dousing the flames that the dreams of his wife brought and making him realize there was no place in her life for him and no place in his daughter's life for the father she didn't know she had.

Twenty minutes later, he was dressed and on his way to the airport. He was busier than he'd been in months. There was little time to think of Brooke or Kari during the day, but his nights were full of them.

"What have we got today, Adam?" he greeted the chief mechanic outside the hangar of Richards's Air Service. Grant's face sported a cheerful smile even if it was painted on.

"Emergency." Adam's clear face was set in austere lines. "I've been trying to reach you. You've got to get a beeper, Grant, or at least a car phone."

"What is it, Adam?" Grant cut off Adam's tirade on current technology.

"Frank's wife called. He's in the hospital—appendix."

"How is he?" Grant frowned.

"He'll be fine . . . but he won't be able to take his flight. I need you to deliver a group to the Niagara Falls Air Force Base."

Grant's eyebrows went up along with his pulse rate. Brooke's features surged into his memory. Niagara Falls was only a stone's throw from Buffalo. "Don't tell me the air force has run out of planes." Sarcasm edged his voice.

"Apparently, they have," Adam said. "This is a group of reporters following the president, who's decided to make a stop at the training facility in Niagara Falls."

"Isn't there anyone else who can make the run?" Grant didn't want the temptation of knowing he could turn around and find Brooke in his line of vision.

"I'm afraid not. It has to be someone with a high security clearance."

"What about Chuck?"

"Chuck's not due back until midnight."

Grant suddenly remembered Chuck was in Dallas at a training class.

"We've got contracts up to our kazoo and more coming in everyday," Adam reminded him. "Every pilot we have is busy. I don't know what's happening, but at this rate we're going to have to begin turning business away." Adam smiled at that. Grant returned it with genuine affection. He remembered when they'd joked about being so busy they could be discriminating about their contracts.

Adam had been with him since they both had left Trans-Global. He was the best mechanic Grant had ever seen, and he believed in the air service enough to work as hard as its owner to make it a success. Adam had no official title. He did everything and anything that needed doing.

"I guess it's you, buddy." He punched Grant's shoulder with a soft fist.

"I'll have to wait for them." The unconscious thought was spoken aloud.

"Yeah," Adam said. "They're due back tomorrow night. Frank had a reservation at the Hilton. Do you want me to change it?"

"No," Grant said. Adam knew about Grant's frequent flights to Buffalo. "I'll take care of it."

"Okay, buddy." His face went back to the chiseled mask.

Adam left him then. Grant knew his mechanic thought he wanted to spend his time closer to Brooke. He'd told him about her. Hell, he'd told everybody. He was so in love, thinking himself so lucky to find love twice only to have it ripped away like a severed arm. He hadn't imagined he'd have to forget ever seeing her again.

Grant stared across the field. Planes taxied in the distance. Waves of heat radiated from the outlying tarmac. The wind caught his hair. A fair wind, one that would be perfect for flying anywhere, except north by northwest.

"Hey, Grant," Adam called from the door. "I've filed your flight plan." He handed him the folded piece of paper. "The weather's a jewel today. You should have no trouble."

"Thanks." Grant took the papers, his mind four-hundred miles away. "When can I expect them?"

Adam consulted his watch. "You've got enough time for coffee."

As if on cue, a bus arrived with twenty men and women in various degrees of business and casual dress. They were loaded down with camera cases, suit-

cases, and garment bags. Several of them carried tri-
pods over their shoulders. A vision of Robyn with her
camera and tripod invaded his memory.

Adam and several men came out to take the luggage
and stow it in the cargo hold. Grant went inside his
office to get his flight bag. It was always packed and
ready for a quick takeoff.

He disappeared into the plane and began the pre-
flight checks. Jerry Asgarth, copilot, took the seat next
to him after he'd made the final cabin count and closed
and locked the outer door. Grant radioed the tower,
and in minutes, they were airborne.

Fifty minutes later, he was on the ground. His grateful passengers smiled as they alighted into the sun of
a crisp autumn morning. He toyed with the idea of
flying back to Washington and returning in time to
pick up his passengers tomorrow. The plane had to be
refueled and checked before it would be ready to fly
back. This would leave him with something he didn't
want or need—time to kill. Unoccupied space in
which to think of a dark-haired woman with lithe steps
and a graceful body that fit his like a fine wine making a meal perfect.

Grant set off walking. He had no particular destination in mind when he started but found himself in
the main terminal building facing a row of telephones.
One was occupied by a uniformed airmen who hung
up and left before Grant completed his internal struggle. He had no memory of lifting the receiver or dialing the restaurant, but suddenly Brooke's voice was
in his ear and his courage deserted him.

"Brooke, this is Grant," he spoke over the lump in

his throat. There was silence at the other end. "Are you there?"

"I'm here," she said, a strain evident in her voice. He knew she was holding back tears.

"I want to see you."

"Grant—"

"I know we have to be careful. I remember everything you said. And I promise this is the last time." He only wanted to say good-bye, he told himself. Brooke didn't answer. He was afraid she'd refuse. "Brooke, will you meet me somewhere?"

"Where are you?" she asked at the end of a silence difficult for them both.

"Niagara Falls, the air force base."

She didn't answer immediately. Grant could almost see her biting her lower lip and tapping her right foot. It was the outward display of her struggle with logic and emotion.

"Stay there, I'll pick you up," she finally answered.

Grant let go of the breath he was holding. "Do you know where it is?" he asked.

"I'll find it," she said with an assurance that told him she'd walk through fire to get here.

"How long?"

"An hour."

Robyn had just changed for rehearsal. Quickly, she slipped out of the leotard and back into her purple suede suit. She didn't want her last time with Grant to be in exercise clothes. Donning the matching coat, she set out to find him. Her feet nearly flew to the car, and within minutes, she was turning onto the New York State Thruway en route to Niagara Falls.

Grant walked to the main entrance and paced like an expectant father. Unsure from which direction she'd arrive, his head swiveled left and right as if he were watching a tennis match.

Robyn parked next to the grassy curb when she saw him. Getting out of the car, she stopped as he faced her. Without realizing it, she was flying toward him, her heels clicking against the asphalt, as she rushed into his arms.

"God! I missed you," Robyn breathed onto his neck. Tears gathered in her eyes.

"I missed you, too." Grant's arms were tight around her. He brought them up to her head and pushed it back far enough to fuse his mouth to hers. Robyn kissed him hard and long, giving herself up to the passion she felt. Ignoring the guards in the small station behind them and the wind pulling at their clothes, they continued in their enjoyment of each other until both of them needed breath.

"We'd better go," he whispered.

"Come on." Slipping his arm around her waist, he guided her to the illegally parked BMW. She slid into the warm interior, and he joined her. He slipped his arm around her neck for one more kiss before fastening his seat belt.

"Where are we going?" Grant asked when they turned away from the base road.

"Fort Niagara. It's a tourist attraction. In the summer, there are hordes of visitors, but after Labor Day the crowds thin considerably."

Grant sat in silence for the remainder of the ride. A shy smile creased the dimple in his right cheek. She didn't know. Jacob Winston hadn't told her, and he trusted him to keep her ignorant of his knowledge. He was satisfied just looking at her, knowing she was his wife. He could see the mannerisms that separately told him nothing, but the combination made her the woman he remembered.

Robyn took the curves with an assurance she didn't feel. Her insides were shaking as she passed the exit that led to the famous landmark and headed for the unpaved road through the woods. Grant had glanced at her but remained quiet. Even when she came to a halt in front of a log cabin and cut the engine, he made no comment. Opening his door, he came around the hood and opened hers.

"Thanks," he said as he took her hand, assisting her to her feet. "I only have until tomorrow. I didn't want my last hours with you to be in a room full of strangers."

Robyn blamed the tears that gathered in her eyes on the wind from the distant bay. Grant leaned forward and kissed her eyes, first one, then the other. The tenderness in his touch made a lump lodge in her throat. She resisted the sob that fought for life. Standing against the open car door, he continued his tender assault on her cheeks and finally her mouth. She leaned into him deepening the kiss until she was drugged with need of him.

"Let's go in," she said, a hoarseness lowering her voice by several notes.

Grant got his flight bag and followed her. The small cabin had two rooms downstairs, a general purpose living area and a kitchen. There was a loft and bathroom upstairs. The fireplace was lighted, bathing the room in warmth. The smell of coffee filled the air.

"How did you do this?" Grant asked, a surprised look on his face.

"Car phone," she smiled and closed the door. "Would you like some coffee? Something to eat?" Robyn didn't wait for an answer. She shed her coat and went to the efficiency kitchenette. When two cups were ready, she handed one to him. He took them both and placed them side by side on the counter.

His arms went around her waist, and he pulled her against him. Her hair smelled so good as he buried his face in the silky mass. "I tried not to call." Agony edged his whispered pledge. "I know it's not good for you or Kari . . ."

"Don't," Robyn told him. Her hands rubbed his back. "Don't worry. We're going to be fine."

He squeezed her tighter to him. She was the strongest woman he'd ever known. She'd survived for five years with the knowledge that he was alive, while he'd been safely protected behind the ignorance of her death. He could mourn and recover. She had to rely on her will to keep herself sane. Grant wasn't sure he was strong enough to handle the same kind of separation.

Robyn pushed herself back. Her eyes were dark and deep with love. He looked into them. They had less than twenty-four hours. He wanted to ask her a thousand questions, he wanted to find out everything old and everything new about her. Yet, there wasn't enough time. In a lifetime, there would be too little time for everything he wanted to know.

Slowly, he bent his head and kissed her. Her mouth was warm, her lips pliant. He tested them, teased, tugged at her lower lip, brushed his lips across hers. "I need you," he muttered against her mouth. "I'll die without you."

His mouth took her then, fully. Five years of longing and wanting poured through him as his tongue met and tangled with hers. He groaned at the whimpers she made, fitting her to him, carving her into his frame until not a sliver of air separated them. His tongue filled her mouth, and she strained toward him, giving and receiving in kind.

His hands were like bands around her, caressing her back and straying downward from the silk of her blouse to the resistance of her suede skirt. Robyn felt his arousal hot against the apex of her legs. She moved against him in an erotic maneuver. Grant joined her in the mating dance as his mouth continued to battle with hers.

When they had to separate for air, his passion-filled eyes bore into hers. Her feet left the floor as he lifted her. His mouth melded with hers as strong arms cradled her. Her fingers ran into the softness of his hair. She'd missed that hair, missed running her fingers through it, feeling its softness, and the smell of his shampoo.

Grant turned with her, carrying her to the narrow stairway that led to the loft. He stood her on her feet in the bright light flowing from the small window. His hands went to the buttons on her blouse. Robyn looked at them as they released the closure one crusading link at a time. When the last one slipped through his fingers, he eased the fabric off her shoulders. The garment fell to the floor. Grant bent, caressing her uncovered shoulders with his mouth. Her head went back, and her eyes closed as thrills rippled through her. His sienna-colored skin merged with the yellow-rose of hers, creating a glow as perfect as the sunrise.

Familiar fingers released the zipper on her skirt, and with the same silence, it joined the blouse at her feet. Robyn pushed Grant's jacket back, his arms releasing her for the moment it took to let it fall. She pressed her lips to the buttons of his shirt before slipping them through the tiny holes. Little by little, she exposed his skin, a study in dark chocolate. The belt bisecting him was freed, and soon, they were naked to each other.

Grant didn't immediately take her to bed, but let his eyes devour the shape of her breasts, the gentle sloping of her waist, and the crest of her hips as they extended into long legs. His hands traced her, pausing to revel in her reaction. It was a memory he would have to live with from this day forward. She was nearly the same. Her breasts were fuller. Kari accounted for that. Her waist and hips were the same curvaceous crescent moons he remembered.

Robyn felt no embarrassment in his open appraisal. It gave her time to feast on him, recall and refresh her memory of how he looked in the morning, how the sun played across his chest and tinged his hair-dusted legs with a reddish highlight. Robyn placed her palms over his flat nipples and stepped closer to him. Five years of sleepless nights spent longing for this moment were reflected in the eyes she lifted to him.

Grant took her waist, a span so slim he could circle it with his hands.

His mouth touched hers, then quickly gorged it, exhausting himself in the satisfaction of holding her close. Any thoughts of taking this slow fled when her naked form welded to him. Heat generated as the electrical impulses in their blood synthesized into a lethal combination. Explosion was imminent, and Grant knew it.

He walked her backward to the bed and joined her there. The mattress was feather soft when Robyn's back made contact with it. It folded around the two lovers, pushing them close to each other, acting like the bread of a sandwich as it wrapped around them.

Grant slid over her, kissing her neck and working his way up the column to her ear. He paused for a heartbeat then his tongue traced the curved arc. Under him, she whimpered as spasms of sensation rocked her. With slow deliberation, he sponged the area purposely avoiding the inner cavity until her arms about him raked down his back. His own body was pained, but he forced himself to work slowly. She was driving him, forcing him to end the torture to them both, but somewhere in the recesses of his mind, he knew they needed this torment.

Robyn didn't know how much more she could take. Grant was hot and hard against her, and she longed for him to end this agony, but he appeared to want it prolonged. He was giving, and she wanted to take, take it now, end the pain in a quick burst, but she remembered this was to be the last time. Pulling herself up, she pushed him back and took position over him. Her hair fell in panels over his face. He smoothed it back, tugging slowly on her head as he brought her mouth down to his. Robyn's mind swam. Grant's hands caressed the curve of her back, and he used his palms to make carnal circles on her buttocks. Her body gripped, and she was tempted to plunge herself over his erection. She kissed his chest, stopping briefly to circle each of his flat nipples until they extended in hard pebbly peaks. Low guttural sounds came from his throat. They pushed her on until she came to his navel. His hands were buried in her hair. They squeezed unmercifully when her tongue dipped into the small spring. A well within him seemed to break, and he pulled her back to eye level.

Reversing positions, he spread her legs and entered her. The pleasure that rocketed through Robyn broke on a ragged gasp. She found his rhythm quickly and frantically complemented it as their hands, arms, and legs worked in tempestuous unison. Robyn held nothing back. Her love, her need of him, her belief in their past and future streamed from her like the dust of a shooting star. She loved this dark man, this man who had crossed time to find and love her. The exquisite pleasure of his touch drove her onward until she had to let the sound in her throat free. His name broke out on a bellowing ring.

Grant heard the wail and knew she was his. She was his like she would never be to another man. And he was hers. He wanted her forever but refused to think ahead of this moment. Brooke's body, clamped around his, drove all other thoughts from his mind except for the mounting hedonism that she evoked in him.

The end came in a blaze, like a star exploding in a fervor of expanding colors. Brooke writhed beneath him, her body alive with sensation as explosion after explosion rocked from one to the other. She squeezed him closer, trying to hold onto the moment a second longer. Grant swayed with her, giving, consuming, driven by instinct to go as far, as high as she wanted to go and beyond. With a wild cry, they collapsed in climactic resolution.

Breath came ragged and hard. Grant's chest rose and fell as he inhaled great gulps of air. He gathered Brooke's head in his hands. Her skin was moist, and her eyes were lazy with love. Tenderly, he kissed her, brushing his lips against hers. Then, he slipped off her, and together they slept.

This time when he awoke, she was there. He wasn't dreaming. Her hair was spread over the pillow contrasting darkly against the white sheets. Grant had never been one to believe in the metaphysical, but something had brought them together again, and he felt there was a solution to their problems. He had to find it. Leaving her and Kari was something he couldn't do. He knew that now, and he was willing to leave everything behind for her like a king abdicating his throne for the woman he loves. Grant's life would be worthless without her.

The last note ended, and the spotlight on Robyn went out. For a moment, there was silence, then the

312   Shirley Hailstock

house lights came up, bathing the stage in a glare of white light. Rehearsal was over. She grabbed her towel and left the stage.

"Aren't you suppose to be away this weekend?" Robyn asked Marianne when she followed her into the dressing room.

"I won't be going this weekend." The short redhead seemed down. Robyn, in her own misery, noticed identical traits in Marianne.

"Did something happen?" Robyn glanced over her shoulder at her friend. She knew Marianne looked forward to these frequent jaunts. She had no idea where her partner went, but she was always high on the adventure before she left. When she returned, depression overtook her. Only chocolate sundaes helped her get over the experience.

"No," Marianne said. "I'll go again soon, but not this weekend."

"Anything you want to talk about?" Robyn asked. Marianne's head swiveled around to stare at her. "Sorry, I didn't mean to pry."

"It's not that. You've never even mentioned my weekends before."

"I have noticed how affected you are by them," Robyn recalled. "But you've never pried into my personal life either."

"Of course, I have. Wasn't I the one who told you to stop grieving and get on with your life?" A sad smile curved her lips. Marianne remembered what Jacob had told her about sending Grant away. Since then, Robyn had begun to retreat into her former shell.

Robyn smiled. "You did it in the nicest way." Marianne returned the smile.

"And you avoided the questions in an equal fashion," Marianne told her.

"Well, I suppose we're a couple of strange ones."

"Not exactly," Marianne returned. "I should have known it would take a man to finally crack that hard exterior of yours."

Robyn returned her stare. "Not today, Marianne, I'm not in the mood." She didn't want to talk about Grant. Her fragile hold on her emotions would have her in tears if she thought about him. Since having left the log cabin and kissing him at the entrance to the air force base, she'd responded like a robot to everything. She went through the motions of living without letting it touch her. Any contact would shatter the fragile wall she'd erected to protect herself from the pain of his leaving.

"You're only in one mood lately," Marianne's voice called her back "And that's cranky."

"It's the weather. October always make me feel a little sad."

"The weather hasn't put those dark circles under your eyes. You forget, Brooke, I've known you too many years. We've gone through four Octobers together. This is the first one I've ever known you to be any different than the even tempered, confident woman who was eager to begin a catering business."

"Okay, it's Grant." Robyn flopped down on the sofa. She pulled the towel from her neck and kicked off her dancing shoes. Her head fell back, and her eyes closed. She should be getting dressed to go home and be with Kari for the afternoon, but she had no energy. "He's gone, Marianne." The words were spoken quietly.

Marianne didn't move. "Why?" she asked quietly. "I thought you were falling in love with him."

"I am in love with him, but there are things I can't explain. Not to him, not to anyone."

"I understand," Marianne said. "We all have secrets only our hearts can share."

Robyn opened her eyes. There was a resigned note in Marianne's voice. "I wouldn't think that about you. You share everything."

"Nobody shares everything." Marianne's stare was direct. "There are things about me you don't know. Some of them you might even hate me for."

"I could never hate you," Robyn told her, knowing there were things she could never speak of to anyone.

The redhead smiled brightly. "I hope not. You're closer to me than a sister. I don't want anything to happen to our friendship."

"And it never will," Robyn told her.

Robyn sat forward. Marianne had taken a seat at the lighted dressing table. With the turn of events in her own life, she wasn't aware that Marianne might be going through her own brand of misery.

"Do you want to talk about something?" Robyn asked.

"Why don't we do something radical?" Marianne ignored her question, abruptly changing the subject. "Why don't we redecorate the lounge or build that photo-chapel we talked about? We have enough money."

"Is that a project to take my mind off Grant or to take yours off . . . him?"

"A little of both. It always helps me," Marianne said.

Robyn knew that. Whomever the man was that Marianne met, he pitched her into depression when their weekends ended. Robyn assumed he was married. Her method of helping Marianne over the rough spots was to involve her in a project to fill her mind and keep her from thinking of him. It usually worked. Now, Marianne was trying to do the same for her.

"Maybe the chapel isn't a bad idea. If we could get it ready by spring, we'd have more weddings than we could handle."

"Good, why don't we get some paper and pencils and sketch out what it should look like? You're always so good at doing that," Marianne said, moving to the desk, pulling sheets of paper in front of her and clearing a spot to work. She began drawing and chatting. Robyn listened but didn't hear much of what she said. She thought of Susan and the wet Sunday afternoon when they sketched out Trifles. What a good friend Marianne was, and how fortunate Robyn was to have found her when she placed the tiny ad so many years ago.

The two women complemented each other. Marianne was good with sculpting vegetables and arranging cold cuts into works of art, while Robyn took to confections. Candy, cakes, and cookies could be anything from the simplest sweets to the most elaborate designs.

Robyn gave Marianne a steady stare. "Marianne,"

she called. Her friend paused, turning to face her. "The man you see—"

"Which one?" Marianne asked. She saw several men, but Robyn knew Marianne needed no additional prompting on which man she meant. He was the only one she was serious about.

"The one whose name you've never spoken. He comes infrequently, but when he does, he leaves you drained."

"What . . . what are you talking about," Marianne faltered.

"I've always known."

"But you never said anything. Never mentioned—" Marianne looked away.

"I know, but lately . . ." she paused. "It's your business. Yet, whenever you've seen him, you're not the same. Is he . . . married?" Robyn whispered the dreaded question.

Jacob married. Her mind went back to him on the night he'd come from Robyn's. He'd admitted it was Robyn he loved. The times he'd held her and kissed her, their hours together over dinner or strolling through the streets of the Capital, she'd only been a substitute for her best friend.

"He's married to his work." Marianne dropped her gaze to the rich pile of the cream colored carpet.

"Is there another woman?"

Marianne raised her head and stared directly at Robyn. "Yes," she whispered.

The look she leveled at Robyn was so penetrating, Robyn wondered if she knew the woman, but decided not to ask. "What about the other woman? Is she married?"

Marianne's head bobbed up and down slowly as if she wasn't really sure how to answer the question. "He doesn't know I'm in love with him. He knows very little about me."

"Then, why does he come to see you?"

"I'm convenient. And there are times when it's necessary. We used to work together, and there are things I still do for him."

"Why, Marianne?" Robyn dropped to eye level. There were tears in Marianne's eyes. "If he makes you so unhappy, why don't you stop seeing him. Tell him you won't do any more work for him?"

"I can't. For the same reason building that photochapel won't get Grant out of your system. It will help you deal with him not being here."

"We're a strange pair. Both of us crippled by men we can't get out of our systems." Robyn's laugh was mirthless. "Well, Marianne, we're a couple of survivors. We'll deal with the pain and the healing. In time, we'll laugh at this."

"Yes," Marianne smiled, fresh tears glistening in her eyes. "Now, let's go make something sinfully chocolate." A smile wavered through her tears.

"All right. I'll meet you in the kitchen. I want to call Will and tell him I'll be late." Marianne left as Robyn punched Will's number into the phone. The bell at the other end rang and rang, but Will did not pick up. Neither was there an answer at her house. He and Kari must have gone out for a snack.

In the kitchen, the two women went to work. "We'll

call it 'Chocolate Thunder,' " Marianne said, grabbing a case of bittersweet chocolate from the storeroom.

"That's good. I like 'Chocolate Death.' It'll be the dessert of the day. We'll have Sue-Ellen make up some cards, and we'll set them on all the tables."

When they had a counter filled with supplies, Marianne looked at her. "Got any idea what we're making?" she asked.

Robyn laughed. The first genuine laugh she'd had in nearly a month. "How about a double chocolate cake, with chocolate icing. We'll make a hot chocolate syrup, layer the cake with slices of chocolate ice cream, pour the syrup over it, and top it with chocolate sprinkles. We'll serve it on those snow white plates in a pool of white chocolate."

"Yes," Marianne agreed. "That is 'Chocolate Death.' " Both women seemed in high spirits as they worked side by side. It was how they'd begun, before there was a Yesterdays, before Grant had walked into Robyn's life, and Marianne had fallen in love with her mystery man.

Marianne was stirring melted chocolate when Robyn went to use the phone.

"That's strange," Robyn turned after replacing the receiver of the kitchen phone. Marianne was lifting one of the chocolate cakes from the oven.

"What's strange?" she asked being careful of the hot pan.

"I've tried to call Will several times, and I get no answer."

"I saw him earlier."

"Where?" Robyn's brows rose. Will never came to the restaurant without telling her.

"He and Kari were walking about the grounds. It was during the photo session."

Because the weather had been so good, the wedding party scheduled for that afternoon had moved into the garden for pictures. Robyn had seen to all the arrangements before the afternoon rehearsal.

"Where were they going?"

"I don't know. They were walking toward the building. I thought they came inside to see you."

"It's probably nothing. Kari likes the restaurant. Will probably brought her for a visit and then took her for ice cream." Robyn trusted Will completely. He'd taken care of Kari since he moved in next to them. They couldn't ask for a better neighbor.

"Kari, be careful. I don't want you to fall and hurt yourself."

"I won't hurt myself, Uncle Grant. I'll be careful." Kari smiled as she balanced on the steps to the airplane.

Tears came to Grant's eyes. It was the first time he'd looked upon the dark-haired child with the knowledge that more than his transfused blood ran through her veins.

He sat down on the slatted bench outside the terminal office. Wind from the airplanes stirred the air, but it was pleasant sitting outdoors. Will sat next to him.

"Thanks for bringing her, Will. I've missed seeing her."

Grant's eye followed the little girl. One of the mechanics was telling her about the airplane. Grant was afraid to get too close to her. He didn't trust himself not to break down and cry in front of her. But from a distance, he could look at her black hair and see his own reflected there. Jacob's visit nearly a month ago had sparked memories. Memories he thought were safely buried. But he had found himself opening the storage closet in his condo as if he were opening a vein. Grief and happiness had mixed with laughter and tears as he poured over the photo albums Robyn had left behind.

Once he had opened the albums, he couldn't stop the memories. Floodgates had been pushed back, and the misery he'd hidden, buried within himself, he now had found alive and waiting on page after page of the albums. Under each photo was a caption. Her neat handwriting inscribed immortality just as her camera had captured a segment of time. *Silver bells, cockle shells, dandelions, and weeds are my only rows* was the humorous caption under a photo of the flower garden she'd planted in front of their house in northwest Washington. *Grant and David, pilot-to-pilot* was another. Every aspect of their short marriage had been recorded in the albums. Even during the period of his captivity in Lebanon, she'd kept up the photographs. Now, he knew she'd left him a record. Something to hold onto when she could no longer be there.

But these weren't the pictures he had been looking for. He had wanted to find his childhood photos. The ones when he was about four, Kari's age. He had found them in the bottom of a box. He was lucky they'd survived after so many foster homes. They'd arrived in the mail one day after he had gone to live with Aunt Priscilla. In another box, he found Robyn, smiling into the camera. He had taken them out and set them on the piano. There he saw it. Between them was the child they'd created. Kari was the best of both of them.

He wanted her, and he wanted her mother. Why should the only choices open to him exclude her from his life? Damn, it wasn't right. Robyn had been doing a job. It wasn't her fault she was good at it. So good, in fact, she had to give up her own identity and go into hiding for the remainder of her life. It was worse than being a prisoner. At least in prison, there was the chance of parole. Robyn had nothing. Nothing but the lives she'd given back to the ten men in exchange for her own.

"So what happened, Grant. I thought you and Brooke would be announcing your engagement any day." Will's voice snapped his dreams. "Then, suddenly, you disappear, and she looks like she won't live past noon."

Grant pulled his attention away from the child. "It got complicated, Will. There are things I can't tell you."

"She didn't turn out to really be a spy, did she?" Will grunted a laugh.

"No, she's not a spy. But you were right about her husband. He is cardboard. She was never really married to Cameron Johnson. He's just a convenient lie."

"I knew it." Will's fist punched the air, emphasizing that his intuition had been proven true.

"That's all I can tell you, Will. The rest is classified."

"Classified? Does she have something to do with the government?"

Grant shook his head. He'd already told Will more than he should. Jacob Winston had told him he was not allowed to tell anyone what he knew. But Will had been his friend since he was a child. And Will knew nothing about Brooke's former life.

"What about Kari? Is she really her daughter?"

Grant's gaze went back to his daughter. "Yes, she's really her daughter. And she was really born in Atlanta."

Will and Grant were quiet for a long time. Each seemed absorbed in the child. The mechanic still was showing her everything about the aircraft, and she, being so inquisitive, continued to ask the same question—why. Grant could hear Kari laughing.

"You and Brooke ought to make up. I'm sure Kari would love having you around all the time."

"If only we could," Grant wished. "If it were up to me, I'd drop everything and go with her. But it would hurt her more than help her. The only thing I can do is go back to Washington and forget we ever met."

"But how can you forget the child?"

"I'll never forget Kari."

"I know. I still think of . . ." Will swallowed hard. Grant knew he couldn't say his son's name. Grant knew the hurt must still be raw. "Sometimes it's hard to remember he's really dead."

"I'm sorry, Will. I didn't mean to bring up sad memories."

"Oh, it's not your fault. You had nothing to do with it. I blame myself. If I hadn't involved him, then he never would have been in the position . . ."

Grant squeezed the older man's shoulder. He knew exactly how he felt. Losing a child was not something you could get over. He'd never had any time with his own daughter. He didn't even have memories he could hold close in order to give himself any comfort. And to think it was an act of desperation that had brought him into contact with Brooke Johnson—his wife. He'd rushed to save a child, never imagining she was his own.

"Uncle Grant . . . Uncle Grant." Kari ran toward him. Her smile was wide, and she held something in her hand. She was dressed in a pink jacket with matching hat and gloves that dangled from her sleeves. Her hair, in two long braids, stretched down her back. Grant stood up, catching her as she flew into his arms. He swung her in a full circle before settling her on his arm and holding her to his chest.

"Uncle Grant, look what I've got." She opened her small palm to reveal a small airplane pin. It was the kind they gave children passengers.

"Why those are the most wonderful wings I've ever seen."

"They look like yours." Kari placed hers against Grant's jacket collar. "See?"

Grant looked at them. "Of course, they look like mine. Here, let me pin them on you." He set her on the ground and knelt at her level. Taking the plastic wings, he clipped them to her collar in the same place as his own.

"Why don't you two visit for a while?" Will said. "I need to make a phone call." Will smiled at the child.

"Graffie, do you like my wings?"

"They're wonderful, darling. One day maybe you'll be able to fly."

"I will fly, won't I, Uncle Grant? When I'm older, you'll teach me, won't you?" The high-pitched voice tugged at his heart.

"Kari will miss you when you're gone," Will said, giving Grant a level stare.

"I'll miss her, too."

Will smiled and turned toward the terminal building.

"Are you leaving, Uncle Grant?" Kari's mouth formed a pout not unlike her mother's. Grant wanted to kiss her.

"I have to go soon, sweetheart." He sat her on his knee, and they continued looking onto the airfield.

"Will you come back to see me? Mother said you were very busy, and you wouldn't be coming to see us anymore."

Grant took Kari's gloves and put them on her chilled hands. "Kari, Uncle Grant has to go away. It may not be possible for me to come and see you for a long time. Can you understand that?"

Kari's pout disintegrated into a frown. Her eyes filled with tears. "But I don't want you to go away. I want you to come and live with us."

Grant hugged the small body to his. He kissed the

top of her head. "It's what I want, too, darling. But it's just not possible. But Uncle Grant will always be thinking of you. And, one day, you will learn to fly."

"Will you come back and teach me?" The suggestion brought her smile back.

Grant fingered the toy wings attached to her collar. "If it's possible, Kari. If it's possible."

The voice was raspy, old. Robyn felt as if it came to her from another life.

"Well, Mrs. Richards, it's been a long time. But I've finally found you."

Fear's cold finger scraped down Robyn's back. Her fingers clutched the phone so tightly color drained from her knuckles.

"I'm sorry you must have the wrong number. There's no one by the name of Richards here." The words were practiced, but Robyn never thought she'd ever have to say them. Her eyes quickly scanned the kitchen. Only Marianne was within earshot, and she had water running in the sink.

"I've made no mistake, *Mrs. Richards . . . Mrs. Robyn Richards.*" The way he said her name made her physically recoil. "I've waited a long time to find you, and now, I'm sure."

Robyn didn't know what to do. She couldn't acknowledge she was Robyn Richards. And, by denying it, she couldn't ask what he wanted.

"Who *is* this?" she stalled.

"I'm a parent just like you. Only you killed my son."

"I never killed anyone." She lowered her voice to a conspiratorial whisper. Marianne finished, and Robyn watched her head for the dining room.

"You have a daughter, Mrs. Richards."

Robyn's knees gave way, and she crumpled onto the chair next to the phone. Her face was as pale as the flour clinging to her hands. "Kari!" she whispered.

"Yes, Kari."

"What do you want?" Robyn fought for control over the shakes that took hold of her body.

"I want justice, Mrs. Richards."

"What are you talking about? I don't even know who you are?"

"But you knew my son . . ."

"Who was your son?" She was out of the chair.

"And I know your daughter," the man ignored her question. "She's a beautiful little girl. Where is she now, Mrs. Richards?"

His continually calling her Mrs. Richards was rubbing her raw. "Look, I don't know who you are, but you've got things wrong. I'm not Mrs. Richards, and I don't know your son."

"You'll never see her again." Each word was punctuated as if he were speaking to a child.

"Who is this?" she demanded. Restrained fear pierced her.

"I know," he said. "I know who you *really* are. You killed my son. And I've got your daughter. You'll never see her again."

"Who is this! Who is this!" She'd heard the click cutting off the connection. Still, she screamed into the phone. Dead silence answered her.

She dropped the phone. Her body was shaking, and she couldn't think straight. She had to do something, but what? Who could she call? What would she say? Who was on the phone? The police. Call the police, a voice in her consciousness spoke.

She didn't know how long she stood there unable to move or do anything. Marianne found her.

"Brooke, what is it!" She took her friend's hands and squeezed them. "Your hands are ice cold." Marianne replaced the phone, then pushed Robyn into a chair. "Who was on the phone?" she asked.

It took a while for her to be able to speak. Then the words came out slow and labored. "I don't know."

The phone rang again. Robyn jumped up. Her eyes widened in fear. If she'd had enough breath, she would have screamed, but her voice was cut short and a terrible pain lodged in her chest. Marianne picked up the phone.

"Jacob."

Robyn snatched the phone from her partner.

"Jacob!" she screamed into the receiver. "Kari's been kidnapped!"

Eighteen

It had been too long time since Jacob had a field assignment. Blood coursed through his veins like rushing wind. Adrenaline pumped through his system. He could smell the danger, taste the adventure. And it was thrilling. He maneuvered the rented Lincoln through the evening rush hour as people hurried toward their homes and uneventful evenings. His evening would prove to be quite different.

Jacob and Grant arrived at the same time. Marianne hadn't left Robyn's side. The redhead had managed to get Robyn home. Since arriving, the phone had not rung, but they'd found a note on the kitchen counter. Robyn's cheeks were the color of kindergarten paste, and she kept looking at the phone as if she could make it ring.

Seeing the two men come into the room together confused her even more. Before she had time to ask questions, Jacob broke the silence.

"Has any other contact been made?" he asked, taking command.

"We found a note," Marianne reported. "The restaurant will forward any calls."

"Where's the note?" Marianne gave the recipe card

she'd found to Jacob. Grant's writing was on the opposite side. Robyn could see it as Jacob read.

He read the words Robyn knew by heart.

21 October

You will lose the one
you love above all others.
As I have lost.

Grant came to Robyn and took her in his arms. "Are you all right?" he asked.

"Grant, it's . . . it's Kari. Kari's been kidnapped." It was the final straw. Robyn dropped her head on his shoulder and burst into tears. Marianne and Jacob looked on.

"Can I talk to her alone?" Grant asked over Robyn's head. Jacob nodded. He led her into the kitchen.

"It's going to be all right, Brooke."

"You don't know that, Grant. There's so much you don't know. So much I can't tell you."

"I know you're my wife, and I've been in love with you since I saw you dance across a stage in Las Vegas seven years ago."

Robyn's eyes dried and came up to meet her husband's. "How?"

"Jacob. He's told me everything. The trial. Gianelli. The Witness Protection Program."

"And Kari?" she asked.

"She is our daughter."

"Oh Grant," she went into his arms. "Can you ever forgive me? I love you so much, I couldn't ask you to come with me."

"We'll talk about that later. Right now, we have to find Kari."

Robyn's smile was thin but confident. They returned to the living room. The activity had increased. Hammil was there along with two other men. They had cellular phones and laptop computers. Everyone seemed busy accessing data by phone or machine. Marianne and Jacob stood near the front hall. They were deep in conversation but stopped when Grant and Robyn reentered the room.

"Brooke, we've got to ask you some questions." Jacob came toward her.

"I'm all right." She lifted her chin in a gesture Jacob recognized. "What do you want to know?"

He started. The questions were fired one by one, and she answered them as she remembered. She repeated everything the man had said on the phone.

"Did you recognize the voice?"

"No, but I have the feeling I know who he is."

"Why?" Jacob asked.

"I don't know. Just that I've heard it someplace before." She put her hands on her temples and closed her eyes trying to pull the voice into focus.

"Where?"

"I don't know," she shouted, bringing her hands back to her sides.

"How long ago?"

"I don't know?"

"Jacob, stop badgering her," Grant interceded.

"It's okay, Grant," Robyn took his hand. "Jacob doesn't mean it the way it sounds." Grant's hand tightened on hers.

"Think, Brooke. Kari's life depends on you remembering."

"Don't you think I know that? She's my daughter," Robyn glared at him then felt guilty for it. Jacob was obviously concerned about her daughter, and this was his way of displaying it.

"Brooke, he said you killed his son," Marianne spoke.

"Yes, but he didn't tell me who his son was."

"There were only two men at the trial who are now dead," Jacob began.

"Gianelli was found with his wrists slashed two days after being committed. And the Devil was executed."

"Who's the Devil?" Grant asked.

"He headed a very powerful organization called the Crime Network. For years, he was reported dead by eye witnesses. Then, he'd surface again after some magnificent kill. A man named Alex Jordan."

Grant was propelled from his position next to Robyn. He stood inches from Jacob. "Are you sure?"

"Absolutely," Jacob said.

All eyes focused on Grant. Sound stopped in the room. The computers stilled.

"Alex Jordan is Will's son."

Grant's voice was like rifle fire in a confined space.

"McAdams doesn't have a son. He's got four daughters . . ."

"Will never married Alex's mother, and for years, he didn't acknowledge Alex as his child," Grant interrupted. "Will's approval was the one thing Alex wanted above all else. He came during the summer, and because we were kind of in the same boat, we became friends." Robyn took his hand, knowing how he felt about losing his parents and belonging to no one. "Alex would do anything Will asked of him. Sometimes, Will was hard on him, not approving what he did when Alex wanted it so badly. There was an obvious love between them, but Will always pulled back, and Alex was forever trying to prove himself worthy of his father's respect. This afternoon Will couldn't even speak his name."

"You saw . . . Will this afternoon?" Robyn stammered. Her attention was on Grant, but she saw Jacob giving orders to Hammil and the younger man now going to the computer he'd brought with him.

"He brought Kari to the airfield. He called a couple of days ago and asked when I was going to be in town. I switched schedules with another pilot and flew in and out this afternoon. Jacob's call came almost the moment I landed."

"Will wouldn't take Kari." Robyn was shaking her head. "He loves her. She calls him Graffie for grandfather, and she loves him," she babbled on. "Will wouldn't do this. There has to be another explanation."

There had to be, Robyn thought, but as Jacob asked question after question, there appeared to be no other explanation. No one outside of that room knew about her. She had never told Will about her past. She had adhered as much as she could to Jacob's rules. The only man who knew slightly more had been Grant—and Jacob had been the one to tell him she was really Robyn Richards. So why would Will take Kari? What could he know? And how could he have found out?

The noise increased as the machinery was turned back on. The other agents were squawking into the phones, and several were punching on the small computer keyboards. Suddenly, it was deafening to Robyn. Grant's hand in hers was the only solid force in the room.

The night wore on. Robyn was tired of answering questions and coming to no conclusions. Where had he taken Kari? Where did they look? Why hadn't they called the police? Something had to be done. Someone had to find out what had caused Will to do this terrible thing, and someone had to save Kari. Suddenly, she knew. None of these people knew Will or Kari. It had to be her. She had to save her child.

"Jacob, I want my old job back," Robyn stepped forward, shouting above the noise.

"What!" His voice silenced the room. The fingers poised above the three laptop computers behind her stopped hitting the keys. The cellular phones, standard issue of the FBI, ceased their snappy whirling rings. None of the harsh voices of the strangers in her living room barked commands into the black plastic handsets.

Grant came up behind her, resting his hands on her upper arms. The gesture gave her strength.

"I want my old job back," she announced.

"Now!" Jacob looked at her as if the pressures of the past few hours had finally snapped her mind.

"Yes, now." Her voice was slightly impatient, but the gentle squeeze from Grant's hands calmed her.

Jacob raked a hand through the dark crop of curls that slipped onto his forehead like an errant cloud. He took a deep breath and for a moment, closed his eyes. "Would you mind telling me why you want to return to the FBI."

"I want to save my daughter's life."

"What does Kari have to do with your old job?"

"Kari doesn't, but somehow Will does," she paused a second. "It's back there, in Washington, locked in the computers of the Major Crimes Bureau. And I have to find it."

Jacob's coat and tie had long since been discarded. He had placed them neatly over the back of one of the wing chairs, but the constant sweep of men and equipment entering and leaving had caused them to fall in a heap on the floor. He stood before her with the collar of his white shirt unbuttoned and the hint of dark hair just below his collar bones. He looked at her with a steady gaze.

"It's been years, Brooke. Even if there was a connection, it would take days to find it."

"Not for me." She saw Jacob's eyes narrow.

"I know you were a computer wizard, but the technology has changed in the last five years. I'm not even sure they have the same equipment. You don't know the passwords to gain access. To say nothing of the security clearance required just to enter the building."

"Jacob, you can cut through the red tape and get me in."

He sighed heavily. The errant curls falling forward again. "I'll have a remote set up here." He turned to say something to one of the men behind him.

"No," Robyn stopped him with a hand on his arm. "It's got to be in Washington. There are files there, access to other computers, and the response time here would be too slow."

She was trembling, afraid Jacob would argue against her going.

"Brooke, Kari is still here. We have no reason to believe McAdams has taken her out of the city. Why do you want to go to Washington?" Jacob took a step closer to her. Compassion entered his voice. "He could kill her at any moment."

"We've got two days, Jacob. He won't kill her until the twenty-first at midnight."

"How do you know that?"

Robyn's hand reached around in search of Grant's solid protection. She found it and held it tightly. "It's on the note," she said quietly.

Jacob's stride was determined as he went to the piano and picked up the damning piece of paper. It was dated October twenty-first. Two days from now. "This isn't proof, Brooke. He's deranged."

"You don't know that." Her eyes flashed. Will had been good to her and Kari. If it hadn't been for him, she didn't think she could have survived the demanding hours at the restaurant.

"All right, he could have just forgotten the date."

"He didn't forget." She knew the date, knew where she had seen it and what significance it had. "The twenty-first of October at midnight was when Alex Jordan had been administered a lethal injection at a federal penitentiary." She pushed aside the eye-for-an-eye thought. They couldn't let him inject Kari and kill her.

"I have to go, Jacob." Tears came to her eyes but

she blinked them away. She was too keyed up now. If she let herself cry, she'd be hysterical in seconds.

"You really think there's something back there? Something we don't know here?" Jacob's gaze was that of a friend, not the official FBI agent who'd guided her into the program.

"Yes, I do," she answered calmly. He stared at her for a long moment. Then, the room seemed to galvanize into action.

"Give me a phone. I'll get us a plane." Hammil snapped a cellular unit in his hand like a nurse slapping a scalpel.

"I have a plane standing by," Grant dropped his hands. "I'll call the airport, and let them know we're on our way," he called over his shoulder as he went to her phone in the kitchen.

Jacob was already speaking into his unit. His comments were crisp and precise. "Get a jacket," Jacob said quietly. His voice was so tender she could almost believe she'd never heard its harsh tones directed at her.

Robyn ran up the steps quickly. She heard Jacob ordering Marianne to stay there and transfer calls. Robyn was in her room before he finished and didn't hear what calls needed transferring. Pulling a brown suede jacket with western fringe from its hanger, she pushed her arms through the sleeves. On her way to the door, she looked at herself in the mirror. Her face was pale and drawn, and there were dark circles under her eyes. Impulsively, she picked up her lipstick and coated her mouth with a rich red color. Then, using the same tube, she dotted her cheeks and rubbed the color into her skin. It highlighted her cheeks and softened her strained look. After pulling a brush through her hair, she left the room and hurried down the stairs.

Grant was waiting for her when she reached the bottom. He had his jacket on, but his face looked as tense as hers. The night had not been an easy one for him either. The room had been straightened. No sign, except the dark impression of footprints on the carpet, gave evidence that anyone had been there. Marianne and Jacob were in the kitchen. They separated when Robyn entered as if they'd been caught doing something wrong. Marianne turned to the sink and began cleaning coffee cups. Jacob's G-Man disguise settled over him like paint.

"What's that?" Robyn asked, the sound of an approaching helicopter taking her attention away from what her mind had registered.

"The chopper's here," Jacob explained. "This way." Robyn didn't blink as he led her toward the door. She stopped briefly to hug Marianne. Then, she followed the two men out into the dark night. Nothing Jacob did surprised her any longer. A helicopter on her back lawn was standard operating procedure for him. Robyn, Grant, and Jacob ducked and ran toward the giant machine sitting on the green grass like a squatting bird. She stepped on the ski and propelled herself into the small cabin. Grant and Jacob followed closely behind. Without a word, the pilot took off, and minutes later, she was high above the city.

It took less than five minutes to reach the airport. She was quickly ushered into Grant's plane. The moment Jacob stepped onboard the doors closed, and the plane began taxiing. After they were immediately cleared and were airborne, Robyn knew Jacob had pulled rank and cleared traffic.

At Washington International Airport, again, the sky was stacked with aircraft, but their clearance was immediate. Deplaning, she boarded a second helicopter which flew them directly to a heliport within the FBI complex. Robyn was seated behind her old computer at the Assassination Bureau, the tiny sign she'd printed years earlier was faded and torn, but taped to the top of a new monitor. An hour and a half after she had told Jacob she wanted her old job back, here she was.

None of them wore the visitors' badges required of every outsider entering the building. And how many rules had Jacob broken getting them into this facility? In addition, the room was clear. Every machine was inactive. It appeared as if everyone had left hours ago. Except for the heat against her hand when she touched the machine, she'd have thought there was no night operation. She knew Jacob's constant telephone conversations while they were on the plane were responsible for the empty area.

She turned on the computer. In seconds, the blinking cursor greeted her. Robyn typed in her access code and password. They took. She looked up at Jacob, her eyes wide but clear. Almost imperceptibly, he nodded. He'd had it reinstated. She wouldn't ask how he knew what her password had been. He'd only tell her she didn't need to know. But she was grateful.

"Is there anyone here who can help me?" she asked.

"What do you need?" Jacob asked.

"I need Will's files. And I'd like all the records,

newspaper clippings, photographs, everything on Alex Jordan's hits. Anything even remotely attached to him. And I need the files on the Network." Somehow they were linked, and she had to find out how.

Jacob didn't waste time asking why she wanted the files. He picked up a phone and issued an order. Robyn knew an entire staff had just gone into action. She'd have what she needed in record time.

"Can I help?" Grant asked.

"Can you use a computer?" Robyn asked.

"I had a teacher once." He smiled and she remembered. He had taught her to fly, and she had taught him a few fundamentals about the computer. For a moment, tension in the room lightened.

"Jacob," she called. "Can he have access?"

"It's against regulations."

Robyn's gaze didn't waver. The strength of what he was doing for her and her child suddenly hit her. Jacob had put the entire U.S. government computer network at her disposal. He'd broken at least ninety of the one hundred regulations against unauthorized entry into the building. And she was asking for access for not one but two people who had no clearance, no authority, and no connection with the FBI. Robyn knew he could lose his job over this. And with what he was doing, very probably would.

"Please," she uttered the solitary word. She couldn't remember ever saying it to the man now facing her. But she didn't want to fight with Jacob anymore. She liked him. If he said no, she'd accept it.

Jacob stared at her for a long moment, then walked to the machine facing her and sat down. He typed something onto the screen. Less than a minute later, he stood. "Your code is FRIEND. The password is BROOKE." Robyn stared at him but he didn't look in her direction.

Grant took the seat Jacob vacated and typed onto the screen. Over his head, Jacob's eyes met Robyn's. She nodded a silent thank you. He walked past her without acknowledgment.

"Go through the menus to Military Service and access Will's records. Find out every place he's ever been stationed. Everything in the file," Robyn instructed. The moment between her and Jacob was gone. She realized he was probably the best friend she had or would ever have.

Jacob sat at the machine next to Grant. "What would you like me to look for?" he asked as he typed his own access code and password onto the screen.

"See what you can find out about Alex Jordan. Anyone he'd been associated with no matter how infrequently. What he liked and disliked. Look for the small details, too. Compile all the confirmed and unconfirmed assassinations linked to him. Create a file I can read."

Adrenaline was pumping through Robyn. She was back. It had been five years since she'd touched a computer keyboard, but it was like swimming, she didn't forget. Her fingers flew across the keys. Information came and went, and she took it all in as fast as the computer would display it.

Silently, they worked. The only sound in the room was the rhythmic tapping of the keyboards. Once or twice, she noticed the doors opening and in came the three men who had been at her house a few hours earlier. They were carrying boxes. Robyn knew they contained the data she had requested.

Someone pinned a badge on her. She barely looked at the man, too engrossed in absorbing the data flitting rapidly across the screen. If she had time, she'd laugh. Jacob couldn't resist being the man he was. He had to comply with regulations as much as possible.

Hours passed as green letters danced across the blue background. She sat for so long that her neck and back began to hurt. She ignored the pain and continued. When or how coffee showed up she didn't know. It was just beside her, and there were empty cups next to her computer. She didn't remember drinking it. Like in the hospital the day Grant came to give Kari the blood, she had no memory of food or drink.

Pushing her chair back, she relaxed a moment. Her head dropped back, and she gathered her hair in a hand-held ponytail for several seconds. Then, she stretched and yawned, her fingers flexed in the air above her head. Sitting up straight, she looked at the men about her. Everyone was engrossed in the work she'd assigned them.

Robyn got up. She joined Hammil who was stacking piles of paper from the storage boxes on a nearby table. Box by box, she emptied the contents and absorbed the information. She soaked up everything. When she finished, she was certain that the Network was comprised of a group of assassins. They were placed throughout the world, probably living normal lives. Some of them were married with families. When the call came through for services, contact was made, and a loving father or a Don Juan type playboy pulled the tools of his trade from mothballs and went into action.

She hadn't yet been able to determine who the leader of the group was, how large a network he commanded, or what connection he had with Will McAdams.

"How are you doing?" Robyn asked Grant.

"There doesn't seem to be anything here we could use. He was a model soldier. His file reads like a man campaigning for the Congressional Medal of Honor. There is nothing here but commendations and awards. From basic training through his retirement, he was at the top of his class or his field."

"What particularly did he excel in?" Robyn poured six cups of coffee into Styrofoam cups. There was no sugar or cream so she passed the revival liquid out to the tired looking men as Grant continued. She peered onto the screen of Grant's computer.

"He excelled in everything from grenades and high explosives to map and terrain reading. During the individual training, he scored highest on the ASVAB and went into intelligence. If you ask me, he was a model soldier."

"What's his I.Q.?" Jacob asked standing up from his machine and coming to stand behind Grant.

Grant scanned through the screens, "One hundred ninety-seven," he said with a low whistle. "The man's intelligent."

"Maybe a little too intelligent," Jacob said.

"I agree," Robyn concurred.

Grant craned his neck to see the two people behind him. "What does that mean?"

"I'm not sure," Jacob answered. "I wonder why a man of such superior intelligence would choose to spend his time making children's toys?"

"Will has always been fond of his girls. When we were young, he supported them in everything from sports to dating. It was only Alex who seemed to expect more than Will could give. His real family lives far away, and they don't visit often. Kari was probably the grandchild he longed for."

"Then why would he kidnap her?" Jacob asked.

"We don't know that he has." Robyn stopped the discussion. "The note doesn't have to be real."

"Face it Brooke. It's in his handwriting. And he's Alex Jordan's father." Jacob's voice was harsh.

She wasn't used to him jumping to conclusions. He was too logical, too much the calm, controlled, think-on-your-feet kind of guy. Jacob came to her, pushing two papers into her hand. Robyn read an account of Will's liaison with a Meredith Jordan before she married and became Meredith Van Buren. The second paper was a copy of Alex Jordan's birth certificate. Under father's name, the space was blank.

"There is another possibility," she added.

"Which is?" Jacob asked.

Robyn moved away from them. She stopped in front of the debris she'd left piled on the floor. "When you staged my kidnapping in Washington . . ."

"What!" Grant was on his feet.

"It's all right, Grant. Jacob was showing me what a dangerous game I was playing."

"Is that why you left so suddenly?"

She nodded. "It worked. He scared me into believing a Network gun lurked behind every pair of sunglasses. I was frantic, and I ran."

Grant covered the small distance between them and hugged her. She leaned against him for a moment, wanting to stay in the warmth of his arms, but Kari's face had her remembering why she was in this room.

"Jacob, suppose someone did find out who I was?"

"Impossible." His comment sounded like a quick snap of the teeth.

"Hear me out," she protested. "Suppose somehow my identity has been found out. Will was watching Kari. Suppose someone came in and kidnapped them both. To force us to think Will is the person who's got Kari, he forced him to write the note."

"Sorry, Ma'am." A voice from behind her arrested three pairs of eyes. Robyn recognized Hammil, the clean-cut agent who had been her escort for Susan's wedding. "We've had the handwritten note analyzed. It's definitely William McAdams handwriting. There are no indications of any stress-related impressions. When Mr. McAdams wrote the note, he was under no strain of anxiety."

"You can tell that from a piece of paper?" Grant asked incredulously.

"Sir," the young man began.

"That's enough, Hammil," Jacob cut the explanation off. The young man's face closed.

The door opened and a cloned agent, molded just like Hammil, stood there. He held his position in the doorway a moment before coming farther into the room.

He went straight to where Jacob stood and whispered something in his ear. Jacob nodded, and the unnamed man left the room. Robyn watched as Jacob picked up a phone.

"Put it through in here and have it traced," he said into the mouthpiece and indicated Robyn should pick up one of the other phones.

"Hello," she said.

"Hi, Mommy."

"Kari! Are you all right?" Relief and fear sliced through her as she heard Kari's voice.

"Mommy, I miss you. I'm fine. Are you coming to get me tonight?"

Jacob's signal told her to remain calm.

"Yes, oh yes, darling. Is Graffie with you?" Robyn's heart hammered in her chest. Grant took Robyn's hand and squeezed it.

Before the child could answer, the phone was taken from her and a gravelly voice said. "She's mine, now. You'll never see her again."

Blood drained from Robyn's face as the line went dead. She started to shake. Suddenly, the brightness in the room was blinding, and the two men across from her appeared to weave back and forth like drunks. Jacob's hand moved in slow motion as the phone left his ear and started an arc. She turned her head, feeling her hair swing around her head and hit her in the face as she looked at the black instrument in her hand. Brighter and brighter the room got until the light was so blinding, she had to close her eyes against it.

She tried to scream. She wanted to say something to Grant, but her mouth wouldn't open fast enough for sound to come through. Then, her knees gave under her, and she felt herself falling. Below her was a dark well. Her body was drawn toward it. She was going to fall into it, and she couldn't stop herself. Down she went, into the blackness of the abyss below. It felt cool, against her hot skin. Behind her was the blinding light, below her the coolness of the dark cave. She went into it gladly. It was comforting, taking her away from the pain of the light and the pain in her head. The coolness would make it go away. She embraced it.

She fell for a long time. There was no bottom to the well. She went further and farther into the coolness of the dark. Suddenly, something caught her. She fought against it. She wanted to keep going. She didn't want to be pulled back into the light. It was painful there. The dark was where she wanted to be. But whatever had her was strong. It caught and shackled her arms. She fought it, struggled against it until she was too tired to care. Then, the darkness swallowed her.

Nineteen

Robyn fought her way back to consciousness. The acrid smell of ammonia assailed her nostrils, and she sat up, fighting the offending odor. One hand knocked the wet vial to the floor while her face turned to come into warm contact with Grant's chest.

She opened her eyes and pushed herself back. She was on the floor. Grant cradled her across his lap while Jacob knelt on her other side. The room was quiet and empty. She looked about for Hammil and the other men whose names Jacob had not given her. They were gone. Only the two men hovered above her.

"Grant, it was Will. He said he'd kill her."

"Jacob told us," Grant acknowledged.

Robyn remembered Jacob was on the other phone while the short conversation took place. She tried to sit. Both men's hands came out to stop her.

"I'm all right," she said, breaking the awkward moment. "Let me up."

They released her and she sat fully up, tucking her feet under her Indian-style. Both of the faces staring into hers looked as drained as she had looked hours earlier when she caught her reflection in the bedroom mirror.

"Do you think he's telling the truth?" she asked not knowing which man she expected to answer. Neither of them knew what Will was capable of doing. She'd been closer to him than either of them. She could hardly believe Will had tracked her for five years, moved next door, and infiltrated her life to discover if his suspicions were true. And, finally, he had. She'd trusted her child to him. He'd been so close and so loving to her and Kari. How could she believe he lived a double life?

"We'll find her," Jacob said finally. His stare was direct. "You thought there was something here that would give us a clue to what he would do."

Robyn and Grant got up. "Yes, what did you find out about Alex Jordan?" They helped her to her feet.

"Not much more than we knew five years ago." Jacob took the seat in front of the backlit computer screen. "He had very few associations. But he did seem to spend a lot of time in Sicily."

"Can we confirm where he was when the restaurant murders took place?"

"We can't say exactly." Jacob turned and met Robyn's eyes. "In Sicily, nine years ago, six American men were killed in a restaurant," Jacob explained to Grant. "The kill was impossible. No windows, door locked from the inside. The food was not poisoned. No marks on the bodies. Yet, they were all dead."

"How did it happen?" Grant asked.

"It's still unsolved," Robyn answered. She spoke almost to herself.

"What happened to the bodies?" Grant asked.

"What do you mean? They were identified by the next of kin and properly buried."

"Can you find the names of the dead and who claimed the bodies?"

"What are you getting at?" Robyn directed her attention to Grant.

"It's from a novel I read called *Lost Companions.*" Grant could tell he made no sense. "It's about a dinner party where everyone ends up dead."

"I understand." Jacob turned to the keyboard and rapidly began striking the keys. The screen flickered. "One of those men was not really dead."

Robyn knew he was connected to a modem and the computer was dialing into another data base. When the Interpol logo came up on the screen, she pulled a chair up. Grant followed suit, and they watched in quiet anticipation as Jacob combed his way through the maze of menus to reach his goal. The list of names came up. Nothing looked familiar to Robyn.

"How about military?" Robyn asked.

"They were all in the military at some point in their lives," Jacob volunteered. "None of them served together and interviews with the families could not produce any links."

"Can you pull up the names of the people who claimed the bodies?" Grant asked.

Jacob pressed several keys in rapid succession, and the list of the dead appeared on the screen. Along side of each name was the name of the next of kin.

"Does anything look familiar? Out of place?"

Both Robyn and Jacob shook their heads.

Jano, Sr., Keith	claimed by	Jano, Jr., Keith
Knight, Joseph	claimed by	Knight, Adam
Lance, David	claimed by	Holden, Jane
McBride, James	claimed by	McBride, Martin
Totten, Earl	claimed by	Totten, Robert
Williams, John	claimed by	Opal, Julia

She went through the names. They meant nothing. "There was a photo." Robyn left her chair and went to search one of the boxes on the floor. She leafed through it and found the black-and-white eight-by-ten glossy.

Three heads bowed over the picture of death.

"Do you know who belongs to the names?"

Robyn reached over and listed the names of the men sitting around the table. They looked as if they were all asleep.

"What day did this happen on?"

"May twenty-sixth," Jacob answered.

"Which was the first body claimed?"

"They were all released the same day, May thirtieth. A hearse arrived for each of the victims. Totten and McBride were the first to leave."

"It's got to be here." Grant whispered.

"You're losing me," Robyn prompted.

"If the assumption is correct, that one of these men was not dead, but only simulating death, then a doctor or a person posing as a doctor had to be in on the job."

"All right. Where does that take us?" Robyn asked.

"Three days is too long a time for a body to simulate death."

"Meaning," Jacob continued, "that the accomplice was part of the medical examiner's office."

"Or posed as part of the office."

"And that's how he escaped. Alex Jordan was either there or someone else was, and he claimed the body," Robyn concluded.

"No," Grant stopped her. "Will was the man there."

"How do you know?" Robyn reacted to his tone.

"I've seen this before." Grant took the photo and looked closer. He stood up, walking about the cluttered room with the picture in his hand. Two men sat on either side of the rectangular table. At the head were two others. Grant came back, straddled a chair and pointed to the man on the far side of the photo, directly right of the head. "This is Will McAdams."

"How can you be so sure?" Jacob asked.

"I knew I'd seen this before." His finger drew a circle encompassing the entire table. "It's in Kari's room. The toy table with the bears sitting around it. There are only five bears but six chairs. This is the missing one."

Robyn gasped. Grant was right. She'd walked by that toy tea party hundreds of times. Kari had moved the bears many times, yet the same chair was always empty. As if it was a message Will was trying to give her.

"Who is this man?" Grant put his finger on the position which had been empty in the toy representation.

"Earl Totten," Robyn and Jacob answered in unison.

"Then, Robert Totten is Alex Jordan," Grant spoke. "What did these men have in common with Will?"

"They were the old guard." It was Jacob's turn to explain. "McAdams wanted to set up Jordan as the leader of a worldwide syndicate of assassins. He proposed a new order, but the old chiefs refused to buy into his plan. He had them killed."

"How do you know that?" Robyn's hands went to her sides and her body froze. Jacob spoke as if he'd always known the men in the photo and of their connections to each other. She was convinced. He didn't need to tell her. "You knew then, didn't you?"

"I didn't know about McAdams's connection." Jacob didn't have to ask her when *then* was. Robyn could tell he'd been aware of the formation of the Crime Network. "When you discovered Alex Jordan's intent six years ago, we'd been aware of the Network's movements for some time. We didn't know who the leader was. He was very adept at eluding us. Now, I know it was because the father-son team swapped the leadership. An action which intentionally misled anyone who might try to infiltrate the organization."

"But it *was* infiltrated?" Robyn was still rigid.

"Yes, eight men had been recruited. They were the best. Some of the most spectacular assassinations were credited to them. When Gianelli ordered the destruction of organized crime, these men were sent. But you discovered the plot, and all eight of them were captured, tried, and remain imprisoned."

"How did Will find out about me?"

"He didn't know for sure, or he'd never have pulled his hand," Jacob explained. "He was in intelligence. He could have contacts and a network so deep, it would be impossible to discover. But still he was unsure."

"He's also proved to be extremely patient," Grant added.

"But how did he find me now? I swear I didn't reveal anything. What happened to confirm his suspicions?"

"I told him," Grant said. He stood up, facing the two pairs of astonished eyes. "Not in actual words. I didn't know for sure until Jacob told me the truth. Each time we met he was very interested in Brooke, even suggesting you might be a spy."

"What did you say," Jacob barked.

"When he came to the airfield to see me," Grant answered Jacob, but his eyes were trained on the pale face of the woman he loved. "Kari was with him. We talked and I told him you were never married to Cameron Johnson. He was a decoy, and your real life was a classified secret."

"Classified," Jacob snapped. "You used that word?"

Grant nodded, glancing at Jacob before returning his attention to Brooke. "Please, Brooke, don't be angry. I didn't know he had any connection with you."

Robyn was angry. How could he have been so thoughtless? How could he endanger the life of his own daughter? She stepped back, taking a long breath. It wasn't fair, she told herself. Grant didn't know what he was doing, and hadn't she mysteriously sidestepped issues that would make him curious enough to confide in a friend? Robyn's shoulders dropped as she let the anger fall away. Grant hadn't been trained like she was. He didn't know how one small sentence could change the course of her life.

"What are we going to do now?" She looked at Jacob. "We're running out of time, and we haven't come up with any method he might use on Kari."

"You think it will be another one of his spectacular kills?" Jacob asked.

Tears formed in her eyes. Both men moved toward her. Jacob stopped, and Grant cradled her against him. "He won't do that." Grant eyed Jacob above Robyn's head. His voice was soft. Robyn responded to it. Craning her head, she looked up at him. "He's here for Brooke, not Kari," Grant said.

"But he said I took his son, and he was going to take my child."

"He won't be able to do it."

"Go on," Jacob knew there was more.

"Will had four daughters and Alex. The girls have children. Children he's seen only a few times. He wouldn't tell me why, but he thinks it is an injustice that his daughters keep the children away from him. Kari is an innocent. It's you he wants." Grant looked down into her eyes.

"Then we have to go back," she said.

"Hold it." Jacob joined the small group in front of the computer terminals. "If you think I'm willing to trade you for Kari, I won't do it."

"It's not your decision, Jacob!" Robyn screamed. "Kari is my child, and I will decide how best to save her life. Not you. I've let you run my existence for five years, and I hate it. This time it's my choice." Her eyes reflected the anger now raging in her body that stepped out of Grant's arms and confronted him.

"All right," he agreed. "We do it your way."

Clarence Darrow Christopher III felt every one of his fifty-nine years. It was four o'clock in the morning. He should be home, in bed with his wife. Instead, he stood looking out of the window of his office at the Federal Bureau of Investigation. A light rain coated the streets of Washington. Street lamps reflected in pools of concentric circles.

What could Jacob be up to? Clarence really thought he knew the man. But in all the years they'd crossed channels between the CIA and FBI, this was the first time anything negative had been brought to his attention. Jacob was straight, bright, honest, a regulations-only man. If there was anyone who could handle the security of the United States, Clarence would have no reservations in recommending Jacob. Despite the incident with Cynthia, they didn't come any more reliable than Jacob Winston.

Yet, tonight, he had let all the years of hard work go right down the drain, the way the rain was going into the openings in the street. And for what? He didn't know. He'd read Robyn Warren-Richards's file. She had helped to put Alex Jordan away, and the United States taxpayers were thanking her for the effort. She was a beautiful woman, both before and after she entered the program. But that was no reason for Jacob to commit career suicide. Unless . . . He refused to

complete the thought. Even Jacob wouldn't be that
stupid.

Well, he had to do it. He might as well get it over
with. Going to the phone, he pressed the button to
summon one of the twenty-four hour secretaries who
manned the station outside his office. Immediately, the
door opened, and a woman of forty stood before him,
a pad in her hand.

"Tell him I want to see him," he said with a sigh.
Without a word she closed the door. Clarence dropped
down into his chair. He glanced down at the folder of
Brooke Johnson, open on his desk. He'd read it and
there was nothing there that seemed to make sense
out of what Jacob had done. He lifted the black-and-
white glossy photo and looked into the sad eyes of a
woman with dark hair framing her face. It must have
been the eyes, he thought. I can see how a man could
get lost in the silent vulnerability spoken there. But
Jacob, he'd thought Jacob was a better man.

The phone rang. Jacob snatched it up. "Winston,"
he said.

"Mr. Christopher would like to see you in his office, Mr. Winston," an efficient voice said.

"I'll be right there," he answered and hung up without a salutation.

Robyn looked directly at him as did every other
pair of eyes in the crowded room. Robyn couldn't remember when Hammil and the other agents returned.
But the room was crowded again.

"Keep working," he said, as his body slowly left the chair. "I have to see Christopher."

Robyn took a step toward him and stopped. "Clarence Christopher?"

He nodded.

"Let me go with you?"

"No!" his voice snapped, then in a softer tone. "You have to stay here and finish what you're doing. If there's any chance at all of finding McAdams, it's got to be here."

Robyn nodded. She knew further argument would be fruitless. Jacob's face was relaxed but closed. He smiled at her and squeezed her arm before walking away.

Jacob closed the door behind him, turning left and walking to the private elevator at the end of the hall. He inserted his key into the security panel and waited for the car which would carry him to Clarence's office. He wasn't surprised to find the director of the bureau in residence at this hour. He'd known it would come to this when they stood in Robyn's living room and when he still had time to change his mind. Robyn thought Kari was in danger, and she was, but Robyn and Grant's lives were also in peril. And he wouldn't let William McAdams win. Not this time. This time he was protecting Robyn, and he wasn't going to let anything happen to her. She wasn't like Cynthia. Cynthia had done everything his way while Robyn challenged him at every turn. And Cynthia had died. And someone like McAdams had killed her.

They were going to find a link, whatever clue they could to determine where he'd taken Kari and what he planned for her. Jacob hoped Robyn was right, and the date on the note was a message of McAdams's plan. But even if it were, they were running out of time, and they were no closer to finding anything than they had been in her living room.

The door to the elevator slid silently open, and he stepped into the subdued lighting of the plush car. Well oiled cables raised him to the executive floor. Then, the doors slid back, and he stepped into Clarence's office.

"Come in, Jacob." Clarence stood with his back to him. He looked out of the window interested in the rain or the street below. Jacob stood in front of the recessed portal of carved doors, waiting.

He'd been in this office many times, but tonight he expected it would be his last. The overhead lights were out, and the room was illuminated by a lamp on Clarence's massive desk. Another lamp poured its yellow glow from a small end table next to the maroon leather sofa. Above the sofa, fifteen years of a man's life were reflected in several groupings of photographs. While most of them coupled Clarence with presidents, judges, and an occasional movie star, his face smiled from a fishing boat and from the background at a picnic.

"What does she know about you, Jacob?" Clarence left his position and came to sit behind his desk. Jacob lowered himself into the chair in front of it.

"Only what she needs to know, sir." The look Clarence leveled at him was not lost. Jacob had rarely referred to him as "sir," yet, tonight, it was warranted.

"Then, why, damn it? Why have you decided to

throw your career into the Potomac and dive in after it?"

"Her child has been kidnapped," Jacob answered quietly. He saw the open folder on Clarence's desk. The contents of that folder had been sealed when she was placed in Buffalo. Clarence must have been extremely concerned to have it exhumed.

"Why aren't you letting the authorities handle this? It's out of our jurisdiction."

Jacob's body left the chair like a bullet. "Our jurisdiction?" He spit the word. "Where is the line for our jurisdiction, Clarence? Can you find where it lies today? Do you know where it will be tomorrow? When Alex Jordan was on trial, our jurisdiction extended to anything to get Robyn Richards to testify. We did everything whether it was within our authority of not. Then, it was all right. What about now, Clarence? She's downstairs, under who knows what kind of stress, trying to find some key, something to piece together an investigation we dropped five years ago, because it may provide a connection to save her daughter's life. And she's got less than two days to get it done. What do you think I should have done?"

"You should have followed the rules. Brooke Johnson should be living a quiet life without the need for constant care from us."

"Clarence, have you forgotten you gave me this assignment?" Jacob reminded the silver-haired man.

"No, I haven't forgotten, but I never thought I'd have you on my carpet at four o'clock in the morning."

"We owe it to her," Jacob said quietly.

"Jacob, what are you talking about. She got the same, better than the same, treatment as any of the members who ever went through the program."

"Did she, Clarence? We took from her. She gave us what we wanted. We put Alex Jordan away. But we took everything she had. We gave her nothing, but an empty shell to exist in until she's too old to care. She walked away from us with nothing, not even the husband she loved."

"Don't lay that at my door, Jacob." Clarence's hand came down hard on the desk, rattling the pencil cup and causing the phone to give a tiny chimelike ring. Clarence was on his feet coming around the desk. "She made that decision without our help."

"What kind of decision would you have made, Clarence, if you were in the same position? If you were a material witness in a federal case, and your government used the fact that your wife was being held in a foreign prison. And, as added incentive, they spring Project Eagle on you. The only attempt to free her rested with your testimony. Would you refuse to testify and leave her there? Or would you take her into the program with you where everything about her is different. Everything, Clarence. She'd be physically altered. The woman you married would cease to exist. A different woman would live in her place.

"And then, everything she liked to do would suddenly become taboo. She could no longer paint. Those hand-drawn Christmas cards she sends out each year would be forbidden. She could never again see any of her family. No more reunions or homecomings. No old college friends or people she worked with. Do you honestly want to tell me you'd opt for that kind of life for the woman you loved?"

"Jacob, we're not talking about what I would do. And that's all past decision now. The truth is we're not doing our jobs. We're no closer to finding who's after Brooke Johnson than we were months ago. For years, we've been running round-the-clock surveillance on her. Do you know how much this is costing the taxpayers?"

"No," Jacob lied. He knew exactly what the cost was.

"The past five years alone have run into the millions. And, if I project it out for the next thirty years, the cost is astronomical. When do you plan to close this? Do you plan to ever close it?"

Jacob remained silent. He knew as long as Robyn needed protecting he'd make sure she got it. Clarence stared at him for a long moment then sighed and went back to his position by the windows. Jacob also knew Clarence and that he was concerned about Jacob's feelings for Robyn. Alex Jordan had been a thorn since Robyn uncovered the Network. McKenzie Cranford had been deputy director, second only to Clarence, and he'd been at the top of the ring Robyn had discovered. Jacob knew Clarence's thoughts tonight were on the scene that had taken place five years ago.

"Unauthorized used of aircraft, unauthorized entry into a federal facility, unauthorized movement of secured files, unauthorized used of government equipment, unauthorized access to sensitive computer information including an investigation in progress." Clarence recited the broken rules as if they were charges against him. "What do you want me to do?" Clarence's voice was low. It held none of the anger of a few minutes ago.

Jacob looked at his friend. He'd turned to face him. Jacob saw the hastily donned shirt still wrinkled from the previous day, his feet pushed into brown leather slippers that had been Jacob's Christmas present to him last year. His hair was uncombed, and he looked older than Jacob had ever noticed before.

"I want you to trust me, Clarence." His voice was friendly, too.

Clarence was quiet for a long time. He and Jacob stared at each other. Finally, he walked back to his desk and sat down. He glanced at the file still lying open and picked up the photo of Robyn. Jacob watched him without words.

"Are you in love with her?" he asked, not looking up.

Jacob sat down. There were several things he could say in answer to that question. He could have told him she was still in love with her husband. He could say he was married to his work. He could lie and say, 'no.' But he met the eyes of the man across the desk directly and said, "Yes, I love her more than a sister, but less than a wife, if that's your point."

Clarence let out his breath slowly as if he were willing himself to control it.

"Does she know?" he asked.

"I've never told her. But I'm sure she knows." Jacob had only kissed Robyn once. But, in that kiss, he'd told her everything. After that, each time he saw her he could see her feelings in her eyes. He knew she loved her husband. None of the warm looks she directed at Grant ever came his way. Yes, he loved Robyn, but his allegiance lay with another woman.

Robyn was not the woman for him, but she was the one who had shown him what living was about. He would be hurt when all this was over, and she was gone from his life, but he could take the hurt. And he would go on. He would stop existing and begin living. The woman downstairs, so full of life despite the sadness in her eyes, had scratched and clawed to have a life. While he had existed from day to day, refusing to get involved because he felt guilty over Cynthia. He couldn't have saved Cynthia. He knew that now. No matter what he did. There were too many people against her. If the men in the helicopter hadn't gotten her, she still wouldn't have lived through the day. Jacob admitted it to himself. He'd done his best, and that's all he could ask of himself.

"Jacob." Clarence's voice pulled him back to the present. "Can I count on you to be objective?"

"Yes, sir." There was no hesitancy about his reply.

Clarence drummed his fingers on the manila folder. The circular seal, ragged on the ends, reminded Jacob of blood. It matched the words, Top Secret, spread across the jacket like a warning sign.

"All right, Jacob. I'll table it for now."

Jacob's body let out the breath he was holding. "Thank you, Clarence." He rose, going back to the private elevator. His hand held the security key, but before he slipped it in the slot, he turned. Clarence stood behind his desk facing him, his hands clasped behind him.

"Before I go, Clarence, I'd like you to know why I'm doing this. Robyn Richards made the highest sacrifice for her country short of dying. She gave up her right to be a human being. Because of her courage and forcefulness, ten men are happily home, living productive lives while she was shot-gunned into hiding. Not one of those men knew of her sacrifice. Not even the man she loved enough to leave. I only hope there'll be someone in my life who loves me as much as Robyn loved her husband. But even if it hadn't been for that, she uncovered a network which allowed us to crack one of the largest assassination rings ever organized. For that alone, she deserves the protection of the taxpayers for as long as necessary, even if necessary means the rest of her life." Jacob hesitated a moment, then turned and opened the elevator.

Clarence watched the doors close. He reached up and turned off the lamp on his desk, then sat down in the dark. When the call had come in tonight and he listened in horror as the details of Jacob's activities were described, he thought of retiring. He'd be sixty-two in three years, and someone else could take over this job. He didn't need the stress. He could stay home with his wife. They could go on a cruise. She'd wanted a vacation for years. But Jacob's comments had changed his mind. He had been right. Robyn Richards had sacrificed a lot, and she deserved better than the lot she'd been dealt.

But there was nothing he could do about that now. A major drug kingpin had been put out of commission and an assassin-for-hire ring had been taken off the streets.

He wasn't sure he could trust Jacob now. He'd admitted he was in love with the woman. And Jacob wasn't a man who loved lightly. Since Cynthia, he hadn't been involved seriously. Jacob had said he could be objective, but no man in love was capable of that.

Clarence Christopher reached across his desk and pushed the intercom button. "Get me Marianne Lincoln," he spoke into the quiet air.

Twenty

It was nearly daylight when Jacob came back. Robyn looked up as he opened the door. His face told her nothing. No indication that he'd spoken with the director of the FBI was revealed.

"If I ask, will you tell me?" she asked, as he resumed his seat in front of the computer screen.

"No," his voice sounding final.

"What's going to happen to you?"

"I don't know." His fingers went to work reestablishing contact with the central computer.

"What did he say?"

"Nothing that will help you find what McAdams intends for Kari."

"Jacob!"

"Drop it, Brooke. He didn't throw us out. So, for the time being, we've got the use of this room and the files. Let's try to get as much information as we can."

Robyn went back to her screen. She pounded on the keyboard. Jacob was the most closed-mouthed man she'd ever met. He could be so stubborn at times. His whole career could rest on this night, and he didn't want to discuss it. Didn't he think she cared what happened to him? Wasn't he aware of how much she appreciated all he'd done for her?

"Jacob?" Robyn got up and went to the desk where he sat. "I care, Jacob. I hope you always knew that."

"I know it, Brooke." He looked at her with one of the few unguarded stares she'd ever seen. His eyes were luminous and open. She could see his fears and wants in the tender expression that held hers. "It will be all right." He took her hand and squeezed it. "It will be all right."

Robyn leaned forward and kissed Jacob's cheek. "You're one of the truly remarkable men I've ever known," she told him. "I want Kari back more than anything in the world, but I don't want your career as her ransom."

"It won't be," he said quietly.

Robyn searched his face for any sign of insincerity. She found none.

"Let's find Kari," he said.

A swelling rose in her throat, and she had to swallow hard to remove it. Without another word, she went back to her machine. Grant touched her hand as she passed. Soon, she was back into the files. She scanned Alex Jordan's information. From the looks of him, she'd have more easily pictured him sitting behind the desk of a large corporation, not engineering the unsolvable crime.

She didn't know how long she worked, but when her head came up again, it was very bright in the room. The clock showed almost noon. Robyn got up from the color screen and stretched. With hands on her lower back, she walked around the machinery.

Where was the clue? It had to be here. Yet, the sun was now shining high in the sky, and they were no closer to a solution than they had been eighteen hours earlier.

What had she missed? Would Will really kill Kari? She pulled the slats of the window blinds apart and looked down on the Pennsylvania Avenue traffic which spanned the wide thoroughfare oblivious to the people in the room above them. People who were tired of pouring over computer files and paper envelopes. Jacob's tie had long ago gone, and Grant's sleeves were rolled up to his elbows. Robyn's sweater had been discarded, and she'd combed her fingers through her hair so often all curl had long ago become limp tendrils of straight hair.

Grant came up behind her. "Tired?" he asked, massaging her shoulders.

"Extremely." She leaned forward as his fingers took some of the strain out of her shoulders. "There's got to be something here, but I can't seem to find it. My brain feels like mush."

"Why don't you take a few minutes to sleep? We'll keep digging," he suggested.

"I can't. If there's anything here, I'd be the one to recognize it. I've spent more time with Will than any of you." She went back to the boxes on the floor. Sitting down, she picked up a set of photographs. Leafing through them, she saw family photos of Will's early life. He was pictured with his children. Four blond girls smiled at her. Another picture had Will and Alex. The child must have been twelve. Then, she found one with Will and a woman who must have been his wife. Robyn had never seen Will's wife.

"Grant, what was Will's wife's name."

"Amanda." He joined her on the floor, glancing at the photograph. "She must have died shortly after that was taken."

"What did she die from?"

"She became interested in local politics. At a rally one evening, there was an assassination attempt. The candidate was missed, but several people near him were hit. Amanda was one of them. She held on for over a week. The bullet lodged in her chest close to her heart. But eventually she died."

"Oh, how awful." Robyn felt sorry for Will.

"Will was away when it happened. He was never quite the same without her. She was the one who got him interested in reading mysteries."

"He always has one in his pocket," Robyn smiled.

"Amanda used to write them."

"Oh, my God! Grant, that's it." The light bulb went on in her head. The switch was thrown and connection was made. "Did you ever read any of them?"

"Just one. *Dinner Companions,* the one that reminded me of the . . ." he stopped.

Jacob joined them. "Go on," he prompted.

"Were they published? Can we find them anywhere?" Robyn asked.

"They weren't published. But I saw them on the bookshelf in Will's library," Grant explained.

"There are eight of them," Robyn said. *"A Week of Knights, Cramped Quarters, A Case of the Nevers, Lost Moon . . ."*

"Yes," Grant confirmed. "Alex used to sneak and read them when she wasn't home."

"Do you know any of the plots?"

"A Week of Knights was about the death of seven men by a character dressed in knight's armor. It takes place in modern-day New York."

"The Stanfield killings," Jacob said. Robyn looked at him. "It's a series of seven killings attributed to Alex Jordan. Go on, Grant."

"Cramped Quarters takes place on a train. A nurse is killed on her way to visit her parents, who are involved in selling U.S. secrets to the highest bidder."

"Genia Novak." Robyn remembered from her research before the Jordan trial. "Genia Novak was a double agent selling secrets. Her death on a train was too spectacular to have any name connected with it except Alex Jordan."

"I don't know any others," Grant said.

"Jacob, what he's going to do to Kari is in one of those books. We have to go back."

Jacob picked up the phone and let the helicopter know they were ready. Grant did the same regarding the plane. With the same efficiency which got her to Washington, she found herself on her way back to Buffalo, New York. Now that she knew what she was looking for, her adrenaline was once again pumping. She couldn't sit still on the plane, and when they finally landed, Jacob ushered them into the helicopter which deposited her back in her yard before taking off again.

"Marianne, has he called?" Jacob asked coming into the kitchen.

"No, it's been quiet all night. Did you find anything at the FBI?"

"Yes, we know he's using the plots to his wife's books."

"What!"

"How are we going to get in there to get the books," Grant asked.

"With all the laws I've broken in the last twenty-four hours, what is breaking and entering?" Jacob asked.

"That won't be necessary," Robyn told him. "I have a key." She went to her purse and pulled her ring out. "Will gave it to me."

Jacob took it. "Stay here," he ordered. Robyn was too tired to argue. The two men went through the back door. Marianne took her arm and led her to the sofa in the other room. She left her a moment and returned with a cup of tea.

Robyn took two sips and put it down.

"You need some sleep," Marianne told her. "You look like you've been up for a week."

"Not yet, Marianne. I've got to find out what's in those books. And where Kari is."

"How are books going to do that?"

"His wife was a mystery writer. The Network used her plots for their kills. Jacob recognized three of them."

"You think he'll try that with Kari?"

"I'm not sure. Grant says he won't be able to do it. But he's killed so many other people . . . I just don't know." The night's strain was taking its toll.

Robyn began to cry. "Oh, Marianne. He has my baby. He's going to kill my baby."

Marianne took hold of her. She rocked her back and forth, pushing her hair back. "Don't worry, Brooke. Jacob won't let that happen. He'll find out what Will's planning to do, and he'll stop him. Kari will be all right."

She continued rocking Robyn as if she were a child and not a thirty-year-old woman. This was how Grant and Jacob found them. Marianne signaled for them to be quiet. "She'll be fine. She just needs to rest," Marianne whispered over Robyn's head.

"Brooke," Jacob squatted in front of her. "I want you to go to bed."

"No!" Robyn's head came up. "I have to read the books."

"You'll be no good if you don't get some rest."

"No!"

"I insist—"

"Jacob," Grant stopped him. "Let her read them. It will take her less time. Then, she can go to bed."

Robyn looked at Grant. She didn't say anything. It wasn't necessary. He knew her, all her secrets. There was nothing they didn't share, and she silently thanked him for his understanding.

Confusion showed on Marianne and Jacob's faces. "Brooke has a photographic memory. She can read the books in minutes and tell us the plot."

The silence in the kitchen grew louder after Grant's comment. Robyn could almost hear accusation, incredulousness, disbelief, and astonishment directed toward her. This was her secret. Few people knew of it.

Since she left the Assassination Bureau, she'd had no real need to purposely use it.

"Don't look at me like that," she demanded. "I haven't changed. I'm still the same person you knew two minutes ago."

"That's why you wanted your old job back," Jacob said. "You went through those files so fast, and you remembered everything you saw. It explains so much; how you could put the Crime Network together and conclude what their movements were going to be. Why didn't anyone know?"

"I didn't tell them. I learned early how people treat you when they find out. They think you're a freak," she paused. "Now, let me read the books."

Grant set the leather-bound books he'd brought back on the table in front of her. "Take your time," he told her, dropping into the space beside her.

Robyn opened the first book. Will must have had them bound. They were type written and the letter 'e' didn't close properly. She began to read, turning the pages more rapidly than any of the other three people in the room could read. She ignored the loud silence and the anticipation of the people around her. Finishing, she quickly outlined the plot, and Jacob confirmed the case adjunct to it. Robyn repeated the procedure five times. Jacob accounted for all but one of the plots.

The book's title was *Trolley Ride to Murder.* The plot had a passenger of a trolley killed and the police baffled by his connection to the prime minister of Great Britain.

"What could that have to do with being here in

Buffalo? The only trolley we have is the one downtown, and it only runs through the shopping district
on Main Street. Anywhere else the tracks have been
taken up or paved over." Robyn looked from face to
face, each one as blank as the other. "As for a public
figure, Kari doesn't know any and neither do I."

"What about five years ago when you first came
here?" Marianne asked. "Did you have any associations before you went into the program?"

"No-no," Robyn bowed her head, holding it in her
hands as she shook. "I can't think of a single . . ."
She stopped in mid-sentence, her eyes darting to Marianne.

"What is it?" Grant asked. "Have you thought of
someone?"

Robyn stood up. She walked to the fireplace. The
photo of Cameron Johnson stood steadfast and un-
changed in its place. But all was not well. Her mind
was tired and fuzzy, but she had heard correctly.
Robyn was used to being careful of her words, even
when she was upset. And she didn't think she could
get any more upset than she was now. But Marianne
had mentioned the program.

"How did you know that?" Robyn asked. Her eyes
bore into Marianne as if she could look into her mind.

"Know what?" Marianne's face screwed into a per-
plexed look.

"I never said anything about a program, and it
wasn't mentioned before we left or since we returned.
Yet, you know I'm part of one. How?"

Marianne looked from Robyn to Jacob.

Robyn closed her eyes and let her head fall back.

Her shoulders dropped in a gesture of defeat. "Oh, no," she cried, turning her back on the room. She hung her hands on the mantel, gathering her anger, fighting for control. "She works for you." It was a statement, and Robyn directed it at Jacob. She faced him, her body in tense control. "You've had her spying on me for five years." Then, she swung her gaze back to Marianne. "It's him, isn't it? He's the secret admirer I thought you sneaked away to see every month? When all the time you were going to give him a report on me—who I was seeing, what I was doing." Robyn was angry with the two people who'd affected her life more than anyone else in the past five years. "I wondered how you knew so much about what was happening to me." She threw her attention back to Jacob. "How you could seemingly materialize from thin air, when it was Marianne, giving you clues to my movements."

Grant watched the exchange without a word. He hadn't noticed the words Marianne had said. Jacob had told him about Robyn, and he assumed, sometime in the past five years, Robyn had confided in her friend.

"Brooke—" Jacob began.

"Jacob!" Marianne interrupted, the note of command in her voice was stronger than Robyn had ever heard it. "I want to explain this to Brooke." She raised her hand to her forehead. "Please, leave us alone."

The room cleared quickly. Robyn paced the sequestered space, her arms folded in front of her.

"I know you're upset, Brooke."

"Upset!" Robyn exploded. "Why should I be upset. I find out my daughter's been kidnapped by the man

I considered my father, a man I trusted has betrayed me and my best friend . . . my best friend . . ." She couldn't continue. Tears were streaming down her face. She buried her head in her hands as she plopped down on a wing chair.

"Brooke, it hasn't been like that." Marianne sat on the lower table in front of her. "I am your best friend. Jacob didn't send me here to spy on you. He sent me to protect you, and up until yesterday, I was doing a pretty good job."

"But you reported everything to him."

"What was I suppose to do? I knew there were people out there looking for you. I didn't know who. And I had to report to Jacob. It was my job." Marianne pulled Robyn's hands from her face. "We only thought of your safety." She handed Robyn a tissue to dry her face. "For a long time, there was little to report. Jacob was only a sympathetic ear. He was there when I needed someone to complain to. He was there to help when things were getting out of hand. I'm sorry. I know you must hate me, but I only did what I thought was right, and I haven't hurt anyone."

Robyn blinked a fresh batch of tears. Robyn had given up control of her life when she went into protective custody. She'd fought for a small amount and thought she'd won a few battles. But she'd been manipulated and ruled by those she had called friends.

Grant's appearance, Kari's kidnapping, Marianne, and Jacob—how much more could go wrong? Robyn turned back to Marianne.

"I haven't changed either," the redhead said. "When I answered your ad, I was sent by Jacob, but it didn't take long before this became more than a job," she paused, her eyes pleading with Robyn. "Brooke, I love Kari, and you're as close as any of my sisters. You've got to believe me."

"I do, Marianne," she said calmly. "I don't hate you." Robyn's anger dissipated. She knew Marianne only had her interests in mind. Jacob had jeopardized his career to help her find Kari, and even if no one around her was who they appeared to be, they had her interests at heart.

Marianne *was* like her sister. She was glad the truth had been uncovered. "How can I hate someone who can turn ham slices into those cute little faces with olives for eyes?" she asked. A hesitant smile made Marianne giggle. A bubble of laughter broke from Robyn. She covered her mouth and tried to stop but couldn't. Suddenly, both women were laughing heartily.

Robyn felt the tension of the past twenty-four hours falling away. The release was wonderful. Tears were streaming from her eyes as her laughter continued. She couldn't stop. Finally, with hands at her sides holding the pain in, she took a sobering breath. Dragging gulps of air into her lungs, she calmed herself.

Grant poked his head through the door. Marianne waved him back.

"They're going to think we've lost our minds," Marianne said, giggles still erupting.

"Let them, it's time Jacob had something to worry about," Robyn told her.

"What about Grant? Hasn't he worried enough?"

"Yes, he has." Robyn calmed herself, wiping her

happy tears away. "Jacob—he's the man who makes you moody after your weekends with him."

Marianne was quiet.

"He's not married, Marianne. You told me that. So what's the problem?"

"There's another woman."

"You know who she is?" Robyn felt this from their other conversation. Marianne stared at her. She continued until Robyn felt uncomfortable. Suddenly, light dawned. "Me!" she exclaimed. "You're wrong."

"Jacob's been in love with you since he first saw you. You have to know that. After the night in the garden when you sang "Secret Love," I thought you were in love with him, too."

"Jacob's not in love with me." Their voices had lowered to conspiratorial levels. "He was in love with a woman named Cynthia. I remind him of her."

"He told me."

"Does he know how you feel about him?"

"No," she shook her head.

"Are you sure?"

Marianne looked her straight in the eye.

"Jacob's not good at expressing his feelings," Robyn continued. "He's probably erected an invisible barrier to keep you from seeing how he really feels."

Marianne leaned forward. She remembered the night Jacob had come to her. She'd thought of herself as a substitute for Robyn. Could she have been wrong? Could Jacob have been thinking only of her?

"How can I find out?" she asked.

"With Jacob you have to be direct. Ask him, although that doesn't guarantee you an answer." Robyn knew first-hand how closed-mouthed Jacob could be.

Marianne thought about that. "I will," she said. "When this is over and Kari is safe, I'll ask him. Now, come on." Marianne stood up, pulling her friend with her. "Let's find out where there's a trolley car around here."

They went into the kitchen. The chaos of the FBI room was duplicated around her counter. Quiet overtook the room when the two women joined the group.

"Are you all right?" Grant came to her.

"I'm fine." She hugged him, knowing how lucky she was to have a man who loved her as much as she loved him. She couldn't keep herself from watching Jacob to see if he looked at Marianne with the same tenderness in his eyes as Grant had for her. All she saw was the wall she knew he had in place. "Have you discovered anything?"

"Nothing," Jacob said. "We've checked the old city maps to find out where trolley tracks used to run. We've also searched for trolley museums in the area, trolley cars being used as restaurants, or tourist attractions. We've come up with nothing."

Robyn's hand suddenly closed over Grant's. Her eyes sought Marianne's. "Crystal Beach," they said in unison. "He's taken her to the beach," Robyn went on.

"When Will first moved here, he worked at the amusement park," Marianne told the group. "It's got a trolley car from San Francisco."

"It's the Trolley Whip, the giant roller coaster." Robyn's voice had the dry dragging sound of a person gasping for air.

Grant put his arm around her. "He won't hurt Kari."

She turned to face him. "No, he wants me. He's been planning this for years, and it's me he wants. Kari is his way of making sure he gets me."

"What do you want to do?" Jacob asked.

"I don't know." In Washington, she was adamant about making the decision herself, now she didn't know how to handle the situation. "Crystal Beach is in Canada."

"I have no jurisdiction there," he said. She heard defeat in his voice.

Robyn looked at the clock on the mantel. It was six o'clock. A mere six hours before Will's promised execution. "The park is closed. We can't even get into it." Tears clogged her throat. She made an effort to swallow them.

"We can get in," Marianne said. "We know the manager at the park. He's a regular at Yesterdays." Robyn's nod confirmed Marianne's comment.

"Call him," Jacob ordered. "I'll get us some authority."

"How?" Robyn asked.

"Clarence Christopher."

"Do you think he'll help?" Robyn could hear Grant's heart beating fast as he held her. She was glad he was here. She needed him, needed his strength more than she'd ever thought.

"I don't know. I can ask."

"What did he say when you went up there, Jacob?" Robyn knew the FBI director hadn't been in his office in the middle of the night without good reason.

Jacob didn't answer. He gave her a look which told

her the discussion between him and Clarence Christopher was a subject she need not bring up again.

The sun had long since dropped behind the horizon of Lake Erie's western shore when the two cars pulled up at the park's main entrance. Another two were at separate locations. Jacob insisted they go in without sirens blaring. Grant held onto Robyn's hand, while Jacob and Marianne followed.

The park manager met them, and they slipped into the darkened area. Robyn scanned every corner for some sign of Kari. It was eerie being in a closed park. Sound echoed with every footstep, magnified by the quietness. She kept looking over her shoulder for someone following her. Robyn had only seen Crystal Beach when lights extended far into the sky, outlining the rides in gay colors. Crowds of people with cotton candy or stuffed animals walked before her. Tonight, the ghostly silence enveloped her.

"Where do you think they are?" Robyn whispered to Grant.

"I don't know. The roller coaster is over there." He pointed to the grimly outlined structure.

Robyn could see the giant thrill machine. It reminded her of a huge dragon. Its fires were dampened for the moment, but with a little effort, it could spring to life and breathe death to the ground.

"I want the lights turned on." Robyn heard Jacob. "At my signal." The park manager started to leave. "Call the fire department, too," Jacob called to the man's retreating back. "And get the rescue squad," he amended. The gray-haired man nodded, and Jacob took the lead, directing them to the base of the roller coaster.

"I'm sorry, Brooke, but if Kari's hurt we'll need help."

She tried to smile. "Thanks, Jacob."

"They've been here," Marianne pointed to empty wrappers from McDonald's. Fresh catsup oozed from the discarded paper.

"All right," Jacob commanded. "Spread out. Hammil, Price, go check the other side." He pointed toward the lower end of the roller coaster.

"It's so nice of you to come, Mrs. Richards." A laughing voice boomed from the darkness. All eyes shifted up, looking for the source of the grating sound. Robyn could see nothing. Her heart thudded against her chest. Suddenly, the lights came on with blinding intensity. Her hands came up, blocking the stabs of illumination. Still, she saw nothing.

Jacob's hand grabbed her arm and pulled her out of the light. Marianne had Grant. They crouched behind a closed concession stand.

"Did you see Kari?" Grant whispered.

"No," Jacob answered.

"Hiding won't help you, Mrs. Richards." The disembodied voice bounced off the stationary thrill machines. "You didn't fly all this way to hide, did you?"

"How's he able to track our movements so closely?" Marianne whispered.

"A good question," Jacob answered. "One I've asked myself since last night when he called Brooke at the headquarters building."

Marianne looked at Robyn. "I don't know how he knew we were there," Robyn explained.

"Come out, Mrs. Richards," Will called to her.

"Why does he keep calling you that?" Grant asked.

"At Alex's trial, it was how they referred to me. The defense attorney made a habit of ending each question with my name. I think they were trying to make the subtle point that you were a hostage, and I was willing to say anything to have you freed."

"Did they know about the agreement she'd made?" Grant directed his question to Jacob.

"With the levels Brooke uncovered, it's possible they knew. The newspapers hinted at it, but it was never brought up in court."

"Jacob, I want to talk to him," Robyn said, looking over her shoulder.

"Brooke, if you have any idea of trying to exchange yourself . . ."

"No," she interrupted. "I know him better than you. Maybe I'll be able to talk him out of this."

"Let her try," Grant said. "Kari's probably scared to death. It'll make her feel better if she hears her mother's voice. If we can get her back without anything more happening, it's worth a try."

Robyn saw the look pass between Jacob and Marianne. Marianne nodded. Then, Jacob looked at Robyn. "All right," he agreed, reluctance in his voice. "But I warn you. Don't try to change the script. We're not going to let him get both of you."

Robyn nodded. She stood up, but remained concealed behind the barricade. Grant stood next to her. She took his hand.

"Go on," Grant said. "I'm right here."

"Will," she called. Her voice was shaky. "Will, it's Brooke." Silence met her. "Will, is Kari all right?"

Again silence.

"Will, please answer me." There was desperation in her voice.

"You killed my son." A thundering voice came back. "And I'm going to take your daughter."

Robyn had never heard hatred in Will's voice. It was there now. A hatred fueled by years of searching and looking for the woman who'd given testimony against his son. The woman who'd uncovered the Crime Network and then disappeared behind the protective custody of the United States government.

"Will, Kari is your granddaughter." Robyn forced herself to remain calm. "Didn't you tell me your own daughters didn't visit? And Kari was closer than any of your grandchildren? Will, you can't hurt Kari."

"I can, and I will. At midnight. The same time Alex died."

Robyn trembled. Grant squeezed her hand and put his arm about her shoulders. "Will, what do you want?"

"I want my son back."

"Killing Kari won't bring Alex back."

"No, but it will make up for living next to you, waiting for a chink in that rock-hard armor of yours to crack."

"Will, it's me you want . . ."

Jacob grabbed her shoulders, wrenching her away from Grant. "No!" His eyes glared into hers. "Just keep him talking. The longer he talks the better chance we have."

Robyn dropped her eyes and nodded.

"Keep her here," he said to Marianne, then slipped out into the darkness and disappeared.

She took a deep breath. "Will, I can't bring Alex back. I didn't kill him."

"He was my son."

Robyn heard the cry in his voice.

"I know, Will," she shouted. "You loved him, and he loved you."

"You took him away. You killed him."

"I had a job to do, Will." Robyn thought she'd appeal to his sense of duty. "I had orders, like you." She paused. "Will, is Kari all right?" Robyn persisted, more quietly than before but loud enough to carry to him.

Jacob came back then. The park manager and one of the nameless agents arrived at the same time. "She's up there. He has her tied to one of the cars. If he lets it go," he paused, looking directly in Robyn's eyes. "It will crash into the cars below. The cars have been welded together, and there's a bomb attached to them. She'll be killed."

Robyn gasped, stepping back as if the words were fists that beat at her. Grant turned her into his arms. "He won't do it, darling. He won't hurt her."

"You don't know that. He thinks I killed his son. He wants my daughter in exchange, and he has her. There's nothing we can do to stop him."

"The fire department and ambulances are here," the park manager whispered.

"Thank you," Jacob spoke in hushed tones. "Could you let them know the situation and have them quietly take up position?"

The manager nodded. "The police are also here."

"Good," Jacob said. "Let them know there's a bomb under the roller coaster, and we need a bomb squad. Show them where it is when they arrive."

"Will treated Alex badly, but he loved him," Jacob heard Grant saying. "I want you to keep talking to him. Remind him she's his granddaughter. I'm sure he loves her, and it's difficult to kill someone you love." Grant kissed her and started to move in the same direction Jacob had.

"Where are you going?" Jacob asked.

"I'm not sure. But my plan is to see what I can do to save my daughter." He was determined. If Jacob had any intention of stopping him, he was in for a fight.

Jacob looked at him a long time. "I'll go with you," he said, then turned to Marianne. "Keep her here." He pointed to the ground.

"I will," she said.

"We'll take the route around the back of the *Tilt 'o Whirl,* then split and approach from both sides."

The men left. Marianne took hold of Robyn. "Talk to him," she said.

"Will, Kari loves you. And I know—I know you love her," she stammered. "Will, can I talk to her?"

The silence that met her lengthened. Robyn fought her tears. She took a deep breath and reined in her fear.

"Will, please! She's only a little girl."

Marianne held onto Robyn for what seemed like hours before they heard the tiny, frightened voice.

"Mommy," Kari called.

Robyn instinctively moved toward the sound, but Marianne blocked her efforts.

"Kari, are you all right?" She struggled to keep the fear in her heart out of her voice.

"Mommy, I'm scared. Can you come and get me down." There were tears in her voice, and again, Robyn tried to move toward her.

"Tell her Graffie will help her," Marianne stopped her.

"Mommy can't reach you, honey. Graffie is there. Graffie will help you."

"Graffie said I'm going down by myself. Mommy, I'm scared." Robyn could hear giant-size sobs coming from her daughter. "Mommy, help me, help me."

"I will, Kari. I will." Tears streamed down her face. Kari sounded so afraid. Her voice was so tiny in the huge space. "What am I going to do, Marianne. I have to go out there. You have to let me. If he takes me, he'll let her go."

"No!" Marianne was adamant. "You heard what Jacob said."

"She's not Jacob's child, she's mine."

Marianne didn't say anything for a moment. When she spoke, her voice was gentle. "I know she's your child, Brooke, but we don't know much about Will's state of mind right now. If you go out there, you'll be a target. And we could well lose both you and Kari. As long as we can keep him talking, it will give Jacob and Grant a chance to do something. Trust them, Brooke."

"All right," she agreed. Then to Will, she asked, "What can I do, Will? What will it take for you to give me back my daughter?"

"You can't have her. She's mine now," he answered.

"But there must be something. Alex has been dead for five years. I've seen you with Kari. She makes you smile. You look forward to seeing her each day. You can't be willing to kill her without a second thought."

"What have you got to exchange?"

Robyn hesitated. This was the opening she'd sought. Instinctively, she knew Will wanted it, too. He wanted to see her in pain, see fear on her face and in her eyes. She knew he wanted to extract everything from her that he felt she'd taken from his son.

"You're not going, Brooke," Marianne repeated Jacob's words.

"What do you want?" Robyn asked the old man.

"What I want you can't give me."

"No one can bring Alex back."

"Then I want you, Robyn Richards. I want you in place of Kari."

"No, Will." The two women heard Grant's voice. It sounded open and free as if he was standing in full view of the park. "You took her away from me once. I won't let you do it again."

"I never took anything from you." Indecision crept into his voice.

"You took Brooke away from me when you set up Alex and forced her to do her civic duty. Isn't that what you taught Alex and me? Always do your duty. Obey orders. Aren't those your words?"

"Alex did what he was told. And she killed him." Will pointed at the ground.

"I won't give her to you," Grant said. "She's mine."

"All right," Will agreed. "I have the child. I don't need the mother."

"Yes, you do," Robyn took a step closer to the light that cut geometric patterns on the ground. "It was me who testified against Alex. Kari wasn't born then. She's entirely innocent in this, and if you want an exchange, it's me you'll get." At that point, she pushed past Marianne's restraining hands and stepped into the light. Marianne followed her. "I'm here, Will." She took a step forward, Marianne at her side. "Let Kari go."

"Go back, Brooke," Grant called. He looked up at the scaffolding. "Will, I'm coming up."

"Don't do that. I'll let the car go," he warned.

"I'm coming up." Grant grasped the painted metal structure and swung his body into one of the X-shaped supports. A shot rang out. Robyn screamed, and Marianne pulled her out of the line of fire. The bullet hit the ground next to Grant, chipping the asphalt and ricocheting blacktop about his body. "I'm not kidding, Grant. I don't want to hurt you, but I will."

"Kari's my daughter, too. I want to spend time getting to know her. I want to hold her in my arms and praise her when she tries things. I want to love her like you loved Alex." Grant swung another foot into the structure.

"Don't do it, Grant," he warned. "I'll let this car go."

Several seconds passed as Grant continued his climb. Robyn got up and went closer to the huge machine. She didn't know where he came from, but Hammil was on one side of her and Marianne on the other. Two other men walked in front of and behind her, forming a human shield.

The sound of the metal wheels of the car against the track was like the scream Robyn let out when she recognized the source. The car started toward the packed vehicles on the ground level. Robyn's eyes riveted to the plunging car. She squeezed Marianne's hands until she cried out in pain, and Marianne pried her fingers loose. Unable to turn away, she watched her child plunge toward death. But the impact she expected didn't come. Turning her head, she saw the grouping at the bottom, rigged to have the top car crash into them, move along the rails as if the park were open and crowds of people were waiting for their chance to go to the top of the loop. Three of Jacob's men appeared. Two pulled the brake stick back while, hidden between the floorboards of the giant death machine, a third did something she couldn't see. The car stopped safely on a cushion of air.

Robyn tried to get through the crowd around her. She wanted to run to the car and get her child.

"She's not in it," Marianne's voice penetrated her thoughts. Robyn's eyes went back to Will. Kari's legs dangled dangerously over the side of the edifice.

"Oh, dear God," she prayed. They all watched Grant as if he were a human fly scaling the wall. Without knowing it, the group inched closer to a small fence which in summer separated park visitors from the spaghetti of cables needed to run the monster machine. Robyn found herself pressed like a sandwich between Hammil and Marianne. They forced her behind another barrier.

More men stole into the park. Like thieves they came under the structure, spreading foam along the ground. Robyn blinked and clamped a hand over her mouth to stifle the sobs she felt coming to the surface.

"Graffie, I'm scared." Grant heard Kari's voice. "I want my mommy." Tears soaked her face making tiny streams of the dirt that covered it.

"I know, sweetheart. Graffie knows. Your mommy is down there." He pointed to the small group.

"Can I go to her?" she hiccuped.

"Soon, Kari. Soon."

"Why did you try to hurt Uncle Grant?"

Will looked at Grant. "Take one more step, Grant, and I'll drop her." Will's voice was menacing.

Grant stopped, glancing down. He saw Robyn push her way to the front of the congregation.

"No!" she screamed. "Will, don't hurt her. She's a child. She hasn't had time to do anything to anyone. It's me you want. I'm here. Take me. Let Kari go."

Grant took another step. Will's eyes returned to him. Grant was very near the top. With another step, his head would be level with Will's feet. He could see Jacob climbing on Will's blind side.

"I warned you," he said savagely and held the child

by her arms out over the ground. "One more step, and she's history." Kari squirmed in his grasp.

"Kari, don't," Grant yelled, then lowering his voice he spoke softly to the child. "Be very still, Kari. Graffie won't hurt you."

Kari responded to his voice, and Grant returned his attention to the man he'd looked on as a hero. "Will, she's your granddaughter."

"Not anymore. She's hers."

"Graffie, I'm scared." Kari wiggled her legs, trying to get back to Will's arms. "Graffie, don't drop me." Kari turned wide eyes at her grandfather. Only the innocence of children could look like that, Will mused. She'd been with him for two days, and she still trusted him not to hurt her. He wanted to press her close to him and hug her small body. But there was the woman below. He forced himself to think of Robyn. She had destroyed his world and taken his son. He would take her daughter.

Will McAdams looked at the child and quickly closed his eyes. Kari continued wiggling.

"Graffie, don't hurt me. Mommy needs me. What would she do if I'm not there? When I was sick, she was so sad. She cried all the time."

Will hesitated. He looked at the struggling child, but he saw Alex. Alex as a baby reaching for him.

"Graffie, I want my mommy," she cried.

Kari's legs began to swing. She attempted to reach safety.

"Kari, don't do that," Will shouted. His arms were beginning to tire. Kari stopped at hearing the tone of his voice. She started to cry.

"Graffie, help me. I'm scared."

Will looked at her. Indecision gripped him. He'd planned this for over a year. He'd waited, methodically following every step, careful to say nothing, betray nothing until he was positive. And now he was.

Grant vaulted over the top. "Listen to her, Will. Don't make another mistake. Don't hurt Kari for something you couldn't give to Alex."

"Graffie, please," Kari cried. "I want my mommy."

She was Alex again. He couldn't keep them separate. He was holding Kari, then Alex would be there. His tiny arms reaching for him, wanting him to pick him up and carry him. But he wouldn't. He didn't want his son to be dependent on anyone. He pushed the child away until Alex no longer came to him. He wanted his mommy.

"I want my mommy," Kari's frightened voice reached him. Tears clouded his eyes, and he started to pull her back.

Grant took a step closer. He was close to reaching Will.

"No!" a voice screamed as if in agony. A shot followed it. Grant heard the collective cry from the ground as he watched Will stumble to his knees. Blood spread over his shoulder and down his right arm. Kari went over the edge. He could hear her scream.

Robyn clamped her fist in her mouth. Behind her there was a scuffle, but her feet found forward motion. She rushed to the scaffolding, jumping the fence to catch her child.

Will struggled to pull Kari up. Grant hurled from

toehold to toehold, trying to reach her before Will's strength gave out. Jacob climbed as fast as he could. Each person was trying to reach the child before she fell.

Marianne got to Robyn and pushed her out of the way. She was prepared to take Kari's weight plus the G-force she'd create by her free fall. A second shot rang out. Marianne screamed, spinning around.

Will's last ounce of strength was tapped as death took him. Kari's fingers slipped free. She fell. The fire department rushed the crash net past the fence, one officer throwing Marianne out of the way. She felt her collarbone snap as she crashed against the support brace. Kari hit the crash net held by six strong men.

Robyn raced to it, pushing aside the big men and reaching for her daughter. "Kari! Kari!" she cried. "Are you all right?"

Tears smeared her face as she reached for her mother. "Mommy," she called. "Mommy, I'm scared." Robyn hugged her, running her hands over her back, arms, and legs, making sure she had not been hurt. She rocked back and forth as relief flooded through her.

"Is everything all right?" Jacob asked from the top.

"How's Kari?" Grant shouted.

"We've got a man down," one of the fire fighters shouted back. "She's been shot!"

"She!" Jacob's voice was a shrill cry.

Robyn whipped around to find Marianne on the ground, her face contorted in pain as blood coated her left arm. Still holding Kari, she went to her.

"Marianne," she called.

"Is Kari all right?" she asked, her hand on her shoulder.

The child continued to cling to her. "Yes, she's fine." Robyn turned to the firemen. "Get that ambulance in here," she demanded.

Jacob's feet reached the ground, and he sprinted across to the small crowd that surrounded Marianne.

He knelt beside her. "The shot," she whispered, one hand holding her broken bone, her face twisted in pain. "It came from Hammil."

"Be quiet," he told her. "I saw Hammil. Where's that damn ambulance?" Two ambulances with red flashing lights screeched to a halt just outside the ring of people surrounding Marianne. Several police cars followed it. Men in white coats got out of each of them and came forward. Two went to Marianne, and two came to Kari. She was welded to Robyn and fought when they tried to separate her. Robyn looked over her shoulder as the paramedics led her away from Marianne and the men working on her. Grant joined them. Together, they took Kari to one of the ambulances.

Marianne's smile was painful. Paramedics hovered over her, checking for other injuries. They had her on a collapsible gurney by the time Jacob managed to reach her again. Robyn looked over her shoulder at the scene of her friend and those with her.

"Are you all right?" Jacob asked her.

"I'm fine," she said.

Robyn knew she was lying. She was in a great deal of pain. Robyn smiled, still clutching Kari to her, as the ambulance sped away with her and Grant.

"Jacob's in love with Marianne," she told him, looking back through the park entrance.

"I know." He put his arm around Robyn and Kari and held them to his side. "I'm glad. For a while, I thought he was in love with you."

Robyn's head fell on his shoulder. She kissed the top of Kari's head. The child had fallen asleep. The past two days and her fear that Will would drop her had taken its toll. She was tired, but even in sleep her arms remained clamped to Robyn.

Grant held them. His family. Everything was going to be all right. He was certain things would work out. He'd make it work out. He wasn't going to be separated from his wife and child again. Neither Jacob nor the government would keep them apart, but he didn't think that would be a problem.

"I love you," he said, hugging Robyn and Kari closer to him. He kissed her and pushed her head back on his shoulder. Holding them for the moment was all he needed. They were safe, and that was enough.

Jacob's face was drawn and tired after two days of nonstop activity. He'd sat in the hospital waiting room until Marianne was out of surgery. The nurse came to tell him she would be all right and wouldn't wake for hours, but he insisted on staying. Finally, they took pity on him and let him wait beside her bed. She slept peacefully as he watched her, holding her soft hand until he, too, fell asleep with his head on the starched sheet.

Marianne woke in the early hours of the morning.

The room was dark except for a soft light above her head. She recognized Jacob immediately. He held her hand loosely. She pulled it free and slipped her fingers into his soft curls. The movement woke him, and he sat up.

"What are you doing here?" she asked, her mouth parched.

"How do you feel?" he asked, ignoring her question.

"I'm thirsty."

He stood up and got her water from the pitcher beside the bed. Then, sitting on the white sheets that covered her, he held her head while she drank through the plastic straw.

"What time is it?" she asked, when he leaned her back against the pillows.

Checking his watch, he said, "Five o'clock."

"You should be asleep," she said. "You look so tired." Her hand reached for his face. He took it in his hand and kissed it.

Marianne bit her lip at the emotions his touch caused.

"How's your shoulder?"

She had a burning pain that threatened to sever it from her body. "I don't feel it much," she lied.

"Should I call a nurse?" His eyes were dark with concern.

"No," she shook her head, biting the misery back. She didn't want him to go. "How's Kari and Brooke?"

"They're fine. Kari was treated for shock and released. They stayed until you were out of surgery. I sent them home then."

"But you stayed." Her eyes were wide when they found his. "Why?" She had to be direct with Jacob. He wouldn't come out and tell her what he felt, and she had to know.

"I couldn't leave."

"Why not? You needed to rest. Kari was safe. My life was not in danger. You could have gone. Why didn't you?" She knew she shouldn't push, but she was past caring. If Jacob was still in love with Robyn, she'd go on with her life and forget him.

"Don't you know?" he almost smiled. "You're so good at reading my feelings."

"I don't want to read them," she looked away. "I want to hear them."

"I love you, Marianne." His voice was so quiet, even in the silent room, she was afraid she hadn't heard him. Slowly, her face turned back to him. He looked scared as if he expected her to reject him.

"What did you say?" She needed confirmation.

"I said I couldn't leave because I'm in love with you." He sat on the bed and reached around her. He leaned forward and kissed her surprised mouth. "I don't know how it happened. I never thought of being in love with you, but for months I haven't been able to get you out of my mind."

Marianne tried to reach for him, but pain shot through her shoulder. She squeezed her eyes closed and waited it out.

"You are in pain." He hugged her until she relaxed. When he released her, there were tears in the corners of her eyes. "I'm going to call the doctor."

"No!" she stopped him. "Not yet. They'll give me

something to make me sleep. I don't want to sleep yet."

He wiped the tears away with the pads of his thumbs. "I don't want you in pain. I was so scared when I saw you on the ground. I thought Hammil had . . ." he looked away, refusing to complete the thought.

"Don't think about it." She caressed his cheek. "It's over, and everything is going to be fine."

Jacob looked at her. "You need to go back to sleep."

"I don't feel like sleeping," she told him. He'd confessed that he loved her. She wanted to talk to him, tell him everything about herself, her family and find out everything about his. She hugged him tighter, content to be in his arms. Then, she remembered the night he'd come to her house. "Jacob?" she began, knowing she had to ask the question.

"Yes," he answered still holding her close.

"That night at my house."

"I remember." She could feel him smiling against her neck.

"You told me you were in love with Brooke."

The gentle nibbling stopped. He sat up straight and stared at her. "I was," he said. Feeling her retreat, he took her hand. "For years," he explained. "I thought I was in love with her, but I wasn't. I'm not quite sure what I feel for Brooke. She's a strong woman, and I have a great deal of respect for her, but she doesn't make my blood boil. I suppose we were together for so long, she was constantly on my mind, but you filled my dreams, making me crazy for you."

"I thought you wanted Brooke, and I was a poor substitute."

Jacob folded her close to him. "You'd never be a substitute."

"I've loved you for years," she told him.

"Oh, my God!" he hugged her. "What a fool I've been. I intend to tell you everyday for the rest of your life. I love you, Marianne."

"I love you, Jacob." She raised her arm around his shoulder and met his mouth as it slid over hers.

Twenty-one

Jacob came through the door of his office and took a seat behind the large desk. Robyn and Grant looked at him from the two chairs directly in front of it. His stare was direct, but not chiseled. He looked . . . *happier*, Robyn thought. He even smiled at her.

"Is it over, Jacob?" she asked.

"It's over. Hammil told us everything. He met McAdams while on assignment in the Caribbean. Several years ago, Hammil's father died suddenly. He left very little insurance, and his mother was sick with cancer. Hammil poured all of his money into her treatments. By the time she died, he was heavily in debt. McAdams found that out and manipulated him, getting him to supply bits of information in exchange for money."

"Where did Will get the money?" Robyn asked. "He lived a very meager life, comfortable but not showy."

"He'd amassed it from the Crime Network and hid it in Caribbean banks. McAdams had plans of reviving the Network and using Hammil as his inside man."

"But didn't Hammil eventually pay off his debts?" Grant wanted to know.

"Not entirely. Most of the medical expenses were paid, but there were massive debts left by his father's failed businesses. Some of his ventures were financed by sources that were less than legal, shall we say."

"How were they going to set up another Crime Network?" Grant asked.

"McAdams had done it before. He knew everything that had to be done, and he was an extremely patient man. When we searched Hammil's apartment, we found files on several key people in the FBI. Most of the records centered on people having financial difficulty. The same method McAdams had used to rope Hammil would be employed to gain whatever information he needed."

"Why did Hammil shoot him?"

"He was at the end of indentureship. With Kari and you out of the way, McAdams had promised to give him all the documents he'd collected regarding his practices here. He'd be free to do his job without the threat of a sword hanging over his head. When McAdams pulled Kari back, Hammil saw his last chance for freedom evaporate."

"I can't believe it's over," Robyn said.

"You're free to go," Jacob stared at her.

"What does that mean," Grant asked.

"Exactly what it says," Jacob returned. "There's no reason to keep Brooke in protective custody. We're sure McAdams and Hammil acted as a team. You're free to become a family again. Go where you like, live where you like, no restrictions." Jacob spread his hands and leaned back in his chair.

Robyn took a breath. She got up and walked to the

window. Outside, traffic buzzed along the street. It had been six weeks since that night at Crystal Beach. It was winter in Washington. Around the tidal basin were clusters of plowed snow. The Japanese cherry trees stood as a bare, black contrast against the white marble monument and distant sky.

Freedom, what a beautiful word. If she wanted to, she could run through the trees with no more resistance against her than the wind blowing her hair. She'd become so used to being careful, to actually be free of the invisible jail was both frightening and exhilarating.

"I can't help feeling sorry for Will," Robyn spoke to the window.

"Don't feel sorry for him," Jacob said. "That old man engineered the deaths of at least two dozen men. If he'd lived, who knows what damage he and Hammil could have caused."

"I hear what you're saying, Jacob, but to me he was a loving father. To my daughter he was the grandfather she needed. Kari and I never could have survived without his kind nurturing."

"I know how she feels," Grant said. "Will was the perfect father figure to me, but to his own son, he was unyielding. Like Brooke, he was there when I needed him."

"It's hard to believe the man who killed a room full of men in a restaurant is the same person who stayed up nights when Kari had ear infections, who went to nursery school with her, and cooked her favorite food."

Robyn didn't ask Jacob how he knew that. He knew

everything about her. Some of it became clear when she found out Marianne really worked for him. Her reports told him when she was sliding off center. It was only at the furthest tangents that Jacob appeared to materialize.

"Brooke, there's another freedom you have," Jacob interrupted her thoughts. "You can go back to being Robyn Richards if you like. We'll correct everything."

Robyn turned to look at Grant. "Robyn Richards died in an automobile accident five years ago," she quoted. "She was en route to Dulles Airport to welcome her husband, a returning Lebanonese prisoner, home."

Grant left his seat and came to take her hands. He followed with the rest of the story, "Grant Richards met Brooke Johnson in a hospital in Buffalo, New York. He immediately fell in love with her and can't possibly live without her."

"And they lived happily ever after." A voice came from the doorway.

"Marianne!" Robyn and Grant said at the same time. "When did you get here?" Robyn asked, coming to hug her.

"This morning," she answered. "Jacob picked me up."

"You will have to get married again," Jacob told Grant when everyone was seated. "When Brooke went into the program all previous records were annulled to give you free and legal rights to remarry."

Grant looked at her. "This time we can do it right, with orange blossoms and a warm weekend in June."

"Maybe we can make it a double," Marianne stilled the room with her comment. She got up and went to perch on the arm of Jacob's chair. He slipped his arm around her to the gaping surprise of the two other people in the room.

"Marianne! That's wonderful." Tears sprang to Robyn's eyes, and she left her seat to hug her friend once again.

Grant got up and shook hands with Jacob. "Congratulations," he said with a smile.

"Where is Kari?" Marianne asked. "I expected to see her here."

"She's with David and Susan," Grant replied. "They were thrilled to find Robyn alive, and they've practically adopted Kari. I think this afternoon they're taking her to see the pandas at the zoo."

"Well, partner," Robyn began. "Now, that we're getting married what are we going to do with the restaurant?"

"Everything is under control. We find we have a staff fully capable of handling things when both of us are away," Marianne smiled.

"I guess Pete has taken the reins and is king of all he surveys."

"I believe that's a true statement." Marianne's head bobbed up and down.

"Do you think we should sell it to him?"

"You'd sell the restaurant?" she asked in surprise.

"I thought you were being reassigned." Robyn asked her. She knew after everything with Will was cleared up, Marianne would no longer have an assignment to protect her and Kari.

"Marianne isn't being reassigned, Brooke." Jacob slipped his arm around her again. "She's being furloughed, permanently."

"I find I like making broccoli flowers, shaping cheese and butter into topiary art, and my confections are always a surprise, not to mention the ultimate chocolate dessert."

Robyn's eyes found Grant's. "I haven't thought about this, but maybe we could let Pete and Sue-Ellen manage Yesterdays in Buffalo, and we can open a branch here."

"That sounds great. Then we wouldn't have to dissolve the partnership," Marianne said. She came around the desk and grabbed Robyn's hands. The two women were ready to sit down and discuss expanding their partnership in Jacob's office. Grant knew that. "We could use . . ."

"I hate to break this up." He stopped Marianne looking at his watch. "But if we're going to meet David and Susan, we'd better leave. You know Washington traffic." If he didn't get Brooke out of Jacob's office, she and Marianne would spend the day planning.

Robyn got up and hugged Grant. "Isn't it wonderful? Washington traffic? And I can go out in it and not wonder if there's someone out there looking for me." She released him and went to Jacob. "Thank you for everything," she said and hugged him. "Marianne, I'll see you soon." Grant caught her hand and led her through the door.

Jacob lifted Robyn Richards's folder from his desk drawer. He took the contents and placed them in a fresh manila folder. *Top Secret* was printed across the cover. Sealing it with red tape he stamped CLOSED across it.

Marianne put her arms around him from the back of his chair. "I'm so glad everything worked out," she said.

"Me, too." Jacob stood, turning her into his arms and lifted her chin. "I love you very much." She opened her mouth to return the sentiment, but he stifled it with a kiss that had her purring like a contented cat.

Robyn awoke cradled in Grant's arms. She felt as if she were glowing, that a light actually radiated from her. But she knew it was only a feeling. The sun must be setting, for the light filtering through the curtains was dim.

After she and Grant left Jacob's office, they went to his condo and spent the afternoon making love. She felt whole, complete as if her soul had been drifting free, without form, for the last five years until Grant found it and restored it to life.

Turning her head, she gazed at him sleeping next to her, his features relaxed. A well of sudden emotion burst forward, giving her no time to stop it or even dampen it down, before it racked her with a force that pierced her core. Suddenly, tears were running silently down her face. She'd felt fate had dealt her a blow, but now that everything was clear and she was free to do as she pleased, she knew the fates looked upon her with favor.

Without disturbing Grant, she lifted his arm and

crept out of bed. His shirt lay on the floor where he'd discarded it. She picked it up and slipped her arms into it as she left the bedroom and padded to the living room. The room looked different now. When she'd been here before, this had been Grant's apartment. This was where she would have remembered him when she allowed herself the luxury of thinking about him. But now she could think of herself in relation to this space.

Outside, darkness blanketed the city like a shroud. In the distance she could see lights dotted against the evening sky. Her eyes fell on the piano. She went to it. The piano had changed, too. Before it held a large vase of flowers, now there were picture frames with Kari and herself. The two photographs added life to the room.

Robyn fingered the keys making a tinkling noise. Then, she sat down. The seat was cool through the thin shirt.

Grant stood in the bedroom doorway as Brooke's hands hovered above the keys. He knew what she'd play before her fingers touched the keys. Quietly, the strands of Chopin's Nocturne in E-major began. He knew it was only a matter of time before she was no longer able to resist sitting down. Since the night at the park when Kari had been calmed, she'd been here several times and each time she seemed drawn to the piano, but she hadn't played it. She played the song with the same intensity she made love. It started slow, ever so slowly, like her fingers on his back. Then, she began the build, a steady drive that climbed and climbed up toward the edge of the world, climbed toward the crescendo of light that drew them into the vortex of expanding emotion. Her fingers shimmered across the keys, bringing the music to life and releasing the rhythms of love until it forced them to cry out in a shattering light that burst into color and carried them over the edge. Then, lingeringly, she prolonged the end, slowing the pace until his heartbeat returned to normal, and the last note of the song died in the reverberating silence of the darkened room.

He loved her. He didn't know how much he'd missed her until he saw her sitting at the piano, wearing his shirt, her hands on the keys. When Jacob explained the reason she pushed him away and was forever saying good-bye, he thought he'd die knowing she was alive and not knowing where she was or how to get in touch with her.

He went to her. Robyn looked up as he came toward her. She took his hand. "I want to talk to you," she said. She got up, and he followed her to the sofa. He draped his arm around her shoulders and pulled her close. "In all these weeks, Grant," she began tentatively. "You've never asked me why I went alone."

"I guessed you'd tell me when you were ready."

She squeezed his hand. She needed something to hold, an anchor. "It wasn't because I didn't love you more than anything else in the world." Bending, she kissed his knuckles. "Part of it was the flying. The other part was Project Eagle.

"Clarence Christopher explained your part in regaining possession of a vital part of a defense system. More than your life and those of the nine other men was at stake. Without that system, he explained, millions could die."

"Brooke, don't you know nothing is more important to me than you? Nothing was *ever* more important than you."

"I know that, darling. I thought I was doing what was best for both of us. According to Christopher, we had to have that system part returned. And flying was your life."

"I . . ."

"No-no," she stopped him. "I thought of having you come into the program later, after the defense system job was complete, but there was no guarantee as to when that would be. By then, you'd have done your grieving, and I was so completely changed . . . it didn't seem fair."

"You don't know the kind of hell I've lived without you."

"At the time, I thought it was better for you," she apologized.

"I can live without the sky, without everything except you. Without you, I'm nothing. Promise me you won't ever make that kind of decision again?"

Robyn's eyes were blank as she looked at him. How could she do that? She loved him too much still to take everything he lived for away from him.

"Brooke," Grant insisted. "You are my life and now Kari is, too. Without the two of you, there is nothing." He pulled her against him. "Promise me, darling. Promise me it's for better or worse?"

"For better or worse," she promised.

Grant kissed her, and for a long time, there was silence in the room.

"There is just one more thing, Brooke Johnson." Grant spoke into her hair.

"What's that?" She could feel him smiling against her.

"I'd like to propose."

Robyn sat up. "All right, propose." She switched the light on.

"Right now?"

"Right now." A smile tilted her mouth.

"You don't want to be dressed in a flowing gown, with moonlight and roses?"

"No, Kari can have that."

"Will you marry me?" he asked, gathering her to himself.

Robyn placed her hand on his chest, stopping the forward motion. "You don't mind that I'm not going back to being Robyn?"

"Not in the least. I've gotten used to you being Brooke, and I'm one of the few men in history who can be a bigamist—legally." He grinned at her.

"I love you, Grant."

"I love you more than I thought it possible," he ran his hand down her cheek. "Will you marry me?"

"Yes," she said, leaning forward and placing her mouth against his. Grant kissed her hard. His hands removed the shirt from her shoulders, and he carried her back to bed.